CW00485004

The Trials and Tribulations of Tiggy Foghorn
A modern day romp through the mysteries of female pleasure

JAGO HARRIS

Copyright © J.R. Harris 2023

The right of J.R. Harris to be identified as the author of the work has been asserted by him in accordance with the Copyright, Designs and Patents Act 1988.

This is a work of fiction. Names, places, events and incidents are either the products of the authors imagination or used fictitiously. Any resemblance to actual persons, living or dead or actual events is purely coincidental.

ISBN: 9798396461147

Also by author Jago Harris:

A Shoe for the Unborn
Available from www.lulu.com

Strangling Sparrows
The second book in the series featuring investigators Joanne Li and Dane Morgan.
Available from www.amazon.com

Humble Thanks

First to my wife Bo, who checked the detail and didn't ask too many difficult questions. Then to fellow author Graham Hunter for his extraordinary knowledge and encouragement. To James Cheadle a photographer who made Prodigy, Idris Elber and Manu Tuilagi look cool but struggled with me. Finally to other friends and family who despite the embarrassment of them knowing that their old fart had written a sexually explicit book, are still speaking to me.

Miami Vice

Tiggy Foghorn, serial philanderer, was in a serious quandary. At 40 something years of age and after what he vaguely remembered to be a 'largish night' he was in an unusually large bed with a naked woman on each side of him.

He tried to focus and after an inordinate amount of thought, the amount that in other people might have solved nuclear fission or world hunger, he thought that one of the women was called Miriam and was from Miami. As to the identity of the other woman he really had no idea and unless he could unstick the eyelid on that side, it was unlikely that he would ever succeed.

Tiggy was in a totally unfamiliar room in what he presumed was the morning and nothing felt quite the same except the tumescence between his naked legs. He was tempted not to waste his normal waking erection but looking to either side he literally didn't know which way to turn or indeed whether he had the motor power to make the first part of the manoeuvre.

Tiggy tried to hear any of the familiar morning sounds he was used to. He realised, to hear anything properly he needed to slide his head out from under the pillow. The dawn in Akaroa was normally a mixture of birdsong and the regular rattle of the metal fittings on the rigging on nearby yachts. This morning eventually he could hear the seagulls and he could tell from the brightness of light coming through the porthole that it was a lovely day. There were none of the other marine sounds he was familiar with and this was not his normal bedroom as the horribly bright tartan cover testified.

Whenever Tiggy had been pissed and woke up in a strange place, which happened occasionally, he had to remember just who he'd been the previous day. This may sound peculiar but Tiggy was a man of many different parts.

Sometimes when he was 'working' Tiggy Foghorn pretended to be Lithuanian on the basis that most people he met in New Zealand would be unfamiliar with the language, culture or history which was what had happened for the last few months, much to the relief of his bank balance. When in character he also modestly referred to himself as being from a minor but ancient Lithuanian family of note and entitled to use the title Count Tolstoy Jergov.

This title gave visiting matrons from Iowa, Melbourne or New York a certain amount of sniggers but generally they were impressed which was the intention.

Tiggy had landed in the east coast of New Zealand around 18 months ago and loved it. Akaroa is a beautiful place a couple of hours travel away from Christchurch, which started as a Whaling Port a few hundred years ago. Unusually it developed a French colonial feel which made it unique in New Zealand and meant that today its restaurants and streets were much sought after by tourists and visitors from all over the world.

Earthquakes and terrorist attacks had reduced visitor numbers for a while but this town felt like such a safe haven that numbers were back to normal within months. This was a mixed blessing for Kiwi locals who were just hoping to make a living without destroying the natural beauty of the place.

Before he'd arrived Tiggy Foghorn had his own difficulties making a living to cope with. He'd moored in Akaroa after an escapade in Noosa, Queensland had gone pear-shaped and meant that he had to leave Australia in a hurry. Return to there in the near future was not an option.

Tiggy thought of himself as an adventurer and Akaroa had often been a home for such men. It had been discovered by French explorers who thought it would make the perfect whaling port and who raised money back in the home country. When they returned, their ships found the Union Jack already flying on the headland as it had already been claimed by their enemies, the British.

Rather than fight the two sides had agreed to combine and make the most of the whale oil coming out of the Pacific which was known as 'black gold'.

Whales were no longer hunted in this part of the world as the need for oil, whalebone corsets and Scrimshaw seemed to have died out in most places years ago except in Japan, where it is supposedly still vital to the survival of civilisation as we know it.

In Akaroa now, the only Leviathans Tiggy Foghorn was interested in were the 20 stone beauties who came down the gangplank twice a week in summer. Their hunting required courage and a steady eye but the chase was exciting. Harpoons were not his favoured weapons and blood was seldom shed but it could be a dangerous sport which required all his native cunning. If he was on target then the rewards were rich but failure could mean imprisonment, disgrace or worse. So far, the risks had been worth taking.

Cruises were the bane of everyone's life locally. The bay was too shallow for the monster cruise ships to come in with 20,000 people but the medium size ships moored off-shore and ferried thousands of people to the dock where they were hustled on to buses before they could spend money in the local shops. The town therefore got all the hassle and virtually none of the turnover. It was made worse by the fact that traditional visitors were put off by all the congestion and were staying away in droves.

Tiggy Foghorn had learned the habits of his prey from weeks of careful observation in their natural habitat in Australia and New Zealand. He saw no benefit in targeting the first groups of passengers to disembark because the tour guides had them on the buses in nano-seconds. They had the protection of the group and weren't easy to pick off from the herd. But he'd found that on some cruises there were rebels who after doing half a world tour and being shepherded from pillar to post, rejected things and went off-piste. These were often independent - minded women who decided to see a few things for themselves. These women of spirit and adventure were Tiggy's favoured quarry.

The Cruise ship *Amazon* had come into the bay last night and blocked out the horizon. Looking at its web site and consulting the clever app on his iPad, Tiggy saw that it contained 4,000 passengers and 7000 crew and that it had been cruising for two months having visited ports in the United States, South Africa and Australia already. It was a luxury cruise with even cheaper cabins costing twenty thousand dollars and Platinum suites costing five or six times that figure.

Akaroa was a new destination for the ship in New Zealand and many of the guests had already come ashore and been pushed on to coaches visiting the Gold Rush Museum, Christchurch earthquake centre and other sundry attractions of that beautiful rebuilt city.

Tiggy Foghorn had to wait for the rebels who his instincts told him would be there somewhere, waiting to surface. But patience is a virtue that all hunters have to develop and Tiggy was impatient to achieve it.

Tiggy was dressed to kill. Which for him was a dark blue blazer, white shirt, club cravat and cream trousers. These were bespoke tailored but slightly faded and immaculately clean as befitted his character. The outfit certainly made him stand out in Pierre's Cafe which had tables lining the harbour. Most staff knew him and admired anyone who could make any profit out these hordes of cruise visitors because they certainly didn't.

The tension was rising and Tiggy had started to worry about his strategy and then he noticed action at the side of the ship. As he'd hoped another tender had left the cruise liner about an hour after the masses had landed and Tiggy hoped that he might see some action.

He watched through his old Zeiss binoculars as the small boat crossed the bay and could see just a few people in the back. He asked Pierre (real name Darren) for a flat white and got out his props. Today that was a Montblanc fountain pen, a small bottle of ink and old leather-bound writing book. The final part of his kit was a thick hardback book which had been skilfully altered and which was artfully hidden beneath the other items.

By the time the boat had disgorged its passengers he had half-finished the coffee and covered the first page of the notebook with beautiful handwritten script. The words were passages from an obscure novel very much in the style of Jane Austin, that he'd memorised some years ago.

Tiggy looked down the quay with his binoculars and discounted the first passengers to land as they were a young couple obviously keen to make their own way. The two women behind looked like potential marks if ever he'd seen one. They were large, colourfully and expensively dressed and could have been sisters.

Tiggy thought he'd become expert over the years at guessing the nationality of passengers by their dress and walk. He was convinced that these were from the US and as they got closer, he heard a loud Southern drawl from one of them that positioned them perfectly as Southern Belles.

"Have you two jumped ship?" Tiggy asked in a lightly accented English as the women drew level with his table.

The pair looked really guilty for a moment then realised by his broad and slightly conspiratorial smile that he was joking.

"Don't worry madam, I won't report you to the captain or have you put in the brig for mutiny – I just hope that you are having fun in this wonderful part of the world?"

The blonde looked down at the man sitting at the cafe table and decided to be a little braver than she'd allowed herself to be recently. She hadn't really talked to anyone other than the men at her golf club and a few married bores onboard since her husband died many months ago.

This guy might look like a bit part actor from a Noel Coward movie but he certainly was different from those grey specimens. He was tall, suntanned and had long dark hair that was greying at the temples just like all those stars she used to see in the movies. Most of those eventually turned out to be gay but somehow, she didn't think this guy

8

suffered from that problem.

Her sister tried to pull her away but she dropped anchor determinedly on the table next to the man talking. The sister was no lightweight but she was definitely outclassed in this competition and sat down with an embarrassed sigh next to her.

Following normal procedures Pierre swiftly came over with effusive greetings, welcoming them to Pierre's fine restaurant and asked the two ladies what they wanted to drink.

"Champagne" said the blonde much to the amazement of everyone, including Tiggy, but he caught on remarkably quickly.

"Pierre, none of that cheap stuff you keep for the tourists ... ladies, if I can suggest some local sparkling wine from New Zealand - it is better and cheaper. What do you think, madam will you trust me?"

She eventually nodded and Tiggy ordered a bottle of Nautilus Methode Champenoise from Marlborough whilst giving them a run down on the local wine scene in New Zealand. Also adding some general recommendations on food such as bluff oysters, blue cod or venison if they were staying and eating in the village. He added that Pierre's was exactly the right place to enjoy such local delicacies. Pierre in the background bowed modestly with a pleased expression on his face and went for the wine.

Tiggy realised that a gentleman such as himself would politely allow the ladies to enjoy their champagne in peace so turned back to his table and started to work. He picked up the Montblanc and went back to his writing with a look of intense concentration.

Our hero's instincts told him that the sight of anyone writing longhand with a fountain pen was so archaic that it would get most observers asking questions. He was not disappointed for long.

"You have lovely writing," the senior sister asked after she had drained one glass and Pierre was offering refills.

"Thank you," Tiggy said with a meaningful sigh. "I find that it is the only way I get my emotions down on the page but I have a deadline which is absolutely crippling me."

"You're a writer?" The blonde asked with real excitement in her voice.

"Very unsuccessful ... otherwise I would have moved on by now ..." Tiggy said with a choke in his voice.

"Where are you trying to get to?" The blonde asked with genuine interest.

"I have a beautiful boat but it is falling to pieces and certainly not fit to cross the Pacific yet. If either of you have owned a boat you know that it costs thousands .... Tiggy looked questioningly over at the two ladies .... "You offered me a drink earlier, perhaps I might have a glass after all?"

It was obvious that neither had any experience of small boats and Tiggy passed over a photograph of a lovely 1920 Riva speedboat with a rare cabin conversion which looked as though it might have been owned by an Italian movie star.

"That is what she should look like but sadly at the moment it is virtually a hulk … but enough of my problems, I should introduce myself."

Tiggy stood tall, clicked his heels and took the blonde's hand. "Jergov"

"I'm sorry?" the blonde said with a giggle she couldn't contain.

"Count Tolstoy Jergov, at your service."

Over the next ten minutes he gave the ladies a modest account of his ancestors in Lithuania – the castle sacked by the Germans, the land pillaged by the Russians, the family sent into slavery and everything else bad that happened to aristocrats in the wrong place at the wrong time. He showed them his cufflinks (bought from a Paris flea market with an impressive crest on) and tried to explain his coat of arms. This included a crown, crossed swords and for some strange reason a beaver. The first two elements were easy but the beaver he explained had been native in his country until they had been exterminated by the Russians during the famines.

At this point Tiggy teared up and his audience saw the deep tragedy in his eyes. The woman introduced herself as Miriam Bender from Miami who had been suitably impressed and taken his hand in hers.

Tiggy couldn't help but be attracted by the beautifully manicured nails, the thousands of dollars of diamonds on her hands and Patek Phillippe watch on her wrist, all of which looked genuine to his untrained but avaricious eye. For a moment he considered warning her about wearing such valuable jewellery when off the cruise ship but managed to restrain himself.

The younger sister had darker hair and similar build. But looked less adventurous, less bejewelled and a lot less impressed with his story. Tiggy, therefore, reserved most of his attention to the blonde called Miriam and couldn't remember the younger sisters name anyway.

It turned out that the blonde Bender sister had made lots of money out of old people's homes in Miami by selling out after the Covid 19 crisis in

10

2022. The virus had depressed values in the sector a little but the low mortality rate in her group of homes and the increase in older people wanting Miami sunshine still meant that she made many millions of dollars profit on the sale.

According to Miriam, George her husband and business partner, had been lovely but boring enough to have been a resident in one of their retirement homes by the age of 40. He had died two months after the sale whilst trying energetically to improve his golf handicap on the championship course in Bermuda.

Miriam herself only really missed him when she realised that there was no-one to talk to over morning coffee or no-one to escort her to the country club every weekend.

Our hero tried to get back to his precious writing a few times but Miriam made up for her lack of recent conversations with men over the next hour. The younger sister barely got a chance to speak but after a couple more bottles of Nautilus, Miriam slowed down enough for her to get a few words in. The sister said that she had been married to a successful farmer with orange groves and vineyards and she was also recently widowed. This world trip was their chance to re-bond as sisters and 'live a little'. It appeared that so far it was working.

After a while Tiggy excused himself and went to the bathroom. Whilst he was in the back Miriam pulled the notebook over to her side and started to read what he had written. The prose was beautiful and although she hadn't read much quality stuff since college, she recognised real talent in the hand written pages. The power of the words almost brought tears to her eyes and she had to push the notebook guiltily back when she heard the loo flush and the door open.

Tiggy could tell that the bait had been taken and that the prose that he'd borrowed from an obscure British writer was good enough to impress most people. He pulled the notebook back to himself possessively and explained that writing had been an important part of the family tradition for centuries. He said that he remembered his grandmother taking him to a huge library in their castle and pointing out all the great leather-bound books on the shelves. She showed him volumes by Shakespeare, Dostoevsky, Dickens and her own particular favourite Tolstoy. It was the love of this Russian author that had made his mother christen him Tolstoy William Jergov much to the embarrassment of the rest of the family.

"Can we read any of your books?" Miriam asked earnestly and even the younger sister looked less threatened and vaguely interested.

"I've only had a few books published and most are now out of print. The modern publishing trade is a disgrace, what with digital and the lack of good quality bookshops anywhere – I really fear that writers of my kind of book are too unfashionable to be published."

"What a pity, those words you wrote today really moved me – I'd love to read one of your books," Miriam repeated wistfully.

"This is one of the few copies left of my last book." Tiggy pointed out the battered hardback he'd brought with him with a sad smile.

The younger sister grabbed it quickly, looked at the cover and held it up triumphantly.

"This is by Eugene Fenton, not by you Mr Jerkoff or whatever your name is."

Tiggy paused dramatically and leaned back. "That is my pen name – the family would not be happy if I sullied their good name with romantic fiction – dreadful snobs, I'm afraid."

Miriam pulled the book off her sister and looked at the fly - leaf which had been doctored by an expert in photo-shop to show an artistic photograph of a younger Tiggy and effusive compliments about the book from some of the leading literary pundits in Europe.

She pointed out the page to her sister who read it through with care, comparing Tiggy with the photograph and becoming gradually convinced. They both looked at Tiggy aka Count Jergov aka Eugene Fenton with renewed respect.

The author rose in his chair and bowed deeply to the two women

"Listen, I have to go." Tiggy gathered up his belongings and started to leave. "Actually, I have got a chance of a making a little money with my next book – maybe enough to repair the hull on the Riva – who knows..."

"Don't go now, have another drink?" said Miriam, rising a little unsteadily to her feet herself. "Tell us a little more ... please."

Tiggy sat down again with apparent reluctance and a certain amount of embarrassment.

"This sounds ridiculous, I know, but some people will pay a lot of money to be in my next book"

"You're joking," said the blonde sister.

"No, honestly, I've got someone who wants me to include a heroine with her name - she's called Evelyn and she's willing to pay ten thousand dollars for that. I've got a guy, a financial advisor called Charles who will

pay a similar amount if the villain has his name – it's ridiculous, really."
"Could you use the name, George Bender in there somewhere?" his wife asked slightly drunkenly.
"Maybe, it's not a bad name really, but for what sort of character?"
"A boring, sycophant with bad teeth and no ambition," the blonde woman said. Her sister looked absolutely horrified and then collapsed in a fit of giggles.
With seeming reluctance and worry about the timescales involved Tiggy discussed things and half an hour later our author had two new characters for his book. The girls had initialled some plausible contracts on his iPad and he had ten thousand US dollars from each transferred into his account in Panama.

Tiggy remembered these recent successes even though his mouth felt like a gorilla's armpit and one eye still didn't open properly. What happened thereafter and why he was now naked and in an unfamiliar bed between two women was a complete mystery to him.
Gradually he tried to reconstruct what had happened. He thought that the author and his two new literary clients decided to celebrate their new relationship despite already having lots of fizz.
The sisters had bought more Nautilus which he drank with the enthusiasm of an author newly appreciated. They then insisted on him trying what they called Miami Slammers and called Pierre over. Before long they were knocking back tall purple drinks with olives on top every few minutes.

He should have realised that these women were serious drinkers and that if he didn't leave soon then there was no chance of him surviving intact. His Achilles heel was cocktails, a fact that he unfortunately always forgot whilst drinking cocktails. Tiggy's thought process was dragged back to the present by a soft hand touching his right thigh and creeping over until it was resting on his erection. He kept his eyes shut but the hand seemed to know what it was doing.
"There you are – good morning, Count Jergov – I see that you are ready?" said a soft Southern voice.
"Ready for what?" Tiggy asked in a croaky and slightly frightened voice.
"Your duties," said a voice from the other side of his body.
Something about this statement triggered another memory of what had happened the previous day and Tiggy started to understand why the

13

sounds of the morning were not familiar. Miriam had said that there were a couple of wealthy friends onboard the cruise ship who would also love to be part of his book and Tiggy started to see a potential goldmine of characters.

He vaguely remembered being helped to the tender and being reassured by the sisters that *Amazon* was moored in Akaroa for a couple of days and he would be able to return home on one of the regular trips made by the tenders.

He didn't recollect getting anyone else as a book character but he did remember that they'd had more to drink in the saloon bar and that both girls had helped him eventually to his present berth.

He didn't think that he'd made love to either sister last night, but he really couldn't be sure. Before he remedied that situation he desperately needed to pee. Tiggy slid out of bed to find the heads and pulled back the curtain on the suite window.

Much to his surprise there wasn't the coast of Akaroa, there wasn't any land at all – just sea and lots of it, stretching all the way to the horizon.

"Fuck!" he said using uncharacteristically common language.

"That's exactly what we're expecting," Miriam said saucily from under the covers behind him.

Tiggy escaped to a loo which was bigger than the main saloon in his boat, sat and contemplated his situation. He appeared to have no clothes, no phone and no-one who would report his disappearance for weeks. It looked as though he'd been 'Shanghaied' but instead of service to his country it looked as though he was going to have to serve two rampant matrons instead.

He seriously wondered whether he was fit for duty. Still, looking down at his distended member he thought that he might as well go down fighting and went back into the suite. He stood at the entrance for a few seconds then dived in under the duvet with an enthusiastic roar.

It was an hour before he was able to speak. The two women were really gentle with him but insisted that they both had satisfaction. This rather unusual ménage à trois did wonders for his libido and both sisters seemed to appreciate his dark arts of lovemaking, so Tiggy lay back between the two women afterwards and asked his kidnappers where on earth he was.

"The good ship *Amazon*," Miriam answered with a smile.

"And where on earth is she?" Tiggy asked remembering to use his foreign accent for the first time.

If the girls noticed his reversion to character, they were too polite to answer but Sister Two said.

"The South Pacific I believe."

"Where is our next port of call?"

"I'm not sure, whether we hit land for two weeks or more, are you sis? The dark haired sister answered with a slight humorous tone to her voice.

"Don't be silly, it's not that long, but it must be ten days before we reach Antarctic." Miriam answered whilst pretending to look at the itinerary in her bag.

The thought of even 10 days as a sex-slave to these two filled him with dread and he decided to escape. He pulled open the wardrobes and couldn't find any clothes that weren't tailored for a woman and opened drawers in desperation trying find anything to cover his modesty. In the end he grabbed a towel from the bathroom and pushed toward the exit but the door was locked and there were no signs of any keys. He tried to pull the door with all his strength and it didn't budge an inch.

"Count Jergov," said a female voice from behind that he recognised. "If you try to escape, we will call security and accuse you of rape and theft. You have no clothes, no proof of identity and I'm sure that the police will have you on record somewhere. If you don't cooperate, we will ensure that you get in serious trouble."

Tiggy thought quickly and realised that it would be difficult to force the girls to give him the keys and to force his way out without creating even more unpleasantness. So he sat on the side of the bed to gather his thoughts and tried to cover his modesty.

"What do want from me?" He asked with more than a little desperation in his voice.

"Satisfaction – after all we've each paid you ten thousand dollars, and we deserve it," the other sister whispered huskily.

Over the next few minutes Miriam Bender propped herself up in bed and outlined their demands whilst her sister nodded in encouragement. Tiggy sat down in the chair by the window and looked at the two extremely attractive women and wondered how long he might survive as some kind of super stud. He was over 40, reasonably fit, extremely well trained but judging by the experience so far, these women would not accept second best.

The blonde's first demands were not unexpected but the rest of their conditions made Tiggy a little more optimistic.

"Firstly, lovemaking of the highest quality is expected. But you will serve just one of us per night."

Tiggy nodded with what thought looked like gratitude but Miriam carried on with their demands like a coach addressing the team before a big final.

"We think that your book idea is excellent and that there are many rich women on this cruise who would be interested in paying to have a character named.

But we demand 80% of anything you make whilst onboard our ship."

Tiggy changed to full Count Jergov mode and gasped dramatically.

"No, that is absolutely outrageous. I am an artist and I'm disgusted by your offer - 10% might be possible as an agent's commission if you find some more characters. This book is not a cheap thriller you can buy and sell like a sack of potatoes - it's a work of genius."

The artist and the forces of mammon spent half an hour going through offers and counter offers and eventually the two parties settled on a 50/50 split.

They started to work out how this arrangement would work on a practical basis. Count Jergov was an involuntary stowaway and yet for this agreement to work he had to be seen, he had to eat and to look respectable. He needed decent clothes for one thing and be able to move freely around the ship. At this moment he didn't even have the clothes he'd arrived in.

Both sisters had suites and the ship was huge so it was unlikely that a stranger sitting with the sisters or sleeping with them would be noticed. Meals and port visits were times of greater risk but his literary team thought that they had four or five days at sea before they had to worry about that.

Tiggy Foghorn was uncertain, which was an unusual state for him. Did the sisters know the full depth of his deceit? Did they know that there was no book in reality and that Count Jergov was a fiction in more ways than one? They had paid the money and it had cleared in his bank account so they had certainly believed him at the beginning. But he realised that their proposition didn't need total belief to work and it could make them both some tax-free cash. Which was an incentive even for rich people.

It was really fascinating to think of it. Foghorn had always seen the sea as his natural element and loved waking up in the Riva with the gentle movement of the tide pulling on the moorings. He had family connections to the navy and apart from his youth he had always been close to the coast or on the water. The sea meant freedom, excitement and opportunity and the sisters were offering him a genuine voyage of discovery.

He thought it through and became his normal optimistic opportunist. This could be Count Tolstoy Jergov's most profitable venture and a nice change from sitting on the quay and waiting for the boat to come in. Our author had done his research and gone directly to the most profitable market.

This could be a comfortable billet in so many ways. To a red-blooded sailor like him the thought of endless food, wine and passion on immediate tap also had an unusual charm.

Tiggy Foghorn had a strange belief in fate. Many times over his last 30 years, his life had been changed by women and though he hadn't always understood the reasons and not always enjoyed the immediate effects, things always seemed to work out in the end.

Tiggy had been taught many wonderful things by a sexy older woman when he been just a callow youth and felt an instinctive love for girls of a certain age and build. Miriam and her sister had that familiar Rubenesque attraction. So he decided to follow his instincts and go with their plan - at least until he could find a safe and profitable alternative.

The Nanny State

Before he was Tiggy Foghorn or Count Tolstoy Jergov, or Eugene Fenton our hero was Terence Foghorn. Terence was born in a small village called Upper Slaughter in deepest Cotswold England, the son of a Royal Navy officer and a retired sex worker. His father had served in the submarine service and met his wife-to-be in Plymouth on shore leave. A joke Terence heard quite often as a young boy was after ten years in submarines his father had gone down almost as many times as his mother. The son was around twelve years old before he understood it and by then he had lots of better things to think about than dirty jokes.

His mother's maiden name (if that is an appropriate title for such a woman) was Antonia Dupont and she was the surprise product of a local girl and a French sailor's illicit coupling on Plymouth Ho after the fireworks celebrating Drake's birthday on July 13th.

The ensuing child was Christened Antonia. The doting mother changed her surname to Dupont to celebrate the father's nationality and give the girl a little more class which was not difficult as Scroggs was the surname she was lumbered with otherwise.

The French father was apparently never identified and the thought of a Frenchman celebrating the birthday of a British naval hero might have been considered a little suspicious – no matter how pleasurable the contact.

Terence's mother to be, Antonia Dupont, grew up to be a fine looking young woman. Handsome would have been a description of her used by the Romantic novelists of earlier years. She was tall, dark-haired and had a cleavage that would have graced the figurehead of the good ship Venus.

Some prostitutes are the result of violence or exploitation but Antonia went into the trade for very different reasons that were entirely voluntary.

Terence learned his mother's life story from a friend of hers many years later and was astonished by the life she had led. At 18 years old a friend of her father had offered Antonia a job as a barmaid in the 'Hat and Beaver' down in the busy part of old Plymouth docks. She'd done well at A-levels and was considering university but really didn't fancy building up a student debt when she had no ambition to be an accountant or engineer. She also felt too grown up to spend all those years with 'kids' and wanted to earn money and be independent as soon as possible.

Antonia had been working at the pub for a few weeks and turnover had already started to go up. She looked like the barmaid from heaven according to most regulars and the landlord knew a good cleavage when we saw one and gave her more money.

Antonia enjoyed meeting people and had an earthy sense of humour which visiting sailors appreciated. Then a smart black guy came in and asked her in the most delicate way possible if she had ever considered doing hostess work because a woman like her could make 500 quid a night.

Antonia had lost her virginity two years previously to a visiting school friend and enjoyed sex. She wasn't naïve and knew that hostess work was not just handing out the sausage rolls at a party. She had high standards and insisted that the men she would be consorting with were clean, polite and generous.

The black guy, who's name turned out to be Harold, came in a few nights later and assured her that her clients would all be 'top-brass' and that she would clear a lot more than 500 quid if she worked for him. She checked him out with a few locals and he appeared to be OK. He was such an up-market pimp that he used the title 'agent' and advertised in the county magazines. After a few days consideration Antonia agreed to give it a try.

Over the next few years Antonia made so much money out of VIP clients that the tax people were after her. A personal meeting with the head of the Plymouth tax department in the suite of the Atlantic Hotel soon helped ensure that her financial affairs were kept in order. In return, she taught the grey-haired accountant a few new things about double-entry that he was surprised to learn at his time of life.

By the time Antonia was in her late twenties she had amassed a small fortune but had decided that a career change was due. As an intelligent woman she realised that hostesses are like professional footballers and often want to leave the profession before their agents want them to. Harold would lose a lot but, in the end, he was powerless to stop his best player leaving the team.

It was at a reception for senior officers at the Combined Forces Club that Antonia first met a tall, handsome, submariner called Foghorn. He was celebrating ten years' service and his grateful crew had bought him a very special present. That present was standing in front of him now and her name was Antonia Dupont.

As he said the following morning after putting on his uniform and travelling back to the submarine base, Antonia had many gifts and wonderful wrapping. He was hopelessly in love and Antonia had found someone extraordinary she could really imagine 'going straight' with.

Six months later Horatio Foghorn and Antonia Dupont were married in the old parish church of Plymouth Reach on a bright sunny day. She wore a white dress as an ironic gesture and he wore a pirate outfit complete with hook which made the ring ceremony a little strange, but they coped. Guests included plenty of hostesses, companions and women of easy virtue. Also, there were many of the sailors and officers who'd been their unfaithful customers.

The service was unique but there was no doubt at all about the couples love for each other. If anyone had looked at the register after the ceremony was complete, they would have seen that the bride had written "sex professional' under profession and the groom had written 'sex amateur' under his.

The reception was at the 'Hat and Beaver' pub which held such happy memories for Antonia and many of the locals. The event was riotous as many of the professionals could get pissed for the first time without worrying about being ripped off by their clients. The rest of the guests were an amazing mix of sailors, punters and even a de-frocked priest, but they all knew how to enjoy themselves. The happy couple toasted each other in the finest champagne and it was obvious to everyone that this was a match made in heaven. Afterwards the married couple retired to bed and didn't make love for the very first time. It was bliss.

In the months afterwards the pair looked round for a home to settle down in. They rented in Plymouth for a while but they realised that they had too much history there so looked in the country. Eventually they had moved to a small stone cottage in the Cotswolds where they thought that Antonia's previous clients wouldn't find her and that Horatio was unlikely to come across any previous shipmates. They were wrong on both counts.

After a respectable amount of time and to show that it hadn't been a shotgun marriage, Antonia gave birth to an 8lb boy who they named Terence. An unusual name maybe, but Antonia had always rather fancied Terence Stamp when he played the baddie in the old Superman films.

The three lived together for many years in total happiness with Horatio away at sea for months at a time and Antonia only doing the odd freelance job over the border in Birmingham. When they were together, they were the most balanced and the most affectionate family anyone could imagine.

Terence's early life had been full of love and his parents had given him everything - except the experience of real life in the raw that they both had had by the same age. So Terence had a sheltered country upbringing and was young for his age in many ways. That innocence would be lost in a way that no-one could have predicted on one fateful day in late July.

When Terence was 12 years old came the social event that would change everything - The Slaughter Kicking Festival.

Like most villages close to each other in England, Upper Slaughter hated Lower Slaughter.

Centuries ago, this meant that young men from the village each occasionally raided the other in dead of night and carried off a pig, a sheep or a woman. An early High Sheriff of the county had been incensed by the fact that this activity and violence didn't make a profit for the estate and banned the raids. Realising after a while that a ban was even more unprofitable, he came up with another idea. With commendable foresight as to what would increase turnover in the pubs he owned, he declared July 29th Slaughter Kicking Day.

Since 1656, the event had taken place on the river which joined the two villages and had a unique character all of its own. Twenty villagers from each community always started from each end at 6.30 a.m. and their task was to paddle a perfect replica of a Viking longship to the opposing village, carrying a cheese, a barrel and a local maiden.

Residents from Upper Slaughter joked that getting a maiden from Lower Slaughter would be well-nigh impossible unless they were below the age of ten years old. The opposing gybes were mainly to do with villagers saying that people from Upper Slaughter had a natural advantage in the river competition because of their webbed feet and hands.

The event normally went on all day and at the half way point on the river there was absolute carnage. The prize had only ever been won once and that was in the 19th Century when most of the lower village had already died of the pox.

The other aspect of Slaughter Kicking Day that concerned the Foghorn parents that year was the violence, drunkenness and sexual freedom that was also a traditional part of the day. Terence was 12 years old but he was still an innocent so Horatio and Antonia decided that whilst they would be attending the event themselves, they needed a nanny for Terence.

A couple of days before the event Antonia still couldn't find anybody local. Most people in the county knew about the battle and wouldn't come within ten miles of it. Police also tended to block the roads coming in and out except for ambulances and other emergency vehicles. On one year they had even had to call in the bomb squad because of a device planted on the river bank by a particularly ambitious villager.

In desperation Antonia had to call an old professional friend from Plymouth who she had trusted implicitly in the old days. Maddie Quimby had gone a little down market since she'd been a hostess working with Antonia but she was still an attractive woman. When Terence met her for the first time he was tongue-tied, which was a problem he learned how to overcome later in rather different circumstances.

Horatio and Antonia Foghorn left their lovely stone cottage at 6.00 a.m. dressed for the battle in steel-toed boots and oilskins. Terence sat at the breakfast bar in his school blazer and shorts and ate his Sugar Puffs, looking across at this woman who was leaning back in his father's recliner showing a lot of black-stocking thigh.

Terence looked up her legs and felt an enormous erection growing which he was convinced would be visible at the end of his shorts unless he could stop it. She seemed oblivious to his arousal and he tried everything – long division, calculus, the taste of school rice pudding – anything to turn himself off but he failed. He was convinced he was going to cream himself unless he could stop looking.

Maddie Quimby had not left Plymouth for years. It was where she had always plied her trade and it was where she felt at home. Though not the newly refurbished dock section, which was designed for tourists – not punters. The town had changed a lot but there was still work for those like Antonia and herself who had been at the top end of the hostess business. But Maddie was finding the competition from younger women a little difficult to handle these days and was having to take clients who were a different class. In fact, the only reason she'd agreed to come to this country bumpkin village was to get out of town whilst two rather violent and jealous clients sorted out their differences.

The other reason Maddie had come was because Antonia had been one of the few friends she'd had in the business and they had both had a lot of fun. She was astonished to be asked to baby sit but imagined that as Terence was 12 years old all she had to do was to was keep the brat off the booze and drugs and open a can of beans at lunch time.

When she had arrived, the son looked like a kid and as scared as a rabbit in the headlights. After the parents left, she tried all the boring questions about school, friends and football with Terence and got no joy. It was a pity, she thought, he was a good looking lad and his parents knew how to have fun, so surely he couldn't be all that bad?"

"Have you had any girlfriends?" she asked.

"Loads" he said with a squeak.

Maddie looked at the youth with disbelief, were all young men this pathetic? She decided out of consideration for her friend and for all the young women in Terence's future who would be horribly disappointed. She decided that this boy needed taking in hand.

"Would you like to learn how to give a woman pleasure?" Maddie asked with a knowing smile.

"Yes, please Miss," he answered, trying to keep the tremor out of his voice.

"Draw the curtains Terence – fuck that for a proper name – I can't call you Terence and I can't stand the name Terry. From now you are going to be Tiggy - Tiggy Foghorn sounds like someone who I could have some real fun with."

She had got rid of his juvenile erection with a couple of shakes of her hand so he could concentrate on his lessons. The first was to how to undress a woman without it turning into a comedy that no-one laughed at.

Tiggy looked back at those lessons with embarrassment but huge gratitude. He'd found practising on Maddie was a nightmare at first. She seemed to have more harnesses, garters and clasps than a shire horse and seeing all that pink flesh nearly brought him off again. She was a buxom woman and finding a way to unbind those wonderful breasts was an art in itself.

At that point Maddie asked him whether there was any wine in the house and despite the fact that it was still only 9.00 a.m. and he had never drunk anything before, Tiggy found a bottle of Blue Nun in the fridge and filled a couple of glasses. He had tried to look cool whilst sipping his wine opposite this lovely woman with huge bare breasts and failed miserably.

Maddie had smiled understandingly and talked to him about sex, women and how some liked their shoulders and breasts caressed, some liked them kissed and asked him to practise on her. After a few attempts he had shown a little more expertise on this and Maddie asked for another glass of wine from the bottle and drained it.

The boy didn't join her – he really couldn't see what everyone saw in this wine-drinking lark and quietly filled his own with some Lucozade from the fridge.

By 10.00 a.m. Tiggy had moved on to Maddie below the waist and he had got a throbbing erection at the sight of the pink folds of flesh and hair (shaved into an attractive heart shape) that guarded her secret place. To him she smelt like the most forbidden animal in the jungle and Tiggy instinctively tried to mount her. Maddie grabbed his balls gently in both hands and told him to hold back and he painfully obeyed.

Over the next hour Terence learned about proper foreplay and Maddie finished off the Blue Nun and started on a bottle of Black Tower. Maddie was kind and patient and Tiggy desperately wanted to please her. To him she looked totally different to the girls in the fashion magazines who didn't have any flesh. She looked more like the women he'd seen in the Dutch or Italian paintings in the Oxford art gallery he had visited. She had curves and shape in all the places that had always attracted men and Tiggy realised that he was lucky to have this perfect example of womanhood to study in front of him for so long. It was obvious Maddie had great confidence in her own brand of feminine charm too.

It wasn't as exciting but the lesson on contraception and how to be considerate to a sexual partner was essential Maddie said. Tiggy practised how roll a condom on without looking ridiculous. This took two or three attempts and Tiggy had to raid his Dad's bedside drawers for more Durex to practice with but he managed in the end.

It was a half an hour later that Tiggy actually put his penis where it was meant to go and he lasted as long as two minutes. Maddy was polite enough to gasp a few times and Tiggy took this as a tremendous success. The lesson on real sexual technique started later and lasted for considerably longer. Tiggy had a few false spurts along the way but carried on manfully until Maddie thought he had at least mastered the rudiments.

Our hero had almost run out of juice by then and Maddie had run out of wine. An old ship's decanter of port had been on the sideboard since Christmas and Tiggy presented it to his teacher with gratitude. She filled a wine glass to the brim and started on the Cockburn with a sigh of satisfaction.

Ten hours after they'd left the cottage a very battered and drunk set of parents returned to the cottage and staggered up to bed. As normal, no one had actually won the trophy because the Viking ships had been sunk, abandoned or scuttled before they had reached the finishing line. There were also several technical objections and the maidens on each side had to prove their maidenhood to the opposition and were now not available for next year. The barrels had been drunk, cheeses eaten and there were three team members from each village hospitalised. Everyone considered it to have been a grand day out.

Terence had learned a game far more fun than Slaughter Kicking and crept into Maddie's bed the following dawn. She threw him out with a smile and said that she would be back in a few months to see how he was getting on with his lessons. She left later by train and if Terence's parents suspected that his innocence had been lost, then they never admitted it to him at the time.

He insisted that all his friends called him Tiggy from that day and they gradually came round. They could tell that he'd changed and the fact that he'd lost his cherry was something he tried not to brag about but couldn't stop hinting at. The fact that it was an older woman gave him maximum points with the other boys as most of them had only fumbled with school girls the same age as themselves.

The fact that he'd had sex *three* times with a woman also made him God-like in their eyes.

Horatio and Antonia refused to use the nickname and only acceded when he refused to answer to any other name. In the end they just put it down to teenage angst he'd grow out of and played along.

When your own father had called you Horatio whatever the history, his dad realised that Tiggy was not the worst name to be stuck with and finally agreed to the change of name.

Tiggy Foghorn stayed in the village for another few years and became very popular with many of the local girls. He remembered his early lessons well and was never just after his own personal gratification, knowing that if the female got pleasure, then he got pleasure too. But Tiggy still had a yen for shapely older women who reminded him of Maddie Quimby – the nanny from heaven. This weakness would lead him to an assignation with the local bishop's wife which would have dramatic consequences for them both and shape his early life.

A Ship of Fools

Back on the cruise ship *Amazon*, Tiggy realised that Miriam Bender was similar to Maddie Quimby in shape and warmth but was unlikely to teach him as much in bed. It was his turn with the sister tonight and though she was also an attractive woman he hoped the farmer's wife enjoyed something a little more exciting than rough ploughing.

What she'd been like in bed last night, indeed what either of them had been like, was shrouded in post cocktail fog but they'd seemed to gasp at the right places and been satisfied with his performance this morning. Tonight, was a different matter and he felt a tremor of erotic nervousness at the thought.

After all these years he considered himself to be a fine artist in lovemaking but one who needed a willing and passionate woman as his canvas. Looking across the suite at the sister he thought that she showed some promise. She was a brunette where Miriam was blonde and not as effervescent but she had a buxom figure and wonderful blue eyes that seemed to smoulder in his direction.

Before that he realised that he needed to concentrate and make some more money.

The sisters had insisted on a cut from anything he made from the Count Jergov writing deal and would be a useful source of information about the ship. But *Amazon* was enormous and he realised that he needed to get dressed and do some exploring himself. Most passengers would have had more than a month to find their way round and the last thing he wanted was to look like a stranger.

The brochure in the cabin was so glossy and colourful that it was difficult to focus, he would have preferred a set of plans. It seemed to have numerous bars, coffee lounges, saloons and at least two major restaurants. He needed to check them out to see where a romantic writer would be likely to retreat in order to write and gain inspiration. He was sure that the sisters would offer to guide him but he felt happier if he did it himself. At the moment he was just wearing a towel and might just stand out too much if he tried it.

He asked Miriam where she'd hidden his gear. She coyly refused at first but he said that he needed food if he was going to perform later so she relented and dragged out a case from above the wardrobe and pulled out his clothes. A quick look at his apparel revealed some wear and tear that he couldn't remember getting. The blazer was just about OK but the cream trousers and white shirt were covered in purple stains which could have been the Miami Slammers. The pen, notepad and Eugene Fenton book were undamaged which was a huge relief to everyone – especially Count Jergov.

Together they agreed that before he made his first public appearance, they needed to get him some more clothes so the two sisters checked sizes and went off excitedly to the fashion shops onboard and locked him in the cabin. He'd warned them against Hawaiian shirts, baseball caps, three quarter length trousers or any other of the fashion disasters worn by Americans on holiday, but feared the worst.

Tiggy may not have been able to escape but he used the time profitably by doing a quick audit of the cabin. He couldn't get in the safe but even the jewellery they'd left lying around was worth thousands of dollars. He recognised some great Tiffany and classic Bulgari designs as well as the expensive watch he'd seen when they'd first met. God knows what she thought valuable enough to put in the safe he thought as he hid a single diamond ear-ring in his underpants against hard times.

Judging by the voracity of the sisters' appetites, his underpants might be an unsafe place to hide stuff on board and he vowed to find somewhere less risky before nightfall.

When the girls finally arrived back with his new clothes later, he rejected many of them as far too Yanky. He eventually selected some cream canvas shorts and a dark blue polo shirt along with his original loafers and at least felt confident enough to go down to breakfast. He wasn't sure that the Count would have been quite this informal but needs must when the devil drives and he was starving.

The breakfast room looked large enough to float his Riva speedboat in and he didn't think that he'd ever seen so much glitter in one place. But the sight of a sumptuous buffet at each end where you could get almost anything made him dribble like a bulldog. He hadn't eaten anything since Pierre's place in Akaroa and that was centuries ago.

Realising that this was their first appearance in public, Miriam took his arm firmly and they queued at the buffet before he attacked it like a wolf. He opted for a huge plate of scrambled eggs and smoked salmon. She ordered a large bowl of prunes and other fruit which gave him a few clues about her digestive efficiency.

Remembering that was his first public performance, Tiggy showed Miriam to her table with very noticeable old-world courtesy. When the dark-haired sister arrived, he stood like an old-fashioned gentleman and let her sit before sitting down himself. He could see looking round that many of his target market had noticed his behaviour and approved. Tiggy was confidently in character as the Count for the first time onboard.

Feeling renewed after breakfast our hero went back to the suite, opened his briefcase and took out the notebook, pen and book that were the tools of his trade and checked them out. The fountain pen was full of ink and he had plenty of paper so he planned to find a place to use them profitably as soon as possible. He bade his farewells to the sisters, promising to see them later after he'd explored the ship a little more.

After nearly an hour of exploration he was able to find a window table close to the bar in the stern. It had lovely views and was miles away from the main bars where the hoi-polloi were busy getting drunk before afternoon tea. It looked a perfect place for Count Jergov to operate his magic.

He started writing longhand, the first chapter he'd memorised so many years ago and the Montblanc flowed with its normal poetry. The blazer and cravat were back, twinned with a new set of cream chinos that weren't quite to his taste but had been the only thing available onboard. Still, he felt that he looked in character and asked the barman for a glass of champagne. He signed *Bender Suite 25* on the receipt added a hefty tip and was relieved when it wasn't questioned.

The first afternoon he wrote for half an hour with an expression so pained that the barman asked if he was feeling alright.

"This second book is being an absolute beast," he said with an accent a little too Noel Coward to be perfect. But then, acting as if inspired, our heroic author put pen to paper and wrote another paragraph. With a satisfied sigh, he shut his notebook and rose to go, waving to the bar in an elegant but distracted way as he left.

Tiggy suspected that by the time he returned that evening most of the regulars would know that they had a successful author as a fellow guest. He needed, however, to maintain his Count Jergov identity more assiduously as he had been danger of forgetting his persona earlier. Even now he wasn't sure whether the sisters believed it, but in his business, it was unwise to change a winning formula too often.

He returned to the same bar at 6.00 p.m. in a more definite Count Jergov mode and ordered another glass of champagne - this time asking what the year was suspiciously, which made the barman hesitant to serve him with the Cava he'd been conning everyone else with. Much to the barman's disgust he had to find a bottle of real champagne and serve it.

Tiggy remembered the slight accent this time and went back to his table to work.

It took nearly an hour before anyone showed any sign of interest and then it was a large, muscular man in a very colourful shirt. Men were not his normal quarry so Tiggy gave him a withering look that normally put off philistines and unbelievers. It didn't work.

"Are you a writer?"

"I try to be," Tiggy said putting down his pen with a sigh.

"Why don't you use a computer, like I do"

"Because computers have no soul, Shakespeare didn't use a computer, Dickens didn't use an iPad even John Steinbeck didn't use a tablet."

"Who?"

Before he knew it and certainly before he invited it, the man had introduced himself as Elmer Flannigan and showed him a photograph of his extensive marina in Florida and his two boats – mainly used for fishing trips. Seeing an opportunity to bait his own hook, Tiggy showed him a shot of the 1920 Riva that he was trying to restore and introduced himself as Count Tolstoy Jergov for the first time on this ship.

Actually, there was a genuine connection between them as Elmer admired the lines of the beautiful boat and Tiggy described its construction, power and just how much he needed to complete the restoration.

"In fact, I am only on this ridiculous leviathan of a ship, writing my second book so I can finish the restoration." Tiggy said with the Jergov accent and explained the principle of the naming characters for ten thousand dollars project.

Elmer picked the other book and asked about it. The Count pointed out his pen name of Eugene Fenton and explained that it was used because of his family reputation and the guy followed normal procedure and looked at the cover photograph and outstanding reviews. Much re-assured the passenger sat down uninvited and read the first few pages of the new Eugene Fenton book on his notepad and appeared to be hooked.

He had chosen his phantom ghost author well. Fenton had written over a hundred years ago and been unpublished in the traditional sense for his entire life – which was tragically but artistically short. After he died in poverty in the slums of Marrakesh a lover had his final manuscript privately published. It was like a more romantic version of a Jane Austen period piece and Tiggy had found a couple of copies on a market stall in

Bury, near Manchester.

The romance wasn't listed by the British Library and if you Googled the author, you got absolutely nothing relevant at all. The work altering the cover had been done using photoshop and the ministrations of a young lad in Sydney who thought it was for a novelty birthday gift. So Tiggy thought that his provenance would stand most levels of investigation and any casual reader could see that Eugene Fenton had great writing skill.

Elmer was visibly moved after reading just a few pages. The heroine is dying of consumption in the workers cottage surrounded by her children. Despite the fact that he looked like a member of the cast of The Sopranos, he obviously had his tender side and was on the edge of tears

"This is lovely, absolutely lovely," Elmer said with a choked voice.

"Thank you."

"I am after a birthday present for my partner – and this could be perfect."

Playing 'hard to get' seemed a little sensible, so our favourite author said that he wasn't sure that there were many characters left and the scope was limited but asked what sort of person were they.

"The most romantic, lovely person you could imagine" Elmer said with a soft smile.

"Describe her to me" The Count asked.

"It's not a woman ... my partner of twenty years is a man."

Tiggy needed to think quickly but realised that it would add more to his portfolio if he added gay men and women to his target market. Gay couples were, if anything, more romantic than the middle-aged women he normally favoured. He asked what sort of fictional character Elmer's partner would like to be.

"Strangely I think that my partner – Neil by the way – would identify with a Heathcliffe type of person. Tall, long haired, with rippling muscles and a rough way with them but obviously with a sensitive nature and cultured manners."

Avoiding any bad taste jokes about Neil being an appropriate name for someone with their taste, Tiggy listened further to Elmer's eulogy and eventually agreed that for 10,000 dollars it might be possible but that contractually it had to be signed up in the next 24 hours or it just couldn't happen.

The only condition Elmer requested was that the Count should write a few words on this specific story and then he would sign up.

The author bought himself some time by requesting a meeting with Neil so that he could get some inspiration about the soul of the person in order to proceed. They agreed to have a few drinks the following day but keep the reason secret, so not to spoil the surprise.

Tiggy met the two sisters in another bar before dinner and they said excitedly that they had met a couple of ladies who could also be potential characters. He was delighted and could see this trip turning into a good earner as long as he could keep the Count Jergov persona fresh and believable. Like most actors he found extended runs a little challenging but the rewards from this performance could be excellent at the box office.

Whilst he'd been roaming the ship he'd not been challenged once and his requests for drink and even gifts had been signed for without question. Having checked quietly in the purser's office he knew that the *Amazon* encouraged everyone to charge extras to their room and that cash was discouraged.

Tiggy had them print an itinerary and saw that the ship was at sea for a few more days until it stopped at Tahiti. The ship would offer a number of trips on that island but move on after a few hours moored offshore.

As Tahiti would be the first call since he'd been kidnapped, Tiggy had to consider it as his first chance to jump ship. He knew that the island was beautiful but his French was appalling and the place was probably too small for him to disappear unless it was an emergency.

Far better would be Dunedin in New Zealand when the ship had done its Polynesian island tour and was on the return leg. This had the advantage of being a country where the culture was familiar and Count Jergov had some successes to his name already.

Dunedin would be reached in eight days' time and Tiggy wondered whether he could last physically as well as artistically that long. So far, he was doing well and he was reasonably confident but he had to pace himself and concentrate or the Count could be dismasted or scuttled.

Dinner that night was actually delicious and Tiggy in Count mode kept up the old-world manners throughout, ordering excellent NZ and Chilean wines and keeping the sisters glasses topped up. He ordered the lobster thermidor with all the trimmings for himself.

The girls each had each ordered something salad-based and ate healthy-looking food until the deserts. Then they attacked the buffet with all the subtlety of a dragnet trawler. The quantity eaten by both was so great that he wondered whether there was a serious risk of a burst when he was on top of the dark sister later.

That night he remembered all of Maddie's lessons about patience and the farmer's wife was a nice surprise. Firstly, she was wearing expensive lingerie that would have turned a Trappist Monk on, secondly, she was surprisingly athletic, despite the pudding overload. Thirdly she obviously hadn't benefited from his kind of attention before and was hugely grateful for the orgasms – which were absolutely seismic.

At breakfast the following morning the look on the two sisters faces showed that they'd talked and that he'd passed the second bed test with flying colours. His first coupling with them both together had been enjoyable but he hadn't really been on top form after all the booze. His early lessons from Maddie hadn't given him any hints about threesomes but everyone was happy with the new arrangement so far. The fact that it was one woman per night from now was a relief.

Reverting to business he told them about his meeting with Elmer and his partner and the gay challenge which they all found fascinating. He told them about the secret fact-finding meeting with Neil later and they were intrigued as to what the partner of such a tough looking guy was like.

When Tiggy did meet him, he was lovely. Neil was tall, slim and the perfect antidote to Elmer who obviously loved him dearly.

Tiggy introduced himself as Count Tolstoy Jergov and the name didn't even raise a smile. Over the next few minutes, he asked Neil about favourite books, film heroes and where his favourite places were. Neil said the sea was where he felt happiest and leaned over to grab Elmer's muscular arm as they talked about special trips they'd done on their boat and the tropical sunsets they'd seen in the US and Caribbean.

Our author rose after half an hour and excused himself saying that he'd be in the bar later. Hopefully Elmer got the message and all Tiggy had to do was to write some sparkling prose as an example of his style. Strangely enough the challenge was quite exciting and Tiggy wondered whether he might be starting to believe his own literary bullshit a little too much.

Foghorn was actually not a bad writer but looking at the Eugene Fenton book and adapting it in some way was likely to be more productive. Elmer Flannigan had said a Heathcliffe type of character would be right, but Neil loved the sea, so a handsome sea-captain might be more suitable. Tiggy looked through the novel for inspiration and got out his fountain pen. After a while he thought that he had a formula and started writing:

Captain Neil Flannigan was a chief officer his men loved. Twenty years at sea as an officer on His Majesty's Frigates had given him a rough manner to those he thought unkind or pretentious but the crew knew that in any storm or any battle he was the man they would follow.

Flannigan was tall, slim and good looking in a weather-beaten way but he was unaware of the admiring glances he attracted in company. Ashore he could be the most gentle of men and often took off his captain's uniform so that he could mix with the normal people his parents had been.

Flannigan had been born in a poor family in Norfolk, England and never had aspirations to be an officer. Whilst he was only 8 years old his parents died and he was sent as a cabin boy to the ship of Captain Nelson who was another officer with humble beginnings

Neil was stricken with grief about his parents and sea-sick most of the first voyage but didn't show his fear to anyone. In the end he got his sea legs and got the respect of all the crew because of his positive attitude to life.

Three months into the voyage the ship was attacked by three French ships off the North African coast and Nelson refused to give way. He stood on the deck in full sight of the enemy and directed operations with Neil Flannigan watching fearfully from the scuppers when a cannon ball hit and Nelson was hit by wooden splinters to his leg. Despite the furious barrage of cannon fire and muskets Neil dashed across the deck to give Nelson a bandage to staunch to blood.

Nelson wound it round his leg and stood up, yelling orders for the helmsman to steer towards the enemy ships. In the end he had a famous victory and never forgot Neil Flannigan ensuring that he got training in the Royal Navy that normally would have been just for the aristocracy.

Fifteen years later Captain Neil Flannigan was in charge of his own frigate but Nelson by then was Admiral and never forgot the cabin boy who tried to save his life under heavy fire ....

Our author drafted what was meant to be the section involving Elmer's partner and then rewrote it in his best handwritten script and in the end, it looked pretty convincing. He did a full A4 page and showed the first part to the girls and they were convinced that Elmer would like it when they met in the cocktail bar later.

When the big guy duly arrived at the table later, he looked suspicious and brutish and Tiggy handed over the sheet of paper with trepidation. Elmer read it several times but his face was difficult to read. Eventually he turned.

"You got it wrong."

"What – this is just a first draft you know."

"His surname isn't Flannigan – it's Davis- but I understand why you used my name. We are not married and even if we were I'm not sure whether married names are our thing. But the draft was lovely and I really think he'll like it. He knows about Nelson, Trafalgar and everything, so that's great. When does the book come out?"

"Hopefully in six months if the publishers keep their promise."

"His birthday is in a month, could you send me something – an extract or something?"

"Probably – would a printers proof do?"

"Sure, that would be really good – I have to say that I'm really excited. Neil is a lovely man as you've seen and he'll just love the book idea."

Over the next few minutes Elmer signed the same contract on his iPad as the girls had done and transferred 10K to his bank account. It might take a little longer whilst they were at sea but judging by the last transaction the money transfer was pretty instant. They shook hands on it and Count Jergov warned Elmer to keep this whole thing secret as he was now almost out of characters and demand was high. Elmer wished him good luck with the restoration of the Riva and left the saloon with a happy smile on his face.

If Tiggy Foghorn had any form of conscience this last transaction would have bothered him because these were genuinely good people. Count Tolstoy Jergov wouldn't have even understood the concept of guilt at all. As far as he was concerned the peasants were always there to give their betters a good time and if these people were rich enough to afford a world tour, they could afford a few thousand dollars to support the arts.

Tiggy was an expert at self-justification anyway and if a pang of guilt had started to bother him, he would have thought of his beautiful boat. All this effort wasn't for him, after all, it was for the Riva, which was a work of art and deserved funding.

Our famous author changed area the following day to meet some new people. Moving around the vessel was like seeing the interior of some drug-crazed fairy palace. Tiggy had never seen so many chandeliers or travelled through so much gold but eventually he found a quiet cocktail bar close to first-class and started his routine.

First, he sat down by the windows and looked wistfully out to sea. Then he got out his pen and started writing longhand on the pad until he had finished the first page. He sighed in frustration and put down the pen and the barman was so intrigued that he came over and peered over his shoulder. Tiggy went into his successful opening scene.

"Second books are a nightmare – please bring me some champagne. The real thing please, not that Cava you serve elsewhere – I need inspiration."

The barman came back with a beautiful flute and an open bottle of Veuve Cliquot on the tray and deftly filled the glass. He was obviously fascinated by our hero so Tiggy looked round and said.

"I am an author - but please don't tell anyone. Count Jergov is my name and I've spent the last few weeks avoiding readers, agents and god knows who else. Please keep this just between us."

Knowing that the barman would keep his secret like any natural gossip would and that his fame would be spread far and wide by nightfall, Tiggy went back to work.

An hour and another glass of champagne later, the floor of the saloon shook and the barman groaned in anticipation. Looking sidewise Tiggy saw a large ginger-headed apparition heading to the bar.

"Luigi, give me an orange juice and make sure it's fresh this time," said a voice about as pleasant as an old-fashioned dentist's drill.

"It's Paco madam and our orange juice is always freshly-squeezed," said the barman piling oranges into a tall glass jar and giving it a jolt with the motor. He handed over a tall glass of the extract and waited for further orders with some trepidation.

"Bring green olives – not black, not pink – green olives and don't take all day," she demanded.

"I'm sorry madam, all we have are mixed olives, but they are the best Italian – I should know madam I'm from Puglia myself."

"I don't give a tinker's cuss where you're from, unless you can get me green olives you can expect another complaint. The Captain and I are already acquainted."

"I'm really sorry madam and I'll pass on your comments to the manager." The barman retreated to the other side of the bar and tried to hide behind the glasses he was cleaning. Tiggy went back to his writing and thanked goodness he hadn't been landed with this harridan. Listening to her accent he detected North Sydney and realised that the cultural revolution hadn't spread everywhere in the Australian continent.

"You're the bloody author I suppose?" his least favourite voice shouted from behind.

Our author turned round and looked at the tight ginger perm, bright red lipstick and thick neck carrying one the largest pearl necklaces he'd ever seen. The woman appeared to be wearing a multi-coloured tent without the poles and guy ropes. Beneath which there were twin ankles each with rolls of fat supporting feet in sandals the size of small boats.

Tiggy liked larger women but the thought of even talking to this one made him feel physically sick. He shook his head in pathetic denial and turned back to his work.

"You can't fool me Count Jergov, I know that it's you cos Miriam Bender told me where you'd be and you don't exactly look like a normal person."

Our hero tried to develop some spine, some courage, to walk away from this horrible vision and stuttered.

"There are absolutely no characters left for my book I'm afraid. I promised the last part to a woman from New York for 15,000 dollars earlier today. That's why I've moved to the quiet of this bar – demand is just too great," Jergov said with an emotional toss of his head.

The woman planted her feet like some sort of malevolent ginger colossus and glared down at the hapless and terrified man, with a determination that brooked no objection.

"I'll give you twenty thousand."

For a while the author again tried to ignore this intrusion and develop some principles but the money was just too good. It was twice what Miriam had paid and in the end the temptation overcame him and he asked her to sit down. Standing up she was just too intimidating anyway but as the seat groaned underneath her, he wasn't sure that the view was less frightening with her sitting down.

He realised that his greed had got the better of him and tried to get a few basic facts about the character. After a few minutes he realised that this woman didn't want to buy this as a present for anyone else, she wanted herself named in the book. Tiggy tried to summon up some of Count Jergov's natural distain but failed.

She signed his iPad contract and arranged the 20K without question and judging by the last contract the money transfer was remarkably quick even at sea. So the Count was considerably richer but now he had to listen to her life story. He tried to delay the briefing till he was stronger or at least until he'd had a couple of bracers but she was determined to tell him now.

Her name was Florence Hasty and she had a life story that she thought would be an inspiration to others. Florence was the daughter of a bush vicar and freelance sheep shearer close to the outback town of Wagga-

Wagga. Her father, Angus Hasty was of Scottish origin, though no-one knew whether his ancestors had come as convicts or officials.

Apparently, the father was a huge red-headed man with a religious fervour that guaranteed high attendance at his church on Sundays. He would pick up local kids in the neighbourhood by the scruff of the neck on Sunday mornings and carry them bodily to church. He was a successful clergyman in a godless time and pagan area and his abilities were noticed by the Church Council. Eventually Angus Hasty had risen to Bishop of one of the largest and most desolate parishes in Australia.

Tiggy shuddered when Florence mentioned the rank that Angus Hasty had reached in the church and also his Christian name. He had a strange premonition that this conversation would not end well and wanted to end it quickly. It was like someone walking on his grave and he couldn't really concentrate on what the Ginger-headed monster was saying.

Tiggy remembered a time of pleasure and of pain before Count Jergov came into his life. It was back three decades and in his English country homeland where he had been for a while an innocent boy called Terence. The youth had been full of hope and surrounded by love in a family that had every advantage. People had called him handsome and academically gifted but he'd thrown it all away because of pleasures of the flesh. Another Bishop called Angus with a wanton woman for a wife had tempted him vilely and changed his future path forever.

Bashing your Bishop

Psychologists say that it is often helpful if boys find something that they are really good at before they leave school. It might be sport, it might be languages or even writing, but it does wonders for their confidence later when they have to join the cruel outside world.

Back in Upper Slaughter 30 years ago, Terence Foghorn had been extremely popular with the local girls for a couple of years. Maddie Quimby had educated him in the mysteries of foreplay and sexual satisfaction, which meant that he was a Premier League lover when all the other boys were amateur players.

Tiggy's fame had spread as far away as Lower Slaughter but even with the two villages combined and new female incomers to school, the total number of conquests he could make was severely limited. He'd tried to make a few quid by capitalising on his skills and trying to educate a few other boys up to degree level. But without an experienced body like Maddie to practice on it was never quite the same. There were some older girls from the village who said that they were willing to act as demonstration dummies but they giggled too much for Tiggy's taste.

Not having a private room to operate in was also awkward. Once they managed to break into school during the holidays and he managed a few lessons arranged before a randy caretaker caught on and wanted to join in. Good weather obviously gave him a few more options and the green pastures of Lickey Hill and meadows alongside the river often had the flattened grass that was evidence of one of his teaching sessions. Increasingly, however, parents who saw daughters returning with grass stains and a glazed expression on their faces, were getting more protective.

His tutor had always promised to come back and check how he was doing with his lessons but Maddie only came back once and for some reason his parents never left them alone together. He was a strapping fifteen by then and they needed him to concentrate on his education. Antonia, his mother, could tell by his underwear that he wasn't exactly celibate anymore, his boxer shorts almost jumped into the washing machine by themselves. So he didn't need any more distractions from his school work and his Mum realised that Maddie still glowed with sexuality that would tempt a saint. Never mind a randy teenager.

Maddie had been perfectly pleasant and never mentioned their first encounter but his parents had changed over recent months and looked a little embarrassed by her. His mum in particular seemed to have forgotten the trade they were both in a few years ago. After a few visits to the pub where Maddie couldn't help eying up the male customers and dropping a few business cards saying 'Maddie Quimby Personal Massage Services' on various tables, his mother and her had a difference of opinion and she decided to leave early.

Maddie Quimby had given Terence one bit of advice before she left to go back to Plymouth.

"Don't believe in love Tiggy, it is a great deceiver and would destroy a sensitive soul like you. Don't take life too seriously either – your mum used to be a great laugh, but look at her now"

He was a bit too young to understand her wisdom really but nodded sagely.

His parents thought that they might never see Maddie Quimby again. Over the years since Antonia and Maddie had worked as hostesses, things had changed and one was now a middle-class housewife and the other was still working in the sex trade. They didn't have much in common anymore and life moves on – or that was what his mum said.

So it was strange, when a few months later he found his Mum in tears one morning reading the paper. When Tiggy asked why, she said that Maddie had been badly injured in a bar when two drunken sailors had been brawling and thrown a chair which had accidentally fractured her skull.

Teenage boys aren't normally much into showing emotion but Tiggy was really upset by the news about Maddie and vowed to remember her advice about life and love for the rest of his life.

One of the stranger changes happening was that his parents were increasingly into religion. For an ex hostess and a promiscuous submariner, they had developed a belief in the Church of England that was extraordinary but totally sincere. This meant that Terence had to go to church in the village every Sunday and rebellion was out of the question. Horatio was an old-fashioned father and Tiggy was not ready to challenge him yet.

Every week Tiggy sat on ancient pews that were so hard that they were a penance themselves. He tried to distract himself by looking at memorial stones set into the walls and imagining himself as one of those heroes who'd died in the Transvaal, Gallipoli or Vimy Ridge he could see around him.

The church was hundreds of years old and made from warm Cotswold stone and one day the sun was streaming through the stain glass windows with shafts of gold, red and blue. It was only when a hard elbow to the ribs woke him that he realised that he'd drifted off with his head resting on the shoulders of a 90 year old woman next to him in the pew.

It wasn't his fault he was knackered, his reputation as the stud of the Slaughters had recently been under threat. Andy Ripley, the new challenger was over 6 foot tall, had the face of a boy-band star and according to Natalie, who was considered to be the school judge of all things male, he had a plonker the size of a Zeppelin. This apparently compensated for the fact that he had the sexual technique of a serial rapist.

Tiggy was determined to prove that no interloper was going to challenge his crown and that he was still cock of the walk. The previous night he had taken Natalie to the local pub to show how mature they both looked.

The Spade Tree Inn had been serving under-age drinkers since before there were licensing laws and Brenda the jovial ex - matron who'd been landlady for the last ten years carried on that policy. She believed that if you treated young drinkers with understanding then they stayed with you for life.

Tiggy could see the disbelief on the heavily coiffured lady behind the bar as he ordered a half of lager for himself and a Gin & Tonic for Natalie, who looked about twelve sitting in the seat in the window trying to look casual. He pleaded with his eyes and she pulled a half from one of the pumps and turned to the optics. The landlady pointed to the list of ten different gins and five different tonics and asked him to make a choice. He nearly panicked but saw a familiar name on the shelf and asked for Plymouth Gin.

Tiggy hadn't really drunk anything since the glass of Blue Nun he'd had with Maddie a year or so back but knew lager was what all the other men in the bar seemed to be drinking. He took his half back to the table, sipped the amber liquid and nearly threw up – it was disgusting.

Natalie had seen her mother drink and managed to put the tonic in the gin without mishap. She looked lovely in her Black Lycra top and Scarlet mini-skirt and Tiggy told her so.

Natalie was one of his earlier conquests and he thought that he'd done pretty well originally but if she was comparing him unfavourably to Andy Ripley then he needed to do better. Tiggy's reputation as the Supercock of the area was important to him so he had decided to pull out all the stops.

One of the other difficult things about his competitor Ripley was the rumour that he had shagged one of the teachers. In terms of school reputation that was the equivalent of climbing the Matterhorn or winning F1. The way Tiggy had tried to compete with that claim was to say to the rumour mongers that the teacher concerned was a Mrs Lally who was 60 years old and smelt strongly of cats. It was Tiggy's first taste of propaganda and the local readers of social media loved it. Ripley spent the next week denying it which made him look guiltier than ever. Other boys started walking past Ripley and going 'meow' and giving him cat food, which made it all wonderfully worthwhile.

Back in the Spade Tree Tiggy only had enough money for one drink and they had shared the table for an hour with his compliments about Natalie's body getting more and more intimate. The pink blush to her complexion showed that at least some of them were working. The problem they had in common with most young people was where to find some privacy as neither of them could go home and there wasn't even a car they could borrow. In the end they had agreed on Lickey Hill and hoped that the weather would be kind.

In midsummer the hill was full of wild flowers and from the top where Tiggy had laid down his jacket, you could see down through the trees to St Barnabas the Younger where he was forced to attend every Sunday. It was a lovely evening and Tiggy had been patient, taking off her top and admiring her body. Personally, he didn't like Lycra as it didn't have the sexiness of removing a top, button by button, but he managed to pull it over her long dark hair without problems. He kissed her breasts and neck tenderly and felt her tremble.

Looking back at that night whilst he'd been in church, he'd thought of it as one of his virtuoso performances. He had managed the condom issue with deft, she had multiple orgasms and he'd had two. He had even remembered to be tender afterwards with her as he saw her back to her home and not just run off and phone his mates. In the afterglow of the sex, she had been lovely and admitted as they reached her garden gate that Ripley was a loser and not as big 'down there' as she had said.

He'd been confident that he'd achieved top gun status in the village again but realised with total certainty that now he needed a different challenge.

Tiggy had barely been out of the village during his 15 years and realised that his fame was really small-town. Whether it was the fact that his father had travelled the world in the navy or the fact that his mother had been adventurous in her youth. Something was telling him that he needed new horizons and new lovers, but in the meantime he the more immediate problem of the dozing in church charge to face.

After church his parents had chatted to other locals and the vicar had invited them and a few other regulars over to the rectory for tea. Tiggy couldn't avoid going with them, after seeing him sleeping in church, his father would be angry. Horatio Foghorn had views about sleeping on duty that were distinctly naval and if he'd tried to refuse, then the Cat O Nine Tails might well have been brought out in earnest.

So Tiggy had agreed to go and as they crossed the churchyard to the old rectory, he felt his jaw locking in the fixed smile he used when meeting devout people. As it turned out the rectory visit was considerably more entertaining than anyone expected. The vicar was extremely excited because he had received a video message from the Bishop, Angus Strange, which he had been asked to show to his church helpers and regulars.

The vicar and his mousey wife Mabel served everyone tea and a selection of fairy cakes in the Parish Hall where there was a large screen used by the Slaughter Film Club and plenty of hard chairs to keep them uncomfortable.

The Bishop's message was meant to inspire his loyal followers and encourage them to raise more money for its many good causes. The Bishop looked like a genuinely good chap of about fifty years with a large black beard shot through with white. But it was his wife who really got Tiggy's attention as she sat next to him on the video with a devoted look on her face.

Diana Strange looked like a 1960's film star playing the part of a doting vicar's wife and for a while Tiggy couldn't remember who it was. He hadn't been born until many years after that time but he'd seen the actress in French films like "A Man and a Woman" and other cool classics he'd seen in this very hall. Then seeing her face again on screen triggered his memory – she looked just like Anouk Aimée when she was playing the iconic girlfriend in the Ford Mustang on the way to Paris in the driving rain. She looked absolutely incredible and to Tiggy's heightened senses, she radiated suppressed sex appeal.

Here was the challenge he'd been praying for. Something worthy of him and all the training that Maddie Quimby had given him. This was no silly schoolgirl or skinny adolescent, this was a real woman who looked luscious. How Tiggy got to meet her was a story in itself.

In the days after the Bishop's message, Tiggy had become obsessed. He spent hours researching and found out that the Bishop's Palace was in Hereford and that Angus Strange had been in office for six years after being on the previous Bishop's staff for two. His wife was younger than him by 20 years and had her own blog dealing with matters of faith and occasionally her passion for organic vegetable growing.

Tiggy became a follower of her blog and made many likes on her Facebook page. After a comment on social media, she had made regarding immigrants and the biblical instruction to "love thy neighbour." Tiggy responded positively and said that he was hoping when older to work with immigrants in the many internment camps that were still around the world.

On another occasion he asked whether Confirmation was still relevant for a young man in today's society and wondered whether a devoted follower of her blog could discuss the matter with her. He said that he was unhappy with some aspects of the traditional church like Bishops and Cathedrals and the male domination of its clergy. He said that he instinctively felt that she was someone who he could relate to and who might give a doubting soul some guidance.

Gently he stalked her and ensured that something regularly appeared on her social media that was kind, supportive or devout. She very seldom answered directly but Tiggy was pretty sure that his comments were being noted. After all, even in the most devout parishes, the amount of people interested in organic cucumber growing was bound to be low.

It took three frustrating months and Terence had to travel to Hereford but finally Tiggy met his angel. He'd only been to the city a couple of times and didn't know it but the cathedral could be seen for miles. The ancient building was already a thousand years old but history really didn't interest him as much as its most recent occupants. The Bishop's home had moved from its original position a few hundred years ago but Google maps on his phone guided him perfectly to the big old Victorian building in a large garden which was now his palace.

Tiggy had chosen a time when he knew from his web site that the Bishop was officiating in the cathedral and gone directly to the residence. As he walked down the gravel drive and looked up at the imposing stone house, he felt his heart hammering inside his chest. He banged the large brass knocker and heard it echo inside, eventually he heard steps inside and the door was pulled open with a creak of warped wood.

Diane Strange was wearing an artist's smock which was covered in many shades of oil paint and had her long dark hair pulled back from her forehead with an old silk scarf.

"You are so much younger than I expected," said Tiggy. "I'm sorry - I'm Terence Foghorn and I've been asking on your social media about the church, confirmation and all kinds of things. But I'm so confused at the moment ....."

"I'm sorry I wasn't expecting you to come here, in person and the Bishop isn't here," Diane said in a husky voice pushing back her hair with a paint-stained hand.

"I know, but I've had a bit of a tragedy and I knew that if I didn't come today then I might not come at all," Tiggy answered with as much desperation as he could muster.

With the invention of a failing grandmother and dramatic confession that he thought he might be gay, Tiggy gained her trust and ended up sitting in her studio. He admired her flower pictures effusively and secretly thought that this woman was the epitome of sex appeal and sophistication. As the average age of his conquests had been around 14 years old so far, this was not surprising. But her long wavy dark hair, full figure and unusual blue eyes were genuinely beautiful and she tried to disguise them whilst on duty as much as she could because male parishioners were often a little embarrassing with their complements. The person who seemed to be constantly unaware of this attraction was her husband Angus, who saw the angels in his stained-glass windows but not in his home. He was passionate about his beliefs but mechanical and embarrassed in bed.

Tiggy had to learn patience. On the third visit to Hereford Tiggy touched her face and she didn't flinch, probably because she had convinced herself that this handsome young man was gay. They were in one of her hothouses at the time and the smell of her orchids was overpowering. After 10 minutes she realised that her top had somehow come off and the youth was kissing her neck and shoulders and she could tell by the hardness of her own nipples and the heaving breaths which she didn't seem to be able to stop, that her body liked it.

Tiggy needed all his control as her body as it lay on the bark floor of the hothouse was as spectacular as his fantasies had imagined. Her breasts were full and white and the silk knickers she was wearing barely covered her pudenda and were glistening with sweat or excitement.

He had to show superhuman levels of restraint not to enter her and go off

44

like a like rocket. He pushed himself in half way as he was trained to and gently increased the penetration and power as it was clear that Diane loved it. Just before he was going to come, he stopped and pulled out a little so he could cool down. She looked devastated until he started again and gradually increased power until she shuddered with orgasm and then he carried on for at least another ten minutes. He lost count of her eruptions and was sure that he had two or maybe even more.

This was a physical and emotional achievement that could never be matched when Terence got older and the memory became more and more dreamlike. But it was an erotic hothouse dream that could always fuel his fantasies when needed.

From Diane there had been little to say afterwards. Her body was ecstatic but her conscience was starting to awaken and the enormity of what she had done was starting to hit her. For her it wasn't a dream - it was a nightmare of her own making.

Tiggy thanked her with deep sincerity and said that it had been a life-changing moment for him. Now he was certain that he was heterosexual and that life was worth living. She quietly dressed and in a few moments, everything was normal again - the orchids were still blooming, the garden outside looked lovely and everything else had been a fantasy.

Back in Upper Slaughter everything seemed normal and his parents were pleased with him as they thought that the visits to the Bishop's house meant that he was keen on Confirmation. Tiggy held them at bay with the statement that he still wasn't sure that Church of England was his favoured religion and that he might have to visit Hereford again and chat with the vicar's wife who he'd got on with far better than the Bishop. He said with a certain amount of truth that he found her approach far more attractive than all the pomp and ceremony of the high church.

Diane Strange was a little less enthusiastic when Mrs Foghorn rang through a week or so later and asked whether she would mind if Tiggy came to see her. Her shameless body was thrilled at the thought but she consulted Angus Strange as to his views and trusted to providence. She said that the boy found the Bishop a little frightening and had been to see her before on matters of faith but that she was uncertain as to the sense of seeing him again. Part of her was excited when Angus said that he thought it would be fine and that he would ensure that that he was out when the boy was coming.

It was a lovely sunny day when Tiggy went for what turned out to be the final visit to the Rectory. Mrs Strange took him out to her precious garden and they sat on a wooden garden seat on the patio looking out over the lovely lawns and flower beds that she was so proud of. Tiggy wondered what her plans were and whether he was on a promise or not. They were a long way from the privacy of the hothouses where they had coupled so successfully and Tiggy's thoughts were interrupted by Mrs Strange asking a question.

"Terence, I really need to know whether you are considering getting confirmed and sincere in your religious beliefs. Or whether your thoughts are purely carnal?"

Tiggy didn't really know what carnal meant but got the drift of the question "Mrs Strange, I am in love with you, you are the most lovely, most understanding woman I have ever met" He emphasised his point by grasping her hand and moving it to his groin where she could feel just how much he loved her. She sighed in frustration or desire.

He didn't know what the flowers were – dahlias maybe or Carnations but they were very colourful and neat when they started. They were flat and bruised an hour later as was Tiggy's body.

It felt like Diane Strange had taken control for the first time and my god she was demanding. This was like the sexual version of a Swan Song or a sweaty Last Hurrah because Diane gave herself to the act like a woman having a last drink before entering the Kalahari. She didn't bother with condoms, she didn't indulge in any chat, she just ground out as many orgasms as she could.

Afterwards, when they were looking round the flowerbed for his clothes Tiggy felt drained of everything and was really rather shocked. Diane fished round in her trouser pockets and gave him the exact money he needed for his return fare.

"That will be the last time we meet Terence – if you contact me again, I'll accuse you of stalking or something nasty – but you've opened my eyes in many ways and I'm grateful. But now I've got to regain my faith and become a proper wife again"

Tiggy thought about trying to change her mind but one look at Diane's face told him it would be pointless. He knew that the world of adults was a strange one so put on his jacket and left the garden, walking round the walls until he found a back gate. He wrenched it open with a creak and found his way back to the station.

Back in Upper Slaughter he had told his parents that he'd decided to become an atheist and went up to his room to sleep. His mother couldn't quite understand why Tiggy was walking with a limp and had some lipstick on his neck but the poor boy looked knackered so she let him go without explanation. The following morning Tiggy came down to breakfast late and his mother tried to interrogate him about his visits but he was adamant about his lack of religious belief now. She had tried to argue but saw from his face that he had received whatever the opposite was of a 'Road to Damascus' experience.

That should have been the end of things in Hereford but fate had an unkind card to play which was going to affect Tiggy for the rest of his adult life and which he was powerless to alter.

About a month later he found a couple of mates from school sniggering in sixth form common room whilst looking at a red-top tabloid newspaper. One of them looked over in admiration and shouted something obscene he couldn't quite catch. Thinking that they were looking at some page three beauty Tiggy ignored them and they were shepherded into the next lesson by the gym master Mr Richards who looked over to Tiggy and shook his head in amazement, or disgust, as he pushed him through the classroom door.

The class went quiet and people turned round and giggled when he came in and he knew that something had happened that he didn't know about. He had a feeling it wasn't anything good.

Then the headmaster's secretary came in with a pink flush to her cheeks and Tiggy was summoned to the beaks study where the head sat back with his normal assortment of stains on his waistcoat and terminal dandruff on his gown.

Tiggy's past life, or at least his past month flashed by in his mind but he couldn't think of anything that would wake up the headmaster like this, especially after lunch. But he sat up straight and tried to look apologetic anyway.

"Foghorn I'm told that you were doing rather well in your mock exams – indeed we had hopes for you to be a candidate for Cambridge entry - but I'm not sure any of that will be possible now."

"What do you mean sir," Tiggy asked, aware that for some strange reason, the worry had given him a hard-on. He remembered being concerned that all this illicit sex at such a young age had given him a tension erection or something even worse.

The headmaster pushed over a copy of the Daily Mail and Tiggy could see the headline -

Bashing your Bishop

Terence didn't get the chance to read the editorial because his attention was grabbed by a photo of a man with a black beard and a Bishop's hat. Also of the shapely white bum, back and face of someone in the missionary position in a flower bed.

Sadly, the security cameras on the back of the Bishop's palace had picked up remarkable detail of the face of the perpetrator and the Bishop's wife in flagrante delicoso. According to the paper, the wife had not revealed anything about the identity of the male congregation member and the editor was offering a substantial reward for his identity.

There was little Terence could say to the headmaster who he suspected was considering ringing up the Daily Mail immediately and betraying him for the reward. Even if he didn't do it, those of his fellow students who could read a newspaper would betray him in an instant.

Terence agreed to leave the school with immediate effect and had gone home. His parents had been informed and given copies of the newspaper by half the village already out of kindness and were stunned. His father was home that week and looked conflicted between pride and disgust but knew that this was a huge problem for Tiggy's mother.

His parents had never been shy about telling him of their own dubious early lives but were horrified by his behaviour. They had got religion in recent years and had the zealousness of many later-day converts. The fact that he had used the excuse of confirmation classes to get close to the Bishop's wife made it inexcusable as far as his mother was concerned. Despite some gentle protests from Horatio, she was disgusted and threw Tiggy out the next morning with just a few clothes and twenty quid in his backpack.

Terence Foghorn had a difficult few days after that. He was only been 16 years old had no qualifications other than being good at sex and being a relatively plausible bullshitter. He dossed down at a friend's for a couple of days to get his head straight and wait for the fuss in the newspaper to die down a little. Then he had decided to follow the one of the family traditions and run away to sea.

The ennobling of Tiggy Foghorn

Terence had hitchhiked to the fleshpots of Plymouth hoping to find his early tutor Maddie who he'd heard had been injured in a brawl. He had only been to the city once and that was as a kid when his parents took him on a nostalgic trip to places they'd known in their youth. Tiggy's only recent experience of cities was Oxford when he and his mates went in on the bus and Hereford when he had visited the Bishop's wife. Neither of which was anything like as big or scary as Plymouth.

A female truck driver gave him a lift for the last 20 miles and kept on looking over at him sideways as if she recognised him. She had a tabloid tucked down the back of her seat so Tiggy didn't know whether his arse and face were still being shown on the front covers or it was his natural animal attraction. Anyway, she dropped him on the ring road and he made his own way from there, crossing over the dual carriageway and following the signs for the harbour.

Where Maddie Quimby was, he really didn't know and the place had changed since he and his parents had been there. The docks had been gentrified and now had upmarket restaurants with tables made out of bollards or upturned barrels with glass tops and titles like the Heroes Retreat and Rumrunner. As far as he could see there wasn't a real sailor or floozy anywhere in sight. The buildings were so clean now that they looked like children's models of the old navy docks and not the working port his parents had known.

He was starting to feel a little uncertain about this whole idea after he'd walked round the quays full of tourists and families three times. He had nowhere arranged to stay and he had very little cash and he was hungry. Burgers here cost a fortune so he just ordered a bag of fries which turned out to be the size of small pencils and in a bag that wouldn't feed a sparrow.

He wandered around for an hour and then walked away from the water until he had re-crossed the by-pass and found a street that was narrow, cobbled and didn't have any illuminated signs offering food or drink. Here he found a pub that looked as though it hadn't been decorated for a few centuries, with paint peeling off the window frames and a crack across the saloon door.

Looking up he'd seen a faded swinging sign that announced to an indifferent world that this was the Hat & Beaver established 1730. Tiggy didn't know it then but it was the very Inn that his parents had celebrated at after their marriage fifteen years previously.

Terence pushed at a door that looked as though most people kicked it open. It had a crack up the wooden base, peeling blue paint and the filthy glass had 'Saloon' etched on it in the style extremely fashionable in Victorian times. He found himself in a pub that the law hadn't changed at all. People were still smoking and he almost choked on the fog of pipe smoke and weed fumes that assailed his senses.

Tiggy pushed his into the room with a determination he didn't feel and collided with a tramp who smelt wonderfully of old urine. He found the bar and ordered a pint of lager with as much courage in his voice as he could muster as he pushed through the crowd of mutants at the bar.

"Is dat Stella, Old Pewsey, Carlsberg or what?" Asked a deep voice that was at odds with the breasts that were virtually at his eye level. Looking more clearly Terence was astounded to see the first trans-sexual person he'd ever encountered in his sheltered life.

"What do you recommend?" He asked trying not to sound too upmarket.

"I recommend dat you fuck off and come back when you've started shaving."

"But I've been shaving for years." The squeak of a response from him had caused guffaws of laughter from the dozen people close to the bar and the landlady had relented and pulled him a pint.

When he tried to pay, he realised that his wallet had gone from inside his blazer pocket and suspected that the vagrant had stolen it. Seeing his discomfort, the landlady had leant across the bar and grabbed him by the lapels and lifted him bodily off the ground.

"What's a matter boy, hasn't mummy given you any pocket money this week?"

"Aargh, aargh," was all he could manage for a while. "Maddie Quimby will vouch for me," said Terence in total desperation. "Tell her that Tiggy Foghorn is here."

The landlady behind the bar hesitated and Tiggy sensed that the name was known but he was pulled closer to the bar as she squinted through the smoke.

"Ang on," said the landlady/landlord. "Aint you da bastard who been screwin da Bishop's wife in papers? ... It's you, I know it's you." The large pair of hands dropped him and he fell to the floor to the sound of dirty laughter coming from all around the pub.

Terence was not used to such celebrity status but rather liked it. When the barkeep threw a copy of the Daily Star across to his partner sitting in

50

the corner he came over and checked the photo of the boy in the Bishop's flower bed against the real thing in front of him. After checking and re-checking the guy confirmed that Tiggy was the celebrity screwer and he was standing right in front of them.

The entire pub was in uproar and it was obvious that organised religion was not very popular in this bar.

Free pints came in from a number of atheists who thought that all Bishops should be screwed too. There was also a shout from an agnostic who didn't know whether to buy him a pint or not. But it was obvious from the continuous uproar that this was the most exciting thing that had happened in here since Trafalgar.

Anything that distracted the landlord from the fact that he had no money anymore was good and he sat down on the sticky leatherette bench seat and tried to be cool whilst he drank the pints lined up on the bar.

There were all kinds of coarse remarks about his last conquest but Tiggy tried to be a gentleman. All he had said modestly was that there no complaints from her and that it was a pity they'd been caught on camera or they would have been at it until doomsday.

After a while the fuss died down and he realised that he was in a strange city and now had no money. He repeated his question about Maddie and the publican picked up a mobile and made a call. She arrived ten minutes later – three years older and with a bandaged head but still his first love. In answer to his first question, she said that the papers had exaggerated everything about her injury and that the brawl had been nothing unusual.

Maddie spent another hour buying him a Cornish pasty and more drink whilst pumping him for more information about the Bishop's wife story. He then told her that he was joining the Royal Navy and going to the recruiting office the following day. After a while she said that it would be the making of him as it had been with his father. Maddie said that she knew the Chief Petty Officer running recruitment rather intimately and she would help if she could.

That night he had stayed at Maddie's flat but she refused his advances saying that "school was over and she got paid for her expertise normally". Tiggy was pissed and randy as a butcher's dog and absolutely devastated by her rejection. He was incredibly frustrated especially when she had someone in her room late that night and he could hear bed creaking and the sighs of satisfaction from her client. Terence had to deal with his hard-on himself which was not exactly what he'd been hoping for when he met his sex guru again.

The next morning she'd come down late and he'd made her breakfast. The orange juice followed by scrambled eggs and bacon had been eaten in silence and it was only after a strong cup of coffee that she started to talk. A quick call on her mobile had been taken in the hall and he could hear her whispering outside. Maddie returned to say that the recruitment office was in the centre of town and opened in an hour. She gave him ten quid and said that he needed to catch the bus at the end of the road and ask for Chief Petty Officer Slade when he arrived.

The navy office was a 1960's classic in steel and glass which was already full of people staring at the posters on the wall showing exotic places and hard-looking men speeding across bays in inflatable boats. Pushing to the front he'd seen a desk with Slade's name on it and sat down in the chair in front of it just before the boy who's turn it was could move in.

When Slade arrived, he was a squat, bandy, red-faced man with a ready smile and Tiggy whispered that Maddie Quimby had asked him to help. A faraway look came into the man's eye and he had asked after her health politely. Terence had answered equally politely and eventually they had got down to business.

CPO Slade had helped him through the paperwork and Tiggy had been a little optimistic with the truth about the level of his academic achievements, reasoning to himself that he would have got the highest-level marks had he stayed at school. The fact that his father had also been in the service helped speed his application but Terence certainly didn't want to serve in submarines. Eventually the paperwork was complete and it was hoped that he could join officer school at the next intake which was in a couple of weeks' time.

Many years later Tiggy would still remember the hurt the young Terence had felt when Maddie rejected his advances over the week he stayed there but his love was unconditional and he forgave her. She'd taught him things about sex and making women happy that some men never learn. It was a skill that would change his life forever and not always for the better. Maddie taught him another valuable lesson before he left Plymouth. One bright Spring morning he was walking past the corner shop newsagent and saw the front cover of the most scurrilous Sunday tabloids still being printed.

"I taught teenage love god everything he knew!!!"

The headline was printed next to a photograph of his beloved Maddie, who was wearing cap, gown, stockings and suspenders, carrying a cane. Realising that this was a follow-on to the Bishop's wife story, Tiggy grabbed a copy and threw some money at the startled guy behind the counter. Luckily there was no photograph of him this time or his life could have been hell.

He felt betrayed in a way that the grown up and cynical Terence Foghorn would not have understood. An analyst decades later would learn of this betrayal and at great expense, use it to explain Tiggy's love of women like Maddie but also his occasional need to exploit them ruthlessly.

Maddie's motivation was easy to see as she probably got a few thousand for the first interview and managed to spin it out for the next few months by running a weekly tutorial column on lovemaking techniques and eventually even an Agony Aunt column on Sunday, which ran for months and was called 'Ask Maddie'. This was incredibly popular and might have run for years had the editor not found out that she was using it to pimp clients for her rather expensive "therapy" sessions.

Tiggy's life changed so much and so quickly that he hadn't had time to dwell on this betrayal. Officer School was wonderful but first he'd had to get through basic training at HMS Raleigh with a square-jawed Master of Arms who didn't take any prisoners and had him doing press ups for fun out on the parade ground or trying to find his kit which had been thrown round the room in disgust by the inspecting officer at morning inspection. If he hadn't already signed the contract and sworn allegiance to the crown, he might have left at that point but gradually he started to learn the way the whole place worked.

Terence was younger than almost anyone else at HMS Raleigh but luckily didn't look it. He latched on to an older recruit who'd been in the forces before and learned how to prepare his kit perfectly. He also started to enjoy the physical side of things and excelled on exercises and on the parade ground. After a couple of weeks, he was given the chance to lead on one of the tasks and his group did well. A word with one of the instructors, telling him that his father had risen to captain in previous years also gave him some brownie points. In the end Terence was seen as having excellent leadership potential and fast-tracked.

The Royal Naval College in Dartmouth was the place he felt that he'd always been destined to attend and he loved the months there. Apart from one night where he was nearly caught in The Angel with the wife of an instructor the stay was relatively unremarkable. His father had been an officer and he felt like he had become a proper gentleman whilst there, learning the manners and courtesies expected of senior ranks.

Tiggy had got quite a reputation amongst his fellow male recruits by being in great demand from just about every attractive woman in Devon. Realising the potential of this Tiggy again made some extra cash by offering lessons on seduction, foreplay and sex techniques to his fellow male students. One of his early conquests had been a rather plain but extremely useful female in the office at Dartmouth who was happy to give him advance sight of test papers in return for favours given. To say that Tiggy sailed through most of the theoretical tests, would be tasteless but true. In fairness though, he was good at the practical tests and ended up playing rugby against the army too.

So Tiggy passed, as expected, with honours. At the formal passing out ceremony only his father attended, his Mum still thought he was something close to the anti-christ because of his religious fornication.

Deck Officer was what Terence Foghorn had always stated as his ambition. He loved the fact that he'd get to travel, earn seriously good money and wear a uniform that would make him almost irresistible to woman. Conflicts like Ukraine and Chinese aggression did occasionally worry him along the way but really his aim was to be a lover – not a fighter.

A few years later Tiggy was in his mid-twenties, he was on a frigate and should have been realising most of his ambitions. At 6ft 2inches tall with a handsome face and thick dark hair he combined the best qualities of his parents, including the deep blue eyes of his mother. He was built like an athlete and extremely attractive to male and female crew members and shore leave was always a pleasurable experience.

Tiggy had achieved a lot of his early dreams, seen lots of places and enjoyed being part of a team but without a battle to liven things up he was started to feel it was becoming routine. He had been in the navy for nearly ten years he was starting to feel frustrated with life and couldn't resist sailing a little close to the wind.

Despite the good salary Terence spent like a sailor and now had built up a debt that needed some clearing. He had always loved beautiful things and the purchase of an Aston Martin Vantage in gunmetal grey had been the extravagance he'd indulged in when last ashore. The car had a wonderful V8 engine that sounded like a symphony – he loved the sound so much that he'd driven through the Dartford Tunnel three times at peak revs just to hear it. He suspected that this meant a couple of speeding fines but it was worth every penny.

The Aston had burgundy leather upholstery that was so sensuous, so beautiful that he wouldn't allow one girlfriend to wear clothes in it. Which caused some excitement when they had arrived at Ascot for the racing and nearly got him in the wrong kind of newspapers again.

Before that he'd used it to take the daughter of an Earl round every Michelin starred restaurant and hotel in the South East, which cost serious cash. She really wasn't worth it as she was elegant, slim but had the passion in bed of a posh pipe-cleaner.

By the time he returned he'd seen the affect a title had on normally sensible people but realised that he didn't have the pedigree or the manners to make it with the English aristocracy. Which was a pity because it seemed to be a licence to print money in terms of credibility. A beautiful and expensive car also impressed most people to a ridiculous level – including Tiggy himself.

A few months later those who had loaned him the money were getting so aggressive that Tiggy had to hide the Aston Martin and needed to leave the UK for a while. In desperation he had started to supplement his pay with various black market deals and was just getting his debt cleared when his frigate and other vessels in the fleet were ordered to sail to Palma, Majorca on a joint goodwill visit with the US Navy. It should have been good news but fate has a habit of kicking you in the goolies just when you think you have found a way to solve a tricky problem.

Many of his shipmates had been blasé about going to the Balearics having been there on package holidays, but Tiggy loved it. Arriving by sea in most places is infinitely preferable to arriving by air with the great unwashed tourists that have often infested Spain. That was the verbal approach Tiggy took in the wardroom whilst pretending to be the travel-weary world traveller that he wasn't. In truth he was absolutely blown away by the warm climate and the beauty of the islands and could see why people had loved them as holiday destinations for centuries.

It was interesting, many of Tiggy's fellow officers had known him for years but they still held him in awe. It wasn't just his success with women, though that was legendary and he always had an incredibly sexy woman on his arm when ashore. It was also because he had always been a little mysterious about his background – dropping hints about aristocratic bastards and undercover agents in his parentage. With him it was believed by many and after a while he had almost started to believe it himself and his personal fantasies had become ever more spectacular.

Sometimes he saw himself as 21st Century James Bond. After all Commander Bond had been Royal Navy and had been incredibly successful with women. He wondered whether his need to buy the Aston Martin had been part of that fantasy in the first place.

The beautiful lights of the Via Maritimo, old port of Palma and floodlit cathedral dominating the town had been wonderful as they moored. He had been looking forward to the various receptions organised for allied navy officers over the following week as a welcome change.

He was on reception duty the first couple of nights and enjoyed meeting navy people in some of the big luxury hotels in the old section of Palma. There was lots of common ground between the US Navy and themselves and being on a frigate had a certain amount of kudos in both as they had always been the fastest and most effective fighting machines. But after a few days, when he had a little more time he'd felt like a change and decided to strike out on his own.

He dressed in his best whites and walked off the ship. After ten minutes he passed through harbour security and walked left to where he could see a large number of private marinas full of expensive yachts. The guy on the security barrier for the private yacht basin seemed mesmerized by the glory of his uniform and hadn't challenged him so Tiggy proceeded hoping that he might meet some big boat totty and have some fun.

In harbours in other places, he'd found that super-yacht owners had beautiful women twenty years younger than themselves who sometimes wanted someone of their own age to play with. Sadly, this time the marina was virtually deserted and he found a small bar at the corner of the quay, sat down and ordered a black coffee and a Lepanto Spanish brandy and looked out at the lights of the harbour.

The waiter took about ten minutes to comply but the coffee, when it arrived, was excellent and the plate of salted almonds and olives really crisp and fresh. The brandy was fire in his throat but slipping down a treat when he was aware of a strange figure at a table a few feet away cursing as a wind from the sea blew some papers off his table and on to the floor in front of him.

As a kindness Tiggy picked them up and couldn't help noticing that it was a part of the plans of some kind of boat. He stood up and took the blueprints to the other table as the man tried to stop the rest of his papers from blowing away by putting a wine carafe on top of them.

The figure looked like something out of a 1920's America Cup picture with his white duck trousers, blue blazer and wide club tie. The finishing touch was a vintage sailing cap at a jaunty angle over a face that looked as though it had seen a thousand sunsets.

"Merci" said the man adding a sentence of highly decorative and to Tiggy, totally incomprehensible French.

Tiggy nodded and returned to his brandy and coffee. The other man pulled out an ancient mobile and had a long and extremely emotional call. Judging by the look on his face afterwards the call did not please him. In fact, despite the dying light of the sunset, tears were clearly visible on the seafarer's sun-tanned face.

The waiter came back and Tiggy couldn't resist asking quietly what the problem with his other guest was. He leant down and whispered that it was the Viscount De Glanville and that he had finally ruined himself trying save an old boat that was very special to him. Weeks later and many thousands of pounds to the worse, Tiggy realised that the waiter had been the first part of an elaborate plan to stitch up idiots like himself and admired its irresistible charm.

The boat *did* exist and had been moored a few yards down the quay. Anybody who's seen those old 1950's classic films with Italian stars Sofia Loren or Gina Lollobrigida will remember that there was always a speed boat on some impossibly blue lake or sunny bay that carried them with great elegance and speed. That was nearly always a Riva and its lovely sleek lines and mahogany deck meant that even today the best hotels in Italy still use them to ferry honoured guests.

When it was light the following day Tiggy had wandered up to the Viscounts boat had checked it over. He was an experienced Navy Officer but this was alien territory. The beauty of the vessel, however, with its sleek lines and gleaming brightwork would have been obvious to a blind landlubber.

Certain shapes are classically beautiful. The 1960's Jaguar E-Type, the Ferrari Dino of the same period and the Riva are considered timeless by many designers. Tiggy shared that love and had bought his Aston Martin for similar reasons. Looking down at the boat he could see that the shape was pure but it was the cabin that made it rare and potentially valuable. He'd only ever seen open topped speedboats in those old movies – this vessel was longer and had a cabin that looked as though a few people could sleep in it.

The Viscount had obviously sensed the interest as he came up the steps to the quayside

"This eez unique – a 1922 Riva by Serafino Riva imself but with a cabin conversion by Benatzi. Sleeps a six and I've spenta fortune on it. Engine is the original Italian Ferrari V12 and it goes like the wind. There is not another like it anywhere"

"What's the problem?" Tiggy asked.

"Tha hull is rotten and bastard shipyard are trying to charge twenty tousand euros to fix it – I've spent thirty already and I'm a broke." The captain left him on the quayside and went below tears again welling in his eyes.

As he went down Tiggy shouted down the hatch that he'd be at the cafe and be delighted to offer him a drink. There was a grunt from inside and Tiggy went back and ordered another coffee.

Whilst waiting Tiggy secretly googled Riva and saw that new Rivas were selling at 3.6 million euros and some original 1920 Riva speedboats were selling at over a hundred thousand. He smelt a deal and a huge profit.

He had tried to check out the provenance of the Viscount himself in the limited time he had available but other than the De Glanville family name having aristocratic connections, he couldn't find anything about the present Viscount.

The Viscount seemed to anticipate this question when he came back to the cafe and volunteered the fact that he had spent many years in Macedonia where a title was not an advantage. He also said that he thought the whole concept of aristocratic titles was a little 19th Century and he tended not to use them. Other people, he pointed over to the waiter and laughed, tended to think it was important.

After a couple of meetings and what appeared to be considerable negotiation Tiggy had agreed to buy a half share in the boat for 70K and the next night the Viscount had given him the papers to sign. He'd scanned the documents briefly but the thought of the potential profit in the boat may have blinded him a little to the detail.

70,000 pounds was nearly everything he had left in his bank account and it really should have been kept safe so he could pay off his debtors in the UK. But he reasoned that by then he would have a couple of months' salary paid in and there was always the Aston Martin to sell if push came to shove. He had another favourite now.

The last night before his frigate sailed Tiggy returned to the marina to find that the Viscount had disappeared. He was also being billed for six months mooring fees and a considerable amount of repairs carried out there. It was then that he realised that he didn't just own 50% - he was total owner of the Riva and had agreed to be totally responsible for its expenses.

After over ten years at sea and having been involved in a few less than legal enterprises himself, Tiggy had thought himself too worldly to be taken in by a shyster like the Viscount. But you had to admire his technique, anyone who could take him for 70K so quickly must be a grand master of the art. You should always learn from a master of their craft and he had tried to analyse just what had made the whole scam so irresistible.

Firstly, the image of an aged and struggling aristocrat was immensely appealing to many Brits and there was a inbuilt instinct for one man to believe another man in tears.

Secondly the boat was beautiful - it may not have been quite the Riva he'd been told – but it was genuinely beautiful.

Lastly avarice – the profit that could be made if he spent enough to get the hull repaired and put it into an auction in California or Nice could be millions.

If Tiggy had known just how complicated and dangerous that process was going to be, he would have abandoned ship right there and then.

By the time his frigate had returned to the UK a few months later things had gone down rapidly downhill. Some of Tiggy's smuggling deals had been discovered and his debtors had been clamouring violently for payment very publicly.

The Navy Office didn't want any scandal and warned him privately that unless he cleared his debts and stopped his criminal activities, he would be cashiered. But if he sorted out his affairs immediately, he would be given the chance to leave without losing his pension.

The last thing he wanted was a dishonourable discharge on his record so he had sold the Aston Martin to pay his local debts and agreed that he would resign after his next voyage, which was to Australia. As his Captain said – Australia wasn't a bad place for a young man with enterprise to jump ship. Luckily the boss had always rather liked young Foghorn and thought that there was not enough 'buccaneering spirit' in today's Royal Navy, so had treated him leniently.

It was now ten years since Tiggy Foghorn left the Royal Navy. He had left surprisingly without a blemish on his record but his early ambitions had disappeared like a fart in a thunderstorm. With no senior officer ordering him what to do he found that his drive had driven away and hadn't been seen since. This didn't really seem to bother him.

After a series of accidental misadventures and Tiggy and the Riva had landed at Noosa, near Brisbane in Northern Australia. With its lovely surfing beaches and national parks this was a very pleasant place to decompose.

Tiggy was living the life of a retired Navy Officer on a very limited income and subsidising it by finding women of a certain age who admired him. It was a quiet life in a beautiful place and he was starting to feel like he fitted in but he hadn't exactly achieved much. He lived on the Riva most of the time, which was in a sheltered berth alongside the quay.

Though he'd tried to generate enough money to repair the hull in the early days, beetles and rot meant that it was an endless task and the Riva was not fit to cross the bay, never mind the Pacific.

The delightful woman who ran the marina was extremely understanding about his outstanding mooring fees as Tiggy seemed to understand her needs on a regular basis. It helped that she was his favourite type having no shortage of curves and long dark hair just like a certain woman from his youth. Her generosity of spirit and loving nature meant that he for the first time could see himself living with the same woman for years – maybe not life – but certainly years. The only sand in his crutch was a large sweaty guy called Ginger who claimed to be her husband.

Terence Foghorn had often been told by his mother not to 'rock the boat' in confrontations with those in charge. That warning should been in his mind a year ago in Noosa when his mooring fees were due.

It was a hot steamy day and Tiggy and Mabel the marina owner were in action onboard and rocking the Riva when there was a roar from the landing stage alongside. The hairiest arm he'd ever seen poked through the saloon door and pulled him bodily out of the boat. He was punched in the gut and thrown twenty yards into the harbour.

By the time he'd swum to the side Mabel and husband were on the quay and Ginger was punching hell out of his wife. Remembering the old Kinks song about being a lover not a fighter Tiggy picked up the heaviest thing he could find on the back of the boat -which was a quart of Aussie Shiraz – and hit Ginger across the head.

The ape barely noticed because the jug was plastic so Tiggy reached in again and found his Gunn & Moore cricket bat and swung it like Botham going for a cover drive. There was a sickening crunch and the husband went down in a spray of blood, unconscious.

Mabel was motionless for a few seconds and then she whispered instructions. They had dragged the husband's body down the landing stage, closer to the office and tried to clean up the Riva with water from the hose. Mabel then called the cops and told Tiggy to get out of the way for a few weeks whilst everything got sorted. Apparently, Ginger had form in the wife-beating sport and she'd called the police before, so she reckoned that if he survived the batting, he would end up inside prison on remand for at least a few months which would give them plenty of time to plan their future.

Whilst he was lying low in a first-floor apartment in Brisbane, Tiggy had plenty of time to consider his existence and knew that he had stagnated. He realised that he couldn't just rely on understanding women to pay his costs, he had to find a way of earning serious money. He had few skills and hard manual work was not an option but his powers of persuasion were legendary.

Tiggy remembered the French aristocrat De Glanville and just how well he had conned him out of 70 grand in Palma. He also remembered the unearned respect his titled girlfriend had received when he'd been taken her round some of the best hotels in the world. He realised that he could learn from the master but he needed a provenance of his own.

Our hero spent the next few days researching. He was in the southern hemisphere so he considered whether he might pretend to be an English aristocrat but he thought it unlikely he could get away with it. With Debrett, Burke and Who's Who the British peerage was so well documented that it was almost impossible. He needed to find something that suited his natural nobility but which was not so well recorded.

After more research Tiggy had developed his own claim to aristocratic roots which he was anxious to test out. For some reason the title Count Tolstoy Jergov came whilst he was dreaming of Maddie and he decided, instinctively, he liked it.

He knew it was rude but reckoned that it would make introductions amusing and that targets would think that no conman would ever come up with such a ridiculous name.

He would be positioned as from a failed Lithuanian noble family, Tiggy reckoned that virtually nobody knew where Lithuania was or spoke the language. Google and other search engines anyone looked at, proved that Lithuania did exist and that it used to have great numbers of noble families. But as the country had been over-run by many other empires it was complicated enough to put off most researchers.

The target market for the new Count was pretty obvious. Wealthy middle-aged women were his favourite individuals and English-speaking women were the most likely to fall for his charms.

He had worked out a number of plausible scams including shares in his ancestral castle, selling Lithuanian titles and of course the financing of his beautiful wreck Riva.

Having decided to target women of a certain age he realised from looking around that cruise ships had a ready supply. Brisbane had been his first test market. There were Pacific Line cruises coming in after south sea Island tours but it was the world cruises that seemed to have the best mix of passengers. Wealth was, of course a primary consideration and Tiggy knew that some of these trips were costing passengers an absolute fortune. And some people did these trips year after year so the amount they spent was enough to restore the Riva twenty times over.

It took three months before Ginger's case reached the courts and by then Count Jergov had made thousands of US dollars in false title sales to US and Australian women who had really convincing certificates to show that they had the right to style themselves Countess or thought that a wing of a fairy tale castle was theirs for a month every year for life. The plan was a great success and Tiggy's act as a Count was so believable that he almost believed it himself.

Most of the lawyers had thought that Ginger would get at least a couple of years for wife beating.

Then Mabel had broken down in court and admitted that she'd caused the problem with her husband and the shit hit the fan. Ginger was released on bail and his only mission was to find Tiggy and get his revenge. So our newly aristocratic hero had to virtually shag his way onto a passenger ship going to New Zealand and quietly arrange to have the Riva shipped there which made a sizeable dent in the restoration fund raised so far.

Amazonian Women

The Cruise ship *Amazon* was the first place that Tiggy Foghorn aka Count Tolstoy Jergov aka Eugene Fenton had been kidnapped by the very women he'd been trying to deceive. He was aware that he was almost irresistible to certain kinds of red-blooded females but abduction was a little extreme even for his taste.

The fact that he had twenty grand from Miriam and her sister already in his bank account before he was kidnapped helped a lot. As did the fact that they were both large attractive women who appreciated his skills in bed. There were two other reasons why he found the shanghaiing acceptable. First was the fact that there were plenty of other targets on the ship who might be interested in paying to be a character in his book. The second was the ship was travelling through the lovely South Seas and he intended to enjoy the readily available selection of fine food and vintage champagne. He thought what gentleman wouldn't appreciate the finer things in life in such circumstances?

As time went on there were dangers in over-consumption. Tiggy had three distinct personas and sometimes after a few glasses of champagne he lost track in his own mind. The one name that no-one knew onboard was Terence Foghorn. Count Tolstoy Jergov was what the girls called him or "The Count" as he was often called when he was introduced to fellow diners in the Starlight Dining Room or Tahiti Lounge.

His pen name of Eugene Fenton was also vital for him to remember when establishing his writing credentials. His discovery of this genuinely talented romantic author a couple of years ago had been fortunate as his books had been self-published and the writer had expired without anyone noticing centuries ago. Eugene was not on any search engine and the work Tiggy had done to falsify the cover so that it had his photograph and glowing reviews was a masterpiece of digital manipulation.

To help with his schizophrenic existence he suggested that Miriam and sister called him Tiggy which he explained had been the diminutive used by his old Grandmother when shouting him in the grounds of their Schloss in the old country. He said that his Nana thought Tolstoy was a jumped-up Russian peasant and refused to use his name in polite conversation – no matter how much his mother had loved his literature. The girls were honoured to be told his nickname but very rarely used it in public as 'The Count' sounded much more impressive when they introduced him.

The women were happily enjoying his attentions on a shared basis and had offered to help by introducing passengers to his book idea as long they had a share in the profits. This newly commercial aspect of their relationship had paid some dividends but he had no doubt that the potential onboard was vast. The average cost of this cruise was about fifty grand for relatively modest cabins and suites like Miriam's were considerably higher. So the chance to become a part of the new book by the legendary Eugene Fenton for a few thousand seemed excellent value.

Tiggy knew he made an impressive entrance when he entered any of the cocktail bars in the late morning or evening. He was 6' 2" slim, dark haired and athletic and about 6 stone lighter than the average guest. His blazer, cream trousers and cravat certainly made him stand out and the leather writing folder and fountain pen he used to beautifully handwrite his works of genius also made him look something from a far more civilised age. Which was the general idea.

He was making real progress. With the two sisters' money already in his bank and the commission from the bruiser Elmer Flannigan to write a part for his gay partner, he had an extra thirty thousand in his account. But the last woman, Florence Hasty, had almost put him off the whole idea and had he been her husband, he would have willingly thrown himself into the jaws of the nearest Great White. When he'd told the ginger headed apparition that was Florence that he had no characters left she'd offered twenty thousand and he'd relented. Tiggy in his guise of Eugene - master writer - Fenton should have had the principles to say no, but sadly the Count was too avaricious to refuse.

Florence Hasty was the worst Aussie harridan imaginable and terrorized the staff whenever she could. She was the only one of his clients who wanted herself to be the hero in the book and she'd arranged to meet him shortly to brief him on her character.

He was so tempted to hide or jump overboard or do something else preferable to meeting her. But the sound of a rampaging rhino coming up the gangway told him he was too late.

"Paco bring me a bloody beer you bloody waster and make it a large one."

The booming voice filled him with dread and Tiggy tried to compose his face as his next victim hauled herself up the stairs. The barman paled and tried to hide but to no avail and the poor serf was forced to look in her direction.

"Are you deaf as well as stupid? Bring me a pint of beer – I'm as hot as a dingo's crutch," she shouted at the bar.

The ginger-headed monster trundled over and sat down opposite Tiggy with a sound of tortured wood and fabric coming from the chair. Our author already had his pen poised over the notepad hoping that her brief lived up to its name but feared the worst and decided to put up a token resistance.

"Having considered this carefully I am not sure that I can accommodate you in this book, madam," the author said quietly hoping for a get-out-of-jail-card.

"You've got my fucking money already, write me in you bastard or I'll sue your arse off." She stood up and loomed over the table like a second row forward and Tiggy feared for his life.

"My god .... madam, well I guess that there must be somewhere ..." Tiggy gathered his notepad close to him and tried to summon up some composure by asking some simple questions.

"... Now Florence, what sort of person are you?... a writer can't just conjure sympathy or empathy out of thin air ...."

"First of all though ... why aren't you on Twitter, Facebook or anything else on my computer – what are you some kind of recluse?" Florence asked with a growl.

Like an aged actor returning to a favourite speech Tiggy recovered his dignity and shouted.

"I loathe the modern media world. It has killed quality literature and closed some of the best publishers – some of whom used to have the vision to invest in the great writers we revere today. Some people call me a technophobe or a luddite but none of my books will appear digitally and I will not use FaceTime or Twatter to promote them. The printed book was good enough for Shakespeare and Dickens – even for Barbara Cartland and it's good enough for me." Tiggy explained with as much righteous anger as he could muster.

The ginger vision took time to process this explanation and finished her pint of lager. After a few minutes she seemed convinced and waved to the barman for another pint. She started her briefing with obvious affection.

"Florence Hasty was a sickly child born in the outback village of Hope Springs, the daughter of a sheep shearer and a vicar who would become the Bishop of the largest parish in Australia. My first memory was being picked up by what must have been a dingo and carried away from home. According to my mother later, she had decided that this world was no place for a weakling and left me outside the shack to see whether I survived – she was a real hard case my mum," Florence recalled with nostalgia.

"Tough love was what she believed in and I survived but if my father hadn't tracked the dingo and shot it with his old 303 then I might have grown up a dingo."

The Count was tempted to attempt a witty response, but stopped himself and concentrated on writing his notes. His horrible imagination kept on conjuring up images of ginger-headed dingos and he had to bite his lip to stifle the giggles.

"I wasn't popular at primary school," she continued "because I was so much better at everything than the rest of those country hicks. The fact that my beloved Papa then became Bishop meant that I was able to go away to boarding school at 10, which seemed to please my mother and she went back to full-time shearing .."

"Didn't you want to follow in her footsteps or become a priest like your father?" Tiggy interrupted the monologue.

"Are you fuckin joking?"

"N... No, lots of kids are inspired to follow their parents...obviously not you, though."

"Don't interrupt I was just getting to the good bits...."

"Sorry Ms Hasty, please continue." Tiggy whispered with barely concealed terror, realising as well that he needed to get back to his note taking, which so far had just consisted of 'Bishop, unpopular, Dingo' and not much else. He wouldn't put it past the Aussie viper to check his notes so went back to his penmanship.

"I left boarding school with excellent results and could have gone to Goolagong University but didn't want to skive off for the next few years with all those upmarket wasters, so I looked around for a way to make some money."

"Training dingos?" Tiggy said under his breath.

"I was at home at the Rectory for a few weeks thinking it though and realised the Papa could have been sitting on a goldmine if he hadn't been a priest."

"You found gold under the rectory?" Tiggy asked with forced stupidity.

"No, you arsehole .... people visited him because of births, marriages or deaths in the family. All times when even poor families will shell out a few extra dollars so that they look good to the neighbours. I realised that the local undertakers were useless and that the whole process could be streamlined. No need for wood coffins, or real flowers as long as everything looked good. So I pushed out the old local funeral director and started to make the most of my connection with the Bishop. Because of the family name being so famous locally I was tempted to call the new business Hasty Death but was advised against it. In the end Florence's Funeral Care was our brand and we were very successful."

"How successful?" Tiggy asked looking up with a suitably funereal look on his face.

"Before I took over the old funeral parlour only made around 10% profit, after I took over, I got margins up to 40% and turnover by five times. I was able to offer a fixed price package which included legal advice, car hire and flowers to families by buying other small outfits that were already in the business. The lawyers weren't always qualified but the punters didn't know that and they didn't have the resources to sue if a will or an estate went wrong.

Front of house in our funeral parlours was very uplifting with sombre music and dark drapes. But behind the curtains it was like a production line and we got the time from cremation to ashes down to 4.5 minutes. Which meant that we could increase the number of funerals per day up to twenty by using my new one-way system.

Within ten years I had opened Florence's Funerals in Melbourne, Sydney, Darwin, Cairns and loads of other places. When we had the forest fires and then Covid we couldn't move for customers but I made sure that our margins increased. We were considering branching out into pet funerals and other religions but I was made an offer for the group by a Chinese outfit that was many millions of dollars so I decided to retire.

That was early last year and because we had a few problems with the accountants I decided to leave immediately and join this world cruise."

"You certainly chose the right business – what with pandemics, wars and natural disasters and everything," our author commented.

"I certainly did."

"And financially, does anyone know where the bodies are buried?" Tiggy asked with a deadly humour he couldn't somehow resist.

As expected, this was met with a blank stare and the Count or Eugene dependent on which side of his personality you were interested in, picked up his pen, notepad and said that he had enough information and left the bar, bowing to Florence as he left.

Tiggy was exhausted emotionally and artistically. He went down the stairs to the sister's stateroom which was closest and intended to lie down on the huge bed and try to collect his thoughts whilst she was at afternoon bingo. First, he stripped off his blazer, trousers and shirt and placed them neatly on hangers in the wardrobe. Thank goodness they were real hangers as negotiating those that only slide into fixed housings were too difficult when a man is tired or slightly inebriated. After his interview with the ginger doctor of death, he was both.

He must have drifted off because three hours later he was awoken by the sister bursting into the room and throwing her dress on the bed.

"I know it's not my turn and we normally meet after dinner, but since you are obviously ready for me, I will certainly take advantage," she said archly stripping off faster than an Olympic swimmer.

Tiggy looked down at himself with horror and realised that his penis was considerably more awake than he was. He sighed and tried not to think of Florence Hasty, opening his arms and wondering just how long he could perform at this level. Whilst she was bouncing up and down on him, Tiggy tried to remember all the commissions Eugene Fenton already had in the bank:

Miriam wanted the character of her husband George Bender to be a boring, sycophant with bad teeth and no ambition.

Miriam's sister (actually named Elsie but a name he had difficulty remembering which was difficult every alternate night) – wanted the character of a rough-handed farmer with a heart of gold called Gabriel.

Elmer Flannigan – his only gay client so far – wanted a heroic maritime character part for Neil Davis his long-term partner.

Florence Hasty – wanted herself in the book as an intelligent and successful woman who after a great struggle with a disbelieving public was seen to be a great saviour of the nation.

Tiggy reckoned that was a total of 50K already in his account and that if he was careful, he might just get a few more commissions if he moved to different sections of the ship and found new targets. Miriam and Elsie hadn't found too many more themselves and Tiggy was now a little doubtful about their likely customer generation. The only introduction they'd made so far was the Ginger Peril and that was enough to put a sensitive author off writing completely.

The more he thought about it, he objected strongly to the 50/50 deal they had struck at the beginning and planned to ignore it when he had chance to jump ship in Dunedin. Agents had always tried to exploit great artists like himself and it was Count Jergov's duty to teach them a lesson.

His calculations were disturbed by a groan of pleasure from Elsie and he realised his efforts had been rewarded.

There was an embarrassing moment later when Miriam discovered that her sister had taken him out of turn and he thought that there was going to be a cat-fight. Tiggy had to promise to still visit Miriam that night in order to bring peace and wondered whether he might need Viagra for the first time to raise his enthusiasm.

At dinner Tiggy in full Count Jergov mode escorted both women to the other dining room and changed arrival time. As he looked down from the balcony, he scanned the dozens of diners hoping that none of his existing contacts were there. It could be dangerous if his characters were aware of each other and started comparing notes. Luckily there were none he could see but there appeared to lots of fresh faces who he might impress with his act.

After helping each woman to her seat like the gentleman he pretended to be, he ordered a bottle of champagne and insisted on pouring a glass for each himself, waving the sommelier away with an apologetic smile. His old-world courtesy stood out, impressing the other ladies and pissing off their partners.

The sisters seemed to have overcome their annoyance with each other and him and looked hugely attractive. Miriam's blond hair was pulled back in what the French call a chignon and she was wearing a blue silk dress that looked like it had come from London or Paris. It showed what a full voluptuous woman she was and the waiter kept on returning in order to look. Sister's dark hair was just hanging loose and she looked as though she had dressed to show her sister off with a modestly cut plum coloured gown that hid her own figure. Tiggy remembered it well enough anyway from the afternoon.

That night he did his duty to Miriam. He did it without complaint and without Viagra despite all of his efforts with her sister earlier.

He was a little proud of himself, as any 40 year old sailor should be who has docked successfully over five times in the last four days. The truth was he found both women extremely inviting and his conscience had almost stopped him taking odd bits of jewellery he found lying around in their suites and hiding them. Almost - but now he just thought of them as keepsakes.

The following morning, he had a bracing breakfast of kedgeree whilst both girls slept in. He then gathered his writing case and went on an expedition to new parts of the ship. The weather outside had changed and a squall was battering the windows, so he thought more potential victims were likely to be inside. His main hope, however, was not to meet Ms Hasty.

Tiggy had done some more reading about the ship and knew that there were six bars or lounge areas on the top two decks and four restaurants. This time he took the lift up to level five as five was his lucky number and wandered towards the bows. He didn't really care whether he met anyone and indeed, would be delighted if he just found somewhere to have a nap. This level of nocturnal exercise was a little excessive and bed on this trip was not always a place to rest.

He eventually found a seating area with a good view of the storm outside and stretched out on a leather Lazy Boy couch hoping for a few hours sleep before lunch.

"Are you Count Tolstoy Jergov?" asked a little voice who seemed to have interrupted the few seconds of sleep he'd managed so far. With a grunt Tiggy roused himself and realised that he'd been spark out for two hours.

"Er ... yes," our hero answered resisting the urge to teach the youngster a few obscene phrases that probably wouldn't have been in his normal vocabulary of words. Looking down he could see a boy of probably around six or seven years dressed immaculately in what looked like miniature US Army uniform.

"Sir, please stay here whilst I find my mother" the boy appeared to salute and marched off at the double.

Tiggy wondered about the level of indoctrination present amongst US kids but the fact that he'd used his Count Jergov name probably meant that the mother had been introduced by Miriam or one of his other clients. He moved off the easy chair and to a table, spreading his tools of trade out on the top and trying to look author-like. At his request a large expresso was brought over and Tiggy took the required dose and waited alertly.

Five minutes later he could hear a female voice barking orders and a figure marched down the lounge followed by her son in perfect step. She was the exact opposite of the type of women who floated Tiggy's boat.

She looked as though she was made of leather thong that had been stretched to the limit. There was nothing that resembled breasts or hips, her hair was cut short and the most complimentary thing you could say about her was that she looked fit. Her clothes were drab green in colour and looked as though they had been sprayed on in an industrial paint shop.

"Jergov?" a voice asked in a voice so authoritative that he nearly thought it was an order.

Keeping in character he stood, clicked his heels, and shook a hand which was surprisingly small and dry.

"Yes madam, how can I help you?"

"My name is Anders and this is my son Dwight."

"Pleased to meet you, Ma'am and you, young sir."

"I believe that you are a famous author and that you are looking for character names?"

"Well, I might disagree with the term famous, but some people seem to think that I am worth reading." Tiggy said with a shy smile and holding up his trusty hardback.

"Explain why you are Count Jergov and that is by Eugene Fenton," Anders demanded.

"Who told you about me?" Tiggy said with seeming annoyance.

"Ms Bender"

"I am from an ancient family with some pretensions to honour and I would be disowned by those left – and there aren't many left after the communists over ran our country – I would be disowned because they don't think romantic fiction is the way a gentleman should make a living – but needs must, so I use a pen name."

"The commies killed your family?" Anders said with righteous anger.

"Only some of them ... but I can't return as my views on communism are too well known to be safe – but back to the book ...."

"Yes sir ..." The woman seemed to brace herself and continued.

"My husband was also called Dwight. Dwight Anders and he would have been a great marine if he hadn't been colour blind. It was a great sadness and he could never understand it as he said. "You don't need to know the colour of the gooks, Arabs and commies down your gunsight, you just need to shoot straight! He was a great man." Mrs Anders ended standing proudly to attention.

"He doesn't sound ideal for a romantic novel." Tiggy commented with surprising honesty.

71

"He was a hard man but he had a romantic heart ... and one night he said that he loved me almost as much as his old Colt Peacemaker. On my birthday he always brought me wild flowers – I'm allergic to pollen but he didn't know that."

The author looked a little doubtful but then seemed to have an idea.

"Err ... listen, it's difficult to fit him in but did Ms Bender tell you the cost?"

"Yeh, ten grand – we're not short of cash, Dwight's gun collection sold for half a million and the plantation is still producing plenty of tobacco despite all those do-gooding democrat scum."

"Is Dwight Senior still with us?"

"No sadly ... he left us only a few months ago ... we miss him."

"What happened?"

"An explosion in his workshop."

"How terrible – how?" Our author had a premonition of just how but kept his mouth shut.

"Dwight was a lifelong member of the NRA, an officer in the National Guard and the most patriotic man you could ever met. It's unfashionable in some quarters but he thought that the USA was being destroyed by Mexicans, Asians and all kinds of undesirables. We fly the Stars and Stripes proudly outside our homes and so do all our workers in Anderstown."

"You have your own town?" Tiggy said incredulously.

"Not all of it is ours but ..."

"I'm sorry, I interrupted Ms Anders please continue about the death of your husband..."

"One of the cops suspected that Dwight might have been making some kind of bomb but his Captain knew Dwight and was a member of the same club or something...anyway the explosion was put down to a gas leak and the local coroner seemed happy."

"Describe him to me physically."

"He was about six feet six inches tall and when I met him, he had the body of a full back but he put a lot of weight over the years. Dwight always loved the military so he shaved his head marine style when he was young which was a pity because he had a lot of lovely blonde hair when he was a boy. Dwight junior has the same – don't you Dwight?" She pointed over to her son who was standing at ease in the corner.

The boy looked uncomfortable with his own non-military hair cut but answered in the affirmative.

"He had lovely blue eyes and always smelt of gun oil, cigars and whisky.

A smell that I've always thought was manly – don't you think so Count Jergov?"

"He loved guns then?"

"As I said he had a great collection of everything from original Colt revolvers right through to assault rifles – even an anti-tank weapon. All American made and in perfect working order – he always joked that if our state was invaded then we had enough firepower to defend Anderstown for weeks. He thought that the second amendment was what made the US greater than the nancy places like Europe who had lost their balls and their assault rifles years ago."

"I'm not sure that Europe thinks that guns are a sign of civilisation," Tiggy couldn't resist saying.

"Come on - even your famous singer John Lennon said Happiness is a Warm Gun – Dwight always loved that song."

"He was trying to be a little ironic I think ... but carry-on Mrs Anders."

Ms Anders carried on describing her loving, heavily armed husband and Tiggy thought that if he was truly an artist of Eugene Fenton's calibre (god, even that word had different meanings now) then a great writer might baulk at including a Dwight for a miserable ten grand. He threw his pen on the table with exasperation and sighed.

"I'm not sure that we have a part in the story big enough for your Dwight. There is a Confederate General who would have been ideal but he's already been reserved for a lot of money. The trouble is this is a romance and most of the people are female, there are only a couple of males important enough to be Dwight and they have gone – I'm really sorry, goodbye Ms Anders."

Ms Anders looked devastated but drew herself up to her full height and about turned. She marched down the lounge in quick order with Dwight Junior behind her and descended the stairs. It was good ten minutes until she returned.

"Dwight used to say that there wasn't a problem you couldn't solve if you threw money at it. So, what about 20,000 dollars?"

"I am not sure that Mr Lopez will except that – he's already paying twenty thousand." Tiggy answered knowing the sensitivities of his WASP market.

"Lopez ... fricking Lopez ... you've got a Mexican playing a General ... you have got to be joking." Anders screamed quietly from her mental bunker.

"He's not Mexican, he's Spanish and it's perfectly logical, he's a Spanish soldier who goes over to the Confederate side and helps them win a couple of battles. "Tiggy said with as much artistic commitment as he could manage.

"Twenty-five thousand dollars is my final offer and you get a red-blooded all-American boy to be your General and not a spic – sorry Spaniard."

Our author stood up and paced the room in pensive torment talking to himself. Anders stood patiently at attention watching his every move.

"General Anders does sound more plausible... it wouldn't need all the Spanish back story," Tiggy mumbled almost to himself.

"I can pay you now ..." Anders said with genuine hope in her voice.

"Listen Mr Lopez was going to give me complete literary freedom to develop his character and I warned him that with publishing being in such a poor state it might take six months even to see a proof ... are you happy to agree to the same terms?"

"Yes sir, we are."

"Right well I'll bring back a contract in an hour and you can transfer the money ... OK?"

"Affirmative. I'll see you later at 1800 hours, but thanks for the change, Dwight would have been so proud to be a Confederate General."

"Please do not mention all this to anyone Ms Anders, Mr Lopez is a powerful man and he won't be happy.

that he's lost his chance to appear as a general."

"OK, consider this to be our state secret," Anders turned and swore her son to secrecy and they prepared to march out at double time.

"It needs to be much more secure than state secrets," Tiggy added and the Anders squad nodded with understanding and left.

Tiggy returned to Miriam's suite a few hours later with the satisfaction of nearly having 75,000 dollars in his bank and the thought of a warm welcome from one of the sisters in bed later. Embarrassingly, he couldn't remember which sister it was tonight and after the literally true, but pleasurable, cock-up yesterday he needed to get it right.

One extra character was to enter the story which would again test the authors ability to confront his principals and still make money. He was again sitting in the lounge near first class, hoping to get some rest when a tall brown-skinned, blonde woman who looked as though she could have been Italian, Greek or even Asian. She asked if he knew Lithuania and Tiggy went cold.

"I was there as a child but the family sent me to England in the 1970's to be educated because they feared that the aristocracy was doomed in

Lithuania," said Tiggy extemporising with the speed of a startled rat.
"But you are the Count Tolstoy Jergov, I have heard so much about?"
"Yes ... but who are you?"
"I am Alexandria De Candole Wolfberg."
"Do you know Lithuania?" Our author asked whilst silently praying to his guardian angel.
"No sadly I don't but my grandfather was there during the war"
"Was he Lithuanian – I'm sorry is he still alive?"
"No, he was German and he died on this exact date ten years ago."
"What did he do in Lithuania?"
"When I visited his house in Panama, I remember that he told me that he was an art curator there and he used to show me his collection. I was very young then but I remember a Cezanne and a Rembrandt on the wall. He was a great man and he said that collecting had been his passion when he was in the army and that he'd had a lot of difficulty getting paintings out of Europe.
"Did he have an art gallery in Panama or something?" the author asked with trepidation.
"No, grandfather thought that there were too many jealous people in this world and that his collection would be stolen if people knew it was there."
Tiggy said nothing and looked again at the woman. Despite the brown skin she had white-blonde hair and he wondered whether she was a second-generation Aryan product. She lived in Panama and was taking a few months off from her job as an investment manager because she had finally inherited some of her grandfather's money after lengthy arguments with the authorities. Ms De Candole Wolfberg didn't specify which authorities but he got the general drift.
"Why did you want to see me? As I said, I left Lithuania many years ago and it is a shadow of its former importance – it's a minor part of the Common Market now I believe."
"Grandpa was a big reader and a bit of a linguist. Despite the war he was an anglophile and obsessed with Jane Austin. He used to read 'Pride and Prejudice' to me whenever he could but I was only six years old and didn't understand."
Tiggy was starting to get the feeling that he would be asked to write about an SS collector who ripped off Lithuanian jews and stole their best art before condemning them to the gas chamber. But that he had a soft centre and a romantic side. He was not wrong.
Our author tried to work what price he could charge that would make him

feel better about taking the dirtiest money he'd ever encountered. Whilst he was calculating the woman sat down and read the first few pages of the Fenton book and read the comments on the fly-leaf which amongst other wonderful compliments described him as a male Jane Austin.

"There are very few male parts in the book as romances in the Austin style tend to concentrate on female dialogue but there is a Jewish banker who appears about half way through?"

"I don't think that would be suitable, "Alexandria said. "Is there not a soldier or a writer or an artist?"

"I don't wish to be crass, but writing a part specially is going to cost you twenty-five thousand US dollars and I would need commitment immediately," Tiggy said suddenly realising what his dirty - money price was.

The woman tried to bargain but our author held firm to his principles and by the end of the day Count Tolstoy Jergov had another character for his book. This time an aristocratic older man who offers expert advice to the two heroines on the purchase of art. He is kindly, good-looking and of immaculate pedigree but tragically dies after ten pages, much to the distress of the girls.

Tiggy retired to another lounge after this interlude feeling unclean but rich. It was difficult with the different currencies but he had made over 100K since he'd been on the *Amazon* and needed a rest. He was to pleasure Miriam's sister tonight he thought - but he couldn't be sure after the mix up earlier in the week and if he got it wrong, they'd have his balls on a platter covered in chilli oil.

Over the next few days Tiggy started to worry that his acting performance was starting to come to the end of its run. As he wandered the ship during the day, he started to worry whether he would recognise any of his clients if he came across them again.

Apart from Florence Hasty who's appearance would be etched in his nightmares he really was not sure what any of them had looked like. Things were most difficult when they went down to dinner because looking down at the hundreds of guests all dressed to the nines, Tiggy couldn't identify anyone.

The other problem was the sisters themselves. After the mistake when Tiggy had pleasured the wrong one he'd thought that the arguments had been resolved. But Miriam had changed and was ripping into her younger sister verbally every time they met. Whether it was just sister bitchiness or serious jealously about him, he didn't know, but his instincts told him to leave the ship before he found out just what the issue was.

Out for the Count

Tiggy Foghorn aka Count Tolstoy Jergov aka Eugene Fenton abandoned ship at Port Chalmers, New Zealand just 10 days after being abducted in the most pleasurable way possible by Miriam Bender and her sister.

No one seeing his departure would have associated him with the aristocratic womaniser or famous author who had entertained so well onboard. Tiggy hoped that no-one saw him at all.

The only possessions he'd had when shanghaied in Akaroa were his English passport, wallet, I Pad and the clothes he was wearing. These and some of his bought clothes were packed in a sailor's duffle bag he'd borrowed from the crew quarters. Now he was wearing a baseball cap, some jeans, a sweatshirt and the all-important hi-vis waistcoat and badge with the ships name on it, purloined from the same source.

He knew from the itinerary that the ship had arranged coach trips from the harbour to places like the Albatross Colony, Dunedin Shopping Centre and the Southern Heritage Centre and hitched a ride dressed like a member of crew and pretended to be asleep at the back.

Tiggy got out in Octagon Square which looked busy enough for him to slip into the crowd, chucked the yellow waistcoat in a bin and gradually got his bearings. He didn't know Dunedin but he could see a tourist office on the side of the square and popped in quickly, looking at the racks of timetables and accommodation guides.

Tiggy had plenty of money but needed to keep a low profile as he had skipped, not paying the sisters their cut of his ill-gotten gains. He'd tried to confuse them by saying that he was staying onboard but keeping away from their suites to avoid the big guy Elmer who'd got nasty. This was eminently believable as despite his lovely nature he looked like a gorilla with a headache.

Tiggy's hope was that by the time Miriam realised that he'd jumped ship, they would be days away from New Zealand and too far away to do anything.

He knew that *Amazon* was in Port Chalmers for only a few hours and that even if someone started a search immediately the chance of anybody finding him on such a big ship was low. Much more likely was that Count Jergov wouldn't be missed for many days and by then he would be a different person and probably thousands of miles away.

As he scanned the racks Tiggy did a quick calculation and reckoned that he had enough money to get the work done on his beloved Riva boat. He needed to find a secure way to contact that shyster at the Akaroa boatyard because storms had been hitting the coast and the Rivas hull wasn't exactly sound. The trouble was he didn't exactly trust the guy.

Tiggy remembered his first visit when the Italian shipwright went below and spent hours poking around in the boat. He emerged wiping his brow with his woollen crew hat and emphasising his point with many Latin gestures.

"Dis iza deff trap – vera leaks everywhere."

The man had demanded twenty grand to make the boat waterproof and demanded cash. Every time Tiggy had tried to negotiate on the price the guy had a sharp intake of breath and refused. As he appeared to be the only guy qualified to work on Riva in Australasia, Tiggy finally had to agree.

That was a couple of months ago and Tiggy had only had enough money to do emergency repairs. Now he had a lot more options but he needed to plan carefully.

That morning in Dunedin Tiggy decided to lie low and do very little. He found an apartment up Harrop Street where the guy was happy to take cash for a couple of weeks rent. Tomorrow he'd go downtown and get some clothes that suited his new image. But now his plan was to go down to the square and get some blue cod and chips and then relax in the vast Victorian-style rooms he'd acquired.

The apartment had two bedrooms, each with en-suite, a huge sitting room and a vast kitchen. Judging by the clothes in the wardrobe and stuff in the freezer, Tiggy reckoned that this was owned by a wealthy Chinese or Thai couple who only visited occasionally. So, the concierge he'd paid was not likely to tell anyone about their informal arrangement which had absolutely no paperwork involved. Which might prove useful if the proverbial ever hit the fan.

After a great meal and a few drinks, he decided to crash early and slid under the sheets. After what felt like just a few hours but was actually 14 he realised that this was the first place onshore he'd slept in for weeks and he'd slept the sleep of the righteous.

He staggered into the en-suite and saw that the ex-Count needed to shower and get some clothes that made him look less like an itinerant deck hand and more like a local. The last thing he wanted to do was look like an aristocrat or an author, in fact he needed to blend in to the background so well, that no one remembered him at all.

Tiggy went down in a lift that had metal latticework sliding doors and out through a big front door with a glass top panel that had the words Highland Bank etched in reverse. He imagined that this part of Dunedin must have been full of banks, solicitors and other professionals originally. Now many of them had been turned into apartments, restaurants and hotels, aimed at wealthy foreign tourists or investors.

Tiggy looked up at the bright blue sky with not a cloud to be seen and knew that it was going to be a lovely day. He turned left into the square and again into the main shopping street and started to wander down Princess Street. There were already tourists looking in the All-Black rugby store and other expensive clothing shops but he didn't want to look like a tourist.

After about half a mile the street started to change and there was a local department store called Farmers which looked as though it had been selling good clothes to locals for centuries. They looked a little old-fashioned but Tiggy bought a couple of check shirts and some denim jeans at half the price it would have cost in Auckland. It wasn't anywhere near Winter yet but he knew that the weather down here could get bitter, so he got some thermal underwear and decent walking shoes too.

Tiggy wandered round for a while in the store enjoying the atmosphere as Farmers reminded him of the visits he'd made to shops in Oxford as a boy. Proper department stores with lots of good local products have died out in the UK and this was a nostalgic reminder of a simpler time when every high street didn't have the same chain stores. Eventually he went back out onto the street, carrying his bags and dumped the sailors gear he'd been wearing in a charity bin behind the supermarket and kept on walking.

He'd only been back once to England since he he'd left the Royal Navy and it had been much changed by Covid and the growth in online shopping. City centres were not the same and the names he'd looked for as a kid were not there anymore. Dunedin seemed to have worked out how to keep enough independent stores open to make the experience enjoyable. Not that he was a shopaholic or anything close but if you had to buy stuff then you should feel good doing it.

The Oxfam charity shop was familiar from the UK and the Kiwi version was just across the road. Tiggy went in, nodded to the woman behind the counter and looked round for anything that might be useful. After a few minutes browsing Tiggy came across an old tweed jacket that looked as though it had been hand tailored for him it fitted so well. Also, a Swan-Dri waterproof coat that looked a few years old but perfectly serviceable in just about any weather other than a heatwave.

The woman like all the people in New Zealand he'd ever met was chatty and interested so he told her he was a Kiwi who'd been travelling for a few years but originally from North Island and she seemed to believe him. The last thing he wanted to look or sound like for the moment was a Lithuanian Count or a famous romantic author.

Back in the apartment Tiggy looked at his clothes and reckoned that he'd done a good job. The shirts looked new, but the old jacket over the top made him look like loads of other locals who treat themselves to a new shirt when on a trip away from home. As a great performer Tiggy had to look the part but first he had to decide what character was going to keep him safe while he waited to see whether there were any repercussions to his trip on the good ship *Amazon.*

He checked NZ TV News when he got back and there were no stories of mystery Counts or false authors so he went out for a glass of wine and lunch to celebrate. One of the great things Tiggy had learned since he'd moved to New Zealand is that the Kiwis do great wine and great brunches and sometimes, he had them at the same time. Going down to the Octagon again he found the Nova restaurant which was right next to the Art Gallery- another aspect of local culture he aimed to experience. First, however, he needed some physical sustenance.

He went down the stairs into a bistro heaving with people, most of whom looked local and looked across at the counter, which seemed to have all kinds of cakes and salads. An attractive girl, with long brown hair tied back in long braid came over and guided him to a small table alongside the glass sides of the gallery foyer.

"While I'm looking at the menu, could I have a flat white please?"

"Sure, are you visiting us, I don't think I've seen you before?" The waitress asked with a lovely smile that almost looked genuine.

"I'm living round the corner for the moment, are you local?" Tiggy answered remembering to keep his accent neutral.

"No, I'm originally from Brazil, but I love it here - anyway I'll get your coffee."

If Tiggy hadn't been sated by a week as a sex slave on the cruise ship, he might have been tempted by the lovely waitress – she was about twenty years younger, and about five stone lighter than his normal taste, but she had a wonderful figure, really exciting brown eyes and moved like a model. Anyway, he looked down at the menu and saw that his two favourites – Eggs Benedict and Eggs Florentine were both on the list.

When his delightful waitress returned, he ordered the Eggs Benedict and a large glass of Kiwi Riesling which added a little bit of fresh tang to the richness of the meal. The combination of wine and brunch is sometimes looked down on by purists but Tiggy's view was don't knock it until you've tried it.

He finished the eggs and ordered another wine looking forward to a relaxed afternoon in his apartment contemplating his navel. His waitress gently persuaded him into a final coffee and he noticed that the restaurant was gradually emptying with locals on their way back to work and there were just a couple of people left in the corner lingering over some muffins the size of footballs.

Judging by her badge, his favourite Brazilian was called Fran and Tiggy could see that she was finishing for the day, putting her Nova apron on the hook and so he made sure that he tipped her twenty dollars and she came over.

"Where else is worth eating or going for drink? I don't know Dunedin very well" He asked her quietly. She mentioned a couple of places but said that she didn't get out much because she was saving for the next leg of her trip."

Tiggy sensed an opportunity and realised that the wine had done wonders for his libido, so he arranged to meet her in the square later and try the Caledonian Hotel for a couple of drinks.

He went back to the apartment and realised just how luxurious this place was and what great value. The few hundred dollars he'd slipped the caretaker was a fraction of what a hotel would have cost and as he walked round, he kept on noticing more nice features. Judging by the tall sash windows and detailed architrave on the ceiling, Tiggy reckoned that this had been built in the early 1800's and been part of a bank or lawyers office before it was converted. Dunedin was settled by the Scots originally and the Hibernian influence was still there everywhere from street names through to architecture.

He checked the TV again. Another big screen was hidden tastefully behind a moving panel in the bedroom but Tiggy didn't think he'd be watching too often. Kiwi TV comprised lots of re-cycled UK and US programmes that he'd seen years ago. The news and weather, however, were good quality and regularly updated. Luckily the Count was still not being mentioned, so he switched off with a sigh of relief.

82

Tiggy was intrigued about his date later. He'd been successful with women for over 30 years, ever since Maddie had taught him so well as a teenager. His career as a serial philanderer was based on targeting women of a certain age and certain size who he had always found to be incredibly grateful. Giving them pleasure had given him money and kept him and his Riva afloat for years. Miriam Bender and her sister had shown him that he'd not lost his power but sometimes he felt like 'The fastest gun in the West' in those old westerns, who always worried about finding someone younger and faster.

The age difference between him and Fran the Brazilian waitress was far greater than anyone he'd bedded. It was going to be an interesting challenge and one where the Count Jergov approach would be laughed out of bed and the famous author angle might be productive or totally ridiculous. He had a couple of hours to plan his evenings approach to the younger generation.

A thousand miles away the cruise ship *Amazon* was on her merry way back to the USA with Miriam Bender and her sister just starting to worry about the absence of their Count. Tiggy had been extremely clever in using Elmer Flannigan as the reason for his disappearance. The man may have been gay but he looked like a thug from one of the Godfather films. The girls saw him at dinner and his tattooed forearms were huge and his hands looked large enough to crush their beloved Count Jergov's lovely throat in seconds. Tiggy had said that he was lying low because Elmer hadn't liked the story he'd written for his partner and had sworn vengeance.

The girls had missed him in bed. Even on alternate nights they had more pleasure in the last weeks than they'd had in years of marriage. Dinner too, was becoming a sombre affair without their Tiggy ordering the most exquisite wines and feeding it to them like a marine version of Jeeves. His gentlemanly treatment of them had made them the envy of the women at the other tables and made him hated by all the males who were delighted by his absence.

Miriam regretted the bad temper she'd been in before he left and worried that she'd driven him away. After three days the girls agreed that action was now required but didn't know what to do. Tiggy was not on the passenger list because they had abducted him originally. The fact that they might be part of a conspiracy to defraud other passengers also gave them pause for thought. They had been convinced originally about the book character idea – indeed they had paid out ten grand each to prove it. But the more they thought about it, the more they wondered.

In the end it was love for Tiggy that made them desperate enough to act. Miriam confronted Elmer Flannigan after breakfast and asked the big brute whether he was annoyed with Count Jergov for some reason. A faraway look came into his eyes and Elmer said on the contrary he thought that he was a beautiful man and a very talented writer. The words he had written about his partner imagined as a 19th Century sea captain had really been wonderful and Elmer couldn't wait to see the book proof in a few months' time. Flannigan was so sincere that Miriam knew that Tiggy hadn't been hurt or thrown overboard by him.

Miriam left and met her sister for coffee to discuss their worries. They tried to analyse the situation and formulate a plan. They didn't know whether the Count was for real and whether he was onboard or not. Looking back on things they realised that they had no way to communicate with him. There had been no exchange of calls, texts or emails between them and just the literary contracts they'd signed as evidence that he'd existed at all.

They thought that he lived on his boat in Akaroa but couldn't be sure. Even his names felt a little unbelievable when his reassuring presence was absent. Count Tolstoy Jergov did seem a little ridiculous now but his explanation at the time had been plausible enough for them to invest in his book. Miriam reminded her sister about the Eugene Fenton book that Tiggy had shown them originally and they compared notes. They both remembered the photo of Tiggy on the cover and the wonderful reviews but now wondered whether it might all have been faked.

They couldn't search the ship so they spent a few hours trying to research their lover in the ships computer room and really didn't learn anything new. Miriam was worried enough to also call an investigator she'd used in the US when she was in business and get him to check the names of Count Tolstoy Jergov and Eugene Fenton. The guy said it would take some time since Europe was not his normal area of operations but he would start immediately. Miriam told him fiercely that he had two days and hung up.

Investigator Brett Lane was not everyone's idea of a Los Angeles private detective. He didn't have a dingy office with frosted windows in a down-at-heel brownstone. He wasn't fat or a big smoker and he had never to his recollection worn a trench-coat or trilby hat. Despite these obvious disadvantages he still successfully dealt with many of the same problems that his fictional counterparts had – marital infidelity, disappearing debtors and commercial fraud were the mainstay of his business.

Unlike Micky Spillane's hero detectives Lane didn't prepare for a case by seducing a blonde or pointing a revolver. Lane normally prepared by running for ten miles down the coast at dawn and then downing a large smoothy.

The call from Miriam Bender had been intriguing as all his previous work for her had been simple checks on the creditworthiness of purchasers who had committed to long term contracts. Some of these had been for retirement homes worth many millions of dollars but hardly complicated stuff. He knew she was on a world cruise and so this must be important otherwise she wouldn't have called. The names she'd given him to investigate sounded like something out of a cheap melodrama – Count Tolstoy Jergov, Eugene Fenton and the nickname Tiggy. He sat down in his office at the end of the garden in his 1920's Deco house in a prosperous suburb and fired up his computer. These days a successful investigator didn't tramp the mean streets trying to find criminals or missing people, they trawled through databases.

Most people leave an electronic trail, created when they use credit cards, access ATM's or travel. Since terrorism became an issue in many countries, cameras and face recognition software mean that you leave a visual trail too. In this case Miriam hadn't supplied a photograph of the target, which made this form of recognition impossible. Lane made a note to check whether they had any shots of the subject and what the investigation was about.

Florence Hasty had visited every bar and every lounge on the ship over the last two days trying to find Count Jergov. She wanted her tame author to amend certain aspects of the brief she had given him and was taking her frustration out on every member of staff she had met. The barman who'd been on when she'd had met the Count had been back on duty and she'd interrogated him viciously without finding out his cabin number or anything of use.

The barman remembered that the Count had signed with Ms Bender's suite number on numerous occasions. But that was the last thing he was ever going to reveal – even under torture from the ginger-headed gargoyle. The Count was a gentleman and generous, neither of which were qualities common to most of the passengers on this trip.

Florence had also been searching for Miriam Bender, the woman who'd told her about the Counts book and the Aussie had tried to get her contact details from the ship's purser. He had also hated Ms Hasty with a vengeance and had hidden behind data protection rather than tell her anything. The Ginger binger had then gone on a new tour of bars and had a pint of Fosters in most of them trying to find anybody she recognised. By evening she was almost comatose and had to be helped back to her cabin by three strong crew men who were absolutely terrified that she might come too.

Florence Hasty woke up the following morning in a foul mood uncertain about the previous afternoon and confused as to what had happened to one of her shoes. She realised that she'd been drinking but her capacity for drink was legendary and only on one occasion had she ended up feeling this bad. That was the Australian Funeral Directors Annual Ball and she'd outdrunk two Irish professionals, won a trophy and celebrated with flaming Sambucas. After that she collapsed in flames and had to be put out by a passing waiter with a fire bucket.

After a large fried breakfast and several mugs of tea Florence decided to try and re-trace her steps but as she was passing the reception, she tried to be polite and talk to the girl behind the desk.

"Excuse me my dear. I'd like to leave a note for Count Jergov, is that possible?"

The girl checked her computer and asked Florence to repeat the name several times but was adamant that no-one of that name was on the passenger list. Florence thought through things carefully and also asked that she check the name Eugene Fenton as he might have checked in under his pen-name. The officer repeated the process laboriously and after ten minutes was only able to find one Fenton onboard and that was a 90 year old Spinster in a wheelchair.

Florence was getting angry and the receptionist was becoming alarmed by this huge woman and eventually agreed to put out a public announcement on all decks.

"Would Count Jergov please urgently come to reception as this is a matter of life and death."

Miriam, Elmer Flannigan, the Panamanian Nazi descendant and the paramilitary Ms Anders all heard the announcement and were shocked out of their complacency. They set off from all parts of the ship at speed hoping to find their literary hero in reception but concerned about the urgency of the message. Had he been there, Tiggy Foghorn aka Count Tolstoy Jergov aka Eugene Fenton would have known that his fate hung in the balance if all parties met and that the Ginger Peril was becoming a major threat.

Back in L.A. Brett Lane had fired up his usual search engines and accessed Interpol and US police and missing files, looking for Count Tolstoy Jergov and found nothing. Knowing that he was of Lithuanian background, he had also looked at their records of the aristocracy. He found that similar to other European countries, many titles had been given as reward for prowess in battle and some went back a thousand years. In fact, it was stated that Lithuania had a greater proportion of nobles than any other. In the 1400's it was the largest country in Europe incorporating many other territories. This split dramatically in the 1700's and Russia annexed most of the empire. In the 20th Century the country was over-run by Germans and Russians and many records were destroyed.

Brett had really never heard of Lithuania but learned that it was now a country of just three million and that it was a member of the EU.

Jergov as a name produced nothing on the further search of nobles. Influential families listed included the Chackiewicz, Pacas, Borkowski, Pacas, Plater and dozens of others but everyone had problems with the spelling and he couldn't be sure that Jergov wasn't an anglicised version of one of them. So Brett came out with very little that supported or denied the existence of a Count Tolstoy Jergov, which was frustrating. He couldn't help thinking, however, that no-one would actually invent a name that was so amusing to a present-day audience.

The name Eugene Fenton was eventually more productive but it took many hours of work before his investigation revealed anything. There was no mention of him in the British Library which supposedly had copies of all published works. Also, no mention of an author called Fenton in the London Times Literary Review, which had started reviewing books in 1820. But an advanced search of literary connections eventually revealed that an author called Wodehouse and a publisher called Penguin back in 1906 had been highly complementary about a book called 'A flame of passion' by a Eugene Fenton and called him 'The male Jane Austin' and urged publishers to back him. Lane thought he'd found Miriam's author but then did some basic maths. Even if Fenton had been a child prodigy, he would have to be over 130 years old in order to be still working. Even with the miracles of modern science, this was not likely.

His last check was on the nickname Tiggy. According to the urban dictionary, Tiggy was slang for a tall, polite but not very intelligent man which confused him. Then he realised that if this guy was older then he probably had no idea of its recent tag. Drilling down further Lane found a copy of the Sun newspaper front page from around 30 years ago where the name Tiggy was mentioned in a sex scandal involving a Bishop's wife. More recently there was Australian report where the authorities were searching for someone called Tiggy who had assaulted a marina manager. The dates were more feasible but there were too many uncertainties to be sure that this was the same man.

The investigator realised that Miriam was in a different time zone, so didn't call but spent half an hour compiling an email to send which outlined his findings so far.

The meeting of all those concerned with Count Jergov in the reception of the *Amazon* was a little strange. Firstly, Miriam had just received an email from her investigator and was still in shock about its content. Her sister was in 'told you so' mode and seething.

Florence had forced the receptionist to make the announcement but didn't know any of the others apart from Miriam who she thought she recognised but wasn't sure. The area was busy with people anyway, so nobody was actually sure who was there because of the tannoy. The main problem in addition was that everyone was there hoping to see the tall, elegant figure of the Count himself.

Everyone had different motives, Miriam and her sister wanted to confront their former bed mate with the accusation that according to their investigator, the Count probably didn't exist and Eugene Fenton died 130 years ago. Secretly they hoped that he would have an explanation and everything would be fine. Elmer just hoped that his plan to get his soul mate's story hadn't been compromised in some way and wanted reassurance that he would see a proof before Neil's birthday.

Anders was there with Dwight Junior hoping that Dwight Seniors legend as a gun-toting Confederate General was still going to be celebrated in the book and that the immigrant Lopez hadn't won his place.

Alexandria De Candole Wolfberg was confused as to who all these people were and why were they so concerned. The Count had seen remarkably healthy a few days ago when they'd made their arrangement but life in Panama had taught her to be paranoid about opening up to anybody. So she held back.

Florence Hasty stomped around the reception area frightening everyone. Even Elmer looked worried by the ginger apparition who stared at everyone who walked into the area. After 30 minutes she tried to get the receptionist to repeat the announcement but she refused saying that the tannoy was only to be used for official purposes and that she would get fired if she repeated it. Frustrated she turned to those around and asked in a voice that would not have been missed by anyone within fifty yards

"Does anyone here know where that feckin' Count Jergov is?"

Miriam and sister decided that discretion was the best part of valour and quietly left before anyone recognised them. But Anders, whose husband had braved everything for the USA, decided that courage was everything and walked over to the woman, stood to attention and saluted. Elmer was a big, tough guy but not hugely confident whether he could beat this woman in a straight fight, so went over quietly and nodded politely to this vision in purple. Alexandria lurked in the background and observed without admitting she had an involvement.

Back in the suite Miriam and her sister decided that the investigators report probably meant that Count Jergov was a fraud and that they'd each lost a serious amount of money. Strangely neither could be angry, Tiggy had been a wonderful part of their holiday and they both had experiences in bed with him that were absolutely life-changing. Sex had just been sex with their husbands, but with Tiggy they had both realised what lovemaking truly meant. They both agreed that Tiggy's excuse for absence – hiding from an angry Elmer – was bull and that he had probably left the ship at the last port of call, Dunedin.

The sisters decided to do nothing for now. They had been guilty in bringing him onboard and could be seen as complicit in part of the fraud, so decided it was best to lie low. As to what Florence Hasty and the rest of the victims might do, they had no idea. But they would be angry and bound to call the police when they finally realised for sure that the Count had disappeared. This would be complicated on the high seas as no force could be relied on to take an interest.

Miriam was worried because she was the link between the Count and two of the victims. Also, he had been seen at dinner with them on numerous occasions and been an extremely memorable part of their group. They realised that they couldn't deny knowledge of him but thought they could claim to be fellow victims who'd innocently recommended him to others and been taken themselves. Which was true-ish though sharing a bed with him might be a little harder to explain. For now, the best thing for them was to lie low and avoid the investigation if they could.

Miriam's investigator had asked for photographs and they realised that they had very little to record their time onboard with the Count. He had been oddly – but now understandably- reticent about people wanting to take their photograph and ducked away with a joke about "no more publicity" or something else modest. The only shot they had was when they had abducted him in the first place and he was sitting pissed in one of the bars onboard. It wasn't very clear but Miriam emailed it to her investigator in L.A.

Florence Hasty looked round at the other victims looking totally gormless in the reception and realised that she had to take charge. She rounded them up and took them down the corridor to the nearest saloon and they found an area where they could all sit.

"I don't think Count fekkin Jergov actually exists!" Florence expounded.

"Yes, he does I met him twice and he was lovely" Elmer said feeling affronted.

"I don't mean that – I mean that he's a freekin shyster, a conman."

"What evidence do you have of that?" Elmer Flannigan asked, still highly defensive of his author hero. "He wrote some lovely words about my partner Neil."

"He didn't want to use Dwight for the story at all - that's not a conman" Added Ms Anders still standing to attention.

Florence could see that she was losing the belief of her audience and that everyone had really liked the Count. She needed a Plan B.

"I'll tell you what. As you can see your precious Count Jergov didn't answer the urgent call from reception. The *Amazon* say they have no record of a Count Jergov or a Eugene Fenton as a passenger on this trip. Go off and try to find him and we'll meet back here at 4.00 o'clock. Is that agreeable to everyone?"

The group couldn't see anything wrong with the idea and agreed to meet in an hour. Florence ordered a pint of Fosters and sat down to wait.

Later that afternoon the head of security and the Captain of *Amazon* were starting to realise that they might have had a stowaway onboard who had defrauded a number of passengers. The names Count Jergov and Eugene Fenton were being used by the potential criminal, neither of which were listed as passengers or crew. There were a number of options being considered:

1. An existing passenger had been using false names
2. Somebody had come onboard illegally and was still hiding onboard
3. The person had left the ship at the last port – Port Chalmers, Dunedin.

It was agreed that there would be a thorough search of the ship. A task that would take days and fraught with difficulty. Also, that there would be detailed check of all the security camera footage taken of passengers leaving and returning at the last disembarkation. The head of security knew that shore visits were always a weak-spot and that almost anyone could get on or off without proper ID in the mass of passengers. These ports of call were generally chosen because they were in friendly countries with a low security risk so checks were minimal.

The officers were not confident except for the fact that the individual apparently looked unusual. A tall, slim, gentleman with long dark hair who looked as though he'd stepped out of a 1920's yachting book would stand out. Disguise was obviously possible but most male guests were a lot heavier which might make a slim guy stand out on the security cameras. The other possibility according to Ms Hasty was a passenger she thought was called Miriam or Muriel or Mabel who'd introduced the Count to her in the first place. Without a surname and with thousands of passengers this was also a difficult search, but one that certain passengers would not let rest.

Blissfully unaware of the problems he was causing, Tiggy Foghorn had gone to a local bank and drawn a few thousand dollars from his account which had an unusually healthy bank balance for once. This is because funds had been transferred from the rather less respectable Panamanian bank he'd used to collect his authors fees.

The NZ account was genuine but he decided not to use any of the credit cards associated with it as he knew that they left a trail that the police could follow.

For now, he intended to stay in Dunedin, chill out for a few days and continue to check the news. If everything was OK then he'd travel by train, bus or taxi back to Akaroa, where he could discuss plans for the Riva and hopefully its final upgrade. First, however, he had a beautiful young woman called Fran to meet and he was looking forward to the challenge.

Francesca Capelle was born in Sao Paulo, 28 years ago, the daughter of a seamstress and a civil servant. Even as a baby she was lovely and won some of the beautiful baby contests run by one of the local newspapers. She looked more European than many others with her straight brown air and big brown eyes. Francesca was well educated because her parents scrimped and saved so that she went to a private school but when it came to college or university, she decided that she would rather travel and see something of the world before she decided on a career.

This gap year became extended, year by year as she travelled through the US, working in restaurants and bars and then across to Europe. In addition to her Spanish, Fran spoke excellent English and French which made her very popular. As did her beauty.

By the time Fran had got to New Zealand, she was a confident tall woman with a figure that a photographer friend had once called luscious and the most unusual hazel eyes that men found absolutely devastating. She'd learned how to use this attraction over the years and her moral compass had often got a little confused. But she reasoned that a single woman in a strange country was entitled to use every natural advantage that she had been given. New Zealand was probably her last stop on what had ended up as a gap decade and she intended to return to Brazil in style.

The man she'd met in the Nova was good looking in the way that some older men get. He was tall, tanned and looked like a tennis player or professional sailor, not like the bulky rugby types much loved by the locals. She didn't know whether he was a Kiwi or a visitor but she sensed that he was certainly good for a meal and possibly a lot more.

The other attraction was that he didn't quite look respectable and Fran had always had a weakness for what her mother had called 'the wrong sort of man'. He had only talked for a few minutes but he had a humorous, roguish twinkle in his eye that was both a challenge and an invitation.

Tiggy Foghorn himself was surprised that he was feeling nervous. He was used to impressing women but this was unfamiliar territory and he wasn't using his Count Jergov persona or trying to be a writer, this was just him.

He'd read some years ago that great classic actors like Olivier or Richardson often felt bereaved when a long run of playing a particular person on stage had ended. His title made him feel important and interesting. His blazer, white trousers and writing folder were his 'props' and he felt a little naked without them.

Tiggy had a small McCallan whisky in the apartment and checked himself in the mirror. He wondered whether he was turning into his father, certainly his height and build were similar and his dark hair was still thick and turning a little grey as his fathers had. But Horatio had a constant look of happiness and good humour on his face which was missing on his own. Part of that was because his marriage to Adele, the former hostess, may not have been made in heaven in the traditional sense, but it was certainly a partnership of great love.

Tiggy had barely seen his parents since he'd been thrown out of school after the affair with the Bishop's wife. His father had approved of his navy career but he suspected that he had found out about his misdoings and premature departure from the 'Nafia' – as he called the ex-navy groups in Plymouth and Portsmouth. But they were still alive and still cared deeply for each other.

Tiggy realised that he might be rootless and loveless but at least he was richer than he had been a few months ago and money always helped him have fun …

He thought back to all those older male stars like Cary Grant or George Clooney and how they had treated those young starlets in the great films. He drew himself up, took a deep breath and went out of the bathroom trying to develop a similar sense of confident elegance. He didn't have his elegant suits or shirts but, in this city, wearing a jacket was seen as formal. The tweed jacket he'd bought from the charity shop fitted him extremely well but he desperately needed a pair of decent shoes as his father had said that you could always tell a gentleman by his shoes and the wealth of a person by his watch. His shoes let him down dreadfully but his Rolex Submariner 515 was old, genuine and a substantial nest-egg if things ever got critical.

Even though it was the norm here, Tiggy felt undressed in his open necked shirt, so looked round the master bedroom for something else. There was one wardrobe door that was locked and he supposed that the owners kept personal stuff there. The wood was mahogany or some kind of local hardwood but he found a knife in the kitchen and after a bit of jiggling, got it open, without too much damage to the lock. Inside were men's and women's clothes in just about every high status brand he'd ever heard of. Sadly, the Chinese man's clothes and shoes didn't fit but finally he found something useful. The Turnbull and Aser bow tie in dark silk had a subtle pattern but was predominately dark blue and the guy had probably worn it with his dinner jacket. Tiggy hand-tied the bow tie with just enough carelessness to show that it was real. Combined with the Wedgwood Blue shirt and tweed jacket it may have looked a little eccentric to locals. But Tiggy felt elegant enough to meet his young lady.

It was a late July day in Dunedin and there was just a hint of Spring in the air as he walked down Harrop Street and into the Octagon. He'd arranged to meet his waitress on the seats facing the gallery at 7.00 p.m. and he was exactly on time. She arrived from the North of the city and he saw her from 50 yards away, she was wearing a scarlet dress that would have looked at home in Rio and turning heads at every corner. She looked like some kind of Bird of Paradise amongst the greens and greys of the locals and ran across the square to him with a broad smile on her face

"I thought you needed cheering up,' she said. "I'm Francesca."

"I'm Terry" he said, thinking carefully about his name. "Tiggy to my friends," he added whilst kissing her lightly on each cheek in the Mediterranean manner.

"Ello Tiggy" she said in an exaggerated South American accent, and waggling her hips in a humorous way.

Tiggy was absolutely captivated by this woman and walked her across the road to the Caledonian Hotel. She slipped her arm through his, in the most natural way imaginable and he felt as though they had been friends for years. The age difference didn't feel to be a problem as she looked old enough to be the trophy wife of a successful man. The mental torture of someone asking whether she was his daughter wasn't going to happen, he was sure.

The hotel looked totally British and the bar as they walked in was heaving with people drinking one of the many beers on tap. Tiggy led Fran to a table and sat her down whilst trying to see what wines or other drinks they served.

"Aperol Spritz please," she asked, pre-empting his request.

The barman didn't seem surprised and was soon mixing the pink liquid in a huge glass and asking whether she wanted Prosecco or Soda. She said Prosecco and he carried on mixing.

Tiggy had a Gordons Export Gin and Feltham's Tonic in a similarly large glass and he brought the two drinks back to the table.

Over the next hour Tiggy got her to talk about her beliefs, her ambitions, her childhood and the state of Brazil's economy and politics. She was an intelligent and witty woman and seemed to enjoy talking about herself to him despite the age difference and he was really interested. He'd never been to South America and Brazil had always seemed so exotic.

Maddie's first lesson all those years ago had been to let women talk about themselves and try to be genuine. Men in her opinion were only normally interested in themselves and sex and not necessarily in that order. This woman radiated something absolutely primitive and at the moment it was radiating just at him. He was being given envious glances by half the males at the bar and Tiggy had to admit that he was really enjoying it. So he let her talk.

The place started to clear as all the early-doors brigade left for home and Tiggy asked what she liked to eat. He realised that working in a bistro all day which served cakes, brunches and European dishes might have put her off the food in the Caledonian which was broadly similar.

Strangely, she said that as a Brazilian she had been brought up on big steaks and that in her home country, meat was cheaper than vegetables. So, she thought that there was an Argentinian Steak House somewhere near the Heritage Centre and would love to try it.

He got the barman to arrange a taxi and paid his bill and loved the reflected envy in the bar keep's eyes as he led Fran out of the taxi and opened the door. It was odd he thought, old-world courtesy was seen as patronising by the feminist brigade, but no woman in his experience had ever been insulted by its use. A fact that had been shown night after night on the cruise ship.

The yellow taxi was driven by a madman who looked Vietnamese or Cambodian and who insisted on accelerating away from the lights so fast that he got wheel-spin and going round corners on what felt like two wheels. The benefit as far as Tiggy was concerned was that Fran had to cling on to him all the way, which was a pleasurable experience for him as her young body felt like heaven. If he could have done it without being crass, he would have bribed the guy to go a few more times round the block, just for the pleasure of it.

The Argentinian Steak House was noisy, dark and full of diners. The head waiter took them across the restaurant to an alcove lined with red velvet. They shuffled round the semi-circular bench seat until they were facing the other tables.

"What is the best Malbec you have?" Tiggy asked the sommelier, who answered with a choice rather too quickly. "Is that really the best?" Tiggy questioned, "or just the most expensive?"

The sommelier wasn't offended as the guy was smiling broadly as he said it but went back to the wine store and found a Bodega Catena Zapata 2015 which anybody with good taste and a thick wallet would like. Looking at his woman, the waiter was in no doubt about this man's taste at all and convinced that she was South American too. Which meant the choice of wine was not going to be wasted on a peasant.

Tiggy checked whether Fran was happy with red and she claimed that was her normal tipple. They both found themselves salivating as the smell of the steaks on the huge flaming grills was wonderful. She ordered a Porterhouse Steak, medium rare and he ordered T- Bone done exactly the same. The Malbec arrived and Tiggy got Fran to taste it. She declared it to be magnificent and it looked so, with a dark red colour and an almost smokey nose. He tasted it and it didn't disappoint, for the first time in months he felt optimistic with the pressure off and a lovely young woman by his side. He ordered another bottle to be uncorked for later.

Francesca Capelle was enjoying herself but the thought of sharing a bed with this older man filled her with a little trepidation and also a bit of excitement. She'd met businessmen in strange bars in strange places and shared dinner and occasionally a bed with them. With them a quick bonk in the half light of hotel room was fine, but this guy was different.

She was worried about her body and all the imperfections normally hidden by well cut jeans or a tight sweater. Fran was convinced that she was getting cellulite like her mothers and that her tummy was flabby because of lack of exercise and too much fast food from the places she's worked in.

This guy, she was convinced, was high class and used to the best in food, wine and women. Fran really wasn't sure that she was in that class, but she should tell from his eyes just how much he was attracted by her. Fran had always felt that she was the most modern of women and part of her thought that being so worried about her body was incredibly shallow. It didn't stop her worrying. Later she felt like a million dollars.

Terry had taken her back to the apartment and they had a bottle of champagne whilst listening to music. She had felt like a teenager on a first date and he was very gentle and understanding. She had never felt in such good hands and he was extremely practised at the gentle art of pleasuring a woman. He was patient and understanding, dimming the lights and carrying her to a magnificent bedroom which looked like something out of House Beautiful and which had silk sheets and the largest bed she'd ever seen.

That first night had been a revelation and she had learned things about her own body she hadn't learned in twenty-eight years. So had the man she now knew as Tiggy and he seemed genuinely in love with every part of it. The following morning, she had been proud to show herself naked as her partner made her feel that it looked beautiful.

He described her figure as being like an Italian film star from the 1970's. Her breasts he said were works of art – maybe a little larger than fashionable in some quarters but those judges knew nothing. She was feminine in the way that the classical artists would have recognised and her hips and bum looked like a real woman's. The rounded tummy, even with its hairline scar, was also admired and after making love she found herself talking about the baby she had lost. He shared her tears and made love to her gently- more gently than before but the intensity of pleasure remained just as satisfying. Tiggy had given her a pride and confidence in her own body that she'd never had before and she was truly grateful.

It was odd she thought just how many women are infected by the images they have seen as kids which are supposed to be female perfection. These are the images pushed by the ad men and fashionistas who are trying to sell something – they are not real. Also, the standards of perfection change every decade with hyper-slim models being the pinnacle every woman aspires to one year then something different the next. Tiggy had a way of cutting through all that crap and making her proud of what she had.

Tiggy Foghorn started to think of Fran as a faithful new young disciple. In fact, the only young disciple he'd had since school and then he'd been young himself so it didn't count.

Previous followers had been in the mould of Maddie and his love for larger, older but voluptuous women was undiminished. But Francesca was beautiful in the way that a Russell Flint painting was beautiful and he loved looking at her naked - she was incredibly sexy but didn't know it, which made her even more sexy.

Her body was a temple that he needed to worship in whenever he could. His attachment to this lovely young woman was dangerous he knew. A healthy detachment had always guided his attitude to females, which he found helped with everything from lovemaking to his conscience after depriving them of money.

Since Maddie had betrayed him all those years ago, he'd loved their company, he'd loved giving them pleasure but he'd never allowed himself to actually love any of them in any real sense.

On the second day in Dunedin Tiggy and Fran had got a taxi down to St Clair where there was a wonderful long beach and a sea bathing pool which he'd heard was unusual. They'd had to buy swimming gear but it was worth it just to see the locals goggling at Fran in her lovely one-piece which really enhanced her figure. Tiggy had only found a multi-coloured pair of surf shorts that fitted him and Fran spent many minutes giggling at the most unlikely surfer on the planet. She couldn't help noticing, however, that his body looked toned and well muscled enough to get a few admiring glances too.

The changing rooms were tiny and more like those he remembered from school but he managed to get changed afterward without too many bruises. They had tea and muffins in the cafe overlooking the pool with the happy buzz bodies feel when they've had vigorous exercise. Fran looked glorious without make-up and just a glow of good health on her cheeks.

Afterwards they walked down the beach for miles and Tiggy gloried in the fact that even in resorts like this, there was a huge amount of space between people in New Zealand. The sky was bright blue with just a couple of clouds on the horizon and things felt good. On the way back Fran put her arm through his and Tiggy found himself wondering what life with a woman like this would be like. She was so intuitive, so 'simpatico' he really could see how it might be possible to love such a partner for a lifetime.

They had lunch in one of the first floor restaurants with a view of the beach and they shared a plate of Bluff oysters washed down with a New Zealand Gewürztraminer which was absolutely wonderful. The taxi back was not a crazy Vietnamese, he was a slow one this time and the driver chatted affably about the All-Blacks, Chinese tourists, the government and all the things locals chat about. And Tiggy was starting to feel more like a relaxed Kiwi with every hour.

Thy shared another passionate night and Tiggy was starting to relax even more. Nothing about him had been mentioned on NZ News and by his reckoning the cruise ship *Amazon* would be in mid Pacific by now and just about as far away from him as possible.

He went out on his own and called the Akaroa boatyard from a hotel giving them authorisation to proceed on the next stage of the hull repair, which meant taking his Riva home out of the water for a few weeks. Fran said that she had taken a few more days off and he was looking forward to spending some more time exploring in Central Otago with her. If anything, she was more loving than ever and Tiggy was increasingly certain that he had found his soul mate. The caretaker had confirmed that the apartment owners were not due back for months so everything looked fine. They had all the time in the world.

That night they sat close together on the couch discussing whether to hire a car and travel over to Queenstown and the lakes. She said that she'd not had time to see the Remarkable Mountains and that she'd love to go there after having seen them on Lord of the Rings as a kid. He agreed though he hadn't really seen the point in all that hobbit stuff when the books had been around and Harry Potter had been more popular. But he pulled her close and joked about them finding their own special hobbit hole to snuggle down in winter.

He couldn't believe he was feeling so affectionate. This wasn't the attitude Maddie had advised him to have all those years ago. 'Have fun but don't fall in love' was her advice and the principle he'd followed ever since. But Fran was devoted to him and she was special.

The following morning, he woke up early which was unusual. He immediately sensed a difference in the atmosphere in the apartment and Fran's side of the bed was empty. Thinking that she was in the loo he turned over, luxuriating in the thought that he had a couple of hours before they had to go. He really needed to keep his strength up if he was going to keep up with these young women, he remembered thinking.

When he woke again, the light was coming through a crack in the curtains and his mental clock told him that it was around 10.00 a.m. He put his hand over to Fran's side of the bed and it was stone cold and he started to get a strange feeling about the day. He shouted Fran, hoping that she was making coffee and got no answer, so he wrapped a towel round himself and checked the en-suite. This was empty of her toiletries and the silk dressing gown they'd bought for her had gone.

Tiggy wandered from room to room and everywhere was so empty of Fran or her clothes that it was almost like she had never existed. He went back to the bedroom to double-check the time and his Rolex Submariner was missing.

With guts churning he went through to the sitting room and the watch wasn't there. He found his wallet with relief on the dresser but it looked thinner than it had been the previous day. Opening it, he found that every

99

bit of cash had gone.

The Rolex had been worth around 50K. Tiggy had been telling her about it to her a couple of days ago. Bragging how he'd got it for a song some years ago from someone who didn't know its true value. He didn't know exactly how much money had gone. But there had probably been around 5,000 dollars in his wallet and a bit more local currency in his bedside drawer.

Tiggy was in denial for a while. He went to the kitchen and made himself a coffee whilst he tried to imagine who else might have robbed them. It took a while for it to sink in, but it looked as though someone had taught him a very expensive lesson. It didn't take a genius to work out who that person was.

He sat around for an hour in a kind of fugue. In his fairy tale, his beloved Fran would come back through the door in the next few minutes with his watch and cash saying that she couldn't leave him because she loved him too much. Sadly, he'd learned not to believe in fairy tales at the age of seven and knew that Father Christmas was a bit unlikely too.

He did a mental run through of every event since they'd met at the Octagon and couldn't think of any point where his instincts had warned him that this was all too good to be true. So, either she was the best con person in the world or he was losing it. The prospect was not good for his future if the latter was the case.

Eventually, Tiggy went back to the Nova Bistro where he had first met her and drank too much wine. He asked the manager where the waitress Fran had gone - the guy said that they were looking for her too because she hadn't been due any holiday and they were short-staffed. When pressed the manager said there were some 'irregularities' his boss had complained about but he was sure that once Fran came back, they would be sorted.

Tiggy had another bottle of wine and managed to talk to one of the other waitresses who he thought had been on duty on his first visit. The Nova was still busy and on the mention of Fran's name the waitress clammed up but looked like thunder. She didn't say anything really, just quietly saying 'bitch' as she passed by on the way to the till.

Eventually and it was a long eventually, he had to admire the style of the woman Fran. It takes a lot to con a conman and Tiggy had been taken hook, line and sinker. To the extent that now he almost felt bereaved because he had really started to love Francesca. Now he felt an emptiness that he'd never known, even when Maddie had rejected him and sold him out to the newspapers.

Tiggy was normally pretty resilient and the next morning he woke up in the apartment feeling a little better and started to think practically. He discounted any form of action against Fran because she would probably be out of the country by now and on her way to Brazil. Anyway, he couldn't complain about her activities without drawing attention to his own.

The missing cash was annoying but if she'd had longer and found access to his account, then he might have lost the 100K plus what he'd made on the *Amazon*. Nothing in his wallet would have given her a clue about that and she'd left the credit cards alone. To be sure he'd gone to the ANZ later, drawn more cash out and changed his passwords.

The watch was upsetting because the Rolex 515 was special and she wouldn't have found it easy to sell in Dunedin. He reasoned that just as a straightforward Submariner, a pawn shop would have valued it at around a thousand dollars. So he consulted his friend the caretaker downstairs and found out the names of a few places where she might have gone. It was unlikely to be a reputable jeweller where they had cameras and needed paperwork to back up any valuable watch purchase. Late afternoon he walked out to one of the most likely places with plenty of cash on him.

Mac's Gold Rush was down a small side street behind the Countdown car park and looked the part. The backstreet had a tattoo place, a cafe much used by cab-drivers and most of the other places had To Let signs outside.

The pawnbroker window had an eclectic mix of stuff including a knackered Fender guitar and amp, a top hat and tail coat outfit and some display cases of silver plate and jewellery. Tiggy pushed his way in and triggered one of the loudest bells he'd heard this side of church. Inside the shop there was very little space between the junk but Tiggy spied a guy hiding behind a glass security window at the far end.

Tiggy stood in front the man who presumably used the name Mac and waited for him to look up from his copy of the Otago Daily Times racing section. Realising that customer service wasn't high on the man's agenda, Tiggy put on his most officer-like tone and decided that authoritative bluster might be worth a try.

"You received a Rolex from a Brazilian woman who was using the name

Francesca. If you return it now, you will be compensated for your loss and no charges will be made against you for receiving stolen goods."

"Who the fuck are you – you're not police."

Thinking on his feet Tiggy blustered.

"I am from Interpol and the woman was wanted in Europe for a number of serious crimes. She has confessed and is under arrest pending extradition back to France. The Rolex belonged to a local politician and we have been asked to recover it quietly as he doesn't want embarrassment of a court case – he was caught sleeping with this woman Tiggy added with a whisper."

"What politician?" Mac asked smelling a lucrative press story.

"I'm not at liberty to say but he is very high in the Wellington party. This woman said that she sold the Rolex here – as I said earlier, I am instructed to compensate you for any losses now or we'll go to the local police and get a warrant."

Mac was obviously suspicious but the fact that the guy thought he had it was worrying. He hadn't had a Rolex, Omega or anything that up market for years so it wasn't his normal trade and the lovely lady who brought it in had been full of shit, talking about having to sell her father's watch to get home to her sick Mum in Rio. He had only given her a thousand dollars which was stupidly low but she had taken it without question and left.

"If I did have a Rolex and I don't say I do, then what would you offer?"

"I've been given up to two thousand New Zealand dollars to buy without any questions asked," Tiggy stated.

"Not sure that anybody would be interested at that kind of money."

Tiggy pulled out a mobile and pretended to fast-dial someone important – moving out of the shop and whispering confidentially outside. When he returned, he looked annoyed and went up to the window.

"Political cases are a pain in the arse - listen I have three grand here, but if you don't find the mystery Rolex now, I can promise you a shed load of problems with your security service – who will not be as understanding."

Mac wasn't blessed with too much intelligence but even he could see that the Rolex was probably bent and that he could make a serious profit fairly quickly here. Tiggy saw that the guy knew something and went back to the front door and changed the sign to 'Closed'. He then came back and was counting out high denomination New Zealand dollars on the counter top. Mac sighed and went back through a curtain and opened an old safe by twisting the dial a few times.

A few seconds later he returned with the Rolex Submariner 515 and counted the dollars. The exchange was made and the only worry Mac had was the risk that the bank notes were forged but he really didn't think that was likely. If it came to that he thought, the Rolex might have been fake too so you have to take some risks in life, don't you? He stuffed the notes down the inside of his under vest knowing that his grasping wife would never look there and smiled to himself.

Tiggy was elated. An old navy mate used to say "bullshit baffles brains" and he had never really understood till now. The watch was his special Rolex Submariner 515 and his bullshit had got it back so he stood to make around 50K US dollars if he ever got it to a reputable auction house. He had all the documentation and one had been sold at Christies for that figure only a year ago so he knew its value. With a warning not to reveal this transaction to anyone, Tiggy left the pawnshop and put the watch on his wrist feeling fully dressed for the first time in 24 hours.

It was now over a week since he'd jumped ship and Tiggy was fairly certain that he'd got away with his Count Jergov activities on the *Amazon*. The Fran tragedy had also receded to a dull ache and he was getting a little bored in Dunedin, so he was restless.

Something ungodly was niggling at him and he realised that he needed some action. He couldn't resist going down to the harbour here to see whether there was any chance of the good Count Jergov having a last stand and maybe making some money. After all, he rationalized, he had been conned out of thousands of dollars and he needed compensation.

He didn't really remember the harbour from the journey in because he'd kept his head down in the coach so this time, he took a taxi and checked the place out properly. Port Chalmers had been offloading ships since the early 1800's and was a working port handling all kinds of cargo.

Cruise ships did come in two or three times a week and this estuary is one of the most photogenic areas imaginable so the passengers normally crowded the rails. Despite this there weren't the tourist attractions or bars immediately on landing in Akaroa and most passengers took the coaches into town.

'The Highland Cow' was the nearest thing to a hotel near the harbour and inside it had a moth-eaten Highland Bulls head on a wooden plinth hung behind the bar and more tartans than you'd get on a US Shortbread biscuit tin. It was dreadful and the Count wouldn't have ever normally have lowered himself to go in there. His alter-ego Tiggy, however, was feeling a little sensitive about the recent past and was happy to reconnoitre it.

He went into the bar and chatted to the owner who surprisingly was called Ranald McDonald and looked like he came from a long line of lairds. After asking about the name the chap said his family had come across from the old country in the late 1800's and done quite well out of farming. The family's Christian name for the eldest son had always been Ranald so they'd kept to the tradition despite the ribbing he got about the name from visiting Americans.

The main reason for the chat was to find out about the cruises, whether they spent any money here in the hotel and whether the dynamics were the same as Akaroa. Tiggy said that he ran a bar on the coast east of Christchurch to explain his interest.

Ranald said that most of the Port Chalmers locals really disliked the cruises because they didn't get any business out of them. The hotel itself got no trade out of them because he had no interest in gentrifying a historic place just to get a couple of tourists from Shanghai or Miami. The only place that got the occasional foreign visitor was the tea-room/bar called the Flying Albatross which was just fifty yards up the hill. Tiggy finished his whisky, thanked the landlord and walked up to the bar a few moments later.

The Flying Albatross was minimalist, modern and beautiful with attractions that appealed to upmarket tourists. They had incredible shots of flying albatrosses and good quality paintings for sale on the walls. They even had a live feed to the Albatross centre a few miles away where at certain times of the year you could see the chicks hatching. From the fashion to the jewellery, everything in there was high quality and expensive – just the sort of place the Count enjoyed.

The following day Count Tolstoy Jergov returned and sat on one of the outside tables with all his normal tools of trade. He knew it was a risk but he needed the adrenalin.

He had introduced himself to the manager at opening time, saying that he was a writer creating a romance about three people on a cruise liner and here for research purposes. He asked that the manager told no-one about his profession and explained that Eugene Fenton was his pen name. Following normal procedure, Tiggy had left a copy of his book on the bar whilst he'd gone to the lavatory and knew by the managers face that it had been seen when he returned.

Our author knew from the timetables that a cruise ship had arrived and had seen several coaches pass him already on the way to town. He, however, was waiting for the rebels who had rejected the standard tours and struck out on their own. Those had been the most profitable targets in Brisbane and Akaroa and he hoped here was the same.

He thought back wistfully to Miriam and her sister who had been his last conquests and couldn't help feeling something like regret. With a curse he forced himself back to the present as he could see a number of people walking up the hill from the harbour.

The Count was in his slightly updated working outfit. The blue blazer and cravat had survived the trip but he'd had to search for a new cream shirt and white trousers which he'd lost en voyage. New Zealand didn't really believe in formal dressing but he'd visited the Oxfam shop again and had some luck. He found light coloured chinos and a white dress shirt, barely worn in another charity place. It was plain enough to wear under the blazer and just needed his old 'ancestral' cufflinks to complete the look.

The bar loved it. Catching passing trade here was always difficult but having someone who looked like Cary Grant playing a 1920's yachtsman outside was wonderful. The first couple of rebels who sat on the table next to him were Hong Kong Chinese which was a new market for our author. The manager came out and the couple asked for the wine list and menu. He then turned to our hero.

"Excuse me Count Jergov, would you like another Champagne?"

"No thank you Henry, the book is being an absolute swine today and I need to focus" Tiggy went back to hand writing in his notepad with an intense look of concentration.

"Don't you find an iPad or computer a more convenient way to write?" asked the woman who was beautifully dressed and sounded highly educated.

Our author sighed. 'It's odd, I know, but it doesn't work for me. Hand written worked for Shakespeare, Jane Austin and Tolstoy and I'm hoping it will give me similar inspiration."

"I've always loved Jane Austin - since I was a girl – she writes on so many levels," the woman added as they ordered wine and food.

"In my humble way, I tried to emulate her with my first book – some critics were kind about my efforts ..." Tiggy handed over the hardback with just the right amount of diffidence.

The couple looked at the book, photograph, critical comments and were impressed. Handing the copy back as if it was a first-edition.

"But now I've got this second book to finish and it's hard. Publishing is in the doldrums and I won't publish digitally. Also, I have an even more demanding mistress than Ms Austin – her name is Riva."

The couple were younger than his normal target by twenty years, a different ethnic background but looked to have loads of money. Which he found often helped iron out the differences.

They admired the photographs of the boat and Tiggy could see the husband quietly Googling (if that's what they were doing these days in China) the name Riva. They both apparently worked for a Chinese state owned company but were based in Hong Kong and were tasked apparently with building up their property portfolio in various parts of the world. They had decided on a cruise to celebrate their 100th property investment in Europe and had been away for a month.

They loved Dunedin and had decided to buy property here whilst values were low and were wondering whether they needed some sort of local agent so they could circumvent the new property investment rules.

Our author learned that 'culture' was a big deal for the wife and Jane Austen had been so important that she had attended a Jane Austin writing course in Beijing and come top of her class. The thought that her name might be included in a book by an author who was considered to be "The male Jane Austen" was too much for her to take in. But she was hooked.

Count Tolstoy Jergov looked to her like the embodiment of the romantic author. The cost of ten thousand US dollars to be part of something that could be the Pride & Prejudice of the 21st Century seemed cheap. This could be the ultimate cultural take-over.

She saw that he hesitated when he heard her name was Li-Meng Yan. He thought for a few seconds then claimed that in the old empire romances between English noblemen and high-born Chinese women had been common. So the name might be included without it looking out of place.

Before the end of the day our author had another 10K contract signed and agreed that a literary tour might be possible to mainland China sometime the next year.

From our authors point of view, he had won what he considered to be his own Booker Prize. The Count had booked a new nationality and a different generation to his scheme and not had to use his skills in bed. He was extremely proud of himself which almost compensated for the loss of confidence that his master Tiggy Foghorn felt when he remembered Fran.

Back in the apartment Tiggy relaxed in front of the big screen with a large Lagavulin, a bottle of which, he'd bought from a Whisky shop as well stocked as it would have been the Princess Street, Edinburgh, it was named after. The smokey taste of the whisky was wonderful and the weather on the satellite map looked excellent for the next few days. He woke up slightly with the urgent music introducing the news:

CW – This is the six o'clock news from Corrie Weepu and Darren MacArthur.

DM – Tonight police are searching for a mystery Count who struck five times on the cruise ship *Amazon*.

CW – This is not a halloween trick or a vampire joke -this Count cost passengers thousands of dollars with a writing fraud.

DM – Police have a photograph of the conman which is of poor quality as you can see, but they think that he may have left the ship at Dunedin. Difficult to believe I know but he is using the name Jergov.

CW – What did you say?

DM – You heard me, Jergov. This is now an international police investigation but officers think that Count Tolstoy Jergov, who pretends to be an author, might be in South Island.

CW - Police are Counting on you to report this Jergov - get it Darren?

DM – Hopefully not Corrie.

They seek him here, they seek him there

On the good ship *Amazon*, the ginger peril Florence Hasty had created maximum disruption with the captain and crew by forcing them to search the vessel twice for Count Jergov or his alter egos.

Miriam and her sister avoided the meetings Florence had with the rest of the literary victims because they didn't want to be drawn into things. They realised their vulnerability having shanghaied Tiggy aka Count Jergov in the first place and introduced the ginger graverobber to the book idea as well. Luckily Florence hadn't recognised Miriam yet but she was pretty sure that Elmer would pick her in any line-out. So she kept a low profile.

It was useful that Florence Hasty could be seen from 100 yards away being the size of a heavyweight wrestler and having bright red hair. They had avoided the dining room on two occasions when they'd spotted her or the large frame of Elmer and hoped to lie low until they reached the US and disembarked.

Brett Lane, her investigator, had sent over some aged press coverage and said that he thought that Tiggy's surname might be Foghorn. But really, looking at it, the idea of anyone changing from Foghorn to Jergov seemed ridiculous. It seemed certain from the findings, however, that the Count and probably Eugene Fenton was a fraud.

Before they landed the two sisters were getting desperate for some solutions and realised that they might have to join forces with some of the people who'd been conned. There was only one acceptable choice. Florence had been so rude that she'd alienated every member of staff who tried to help. Ms Anders was like an alien species with her quasi-military dress code and cadet son Dwight. Elmer Flannigan may have looked like a bruiser but he was actually a darling and they decided to talk to him before they landed.

Elmer couldn't believe that he'd been taken for a sucker. The Count had been so sincere about his Riva boat, so much in love with its beauty and the words he'd written about Neil were so sincere, that he surely couldn't be all bad? But he loved boats and understood why someone might go off the rails if they thought they might lose a lovely thing like the Riva.

Elmer remembered a sail boat he'd had as a kid. It was a 12ft Wayfarer, clinker built and made from overlapping planks of teak that had been varnished to a shine for years before he'd been born. It had one mast and an old canvas sail that had faded from red to dusky pink. When he first tried it, it was like finding an old friend and it sailed beautifully in almost every sort of wind.

When Elmer had been coming to terms with the fact that he was the toughest looking guy in college but also gay, he would take the boat out into the creeks and dream. When the boat was washed away in a storm he was devastated, it was like a friend had died. He had seen the same love in the eyes of the Count when he was showing photographs of the Riva. It was hard to believe that he was a heartless conman.

Onboard *Amazon*, Elmer realised that Florence was getting nowhere with her attack on everyone official and backed away from her group. He eventually told Neil about the whole scam and he was first incredibly annoyed that he'd been taken, then philosophical about the whole thing. The funny thing was that Neil was incredibly turned on by the idea of being portrayed as a muscular sea captain and grateful that Elmer had tried to give him such a thoughtful gift.

Miriam saw Elmer and Neil at breakfast and suggested a meeting. They had met a few hours later, both sisters and the two guys attended and Miriam led the discussion. She said that she regretted introducing the Count and admitted that they had also been taken in by his scam and paid out the money just like them. She obviously didn't admit that they had been behind his kidnap or that they were originally on a cut of the profits. Somehow Miriam didn't think that it was relevant and as a well known politician once said "Sometimes it's best to be economical with the truth."

The four knew that Florence Hasty was not anyone they wanted to work with and agreed that if they wanted to find Count Jergov they needed to inform the Head of Security of *Amazon* what they knew as quickly as possible. They met him and the Captain later and found them in complete denial.

The Head of Security at first tried to claim that they had no responsibility because the Count was not a passenger. Then that it was probably best left to when they landed in the US and to pass in on to the local cops there. Elmers's brother was a cop and a quick call revealed that they wouldn't be able to handle this because the crime took place thousands of miles away in international waters.

It was obvious after half an hour of heated discussion that most law and orders authorities were likely to deny any responsibility because jurisdiction was such a complicated issue.

Miriam and Elmer turned on the security officer and pointed out the ship's responsibility in no uncertain terms. This company had allowed this man to come onboard illegally and perpetrate these crimes in full view of staff. There were many wealthy and influential passengers on an expensive trip like this and they expected security and protection from criminals. The ship had failed at every level and the officers themselves might be liable to a type action by some extremely aggressive lawyers that Miriam knew.

The Captain paled and ordered the Security guy to co-operate fully. He considered for a while then said that they suspected that the Count had left the ship at Dunedin because some crew clothing and an ID Tag had gone missing at that point. Some footage from the harbour cameras looked as though it just could have been someone trying to sneak off but with 5,000 crew and rotation of some every few months, they really couldn't be certain who it was.

The Captain concluded that the only action that made sense now was to contact the police in New Zealand immediately and ask them to start a search for Count Jergov. They had some contacts there who might be willing to act but it was still going to be low priority for most police. The only hope would be to offer a reward and hope that the media gives it some exposure. The guys had over a week to disappear but New Zealand's a small country and perhaps we'll get lucky.

Miriam supplied the one shot they had of Tiggy along with the report the Brett Lane had sent over and the officer went to the radio room to speak to his contact in NZ.

Police Sergeant Lawrence was on duty in Dunedin Police Headquarters at 21.00 hours when a strange call was put through by reception. It was difficult to believe that it was from a ship on the other side of the Pacific because it was so clear. He'd seen the *Amazon* in port the previous week and knew that it was a cruise ship of enormous size that visited a couple of times a year but had never talked to any of the officers. The Head of Security had been a cop in a previous life and knew that this sort of enquiry was going to generate pages of paperwork so kept his request simple. Sergeant Lawrence did as requested and passed on the story to the local TV channels, hoping that it would get exposure on the earliest news broadcasts. With a strange one like this, he expected some of the more sensational stations to run it within hours.

Later in Dunedin, Tiggy had used the TV remote to freeze the shot on the broadcast so he could work out whether anyone might recognise him. He had avoided photography onboard but someone had obviously caught him slumped at the bar and though it was blurred it was dangerous for the Count. The Chinese couple he'd conned recently or the bar staff might recognise him if he came back in blazer and full gear but he doubted whether anyone else would. So it was going to be civilian clothes for Tiggy Foghorn for a while.

More upsetting was that the Count Tolstoy Jergov persona was blown. Tiggy had worked hard on this identity in Brisbane whilst he was in hiding waiting for Ginger to be sentenced. He had made well over a hundred thousand dollars for himself during the last year and he was like a rich uncle who kept on providing. Now he had to die and Tiggy was feeling the loss in more ways than one.

Tiggy decided to move out of Dunedin as soon as possible and not leave a trail that the police could follow. The apartment was lovely but it had associations with a certain Brazilian woman that weren't exactly positive.

He had plenty of money in the bank account he'd used to take all the literary payments from his victims. Money laundering legislation had made secret money a little more difficult in recent times but Tiggy had a Panama account that he'd opened in his smuggling days that didn't tell anybody about anything. But the boatyard was demanding money on a continuous basis and he wasn't sure that he had enough in the fund.

Tiggy finished the bottle of Lagavulin in the apartment he'd started to think of his own and planned. Despite the death of the Count, he still needed a challenge and reckoned that he could out think any hick police force who were after him ...

Eventually he decided to keep away from the coast and look for somewhere else he could make serious money. They had started work on the Riva hull in the boatyard in Akaroa and it would be a few weeks and many thousands of dollars before it was fit for auction. He probably still needed a couple of big earners before he could get out of the country in style.

Francesca Capelle was sitting in Christchurch airport terminal on her way to Auckland when she saw the news on the big screen monitor and thought she recognised someone. It was odd, she thought, how much she'd enjoyed their days together, but she'd enjoyed Tiggy's cash and Rolex even more. The exciting thing she'd noticed was the surname on the credit cards in his wallet had not been the same as that he'd used when introducing himself. Strange that, she thought and stored it in her memory banks for future use.

After her various other schemes over the years and the pocketing of everyone's tips at the Nova bistro, Fran had nearly enough money to go back to Rio in style but not quite enough. The Rolex had been worth lots more than the pawnshop had given her, she knew that but she was under pressure to get out of Dunedin and the Bastardo of a guy sensed it and she just had to take the thousand. So she felt a little cheated by him and the guy Terry or Tiggy or whatever the guy was called who it belonged too. Perhaps she needed to deal with that – it was like an itch that you can't scratch as her father used to say back in Brazil – you just have to scratch it, or it will drive you crazy.

Francesca was being eyed up from across the terminal by a business man who looked very sure of himself. Judging by the suit he was probably a European and being an expert on such things she bet herself that he was English – probably a computer guy or even more likely an advertising guy about to go to head office in Auckland. He was carrying a very elegant overnight bag that looked like it cost more than she'd been paid last week.

The bet was that if he was English then she would agree to dinner and who knows what afterwards. After all, she didn't have anything booked in the city and hadn't got onward flights organised yet. If she lost the bet and he was French or Italian she would agree to dinner and who knows what afterwards but not feel as clever about herself.

She smiled over at the guy in that uncertain way that she'd used many times before which meant "I'm in a strange country, I'm helpless, please come and help me."

After looking over and seeing her dropping her papers on the floor in the most pathetic way imaginable, the guy finished his mobile call and walked over picking up her stuff and putting it on her table at the same time.

"Hank you, hank you Senor, muchio grathias," Fran burst into a speech of such incomprehensible South American Spanish that even her parents wouldn't have understood and then added "Hawkland, Hawkland?" in a desperate questioning manner and the guy confirmed he was going to Auckland too. She smiled with such tender joy that no man could refuse her help which was the general idea.

As to her bet with herself, well, the man said his name was Bryn and he was Welsh which she thought was British and maybe part of Europe but she couldn't be sure. Also, he hadn't said what he did for a living and so didn't know whether it was advertising or computers.

Still, she was prepared to give herself the benefit of the doubt because he was a good looking man who was probably on expenses and with a wallet full of money. Now she was noticing such things, she saw that he was wearing good shoes and a Breitling watch that she'd seen in the shops for five thousand dollars. This time she wasn't going to be ripped off by any Kiwi shyster when she sold it.

The tannoy announced the departure of the Air New Zealand flight and the two walked together upstairs to the departure gates. Fran tried to look helpless at every turn though Christchurch is as simple an airport as anyone could devise. There was always a chance that the guy was married or gay but he acted straight, wasn't wearing a ring and her instincts told her he was single or at least up for a bit of fun

She had already checked in her luggage and already had a boarding pass so the check at the gate would be minimal as this was an internal flight. In terms of her target there were certain points of weakness in her plan to use him for a meal and accommodation in Auckland. Firstly, they already had allocated seats so they could be many seats apart on the journey. Secondly it looked as though he only had an overnight bag so probably wouldn't have to collect luggage like she did. This was going to need all of her acting skills to reduce the chance of them being parted in the normal airport rush in arrivals.

She'd enjoyed the last few days in Christchurch. A few years ago, it had a massive series of earthquakes which destroyed lots of the original buildings and she'd seen the ruin of the old stone cathedral. Now there was new building everywhere and some of the coolest architecture she'd seen since Rio. The river Avon still ran through the middle of the city and at night the bars were heaving with people her age having fun. There were trams, gondolas up to the mountains and loads for her to do.

Fran knew that many people had died during the quakes and that Christchurch had also had a major tragedy when a terrorist gunned down a load of people. But the place had great spirit and it felt like a frontier town. She'd heard that after the shops were destroyed that people took shipping containers from the port, painted them crazy colours and opened up selling from inside. They became a symbol of the resilient local spirit. Covid and other challenges had done nothing to dampen that.

Fran was now boarding the plane to Auckland a couple of steps behind Bryn the Welshman and was pleased to see that he sat a couple of rows in front of her allocated seat. As she passed, she smiled down at him giving him every impression that she really needed him in this confusing world.

It was an incredibly short flight and after landing she pushed past him so that she was ahead when it came to the horribly complicated matter of finding her luggage. Predictably Bryn ended up wheeling her luggage on a trolley out of the domestic terminal and trying to answer her questions about 'Hawkland'. If only Bryn had realised then that he was going to buy Fran dinner and offer her a bed for the night in one of the best hotels and that it was all preordained. Then he might have been a little less awkward at the beginning.

The following morning Bryn the Welshman woke up exhausted and late for his meeting with the Art Gallery. He wasn't in computers or advertising as Fran had predicted and he wasn't English as she'd presumed. Bryn was an insurance investigator there to check damage on a minor work by Picasso that the gallery had claimed on. Somebody had cancelled his automated alarm call and someone had drugged his drink or something as he couldn't remember making love to the most beautiful woman he'd ever met.

Bryn called the gallery on his mobile and apologised. Then realised that there was no sign of Fran or her luggage and it was already lunchtime. He had to check the time on the digital clock by the bed and then on the TV because his watch had gone. He realised with sick feeling in his gut that his wallet was nowhere. He checked in his suit jacket and under the bed and it was gone.

After leaving Fran had changed. She'd worn an extended beanie hat in bright blue with Otago Highlanders printed on it. Her hair was pushed inside and it was so low on her head that the camera couldn't see her face at all. Which was the general idea.

She loved people who had their credit and debit card PIN numbers written small on the back of a business card in their wallet. She loved Bryn whatsisname to death and drained both his accounts at an ATM at International Departures to show just how much.

Count Tolstoy William Jergov was dead. He'd been exposed as a bounder and a charlatan by New Zealand News and he was being pursued by the powers of darkness otherwise known as the police.

Tiggy missed him like a boy misses a black sheep uncle who's always getting into scrapes but always a lot more entertaining than his parents.

It was funny he thought his own parents couldn't have been more entertaining originally. One was a highly successful sex worker, the other a randy submariner who'd known how to raise hell when he came ashore. Yet they both turned into pillars of the church and respectable members of the community and totally boring.

Tiggy gave himself a good talking to over another bottle of Malt. There were great dangers in the world – global warming, pollution, world hunger, political correctness. Of all these the most ridiculous was political correctness. The Woke generation had a lot to answer for – they were offended by everything except offence. It had to stop.

Tiggy Foghorn loved women. Not the androgynous, flat chested excuses for women who were embarrassed by their own sexuality. He loved larger women with hips and breasts that moved when they walked. Women who were passionate and happy – not diet worriers or exercise freaks. Real Women who knew they were better than men - even the thought was starting was starting to give him a hard-on.

The few days with the Brazilian woman Fran he realised had been like experimenting with a new sexual position. Good sometimes stretching yourself to, but in the end not as satisfying as the tried and tested angles. An even better analogy he thought was becoming vegetarian for a few days and then realising how much you enjoyed good, red meat.

The next day Tiggy Foghorn caught a bus across the country to Queenstown where he hoped he might be able to become really carnivorous again. He paid for a single and within a few minutes they were heading out of the Dunedin suburbs which were like loads of US towns – full of car dealerships and DIY stores. He'd never travelled inland in New Zealand before and was hoping to see some of the real Central Otago. So far, apart from the old rugby ground at Carisbrook it looked the same as everywhere else. Eventually the industrial estates thinned out and the bus was on straight roads that were empty apart from the odd enormous lumber wagons hauled by big American Tractor units like Kenwood or Mack.

It took a couple of hours before things started to look interesting. Then around the town of Lawrence he started to see some vineyards and the country started to change. Tiggy lost track of the stops but most towns were like mid-west towns in the US and not exactly works of architectural value. But further into the journey he started to go through big fruit growing areas and started to see mountains in the distance.

Central Otago is famous for its mountains and lakes. The Remarkables and Southern Alps were both featured in the Lord of the Rings and loads of other movies from the 1990's onwards. Tiggy was relieved that he was starting to see evidence of those ranges-indeed the bus went over some passes he found it difficult to believe that any coach could make. As the timetable operated five times a week, however, he had to believe it.

Within a couple of minutes of the scheduled time, Tiggy realised that he was on the outside of Queenstown and in the first traffic jam he'd ever encountered in New Zealand. The bus was crawling into town behind five tourist coaches and a load of mini-buses all going the same way. Looking up he could see the mountains on the side of the lake and loads of bright coloured hand-gliders or parachutes floating down from the tops. The driver made his announcement and opened the doors with a hiss. Tiggy stepped out, dragging his case and touched his toes to stretch his stiff back. It had been a long journey and most of his fellow passengers were gap-year kids who had slept most of the way. But looking down the wonderful blue lake with mountains each side he could see why it was so popular.

"Which is the best hotel in town," Tiggy asked the bus driver companionably as they stood side by side uncreaking after the journey.

"What for you?"

"No, I have a female friend visiting in six months – who has a lot more loot than I do" Tiggy answered with a smile.

"Well, the problem round here is that all the hotels are owned by the tour companies, so they're full of Chinese and Yanks most of the time."

"Where would you stay if you won the lottery?"

"Not here."

"Where then?"

"Probably the Invercastle Arms Hotel on the banks of Lake Wanaka. That's where Sam Neil had his party and the All Blacks' captain stayed there for a week last year. That's where I'd go."

"Cheers, I'll check it out."

"Hope she's got loads of money. I've heard it costs thousands there."

Tiggy stored the information shook the driver's hand and worked his way across town for his regular visit to Tourist Information to find some accommodation for himself. It was seriously crowded.

"Kiora, how can I help you?" asked the lovely girl behind the counter who looked as though she was at least part Māori. Tiggy was about thirty years older than the kids she'd been greeting and couldn't help but admire the sincerity she maintained every time she said it.

"Kiora, I'm originally Kiwi but I've been away for some years and didn't realise how busy it'd got here. Wow, any chance of some reasonably priced accommodation – I'm not on a tourist budget," Tiggy added with a smile.

"How long for?"

"About a week, maybe – it depends on costs."

The girl searched on her computer for a couple of minutes.

"Listen this isn't on any official list but it's an Auntie of mine who prefers Kiwi guests. This is the number – hope it helps."

Tiggy was happy that his travelling Kiwi identity had been believed by a local, picked up the print-out and pushed through the office which now had around fifty people of all kinds of nationality in it and exited with relief. This was crazy, he thought New Zealand had a population of only six million and most of them were in Auckland area. Queenstown was the first time he'd felt truly crowded out.

But looking around at the scenery he could see why.

He needed to check out his B&B as soon as possible and for the first time he used the satnav on his new phone. According to the App it was only a five minute walk, so he went to a cafe at the side of the lake and ordered his usual flat white coffee. The only thing he'd been able to eat at the bus journey stops had been Jimmies pies or muffins. He'd had one Cornish Pasty which had reminded him of his childhood holidays in the West Country but now he needed something more. The prices on the menu were eye-watering but the view made it good value and he ordered a seafood pasta dish which sounded interesting. Whilst waiting he called the B&B emphasising his Kiwi credentials and got in for the next three days at an almost reasonable rate.

During the time on *Amazon*, Tiggy had an excess of food but that had been days ago and he was ravenous. But what he saw through the plate glass of the restaurant on the big TV screen inside almost made him vomit. The unsettling sight of Florence Hasty – the Ginger Binger who'd nearly put him off big women and life in general being interviewed on TV. He couldn't hear the sound but decided to get out whilst he had the motive power to do so. Tiggy left fifty dollars under his cup and made a hasty exit.

A few hundred miles away a Hong Kong Chinese couple saw the same interview and the husband followed the story on his smart phone. His

117

English was perfect but he couldn't quite understand what the ginger headed woman had been complaining about. Whatever had happened it had appeared to have taken place on a cruise ship called *Amazon* which they knew was a very expensive vessel specialising in world tours. The ship they had been on was a much smaller vessel so they couldn't see the relevance.

It was only when the name Count Tolstoy Jergov came up on the sub titles that he remembered the conversation with the elegant sailor and pushed the I Pad over to his wife. She had been dreaming of a part in the authors new book ever since their meeting at the Albatross Cafe and was shocked into silence for a while. Then she cursed in gutter mandarin and they called the local police and were about to contact their consul in Auckland when they realised that the last thing they needed at this stage of their careers was a loss of face of this magnitude.

Sergeant Lawrence had done everything the Head of Security on *Amazon* had asked and got the Count Jergov name mentioned on local TV and radio which is where his job ended as far as he was concerned. After all no-one knew whether Jergov was in Dunedin or indeed whether he was in New Zealand at all. Certainly, nobody of that name had passed through any official channels so he thought the job could be filed in the bin. Then he had been sent a copy of an interview with a woman in Australia and had a call from a Chinese couple who'd been touring New Zealand and Max knew that Count bloody Tolstoy Jergov was in the country.

118

A New type of Romcon

Tiggy took a while but he found the B&B recommended by the girl in the tourist office. On the way he had a severe shock. There on a huge plasma screen on the wall of a bar, he saw the terrifying sight of Florence Hasty. It was too far away to hear the Aussie cow but it took a while to retain his cool and become the relaxed Kiwi traveller again.

In contrast, Tiana Mathews when she opened the door was a perfect older version of the beautiful girl in the tourist office and smiled agreeably when he repeated the traveling Kiwi story he'd used earlier.

"Yis, this town is crazy and I'm glad that my husband bought twenty years ago. It's mad all year now and full of Chinese, Americans and just about everyone ... not that I'm against em ... but just too many."

Tiggy settled a week in advance for a lovely double room with a loo, TV and nice view of the lake. He said that he was here for a rest and would be out for most of the time walking or reading in his room and wouldn't need any food. She nodded and gave him a set of front door keys saying that there were no other guests at the moment and they lived in an annex at the back so he would have plenty of peace.

He sat down with a cup of tea and a plate of shortbread Mrs Mathews had brought him and enjoyed the view of the mist rolling down the mountains opposite to the lake. It was getting late but there were still a few boats on the lake and the big steamer that did regular trips was just returning to the quay. There was obviously plenty of money round here but the boats were not as luxurious as they'd been in Akaroa or Brisbane and if he was going to find another illicit source of money, he sensed that this was not the place.

He checked the evening news to see whether he was famous and there was no repeat of the ginger apparition he'd seen earlier. Thinking it through, she might have been on CNN, BBC or one of the other channels broadcast worldwide. Restaurants like that tended to aim at foreign tourists and have coverage of news and sport that appealed to them on big screens. Hopefully that meant that Count Jergov was not famous here and the coverage he'd had on local news was a fading memory.

Tiggy watched the news twice that night and there was no mention of the Count or any of his aliases, so he hoped for the best.

After a good night's sleep Tiggy had a call from the boatbuilder in Akaroa which spoiled his day. Apparently there had been a fire caused by the boats ancient generator and electrical system which had done a huge amount of damage to the engine and stern. The photograph of the blackened stern and engine compartment filled Tiggy with despair. According to the mechanics the boat had been back on its moorings and hadn't been covered by their insurance. Tiggy hadn't insured anything since his Aston Martin so he knew he wasn't covered personally

What made the whole thing twice as frustrating was the Ferrari engine was one part of the Riva which had been in good condition after the work a few months ago. The guy at the boatyard made him angry and Tiggy vowed to get his revenge. In the meantime, he wanted an eye-watering amount to repair the engine and wiring and Tiggy wired through his authority.

Looking at the photos of the Riva from the front, however, it looked magnificent and the work on the bows and cabin superstructure had really worked well. He realised that the Riva was an expensive mistress and he needed to make even more cash soon in order to feel secure.

The only reassuring thing was that classic Rivas were going up dramatically in price every month. The rich man's money that had previously gone into classic cars had also moved into boats and now those with super-yachts worth billions were searching for classics they could use in-shore. His Riva was unique and he was convinced that with the right provenance it could make enough to pay for a well-deserved retirement. His was a young man's game and though he was only in his 40's he needed to make enough to hang up his blazer and fountain pen and relax somewhere warm.

First Tiggy had some creative thinking to do. Count Tolstoy Jergov had been exposed as a bounder and a cad in New Zealand and needed to be buried in the ancestral tomb. Now he needed another persona that might work as well.

It was still early in the day but Tiggy Foghorn always thought better with a drink in his hand. He looked out of the window at the lake and mountains and could see everything with startling clarity. It looked as though it was going to be a brilliant day so he locked his room and went down the drive to the main road into Queenstown. People were already throwing themselves off the hills behind on brilliantly coloured hand-gliders and he could hear boats starting up on the lake. Buses were also starting to queue down the road. It was all far too busy for Tiggy so he walked as fast as possible across the line of traffic and in the direction of the lake.

It was difficult, but eventually Tiggy found a bar that wasn't already infested with tourists. He ordered a plate of his favourite breakfast and a flat white whilst he looked at the wine list to see what was going to give him inspiration. The bar didn't have a view of lake or mountain but after half an hour he realised why it still had plenty of people – most of whom looked to be local – eating there. The food was wonderful.

The brunch at the Nova in Dunedin had been good but this was twice as good. The eggs were almost orange and the sauce was so rich that you could almost stand a fork in it. Tiggy almost ordered another plate but he was feeling the strain on his waistband after all the meals on *Amazon*. If he wanted to play the part of the tortured author or disgraced aristocrat, he certainly couldn't do it looking like a fat slob. To help his thinking he took advice from the man behind the bar and had a large glass of Wooing Tree pinot noir. It was still early but as Tiggy's father, Horatio Foghorn used to say, "the sun was always over the yardarm somewhere in the world".

After half an hour Tiggy hadn't had enough inspiration so ordered another glass. He was starting to feel nostalgic for the simpler times on *Amazon* when he'd had two passionate sisters, Miriam and Elsie to keep happy. They were rich but they were also passionate and grateful for his skills in bed - which was a perfect combination as far as he was concerned.

Thinking about them had given him a slight stiffy and he had to adjust his seating position in order to accommodate it. It had also reminded him of something connected with the girls that he needed to deal with. After tipping the waitress generously and paying the bill Tiggy had a few words with the patron and walked into Queenstown.

The shop certainly wasn't aiming at the mass tourist trade and had a beautiful Bentley Continental outside that was almost as lovely as Tiggy's Aston Martin. Tiggy looked in the window seemingly nervously and eventually pushed open the door and found a counter with an elegant older man behind it.

"Good Morning." I don't know whether this has any value, it used to belong to my wife." Tiggy pulled out the single Bulgari earring he'd liberated from Miriam's cabin. "My wife ... sadly dead since last year, had a terrible habit of losing stuff and there's only one, I've been carrying them around but," Tiggy ended with a sad shrug.

"I quite understand sir, just excuse me whilst I look at it more closely." The manager could tell the quality by eye but needed a few seconds peering through the glass to work out how he could most successfully rip off this country hick who smelt of drink already and was probably a wealthy wino.

"I'm afraid it's not worth much as a single piece," the manager said after a few minutes on his glass.

"But it cost us thousands of dollars in Rome when we were on that last cruise ... Miriam loved them," Tiggy complained. "And I was hoping that these other things might be of interest too." Tiggy pulled out another single diamond ear-ring and one small ring with emeralds that the sister had worn on her little finger.

"My goodness sir, your wife was a little accident prone, wasn't she?"

"A little ... but she was lovely and the ring was just something I found under the bed after we'd given all the rest of the jewellery to our daughters."

It took a further ten minutes and an excellent display of emotion from our hero for a figure to be reached that was just about worthwhile. Tiggy asked for cash as he said he didn't want any problems with death duties and walked out of the shop with a wad of New Zealand dollars that felt reassuringly thick even if they were a little less than he'd hoped.

The truth was Tiggy had wanted to get rid of the jewellery ever since he'd left the *Amazon*. He'd hoped that he'd not been too greedy in the number and type of items he'd pocketed. Miriam in particular had been careless with her stuff and having one ear-ring left probably meant that she'd claim on insurance anyway.

The ring he'd liberated from the sister's suite had been worth more than he'd anticipated as the quality of the stones was excellent. But it was small enough to be lost without trace in a suite that vast. So he thought his chance of being blamed was low.

His hope was that all the stuff he'd sold would be claimed for and that none of it was so valuable that it would appear on any international lists. His suspicion was that the Bulgari would be broken down into individual gems and be turned into a new design. So here again he thought even if the Count was blamed then any connection with this transaction was unlikely.

Tiggy walked back into the centre of town and found it relatively quiet after the chaos earlier. Presumably because all the coaches had left for their various tours and even the kids were away on the Shotover River or Bungee Jumping somewhere. It was wonderfully quiet.

He'd had confirmation on his smartphone that the yard had received his money and would start the new repairs over the next few days. This was a reminder that the morning he'd designated as for planning his financial future had gone by with no progress.

Tiggy decided to find a quiet bar to help his 'little grey cells' operate at peak efficiency. He'd only learned one thing of potential use in the last few hours and that concerned the Bentley Continental parked outside the jewellers.

The bar was called *The Travelling Kiwi.* Despite the name this turned out to be run by an Englishman who was from a small village in Warwickshire. He was called Michael who had run bars everywhere from Singapore to LA to London before he found a derelict police house in the backstreets of Queenstown and set up a micro-brewery. He was the opposite of Tiggy, physically being short, stocky and ginger but they got on from the moment they met.

Tiggy said little about his own background other than he was a writer. Over the next hour they discussed favourite writers – his were Hemingway, Conrad and Greene. For professional reasons Tiggy said his were Jane Austin (which got a weird look from the landlord) Steinbeck and Le Carre which got a more understanding nod.

Over a jug of the brewer's stout, Tiggy pumped him for information about tourism and wealth in the area, explaining that he was writing a romantic novel about a wealthy and titled woman's battle for poor people despite the opposition of a domineering father. The plot sounded a bit thin to both of them but after another jug it started to make more sense. Michael confirmed that the nearest hotel with real five-star luxury was in Wanaka.

Back later in his B&B realised that he needed to travel to the other side of the region to a 5 Star hotel on the side of Lake Wanaka. He called a number on his mobile and arranged a number of trips to the area and agreed a price.

First, Tiggy had to decide who exactly he was on this trip and how he was going to help finance the ever-increasing costs on the Riva. The formula he'd developed all those months ago and which had been successful on *Amazon* was:

1. Aristocratic credentials from Lithuania – a place with real history but difficult to research.
2. A tragic family past to tug at the heart strings
3. Plausible things that a tragic aristocrat might sell – titles, time share in castles,
4. The Riva and its genuine need for funding
5. The fictional romantic book

He'd already accepted that for the moment the Count had to die and that any claim to an aristocratic pedigree might be dangerous in this country whilst any investigation was taking place. Without this noble background

123

he would find many of the other sales pitches difficult apart from the Riva. And in this country, he suspected that there was less respect for a noble background anyway.

Unless he could find a ready supply of wealthy U.S matrons – difficult away from the cruise liner ports – he had to consider change.

The book had been the most successful of all his pitches and he realised that of all the identities he'd used the authors name was least risky. Eugene Fenton hadn't been mentioned in any of the news broadcasts and might still provide some profitable work. But Tiggy had to find a look to replace the tragic aristocrat dressed in blazer, cravat and cream trousers which had made the whole pitch so memorable.

He looked in his wardrobe and realised that most of it was useless apart from the dress shirt and the silk bow-tie he'd borrowed in Dunedin. Queenstown was not ideal but he decided to walk down later that day to see whether there was anything for sale that might help. Punters expected authors to look eccentric and he also had to look like a highly successful author or no-one would pay to be in his book.

He normally started with the charity shops and there were three. Two were full of bric a brac and floral dresses in huge sizes but the third showed real promise. At the back he found some English brogues that were worn but looked as though they had been lovingly polished for decades. They were his size and he put them on with no superstitious need to know who's owned them last. They were now part of his persona.

A cream linen jacket cost him serious money. Ten dollars was all the Jaeger suit cost and it was really high quality. The trousers would be dumped in the nearest bin being about four inches too much round the waist. But the jacket fitted him well and went extremely well with the wide silk op-art tie that looked as though it had been hand-made in the 1970's.

The only new stuff he bought were a couple of sea-island cotton shirts, socks and underwear plus a cashmere sweater. The cost for all these was an outrageous 200 dollars.

The next day he dressed carefully in his new outfit and looked at the result in the mirror. Our author had deliberately not shaved since Dunedin and had a respectable growth of stubble which he was pleased to see was still black. The only beard he'd had before was on leave from the Royal Navy – who tolerated beards in those days – and people said that he looked pretty good.

He wore a mid blue shirt with the dark silk bow-tie he'd borrowed from the apartment and some dark trousers. With the cream linen jacket over the top Tiggy reckoned he might look a little louche or eccentric but he was ready to give it a try.

The weather was looking good for the day, so he went out of the house carrying the jacket and walked down to the corner. There as arranged was his driver and the Bentley Continental looked wonderful.

Tiggy had phoned the guy the previous day from outside the jewellers and told him that he needed driving around the district for a week. The car was magnificent in very similar colours to Tiggy's Aston Martin – gunmetal grey with cream leather interior and he loved it. The jeweller had said that the Bentley was owned by a failed property developer called George who owed him money and left the car outside the shop to give it a bit of class.

He introduced himself to George and sat in the back with the familiar tools of trade he'd used before – large leather notebook, fountain pen and hardback book. He asked to be taken to the Invercastle Arms Hotel in Lake Wanaka and George agreed. Tiggy could see that his driver looked embarrassed and eventually realised that he needed money for petrol before they could go anywhere. Tiggy took a risk and handed him five hundred dollars in advance of his fee.

The man was obviously embarrassed but said that he had made and lost a fortune after Covid and been ripped off by an unscrupulous wife who now lived in London. He lived in comparative squalor and only still had the Bentley because his wife had never known about it. He'd lost the Ferrari and classic Alfa Romeo to the wife's avarice. But because the Bentley was old and she thought that it belonged to the jeweller, she hadn't taken it. George said it was the love of his life but that he couldn't afford to put petrol in it.

Tiggy commiserated with him and said he was also in trouble because his agent was complaining about the lateness of his book – which should have been finished six months ago. Which is why he was hiding out in New Zealand avoiding everyone. Tiggy confided that the advance he'd been given had almost run out and that he had to finish this month or he would be in trouble.

The journey to Wanaka was longer than expected and the Bentley coped admirably with hairpin bends and steep gradients which led to views that were so spectacular that he asked George to stop.

He seemed incredibly high and was looking down a long valley in incredibly clear weather. So clear that George pointed out that you could see the airport twenty miles away at the very end. Tiggy tried to look as cool as a successful author would but failed miserably – it was spectacular and now he was away from all the crowds he felt extremely lucky to be alive.

Back in the car Tiggy admitted that his name was Eugene Fenton and that he was famous in some quarters for romantic novels. He repeated his diatribe about the horrors of digital, ebooks, social media and computers, re-enforcing his image as a wealthy technophobe who just wanted to be a male Jane Austin. George tried to look impressed in the rear view mirror but failed.

Tiggy appeared to be note-taking on the way over but was really just memorising another section of the Fenton book so he could hand write a different section with the Montblanc which had captured hearts on *Amazon*. This was the big test – Eugene with no added nobility and breaking into new markets in a strange country.

Tiggy would not have admitted it - even to himself - but Fran had dented his confidence a little as far as the other sex was concerned. Maddie's advice to have fun but never fall in love had been forgotten and he was paying for it now.

He needed larger females of his own age to play with. Tiggy was hoping to meet a few over the next few weeks and prove his point. After all he had given a fair number of them pleasure over the last few years and they had shown their gratitude by contributing towards his Riva fund.

The final few miles to Wanaka were spectacular and as they descended, he could see the lovely lake and town surrounded by vineyards and mountains. George knew that the hotel was a few miles outside the town as he had eaten there many times when he had been rich. Tiggy asked him to drive to the front door and play the chauffeur bit to the hilt. It was mid-morning and the sun was getting hot so he put on a jacket and a battered Panama hat and got out of the car, giving the receptionist just enough time to clock the car and see his outfit.

"It's a few years since I've been here, is it possible to find a quiet shady place outside where I can work? Do you have a split of champagne too?" Tiggy asked with a deep English voice that he'd last used to order new naval ratings around.

"Yes sir, are you staying with us?" the receptionist asked, automatically sitting up more straight at her table.

"Not yet, but if you have a suite and I make progress over the next few days, it would be a delightful distraction."

The woman summoned a waiter who led him through the bar and out to a lovely garden where there were tables under the ancient pine trees. Tiggy deliberately chose a secluded table in deep shade away from the main area and noticed through the glass that George was chatting to someone. He presumed that his request to keep his profession secret had been blown and that most staff would know that he was a famous author soon.

From behind his vintage Ray-Bans (sourced at Scotties barely used emporium) our potentially famous author could see the verdant pastures of the Invercastle Glen Hotel rolling down to the lake. Separating the residents from the hoi-polloi was a ha-ha of quite impressive proportions. If Tiggy could have had it full of alligators he would be even happier – he didn't want to waste his skills on guests who couldn't afford it.

Judging by the wine list this wasn't going to be a problem. There was vintage Krug at a markup that would have had a lottery-winner gasping and even local Marlborough wines starting at 90 dollars a bottle. Tiggy asked for a split of Nyetimber English on the basis that it was award winning champagne and they probably wouldn't have it. When the Sommelier confirmed this our hero protested loudly and quietly asked the man to bring a bottle of local stuff that was "equally good value."

Tiggy had found in the best restaurants, sommeliers very seldom rip you off if you ask their advice politely. If you show a little knowledge and not arrogance you normally get some good stuff.

In this case the man – who looked from the nameplate to be Italian – brought a bottle of Deutz from NZ which was not on the list but very good. Tiggy sipped it appreciatively, asked a few questions about its parentage, and gave the man a grateful smile and a 20 dollar thanks.

It might have been the fizz but Tiggy was feeling quite confident about his new image. After a trip to the loo he reckoned that the bow-tie and expensive shirt, combined with the linen jacket, made him look successfully eccentric. Not up to Count Tolstoy Jergov's level but pretty good and as always, the Rolex Submariner 515 on his wrist was a confidence booster and a visible asset that might be recognised by some. The only thing that was starting to nag him was his libido. The hiccup with the young Brazilian was almost forgotten and his dirty mind kept reminding him of successes in recent years with older women of a certain size and demeanour. Looking across the lawn he could see that the tables were filling up and that one in particular was looking promising.

A few hundred miles away Sergeant Max Lawrence was pissed off. He'd hoped that getting local media to run the Count Jergov story was going to be enough to please everyone on the cruise ship.

He had enough local problems in Dunedin to deal with including a drug bust in the university and a major fraud affecting a number of foreign tourists. This was a law- abiding city normally but for some reason things were going crazy, so the last thing he needed was the complication of an international case.

Max had tried to kick the case upstairs but his lazy boss used the fact that he knew the security guy on *Amazon* to instruct him to carry on. The fact that an influential Chinese couple had been put through to him made his involvement in the case certain. If he solved it quickly – then the boss would be happy to go on TV and take the credit. If he failed ....

With a sigh, Max opened his laptop and started a file for Count Jergov. What warped sense of humour came up with that name? And what brainless idiots were daft enough to give him thousands of dollars?

Max Lawrence was a stocky guy with a large moustache who was built for comfort rather than speed. Over the 20 years he'd been a cop he had dealt with all kinds of problems from multiple fatality air crashes through to special protection duties for Presidents and Royals. He had achieved a great reputation during all of them for being cool under pressure and getting the job done. An inability to toady to superior officers and suffer their mistakes silently had, however, made him a little unpopular amongst the most senior ranks.

First, he put in the file everything that the cruise ship officers had said about him:

White, Caucasian male around 6ft 2inches tall, approximately 13 stone weight with dark hair, clean shaven, tanned complexion with blue eyes. Around 40 years of age.

Possibly Lithuanian national, uses title Count Tolstoy Jergov also uses nickname Tiggy.

Has possibly defrauded a number of passengers by charging them thousands of dollars to be named in a new book.

Claims to be an established writer with the pen name Fenton – though some investigations claim that this man died over a century ago.

Dresses in eccentric but very old-fashioned clothing such as blazers cravats etc.

Lawrence reviewed the information given by the Chinese couple who met a similar man at the Albatross Bistro and commissioned him to write a character in a romantic novel. The physical description seemed to match and he was wearing old-fashioned clothes. They added that the man showed them a copy of a book with his photograph and glowing reviews which looked extremely convincing. Similar to other victims they signed a contract on his tablet which looked authentic and transferred the money immediately to a bank in South America. One other new fact was that the criminal claimed to be raising money for some kind of classic boat.

One complication was politics. The Chinese couple felt obliged to report this to the police but insisted that they remain strictly anonymous. They worked for the Chinese government and reckoned that if their problems became known by their employers, then it would be very damaging to their careers.

The cruise ship had sent some kind of photograph originally but looking at the shot now Max really couldn't imagine that it was usable again. All you could see was a man hunched in a bar somewhere with dark hair and a face that could have been anyone. He made a note to see whether the photo-enhancement people could do anything with it but didn't hold out much hope.

There was a couple of technical issues he also needed to check. If all his victims had signed contracts was there any anything really illegal going on? Also, if they transferred money then there must be a money trail and with all the money-laundering legislation there had been in place for the last few years, he should be able to find it. But these checks were extremely formal and took ages, Max sighed and sent a few emails.

The sergeant tried to imagine what such a fraudster might do next in New Zealand. If his primary market was female foreign tourists then other cruise ships visiting the ports were a likely source. Looking at his database he realised that in addition to Dunedin ships visited Auckland, Christchurch and Akaroa as destinations where tourists took tours onshore. He sent an email to his equivalents in police offices nearby with a description of the Count and his modus operandi and asked for immediate checks.

In terms of other favoured targets, New Zealand had thousands of hotels, guest houses and tours catering for tourists but in terms of high-worth customers, it was a more difficult job as there were many expensive houses for rent that were not on any standard web site or directory.

The search for anyone who had used a passport in the name of Jergov entering or leaving the country had revealed no-one of that name. The Lithuanian consul had also been contacted but had not responded so far. Max was not holding his breath while he waited as the nearest city with a Lithuanian embassy was Sydney. Part of the problem with all Max's telephone calls was that most English speaking respondents spent a few minutes giggling at the name before realising that it was a serious question.

By the time he'd been working on the case for a few days, Max was starting to lose his normal sense of humour. His legal department had spent hours on the one example of the literary contract they had been given and had come to no real conclusion. They wanted to submit it at great expense to another set of lawyers with specialist knowledge but suspected that if Count Jergov actually did some work on the project using the names involved, then what he had done was not illegal.

Max knew that like most lawyers, they wouldn't commit themselves and that referral to any specialists would cost more than the Dunedin annual budget for peripheral things like police officers.

Max had been more hopeful about bank transfers into Count Jergov's account from some victims. Banks in places like Switzerland, Luxembourg, Cayman Islands and other 'Offshore' facilities used to have all kinds of dirty money from Nazis and Russian oligarchs to corrupt African Presidents and drug runners. Most of these had to change their ways in the last half century because of money laundering legislation which was agreed worldwide.

Max knew that enquiries to any of these would take shed-loads of paperwork and probably take years but after a brief conversation with a specialist he realised that his chance of getting an honest answer was zero. Panama hadn't even pretended to agree to the freedom of financial information legislation and Count Jergov banked with the Panama Gulf Bank.

Most police forces rely on the media to help them find criminals but the public forget about such things incredibly quickly. Max sent a request to the TV and press people he'd contacted before asking them to re-run the Count Jergov story again as the police had more evidence that the conman was still in New Zealand. He had a fairly instant OK from the news programme that they would run it the following day unless there was any other juicy disaster that took precedence.

So Max couldn't think of anything more he could do for the moment and was closing down the computer to go home for a beer and bit of civilised conversation with the dog when a call was put through from the switchboard.

The voice was twice the volume of most things he'd heard this side of a thrash metal concert he'd taken his sons to a few years back. It was also an Australian accent that was about as pleasant as an old-fashioned dentist drill. The woman claimed to be a person of great importance and said that she had been defrauded by Count Jergov and was now back in Sydney. Her name was Florence Hasty.

In the garden of the Invercastle Hotel in Wanaka our author was feeling strangely elated. He had consumed most of the bottle of champagne before lunch and realised that it was important that he didn't peak too early. George was returning with the Bentley around 3.00 p.m. and he hadn't had any interest from the other guests. Fizz also made him randy, which after the enforced abstinence of the last few days was not exactly helpful as authors are supposed to be abstracted and committed to their art - not slaving around like a dog after a bitch on heat.

The sun had moved round and Tiggy ordered some food to soak up the booze and moved further into the shade. There was the distant drone of boats on the lake and the buzz of bees in the bushes and Tiggy put his pen down to rest his eyes against the glare.

"Sir ... excuse me sir ..."

The voice was insistent ... "Sir I have your food." Tiggy woke up with regret, just having renewed his first acquaintance with Miriam and her sister in his dreams. Embarrassingly his hard on must have been visible to the waitress through his thin trousers and she scuttled off like a startled ferret.

It took a while but he managed to get some steak down himself and drink a coffee. Looking at his watch he realised that he'd probably been dozing for 30 minutes but felt considerably fresher.

"Is it true you're a writer?" said a soft female voice from behind.

"Er .. no .. not at all ...." he said defensively.

"Well, your driver said you were ..."

"He was supposed to keep that confidential as I have a deadline to meet and daren't be distracted by agents or fans ... I'm sorry to be rude but I must carry on working." Tiggy couldn't quite see the face as he was blinded by the sun but her voice had the accent-less English much favoured by expensively finished woman from the US or Europe.

He shaded his eyes with his hand and started to wonder whether he had

131

been visited by a fantasy angel or hallucinating. To cover his surprise, he picked up the Mont Blanc, opened up the leather writing case and started to write the new passage he'd memorized on the way over. The Fenton section had been dealing with the heroines battle with 17th Century prejudice against women and the appalling indignities suffered by a maid servant made pregnant by the Lord's son. It was standard romantic novel stuff but even Tiggy was moved by the prose and hoped that anyone else would be too.

The female moved opposite his table and was politely waiting. When Tiggy looked again he realised that his initial shock was well deserved. The woman in front of him was the spitting image of his first love and sex guru – Maddie Quimby.

Around twenty-five years ago Maddie had taught him some valuable lessons. The sex instruction in his parents' cottage had been a masterclass which he'd learned from as a boy and which he still used today. That had been all about giving females the pleasure they deserved but very seldom got but later when he'd been staying with Maddie before joining the navy she'd talked about men in general.

After ten years in the hostess business dealing with mainly with top-end clients, Maddie split men into three basic categories:

    1. The Grabber

This man was basically a smash and grab merchant with no conversation and no technique. Maddie said that her record for the fastest client visit was six and half minutes including penetration, payment and tip. This was a regular and Maggie said that one week in a fit of humour she asked him whether a wank administered by himself might have been just as enjoyable and a lot cheaper. The man looked shocked and insulted that she thought him a wanker and assured her that sex was what he wanted.

    2. The little Boy

Maddie said that an Admiral of the Fleet had been a prime example of this category. He used to sidle in looking sheepish and loved being treated like a naughty boy. With these people the sex quite often needed to be with Maddie dressed up as some form of authority figure such as matron or teacher. Followed by some form of punishment such as the cane or an extra 50% on the bill.

    3. The Deviant

This was the only type of client that gave some Maddie some headaches and, in some cases, bruises. It was also why she kept a cricket bat and some handcuffs under the bed. She remembered the joke told to her by an early client. 'Why is Lobster Thermidor the same as a blow job?' The answer being. 'You don't get either at home.' So, some deviants just wanted a bit of oral but others wanted anal and others .... well, even Maddie refused the violent or SM clients because the idea made her giggle despite all the interest in the book 'Shades of Grey'.

Maddie accepted that her definitions might have been slightly biased because she was a sex worker but really the types of men she'd described made sense to Tiggy too. Men and women are both selfish in different ways and Tiggy's success with women had been partly because he was genuinely interested in them also because his lovemaking technique was unselfish and practised.

Tiggy realised that despite his recollections the woman who was the Maddie look- alike was still standing in front of him awaiting some kind of answer.

"I ... I'm sorry what was your question ...?"

"I said what is it you are writing and why are you writing it by hand?"

Trying not to be bored by the same old question he put the pen down with a sigh. "I've tried computers ... I'm not a technophobe. But a fountain pen suits my writing speed and my thoughts flow better. Shakespeare managed thousands of words with a quill pen and Jane Austin I believe used an old fountain pen."

"What might I have read of yours?"

"Nothing. I suspect nothing ...," he said with just enough arrogance.

"Do you mind if I sit down?" She didn't wait for an answer and sank into the seat opposite and Tiggy got an enticing glimpse of sunburnt thighs and a wonderful cleavage. Some exotic fragrance drifted across the table and Tiggy looked across and pretended annoyance.

"I don't like ebooks or Kindle and I suspect you do. Digital has been the death of decent publishing worldwide and my last book was published traditionally – who knows what will happen if I don't meet the deadline with the next."

The woman didn't comment and Tiggy looked across at the thick dark hair and beautiful Irish blue eyes and voluptuous figure that could have been Maddie re-born. The only difference was attitude and this woman had the education and arrogance that spoke of a very different upbringing.

Sadly, all Tiggy could think of was seeing her in bed.

The waiter brought some more food and she ordered a Spritzer. Tiggy asked and she confirmed that she was staying at the hotel and had been there for s few weeks already. She said that her name was Adele Lang and Tiggy stood up and kissed her hand without offering a name in return. Seeing no reason to change a winning formula our author excused himself and went to the lavatory inside allowing just enough time for anyone nosy to look at Eugene Fenton book and it's glowing and totally falsified reviews. Using this old trick might be risky but Tiggy thought it unlikely that anyone from *Amazon* would have exposed him. Or if they had, it would be painfully obvious pretty quickly when he returned.

Looking in the restroom mirror Tiggy almost expected to see the Count and reminded himself to be his new self and not drink any more booze. He went out and was relieved to see that his new fan was still setting at his table and was looking with respect in his direction.

Adele said that she was a politician normally working in Brussels and as Tiggy didn't actually stop her she then felt she had permission to talk about her favourite subject – which was herself.

Apparently, Adele Lang nee Hughes had been born in London forty-five years ago and educated privately in the UK and Geneva. She had worked as a PPS for a labour politician who'd become a MEP in the 2000's and eventually was fast tracked to be a candidate herself. In those days the vote figures for European elections were incredibly low and much to her surprise she was elected for Leicester Newton despite the fact she'd only visited there a couple of times. She'd got in also because she'd married Terry Lang who was well respected in the area and who backed her.

She'd become a serious Euro MP who knew her way round the gravy train that was Brussels and Strasburg within months. She eventually realised that her husband had been useful once but that he was now a boring Eurocrat who would only hold her back. His constituency had excepted the divorce as evidence of the pressure she was under doing work for them and she was re-elected in the last election before the UK vote on the EU.

Adele could see what was likely to happen and used the fact that her father was Irish to apply for an Irish passport. She got this within a few months and told her family she was moving to Dublin.

Brexit had taken longer than even she'd anticipated but she didn't care. She'd been pulling in her salary as a British MEP and served on a number of lucrative consultancies in Brussels and knew that she would be compensated generously when she finally left. The payout had exceeded her wildest dreams.

During the days she was a regular in Dublin she practised her Irish accent and brushed up her Irish credentials. Her father Paddy Hughes had run an international construction business but loved the fact that he'd been born in Cork. Like most ex-patriots he'd become more Irish the longer he'd been in London.

It hadn't taken long but Adele's own version of soft power had got her in Brussels again but this time working for the Republic of Ireland. She hadn't intended to sleep with people of influence to get there but it had helped establish her credentials she said with a smile.

According to her she'd done incredibly well for the last couple of years and was pulling in a lot of Euros as a senior researcher working on the Celtic influence on US trade.

Adele paused for the first time and Tiggy thought that he might get a word in but realised that the woman was obviously moved – deeply moved by something and our hero had the good sense to keep quiet. At the moment she was on sabbatical from Brussels and had been for the last six months because of something terrible that had happened during work. Apparently, she had been working on a paper dealing with the Celtic fringe in New York with a Greek guy called Manolo who had been in charge of a number of sub-committees she wanted to be on. They had been working late in one of the top meeting rooms in the European Parliament building and it had been a hot day. She said that she had been wearing a mini skirt with and loose top because of the heat and before she had time to pull away, she found that the Greek guy had slipped his hand through the gap in the front of her silk top and cupped her left breast.

Tiggy really didn't see why this should be a problem to a woman who had, on her own admission, used her body to get to the top. But had the sense to look shocked and understanding.

The upshot of this outrageous assault was that Adele was given a year of paid compassionate leave by the EU and the Greek was fired from his job.

She had decided to fulfil a lifetime ambition and come to Australia and New Zealand whilst she was recovering. She said that her lawyers were still working on the compensation figure but that it would be substantial.

Tiggy had been instinctively pro-Brexit in those years leading up to 2020 and now knew that he had been right. He'd suspected that many of the

135

institutions were bureaucratic and self-serving and that many of the politicians involved were milking it for all they were worth. Everything this woman said backed that up to the hilt. The fact that she admitted sleeping with the right people to get the Irish job but got the poor Greek guy fired for a simple grope was grossly unfair. Still, he was probably back in Brussels himself by now.

Tiggy kept a neutral expression and let her finish, thinking that despite all the doom merchants and real challenges the UK had done pretty well in the years since the split. Now he had his own separation campaign to plan which was to separate those lovely thighs in a way that was mutually satisfactory.

First as an act of faith he picked up his telephone and delayed George's pick up. Things were looking better and there was just a chance that he might have a productive trip. But he needed to be patient if he was going to make the most of this enticing prospect. He looked over at the woman who was waiting expecting sympathy.

"You've had a terrible time but I'm in a really embarrassing situation at the moment. As you heard I have just delayed my driver because I have to finish one more character part today or I will lose a substantial amount of money. I talked to you ... well, you remind me of someone very special I used to know – a woman who was my muse, my inspiration."

Adele was part affronted but mostly flattered.

"Alright but I'd love to talk to you more about writing as I've always thought that I'd love to write a book about Ireland."

With an exasperated sigh our hero added.

"I'm a romantic writer that some critics have been kind enough to say writes like a male Jane Austin – surely after your recent experience romance is not your thing?"

Adele leant over towards him and flashed those lovely blue eyes at him.

"That's not true. If anything, I'm more romantic than ever and Austin was a huge writer for me when I was a girl."

"How long are you staying here?"

"At least another week."

"I'd love to talk – as I said you remind me of someone very special but if I don't get this done it will cost me ten thousand dollars."

"That's a lot of money for a few hours work."

"As Whistler said to Turner – it's not the time taken to do it now, it's the years building up the skills in order to do it." Tiggy was really proud that he'd remembered that one.

Adele Lang looked suitably impressed too and started to rise offering Tiggy an enticing glimpse of those sun-burned thighs again and our author stood too and kissed her hand whilst looking deeply into those eyes and trying not to look down a cleavage that had already cost the EU so much money.

Tiggy arranged to see her the following day for afternoon tea in the garden and looked meaningfully at the Rolex. He only had an hour before the Bentley returned and went back to his notes with a look of intense concentration.

His driver rang and Tiggy wandered out of the garden looking like an author inspired. After a trip to the loo, he went to reception and asked to see the menu and wine list. Tiggy hoped that he was going to sample both over the next few days at little cost to himself. Just as he was wandering out to the car the sommelier rushed over and said that he could get the Nyetimber Tiggy had requested but it would take a couple of days. Tiggy agreed and smiled at the man with gratitude just requesting that he ensured that it was a good year.

Back in Queenstown he was dropped at the corner of the road and went up to the B&B. He stripped off his finery and had a long shower turning on the TV as he emerged looking for any news about the legendary Count Jergov. There was nothing so Tiggy dressed in the nearest thing he had to off-duty clothes which was some chinos and a blue shirt, and as he'd seen the weather, he put on his charity shop Swanndri coat.

As he left the house and started walking it got darker and a squall hit. The temperature seemed to have dropped by 10 degrees and the rain almost felt like hail. The mountains opposite were invisible in cloud and he could see boats running for shelter down on the lake. He knew it was early Autumn but the weather at the hotel had been positively Mediterranean and the contrast was amazing. It was a good time to get out of the weather and have a few beers.

The Travelling Kiwi was a bar he'd been into and liked because it didn't have screens showing rugby or sailing and it had its own micro-brewery. One of the few things Tiggy hadn't liked about New Zealand was its beer – which was gassy, tasteless and served so cold that you didn't know that. This place brewed and served real beer that tasted European and Tiggy ordered a jug of Landlords Stout which was around 7% - strong enough to be treated with respect.

After a few minutes Michael came over and asked him about his day remembering that he was a writer. Tiggy repeated that he was researching rich women for a new book and that he'd been across at the Invercastle Hotel in Wanaka meeting a few. The landlord being a randy sod presumed that he was also trying to get his leg over and they had a very blokey conversation about what they would do if they hooked up with a rich widow. Tiggy reminded him about the ambition most young blokes had which was to marry a rich woman who owned a brewery. Michael said that he had a brewery already so all he needed was the wealthy woman. They laughed like schoolboys and the landlord ordered another jug.

Tiggy was starting to feel the buzz of the alcohol but ordered a large pie filled with venison which arrived with Kumara chips and he started to feel that everything was good in the world. As much as he loved women, they were a complicated breed and he enjoyed evenings like this as much as sex. Well almost as much.

Tiggy had been in the Royal Navy for years and had found the fellowship fantastic on board but the social life ashore was wonderful. He knew that he had been born good-looking but the uniform made him almost irresistible to both men and women. Looking back, he wondered whether he could have kept going and retired as captain like his father. Or whether the chance to make a bit of extra money and live above his means would have always tempted him to the dark side. He often blamed the Riva for his plight but if he was honest, he'd gone off the rails well before he was conned by De Glanville in Palma.

Tiggy realised that he had been lost in his own thoughts for ages and that Michael had gone back behind the bar and was serving some locals. A ping from his phone woke him up with the news from the boatyard that they had repaired the engine and were demanding more money. He responded with a request for completion dates and further costs and was told that the boss would be in touch soon.

He hated the boatyard guy with his false Italian credentials and smarmy good looks. But he was the only person in the country whose work on the boat would be approved by the parent company. The only good thing was that classic Rivas were going up in price exponentially and he knew that his unique model could make enough to keep him in luxury if he could feed this money pit for just a few more months.

One source of money called Adele Lang – the English turned Irish turned Europhile - was looking good. The fact that she looked like the angel of his youth was an omen and the fact that she was awash with compensation made her even more lucky.

That night Tiggy slept the sleep of the wicked. He needed to get fit for the next stage of his plan so he went up the hill to the leisure centre and signed in as a visiting Kiwi from Grendon in North Island and swam for an hour. Many sailors never learned to swim in the old sailing days because they thought it was unlucky but Tiggy swam fast and well in the speedy lane that was normally reserved for athletes. The New Zealanders really believed in exercise and had invested in great facilities back in the early 20th Century. One of the reasons they produced so many good sports people he thought.

Afterwards, invigorated, he dressed in his author outfit swopping the bow tie for a flamboyant silk kipper he'd found a few days ago. Thinking positively, he also packed a few overnight things in a small bag in case he got lucky.

Looking back on it a day later Tiggy wasn't sure who'd had the better part of the deal. Adele Lang had certainly demanded value. The afternoon tea at the hotel had been quite civilised and he'd talked over tea and cakes about the book and the people who'd already paid to be in it. With total honesty he'd mentioned that a number of people had already paid up to twenty thousand dollars to be featured including a retired business owner from Miami, a successful business woman from Sydney and a gay marina owner from Florida.

Our author had said that he was embarrassed about the success of the whole thing. Adele had first looked indifferent but gradually warmed to the idea when she thought she might be able to screw a good deal out of him. He sighed and claimed that there were only two characters left – one female, one male and that they were both powerful personalities and almost impossible to cast. She'd taken the bait and invited him to dinner.

Dinner was wonderful as were the two bottles of Ripasso he'd helped drink before he pretended to pick up his mobile and order his car. She'd stopped his call with a melting look from those lovely eyes and a hand that touched his thigh under the table and found indeed that he 'was pleased to see her.' Tiggy protested that he needed to finish his book and Adele said that she wanted to be part of it.

After much haggling they agreed a fee of 15,000 dollars and much to his surprise, she opted to make her father famous and not herself. Paddy Hughes was to appear as a powerful and successful European entrepreneur who buys Harlestone Manor and courts one of the main female characters in the romance. For a woman used to dealing with vast amounts of Euros, it seemed easy for her to sign the contract and transfer the money to consummate the deal.

They ended up outside in a darkened garden lying on sun loungers feeling like characters in their own story. The stars were unbelievable here and Tiggy pointed out various constellations before asking her to take every stitch of clothing off. Much to his amazement she complied.

Her body actually was even lovelier than his guru. Dress size 14 or 16 and perfectly shaped like a woman in a Dutch master or Italian fresco. He could see the goosebumps on her skin in the moonlight.

Tiggy was ready to put every bit of the knowledge that his guru had taught him into one final performance.

"Adele, I don't want anything from you, I don't want you to do anything – the next half an hour is all about you."

He spent time gradually waking up parts of her body with a caress, a kiss or a word and pushing her hand away when she tried to touch him. He hadn't intended to bring her to a peak yet but when he'd turned her over and was working on her buttocks and down between her thighs, he felt a shudder and knew that she'd climaxed early.

Tiggy turned her back over and slowed for a few minutes, knowing that if he was patient, he would get an even more explosive reaction later. He entered her in the missionary position five minutes later with his arms taking the strain on the arms of the sun lounger. He found her wonderfully wet but went in part way and slowly until he found her spot, gradually increased power using her gasps as a guide.

Looking back, he reckoned that he didn't put a foot (or maybe a dick) wrong all night. She had pleasure at a level of intensity that drove them both inside as she was so loud. Over the following hours she had extraordinary stamina and ended up taking control.

About three o'clock in the morning he went to the bathroom, had loads of water and a little blue pill. It was now her mission to turn him on if she wanted more pleasure herself. She danced, she licked, she sucked and she rubbed herself on him and he rose to the occasion. They only stopped when they were both so sore, they thought they might damage something permanently.

Tiggy sneaked out at first light having texted George and slept the sleep of the truly exhausted in the car having achieved a personal equivalent of

140

a double triathlon. He was woken on the outskirts of Queenstown and crept up his street floating with exhaustion.

He staggered up to his bedroom feeling as though he'd respected the memory of his early sex goddess, Maddie Quimby, in a way that she would have appreciated. Also having accumulated an extra 15K dollars in the Riva fund – which he suspected she would also have loved.

Our hero slept for another six hours and was only woken up by the smell of cooking in another part of the house. He was ravenous but before he went out, he put on the NZ News Channel where his favourite two – Andy Burnham and Carol Weepu were doing their normal unique slant on the day's headlines:

A.B. The legendary Count Jergov is still in our country and he's defrauding tourists.

C.W. Who? Did you say Jergov?

A.B. I did. Over a week ago we reported that police were looking for a cunning fraudster who used the name Count Jergov.

C.W. This is a photograph of the conman that has been enhanced by our experts. He pretends to be an author and police ask you to call this number if you know where he is.

Tiggy turned off the set in panic and wondered whether anyone in Wanaka was watching TV. The photo enhancement that had been done was a surprisingly good job but hopefully the new beard might help his disguise. It was obvious that the hue and cry was on with a vengeance and he needed an escape plan that got him to the Akaroa boat yard safely and quickly.

Having a painful Brazilian

Francesca Capelle had receded from Tiggy's memory like you gradually forgot a nasty kick to the balls but she had not forgotten him.

Despite the extra cash she'd got from Tiggy and the Welsh guy she'd ripped off she'd still not left the country or gone home to Rio despite all the promises she'd made to her parents and herself.

Part of this was because she thought that she'd taken too many risks by being greedy and emptying the Welsh guy's bank account at the ATM.

She'd been wearing a ridiculous woollen hat which should have covered her up from the cameras but the police had been very active round town since, and she was worried about high security areas like airports. The guy Bryn been some sort of insurance investigator so she wondered if he had some influence with the cops and they were giving the case special attention.

She'd held on to his Breitling watch and was wearing it rather than trying to sell it because she didn't want to visit any more shysters and get ripped off like happened in Dunedin. It was a risk but she loved the watch and after adjustment it fitted her like a glove.

There was an even more compelling reason for Fran to stay where she was. Looking through a glass window of a bar she'd seen a TV News broadcast which appeared to show a photograph of her lover in Dunedin. The shots weren't 100% clear but pushing in the bar she'd seen that the police were after someone with a weird name like Jergov who had conned people out of thousands of dollars. Her instincts were that it *was* her lover and with what she knew about him, there might be an opportunity to screw more out of him.

Fran had enjoyed the lovemaking with him more than at any time in her life and the experience had been life-changing. He'd been wonderful for her self confidence and always complementary but there was something about him that didn't ring true.

He always paid cash and he had lots of it – at least he did until she'd stolen it and he'd always been a little vague about his name and nationality.

She'd seen the name on his credit cards – the ones he never used. So, they were either stolen or his own that he didn't want to use. As Fran herself knew, using a credit card was like leaving a digital trail that anybody can follow.

For these reasons Fran stayed in Auckland and kept her head down. She got a job in bar as she had done so many times and in so many places round the world. No paperwork and payment in cash.

Auckland was a big city and she loved it. She'd opened an account with a local bank which was associated with her bank in Rio and was able to put in a considerable amount of cash that she'd got from her various slightly risky enterprises. She got new local cards too and telephone banking that made her look more normal but tried to avoid leaving any kind of trail.

Auckland- The City of Sails - had an energy that reminded her of Sydney where she'd also worked but it was tame compared to the manic chaos of Rio, the city she was planning to return to soon with enough to buy an apartment in one of the better areas.

Her gap year may have turned into ten years but she'd made money everywhere – not always legally- and stashed it away in her Brazilian account. In the past, Fran tried to be careful to bend the law and choose victims who were rich enough to afford it. She'd tried not to take too many risks or commit crimes that would have the police seriously on her tail. But over the last few weeks, she feared that she'd overstepped the mark and tempted fate.

Fran had developed one healthy habit since she'd been staying at the hostel and that was running. It may have been the impending 29th birthday that she worried was terrifyingly close to 30 which had been the age that had seemed so old when she was a kid. He mother had been grey-haired and fat at that age and Fran had vowed never to be that unattractive.

She bought trainers and Lycra shorts and started running. Every morning she put her valuables in a small back pack and hit the road about 7.30 a.m. The first day she was knackered after 100 yards but gradually she increased distance and now was doing a couple of miles and feeling good about herself. She found that any worries about police or people she'd robbed that had bothered her overnight suddenly got themselves in perspective and she was more confident.

One of her favourite routes went downhill from the hostel crossing a number of intersections and eventually ending up at the place she called the Americas Cup harbour because of the winning yachts on display. Wherever she ran SkyCity the huge tower was an excellent landmark if she ever got lost but the waterside areas were more attractive than anywhere else. There was a ferry going to all kinds of places and boats everywhere but if she timed it right then the actual quayside where the old Americas Cup winners are on display was empty of tourists. She would then have a swig from her water bottle and then set on the return jog which was uphill and more cardio challenging.

After a shower and fruit breakfast she'd look at some TV or read the paper to see whether Tiggy or herself had made the news. Then she'd walk to the Murphy's Bar where she worked lunches and evenings. The place was seriously Irish and got a bit loud on sports nights but she reckoned that it was the last place an upmarket Welsh guy like Bryn would ever come, so reasonably low risk.

Bryn Edmunds was actually still in Auckland and feeling considerably poorer than when he'd arrived. The Brazilian woman had taken him for an absolute plonker and for a substantial amount of money too. He'd been late at the gallery where he was supposed to start the process to authenticate a Picasso sketch and the pay out for its theft.

This delay had nearly got him fired and only the excuse of a violent attack of food poisoning had kept him safe. He certainly looked the part when he'd arrived as the girl had obviously drugged him the previous night and he was white and shaking.

Bryn reckoned he'd got the worst reward possible for helping a woman in distress. Despite buying her dinner and getting all the right signals he'd not slept with the most beautiful woman he'd seen in centuries.

She'd taken his wallet and he'd been prepared to live with the shame of her nicking his cash but the watch was a Breitling he'd been given for his 21st birthday and incredibly important to him emotionally. The shame didn't stop there, she'd gone to an ATM and cleaned out his account which meant that he'd had to admit to the bank that he'd written his PIN on a piece of paper in his wallet. They were not happy.

The final indignity was having to go to the local police. One of the rising stars in the art insurance business and a Welshman turned Australian citizen being ripped off in the oldest scam in the world was something the Auckland police were going to enjoy. They did, for hour after hour after hour.

Bryn had to describe his assailant and the fact that his description sounded like every man's fantasy – probably Brazilian or South American. Tall with good bust and lovely bum but slim waisted. Also, long brown hair, pale complexion and wonderful hazel eyes. One of the police officers suggested that it might be safer to not take strange young women to his room in future. He thanked the sergeant for his advice whilst mentally eviscerating the smart-arse.

He went through hundreds of mug-shots and saw no-one remotely similar but the more friendly of the cops said that he'd check for any recent similar thefts and let him know if anything cropped up. Bryn had at least a couple more days in Auckland on the claim. At least his new credit cards had arrived quickly and he was able to enjoy the city without having to borrow money.

He was a keen sailor and had loved watching the big competitions on the TV for years. The Americas Cup had been a favourite ever since he was a kid. The battle between the US and Great Britain started nearly a century ago and he remembered the paintings and early film of those beautiful J Class yachts owned by some of the richest men in the world battling it out. Then the boats looked more like clippers than yachts but after the millennium things changed in a big way.

More nations got involved and the Kiwis managed to win it several times with yachts that still looked fairly traditional – some of which were regularly on display down at the harbour.

The boats got more like F1 racing cars after that but Bryn still liked seeing the original boats and had vowed to go down to the harbour when he got a few minutes to spare.

Bryn was quite happy in his own company and spent a day compiling reports in his bedroom and talking to his head office in Sydney. Luckily no-one there had heard about his embarrassing encounter with the Brazilian woman and he hoped that it stayed that way. He'd been able to confirm that the sketch in question was a genuine Picasso so the gallery was happy and he booked a return flight back in a couple of days, vowing to see a little of the city before he returned.

Early the following morning he hired a bike and decided to drift down to the harbour and have a leisurely breakfast. Then he planned to look at what ferry services were running and take some trips over to the islands. He hadn't cycled for months and even though he was fit, he found that his leg muscles ached after a couple of minutes so decided to have a coffee and consider things. He found Carlos' Trattoria down at the harbour and ordered a Flat White.

It was a lovely Autumn morning and Bryn was looking across at the winning yachts and enjoying the sea breeze flapping the flags on the many boats moored in the marina. The air seemed so clean in New Zealand and he was convinced that it made the skies brighter and the coffee taste more of coffee. He was in a little world of his own when a lovely sight disturbed his reverie.

The woman was tall with legs that seemed to go on for ever and a figure that Lycra was made for. Her long brown hair was pulled through a baseball cap and her face, visible as she tilted it back to take some water from her bottle, was absolutely beautiful. The last time Bryn had seen it had been in his hotel bedroom when he had really thought he was on a promise.

Much to his amazement Bryn's heart was going like a hammer and he could barely catch his breath. He'd forgotten just how devastatingly lovely she was and part of him just wanted to look – to look at the woman who he might have shared a night with.

Bryn wasn't bad looking but this girl was in a different class and everyone male in the cafe was looking as she had a further swig from her bottle and put it back in the pack. He had to pull himself together and remember that this lovely had cleaned out his bank account and stolen his watch.

Before she'd put the pack back on, he'd put a few dollars on the table and rushed across to where his bike was locked up. She was obviously going on with her run and his hands were shaking so much that he could barely get the lock open. He did it and threw the lock down and got on the bike just as she set off uphill. It took only a few seconds but at last he got the bike in the right gear and started to follow her uphill.

He had his mobile in his backpack but couldn't stop to get it out as she was running down alleys, crossing intersections and going up one way streets and he daren't lose her in the crowd. Fifteen minutes later she pushed open the door of a small tourist hostel and went in. He wondered what to do next, but got out his phone and waited.

Bryn had few doubts that it was the same woman but wondered how to prove it. Almost without him noticing she slipped out half an hour later and he just had time to take a couple of shots on his iPhone. This time she was wearing a green top and black shirt and walking at speed down the road, Bryn followed her on the bike until she entered an Irish bar with the original name of Murphy's Bar at about 11.00 a.m. He parked himself on the edge of a car-park and waited, looking at the shots he'd taken on his phone, which were just about good enough for him to recognise her but he doubted whether the police would be able to use them.

After a while he lost patience and went in the bar, thinking that the cycle helmet might make him a little more difficult to recognise. The inside was dark and covered in the Irish memorabilia he'd seen in pubs all round the world – Guinness posters, old rugby shots and black and white photos of poets and peasants. Someone – not Fran – greeted him as he entered

146

and he ordered another coffee. He sat in a booth away from the window and kept his head down whilst trying to see her out of the side of his eyes.

Eventually he spotted her on the far side of the bar and realised she worked there as in addition to the green polo shirt he'd seen earlier; she was wearing an apron with the bar name on it.

Bryn thought that a Brazilian with apparently poor English getting a job in an Irish bar was a bit unlikely. But when you looked as good as she did, the manager probably had made a lot of allowances. More likely, she was nowhere near as helpless as she had made out in the airport or hotel. You could tell from her demeanour earlier; she was confident and a good enough actress to convince anyone of anything.

One thing that gave him a little hope was the watch, which looked large on her wrist in the photos and he was hoping was his Breitling. If he got that back, he was almost prepared to forgive the rest of the theft as it was a reminder of his parents who'd died a year back.

It was still only about mid-day when he paid and left and he tried to work out his next course of action. Logically she'd be there for at least another couple of hours, so he had time before she left. First, he had to try and contact the cops and get some action out of them. Which unless he could find the incident number or the name of the one friendly officer was going to be a pain.

First, he had to have faith in his logic and leave the bar area and go to his hotel where he had a note of the names and some more respectable clothes.

Fran was enjoying most things about the bar job apart from the attentions of the manager. His groping was getting persistent and though he'd been understanding in the interview and pretended to believe the fact that she was half-Irish and therefore employable, this had to stop. She realised that she was probably going to have to make a fuss to make life bearable.

It would be a pity because she could do the job standing on her head but he wanted her to do it lying on a sack in the stockroom instead. The irony was that the manager wasn't Irish either but he was a big, hairy and raw-boned oaf who looked like a bog-trotter, so he got away with it.

She'd checked the local papers that morning looking for anything that referred to her crimes and was starting to hope that she'd got away with her excesses at the Welshman's ATM. He'd got a lot of money in that account and she was surprised that the bank had allowed her to withdraw so much. Perhaps he was on business expenses and often drew out large amounts she thought – but it was certainly enough for her to get a ticket home and travel in style.

The bar manager tried it on again when she was going through the apparently religious experience of pulling a pint of Guinness. She got to the half way point and paused in the prescribed manor when she felt him hard against her behind.

"Listen you gob-shite, you won't turn me on in a month of Sundays like that – I prefer women."

Fran did in a reasonable version of the insult she'd heard on Father Ted via YouTube in an attempt to become more Irish.

"You ... you fuckin cow ... you could 'ave told me you were a pillow-biter," the oaf of a manager whispered behind her.

"You didn't ask," she snarled, finishing the pint with a shamrock on foam.

At least that kept him away for the rest of the lunch session and she could see him complaining to a couple of locals who always propped up the bar at the far corner pretending to be Irish. They normally turned into gibberish by closing time but after three pints and three chasers in they were all looking over and probably thinking 'what a waste'.

This bar, like the one in Dunedin, had a policy of putting all tips in a big jar behind the bar so that they were shared with people like the kitchen staff who normally didn't get any. This had made Fran a surprisingly large amount when she'd made off with all of it the night before the big share in the Nova in Dunedin.

Now she planned to do something similar at this place and judging by the size of the jar there already, it could be a bonus. Checking it out she knew that the policy here was different and there was a split at the end of the working week. Weekend staff having a separate arrangement.

That meant that two nights time was the best for her to indulge in a little personal profit-sharing before she did a final exit.

Fran looked at the lovely watch she'd acquired and realised that her duties were over for the lunch time. There were only a couple of hours for her to get back to the hostel, have a shower and get ready for her evening shift. On the way she planned to call in to a travel agent and check out flights then to do a little clothes shopping. Auckland had some wonderful shops and there was nothing like the thrill of spending somebody else's money to bring out the shopaholic in her.

The red dress she'd worn when she'd first met the guy in Dunedin had been lucky, but worn on every occasion she'd try to entice anyone for the last six months. Tiggy had seemed to love her wearing nothing most of all and the thought of those nights still gave her something to be moist about. Calling into Zarbo, a high fashion boutique, gave her a few more ideas and she bought an electric blue dress and some Choo shoes that made her look a million dollars according to the gay guy in the shop.

Back in her room she switched on the TV whilst waiting for the shower to heat up, heard the urgent music of the 6.00 o'clock news and realised she was late for Murphy's.

The evil Count Jergov is still stalking the country according to police. They seek him here, they seek him there, but they can't find that evil Jergov anywhere ...

The rest of the announcement was lost to her but she couldn't stop looking at the photo. Somebody had done a brilliant job on the photograph she'd seen a few days ago and she was convinced that it was the was the guy she'd shacked up with. Her brain switched off whilst she thought back and she knew she could get more detail online. In the meantime, she needed to get a move on and get to the bar or she'd be fired before she had chance to get her bonus.

She was ten minutes late at Murphy's and the manager loved it. A new set of pseudo-Irish derelicts were sitting in Neanderthal Corner and he threatened to fire her two or three times loud enough to impress them. She knew he wouldn't because the real customers loved her and she'd ended up pouring Guinness and Jamesons better than he did.

Fran had a lot to think about. The photo on the news had disturbed her and made her wonder whether she had been infected by something in Dunedin that she'd only read about. Tiggy or whatever his bloody name was had genuinely seemed to care about her and there was just a chance that she cared a bit more for him than was comfortable. Don't be bloody stupid she thought to herself as she pulled yet another Guinness and the locals were settling down for another televised rugby match. She better watch it or she'd end up with someone called Jergov and lot of little Jergov's.

Fat chance of that she thought and went round the bar to enter the next order on the till. At least the tips jar was looking even healthier this evening, she thought.

A few yards away pretending to be Irish was a Welshman turned Aussie called Bryn Edmunds with a Kiwi called Dane who was pretending not to be copper.

Bryn had finally got through to the right policeman after braving the usual telephone filtering system, there to filter out idiots, time-wasters and those with a really urgent enquiry. Constable Dane MacArthur had joined investigation division after three years in uniform and was in his mid-20's – roughly the same age as Bryn and had agreed to meet him at 7.00 p.m. Bryn said that he'd actually seen the woman that had ripped him off and had emailed the shot. The thought of not having to raid a fetid drug den or try to arrest a huge Māori – which had been his task the previous few days obviously appealed. After all, having to investigate a woman who looked like she'd won the Miss Brazil contest in an Irish bar, where he'd be forced to have a few pints, was not the most difficult job.

As Bryn and the cop sat in the booth at Murphy's they could see the woman at work.

"Are you sure it's the same woman?" the cop asked

"Yes ..., how on earth could you forget a body like that?" Bryn answered.

"She slept with you ...?" Dane asked more in envy than professional interest.

"I ... I don't think so ... it was all going so well; she was in the room but I ended up waking in the morning with a mouth like a ..."

"So, you think she drugged you?"

Look at her ... if there had been a chance of screwing that, don't you think I'd have done it?"

The cop looked over and nodded in total agreement and made a few notes.

"Listen we have a number of difficulties proving any of this - the CCTV at your bank didn't show enough for a positive ID and nowhere else you went with her is likely to prove criminal intent. The restaurant and hotel might have footage but she probably wouldn't deny being with you. All we can do for the moment is quietly find out more about her and see if she has any kind of record."

Bryn could only agree with the cop's assessment and that the first thing was to find out who Miss Brazil really was. Constable MacArthur promised to visit the hostel as soon as possible and run the woman's name through the system.

It was actually the following morning when Bryn was enjoying his morning constitutional down to the harbour that the policeman gave him a call.

"Listen, I managed to slip into the hostel last night and make a few enquiries whilst she was still at the Irish bar."

"Brilliant, thanks for doing it so quickly – what did you find?"

"Her name is Fran – Francesca Capelle to be exact and I saw her passport – she is Brazilian as she claimed but we have nothing against her on our system and she's been in New Zealand for two months."

"What about in other places, Brazil for example?"

"Well, we could check internationally but that would take months and we still have that basic problem?

"What's that? "Bryn asked with increasing frustration.

"We haven't got any proof she stole anything from you."

"What about my watch?"

"You didn't mention anything about any watch sir – what do you mean?"

Fran was on her last day of work and she had booked her air tickets for Sunday. First Class Air New Zealand looked wonderful but crazy money but she thought that after ten years away she deserved Business Class. After all, she reckoned that most of the most rewarding men she'd met over the years had flown business class. So why shouldn't she.

She'd only put it a small percentage of her own cash tips in the jar at Murphy's. In fact, she'd taken out more than she'd put in. Fran justified this in her own mind by remembering that she'd generated loads more happy customers than the miserable bitches who normally worked there. Also, she was leaving and wouldn't have any more chances to earn – they would. The logic may have been a little flawed but it suited her.

She was actually a bit miffed at the end of the shift that she couldn't take all the tips but there were too many people waiting for their share. The bottle wasn't full and she could see a number of the kitchen skivvies looking dismayed at what appeared to be a poor week. The manager also looked a bit surprised but managed the share-out without comment.

Fran picked up her share pushed it in a side pocket and said a cheerful goodbye to her mates, pushing her way out of Murphy's and on the street which was still full of revellers enjoying their Friday night out.

"Ms Capelle?" a guy pushed in front of her showing a police warrant card.

"Y … Yes" she answered with a sick feeling in the pit of her stomach.

"I need you to accompany me to the station immediately Ms Capelle."

She was escorted to a police car and pushed into the back seat in the safety conscious manner she'd seen on so many movies. The station was a modern building and the process at the beginning went by in a blur.

Fran was vaguely aware that her possessions had been taken away, she had been and put in an interview room. This was grey and had a mirrored wall that everyone knew had people watching behind. At the door was a uniformed constable and eventually she was joined by two more senior officers – one of which was called MacArthur.

He turned on the recording and said in a friendly manner. "You are not being arrested yet Ms Capelle but you have been accused of theft by a number of people and I would like to get your version of events before I take things further and talk to your consul."

"Who has accused me?" Fran asked with as much arrogance as she could manage.

"Murphy's Bar first of all."

"That's ridiculous and that manager I was going to report for sexual harassment."

"So, you deny that charge, Ms Capelle? "

"Totally"

"In which case, perhaps you could explain why the twenty dollar note which we invisibly marked in the till was in your bag?"

"The manager ... he probably ..." Fran started to run out of English and uttered a stream of Spanish that would have been incomprehensible to anyone.

Constable MacArthur waited for her to run out of steam. "Also, a Mr Bryn Edmunds accused you of the theft of a considerable amount of money and some valuable possessions."

"That's crazy – he was a man who tried to get in bed with me a few days ago and I refused. I didn't take anything." Fran managed to squeeze a few tears out of those beautiful eyes but the policeman was impassive.

"In which case, perhaps you could explain why you were wearing his watch?"

"That's my watch" Fran sobbed.

"No Mr Edmunds has showed me the registration documents for the Breitling watch which were emailed from his home and they match the one you were wearing."

Fran knew that she had been trapped and presumed that they had evidence of her at the ATM. In her panic she could only think of one way out and said. "Can I speak to a senior officer please. I have information on a major criminal who has been on National TV – His name is Count Tolstoy Jergov."

Max Lawrence had been trying to mind his own business when the call came in from Auckland. Most of his police work was dealing with crimes in Dunedin and the Otago region. Yes, there was the occasional crime involving a foreign tourist but international stuff was a rarity. That's the way he liked it, he knew his patch and got crime solved here.

Since he'd been lumbered with the Count Jergov case he'd been getting calls from the US, from Australia and all round the bloody place demanding action. The latest of which was some sort of senior politician from Europe on sabbatical over here (what the hell was a sabbatical anyway?) and who'd been tricked out of fifteen thousand dollars by the legendary author. This Ms Lang was threatening to contact our illustrious head of state unless she got some action.

The most annoying, however, was a Ms Florence Hasty who'd insisted on Face time, Zoom or some other visual contact when she had a face most suited to radio. She seemed to be calling every couple of days and claiming to be the spokesperson for three or four other poor suckers who'd been taken in by Count Jergov. She hadn't added anything to his knowledge of the conman but she was far too close for comfort over the Tasman Sea for Max's liking.

The two sisters from the US and the guy from Miami had also teamed up and had been more useful in terms of information. Max had been honest with them from the start, passing on the information that according to his legal department Count Jergov's contracts – that they'd all signed – looked reasonably watertight and that all the man had to do was to write a few words and he'd be legit. The other point Max mentioned was that as the funds had gone to a Panama bank, there was virtually no chance of recovering the money. Obviously, Max said that there was a fraud charge that might be brought in terms of pretending to be Eugene Fenton but only if they had total proof that he had intended to deceive.

Miriam and Elmer were not surprisingly discouraged by this conversation and understood that Max was doing his best. They said that they'd continue with their investigation locally and let him know if they discovered anything else.

Sergeant Max Lawrence thought that the man named as Count Jergov or Eugene Fenton more recently had been as close as Wanaka in the last few days. He'd put the photo-fit and other details on the system so theoretically anybody might pick him up on a train, bus or plane. But nothing had come in yet and if the illustrious Count was as clever as he thought himself then he wasn't likely to travel looking like Jane Austin.

Only a strange call from Auckland Police had shown any promise and Max wasn't sure whether it was real or not. After TV broadcasts requesting help with a runaway, criminal police got all kinds of cranks as well as a few genuine calls. Much to his amazement the Captain didn't want to go up to Auckland and take all the credit (he must have a masonic dinner dance to go to Max thought) and ordered Max to go immediately to interview the witness. Timing was an issue apparently because the witness was due on a flight in 48 hours.

So Max found himself in an interview room, identical to the one in Dunedin except for the choice of beverages. Being the big city, you could get Expresso, Cappuccino and all kinds of other coffees but by the look of them, they looked like mud in a mug, just like at home. A nice detective called MacArthur gave him the background on the woman but he hadn't prepared Max for the power of this woman.

As she came in with a tear in her eye he felt an almost overwhelming urge to give her a hug but realised that might not be considered appropriate in the force. She was tall, shapely and had the most angelic face Max had ever seen. This woman had the figure and face of a movie star of the 1950's and would have won beauty contests, if such exercises in male-dominated, sexually exploitative and politically incorrect scandals were still allowed. Sadly, they had been banned years ago and Max could only regret it.

At 54 years old Max was happily married with kids and loved his wife to bits. Some women, however, have the power to wake up the caveman in anybody. Francesco Capelle was such a woman and Max had to concentrate hard on regulating his breathing and stopping his heart fluttering so much that it was flapping his shirt front.

"Ms Capelle, you claim that you have information that might lead to the arrest of a Count Tolstoy Jergov – is that correct?"

"Si." Fran said with enough emotion to make those magnificent breasts heave with emotion.

"What is that information?"

"I ya said to misser MacArthur, I needa deal so I ged to Rhio an da Mama."

Max nodded to her and went out of the room to find Dane MacArthur. After checking what the strength of the charges were against Fran – only minor theft provable though she was likely to be guilty of much more serious charges of theft according to local police. Max told the local force the extent of the fraud involving Count Jergov – over a hundred thousand dollars worth of defrauded foreigners - some with influence in high political quarters.

Dane MacArthur had been in hysterics when Max had first gone to the viewing booth because of Fran's ability to turn on the Brazilian vamp accent and flash her assets whenever she needed it. Max was warned not to be taken in as he knew that this was an intelligent woman who'd been speaking perfectly good English for years.

Both officers had to consult their superiors but, in the end, it was agreed that if Fran could give valuable information on Count Jergov, then she would be allowed on the plane to Rio. This was the right decision as the Auckland police case was not great and even Bryn Edmunds had said that he didn't really want the embarrassment of a court case as long as he got his watch back. This had happened and New Zealand as a country would not miss Ms Capelle nor would she be allowed a visa to return.

Max returned to the interview room over an hour later and sat opposite

"I have been given authority to discuss a deal Ms Capelle but what information could you give that might lead to his arrest?"

"I know iz namba." There was then a stream of incomprehensible Spanish which meant more breast heaving and flashing of eyes.

'Ms Capelle, we know your English is perfectly good so less of the Viva Zapata accent please or we'll throw you back in jail." Max shouted in good basic South Island drawl.

Fran herself had been in panic-mode and tried to cover it up in the normal way by resorting to talking patois that even her mother would have had trouble with. The normal tears and hysterics seemed to have no effect on this new cop who looked more like a country farmer than a policeman. She realised that she was cornered and that she had a choice. Betray a man who'd loved her dearly and given her the best loving she'd ever had. Forget that he'd given her even more than that – he'd given her self confidence with her own body that was life-changing. The choice was difficult but sadly not that difficult when her survival was at stake.

"His name was British I think – nothing to do with a Count," she said in perfectly modulated English.

"That's good, but what was the name?" Max asked whilst trying to hide his impatience.

"I saw the name on his personal credit cards – the ones he tried to hide when he was in New Zealand."

"How did you see those and what was the name?" Max asked again with even less patience.

"We lived together for a week when he was in Dunedin - we were lovers."

"How do you know he's the man we're after and what was his name?"

"He was the man you call Count Jergov – I recognise him from the photos on TV."

"Where was he from?" The policeman hoped it wasn't from Lithuania as he wasn't quite sure where that was.

"He was either from New Zealand or British – I'm not sure."

Fran knew that this was an extremely risky game. She had never known whether the credit cards in Tiggy's wallet were his own or stolen. But she couldn't show any lack of confidence and the policeman seemed satisfied for the moment. She only had one trump card and that was the name itself so she said that she would only reveal it when she had a written pardon, her passport and the tickets home in her hand. The cop nodded and left the room.

A few minutes later she was taken to some form of holding cell and given some food. She guessed that the police would check her story and Sergeant Lawrence would talk to his boss. If it was legit then she might get out of the country. Only time would tell.

The search for a silent Foghorn

As he looked in the mirror for the fiftieth time Tiggy Foghorn realised that he was a little bored lying low in in Queenstown but at least his beard was becoming interesting.

It was a couple of days since the TV News had tried to expose the nefarious Count Jergov but a really short farmers haircut and the full black beard had made him a little more confident that he wouldn't be recognised as the evil aristocrat.

Judging by his tightening waistline caused by the addiction to the beer, venison pies and fish & chips that the bar served daily, he was trying to alter his appearance in other ways too. The swims at the leisure centre were good for fitness but obviously not good enough to keep his figure. If his excuse was that he was working on his disguise, then it was working. When he looked at the full length mirror, he almost didn't recognise himself.

He found it difficult to be serious and remember that lots of people might be after him – not just the police. Thinking back to the good ship *Amazon* he thought that Miriam and her sister Elsie would probably shrug the whole thing off as a valuable learning experience. They had both had plenty of five-star fornication whilst he was there and he thought that they would be understanding.

Some of the others hadn't had the same benefits. Elmer Flannigan may have been gay but he was not one anybody would like to get on the wrong side of. One significant extra danger was that as a marina owner he might remember the Riva that the Count had mentioned he was trying to restore and use it to find him. Hopefully he was now miles away with his sea captain.

The Ginger Merchant of Death, Florence Hasty, hadn't shared his bed. Here Tiggy mentally tortured himself as to whether he would ever have shared a bed with her if she'd offered more money. Even the thought sent a shudder of bowel-clenching fear through him and he knew he would never have done it. In terms of likely threat to his discovery, he thought she was a higher risk as she'd be home in Australia by now and closer.

His analysis of the rest of the cruise people were that they were mainly back in the US or South America by now and therefore less risk. Ms Anders & Son, the gun loving family of Dwight would probably only be a threat if he ever visited the deep south or voted Democrat.

Ms De Candole Wolfberg, the grand-daughter of a likely Nazi who hoarded stolen art in Chile or Peru or Panama – he couldn't remember which – could be a serious danger if he ever visited his secret bank in Panama City. Otherwise, he reckoned the money involved wouldn't make it worthwhile for them to cause too much hassle with the authorities and risk exposing their own dirty tricks. But the young woman was smart, rich and if she decided to be vindictive, then he could be dealing with some extremely nasty people indeed.

Overall, he thought his ship-board activities could create some risk of pursuit but as long as he kept his nose clean for the next few weeks, he reckoned the risk of discovery was relatively low.

There were more than just his shipmates who'd been taken in by the Count or his alter ego. The Chinese couple were young, tech-savvy and an unknown quantity. His hope was that if the importance of losing face was as high as he'd heard, then they would try to cover the whole thing up and not be a threat.

His most recent conquest in Wanaka was difficult to gauge as she was a politician and in Tiggy's opinion they didn't conform to any set of rules that human beings follow. Hopefully as she couldn't get any profit out of accusing him of molestation as she had with that poor Greek in Brussels, she'd be grateful for the bed action and forget him. She certainly got value for money out of him and was due to finish her year of 'sick-leave' soon and return to Dublin and Brussels, so he hoped that distance would reduce any threat from her.

Tiggy continued his personal risk assessment process. If he was honest his daily trips to the Travelling Kiwi were a risk as he had told Michael the landlord, he was a writer and interested in wealthy women, before he went to the hotel in Wanaka. He had to have some pleasures and he enjoyed the craic and the beer too much to give it up immediately.

Another concern was George, the guy who had driven him over to Wanaka in the Bentley. For the moment Tiggy reckoned that he was OK because he'd been paid inordinately well for the week and had been told that the following week was likely too. In Tiggy's experience there was no way better to ensure silence, than to offer the possibility of financial reward in the future. By the time that George found out he wasn't needed, Tiggy needed to be gone.

As he walked back through town after a mainly liquid lunch he was struck again by the beauty of this place. The sun was sparkling on Lake Wakatipu, the mountains reared up on every side and the sky was a brilliant blue. The crimson and blue hand-gliders were floating above as mad buggers threw themselves off the hill. Sane people messed around in boats or lined the harbour drinking wine or coffee.

This place was a paradise, apart from the thousands of tourists who only spent 1.46 days on average according to the stats, but screwed up the traffic and didn't spend much in the town. A wise backpacking local who Tiggy had met on the bus, had said that this place was doomed the minute it had to put traffic lights in the centre of town.

Tiggy had paid for two weeks at the B&B in cash when he arrived and knew he could leave at any time. His lovely landlady was unlikely to be a problem as she had only really seen him at the beginning but he would leave flowers and a thank you note when he left. She was single and so attractive that Tiggy wished that he had had chance to express his thanks in a more physical way but he knew he didn't have the time. After the marathon that had been the Eurocrat in Wanaka he had almost recovered his libido but he knew he must resist temptation.

He sat in the chair in the bay window of his room and tried to plan his exit. There was a small airport in Queenstown which did flights to Christchurch and he was really tempted. The flight was brief and through stunning mountain scenery that a few locals had said was one of the most scenic in the world. Also, as it was internal, he suspected that security would be low but in the end, he decided the risk was not worth it.

It was whilst he was propping up the bar for yet another final drink at the Flying Kiwi that another solution to his transport problem appeared next to him. Gerrard Walter was an ex-Kiwi schoolboy rowing champion, ex-champion rally driver, ex-husband to three wives and generally good sort to have in a pub. He was now about five feet five inches everywhere having put on shed-loads of weight after giving up rowing. He was shaven-headed and big bearded and he was probably one of the most entertaining men Tiggy had met in years.

Unusually for a man who loved bars and pubs, he didn't drink. Tiggy wondered whether he'd had a serious problem in the past and been given the gypsies warning but it didn't matter. Given half a chance he would tell jokes like a pro or play the piano in the corner like Errol Garner. He introduced himself to Tiggy on the second time he went there and they became good buddies. Cars were a subject they both liked talking about and when Tiggy mentioned the Aston Martin he'd owned briefly in a past life they had a highly entertaining row about the merits of Ferrari, Porsche and Alfa Romeo verses the old British names like Jaguar and Aston.

Gerry made his living out of cars and had a small dealership on the

159

outskirts of town selling unusual Japanese and European imports with some sort of exotic tuning or modification that made them particularly quick. Tiggy said he was after something more modest and cheap enough for him to write off financially at the end of the month when he might be leaving the country. Gerry said he'd think about it and Tiggy said this was a cash deal and he was running out of loot, so to remember that his Aston Martin days were long past.

Tiggy considered the other options of getting out of town and closer to Akaroa, where the Riva was hopefully nearly finished. Bus was the only other public transport available but it would take around 5 hours and have around three stops before he reached Christchurch. Then he would have to take the infrequent cross mountain mini-bus which went across to his destination. It would be a cheap, relaxed and relatively secure method but Tiggy wasn't sure he needed the scenic tour.

If Gerry came up with a reasonable car, then it would be the best option. It's a long drive and bits of it on the Canterbury Plain are pretty boring but the roads are good and normally empty. The attitude in New Zealand to documentation is a lot more relaxed and Tiggy thought that insurance was optional. He'd check that with Gerry but the more he thought about it a car was the right option.

The first coffee the following morning down by the lakeside and Tiggy was feeling rough. He'd arranged to meet Gerry at the nearest coffee house to the end of his road and the morning was far too bright for a Gentleman of Tiggy's drinking habits. Gerry was bright as a button and Tiggy could see him from across the lakeside park, wearing a bright yellow T-shirt which appeared to have a cartoon smiley face on the front. He looked so big that it looked like a big yellow planet moving to eclipse the sun and Tiggy had to shade his eyes.

They shook hands and Gerry ordered a huge Cappuccino and a Blueberry Muffin the size of a large loaf. Tiggy asked for a flat white.

Gerry looked at his lack of appetite and general apathy pityingly and tried to get down to business.

"Listen mate, I've got a Subaru Outback diesel which is 10 years old and done about 80K miles. It's a four wheel drive estate car jacked up a few more inches than the standard estate and it will go anywhere."

They negotiated on price for a few minutes and Gerry ordered a full breakfast to be consumed after the muffin. Tiggy knew that the guy was a non-drinker but the amount he was eating was heroic. Tiggy relented and ordered an Eggs Benedict as always. They agreed on price eventually and he relaxed over his second coffee, feeling just a tad more human.

The following morning, he left at 5.00 a.m. in the dark green Subaru. He instinctively liked the car; it had been looked after well and had brown leather seats that were worn but extremely comfortable. The 2.5 litre diesel engine was powerful and the fact that it was a 4X4 meant that he could be reasonably adventurous in terms of routes. He'd found the difference between main routes and secondary ones over here to be huge with some of the latter being no better than cart tracks. It would be good to be able to get off the A roads if necessary.

Tiggy was out of Queenstown and filling up with diesel well before breakfast. The boat situation in Akaroa was still worrying. The pretend Italian Roberto Carlotti who ran the boatyard was a shyster of the highest order and couldn't guarantee anything in terms of price or completion. Since the engine fire all those weeks ago he'd demanded more money twice and refused any conversation about insurance or compensation.

The Riva had been back on Tiggy's berth when the accident had happened which was complicated because he hadn't paid for months. According to the boatyard it was caused by Tiggy's ancient electrics, it was more than Roberto's job was worth to let him have it back until fully repaired etc etc etc. As it couldn't go to auction without his seal of approval, Tiggy was up the proverbial creek without the proverbial paddle.

So Tiggy needed to get there as soon as possible and check it out. He also needed to avoid drawing attention to himself and think of where he might stay whilst his boat was in dock. He had a couple of technical questions with own status to think through as well.

When he'd arrived in New Zealand six months back, he'd been on the run from that neanderthal husband of the marina owner in Australia they'd thought was safe in prison. When he'd got out of clink early and the wife had blamed Tiggy, he'd had to make swift exit from the country.

Tiggy got out of Brisbane by seducing a female member of a ship's crew and staying in her cabin until he could jump ship in New Zealand. Which he did without ever having ever having to show his passport. Security in those days had been relatively lax between the two countries especially with regular cargo vessels.

Tiggy had effectively been off-grid ever since. He had a local bank account which had informal connections with his secret bank in Panama and he paid cash where ever possible. But very few people knew his name and even fewer knew where he was. Which is exactly what he was hoping was going to help keep him safe.

A few hundred miles away that safety margin was about to be tested in a way that he couldn't possibly have predicted. Much to her surprise Fran's demand to the Auckland police was agreed to and her documents were returned to her within an hour and she was promised a pardon that would be given in the final exchange of information.

Sergeant Max Lawrence had been under pressure from the Australian gorgon Ms Florence Hasty, despite instructing his office never to give out his mobile, she'd phoned twice whilst he'd been in Auckland and was threatening to catch the first plane over from Sydney. He had put her off by saying that an arrest was imminent and that he'd call her in the next 24 hours. Also, the fact that there was every likelihood that Count Jergov wasn't in Auckland – he could be anywhere by now, including out of the country. This seemed to mollify the monster briefly.

A much more co-operative Miriam Bender had also been in touch from the US to say that her investigators had passed on some extra information about the good Count Jergov and that she would email his report.

Personally, Sergeant Lawrence thought that his key witness, Fran Capelle was probably guilty of the misdemeanour's she had been accused of and probably a lot more. A lifetime of interviewing suspects had given him an instinct for such things and he could tell that she was scared of them finding out something – and it wasn't just the theft of a watch.

When off duty later he went to Murphy's the bar that she'd been working at and had a few pints of Guinness. It wasn't his choice of beer as he had been brought up on Speights served ice cold in the way that Kiwis like. But he'd been to the old country 10 years ago to celebrate his 40th and along with the mandatory trip to Scotland to find where the Lawrence clan came from, he'd gone across to Dublin and tasted the real stuff. He'd never had such expensive booze as when he'd been in Ireland and couldn't understand how a nation of legendary drinkers, allowed their home country to be so expensive. Yet every city from Bangkok to Rio to Auckland had an Irish bar somewhere. Max wondered whether it wasn't the nation's most successful export and whether they had all been set up by the Guinness company.

The manager was a bit of an arrogant idiot until Max flashed his warrant card and mentioned the fact that Fran had accused him of molestation. He knew that would bring out the aggression in the pseudo paddy and it did. Over the next ten minutes the manager said that Fran had tried to sell sexual favours to him (looking at the ape in front of him - a million dollars would not have made that plausible) also that she had short changed the bar in terms of tips and finally that he had caught her trying to take money out of the communal tips jar. All of this minor stuff seemed highly likely but not what Fran was worried about.

Outside he gave the local cop MacArthur a call on the mobile and mentioned his suspicions. MacArthur said that the big crime had been the emptying of a visitor's bank account of several grand but they had no proof, also that the victim definitely didn't want to press charges. MacArthur sounded annoyed and said that Max should stop any further investigations on Fran because his boss just wanted her out of the country. That applied just as certainly whatever information she gave about Count Jergov.

Max had a glass of New Zealand Pinot Noir on the way back to his lodgings and still couldn't get the taste of Guinness off his palette. So he had another and a bag of local fish and chips and started to feel normal. In the morning he was due to see Fran the suspect and get as much out of her as possible before he accompanied her to the airport. She would then catch her international flight to Rio de Janeiro and he would catch a local shuttle back to Dunedin.

Francesca Capelle knew that her lover was special and that really, she should have more loyalty but she was genuinely worried by the older cop, who seemed immune to her charms. Brazil felt so close now and the thought of being imprisoned here was scary. She held out for as long as possible but the cop kept on asking for names, names, names. At the airport she was convinced that they were going to pretend that she could get on the plane and then pull her off at the last possible minute. She had taken thousands out of the guy's account whilst wearing a stupid woolly hat and she couldn't believe she'd got away with it.

"His name was Foghorn." Fran blurted on the security office at the airport, "Mr T Foghorn."

"Are you taking the piss? What kind of name is that?" Sergeant Lawrence asked in disbelief.

"Honestly the name T Foghorn was on his credit cards."

Max thought that she was in some sort of bizarre fantasy or cartoon and went outside to phone Auckland police again. MacArthur agreed that it sounded unlikely but that Ms Capelle needed to be out of the country on the next flight or he would be busted down to constable and he suspected Max would be next on the demotion list.

Chief Inspectors in both regions had apparently talked and decided that she wasn't worth the paperwork and needed to be out of the country without delay. In total frustration Max went back in the airport office and slammed her documents down on the desk. He told Fran that if she ever returned to New Zealand that he would personally ensure that she would be thrown in the high-security jail in Greymouth and that she would never get out. Fran totally believed him and scuttled out of the office to the departure area.

Sergeant Lawrence had never been as close to resigning from the force. He had less respect for the higher ranks than he had for the rule of law. If it had been up to him, he would have sweated Ms Capelle for a few more hours until she came up with a name for Count Jergov that wasn't as ridiculous as T Foghorn. By now she would be on her flight to Brazil and he needed to catch the shuttle back to Dunedin and decide whether this lead was a dead end.

The Subaru had been travelling for two or three hours and Tiggy was really enjoying it. The idea had not been to travel directly to Akaroa but stop somewhere overnight where he could collect his thoughts and make a few calls.

He'd only been away from Queenstown for a few hours but certain people had already started to miss him. A barman called Michael was wondering where his daily drinking buddy had gone since he'd missed his lunchtime session. A certain politician from Brussels called Adele Lang had found George, the man who'd driven Tiggy over the Wanaka and was hoping to subject him to questioning regarding a certain author called Eugene Fenton. She'd seen a TV news broadcast about someone who'd been pulling some sort of writing fraud recently and the photograph looked a bit like her recent bed mate. The only link had been his driver and luckily the hotel reception knew roughly who he was and found a business card. So far, the messages she'd left on this number had not been answered but she was a persistent woman and had a few other contacts she might use. It would be a pity if he turned out to be a shyster because the night in his arms had been orgasmic and the idea of commemorating her Irish father in a novel had been worth the 15 grand she'd paid out.

She just had to ensure that it happened and wondered whether it was time to phone the number of the guy who worked in the New Zealand First Ministers office. Adele was reticent about revealing all the facts about her night with the author as she would have to if this all got too official. She'd been given huge compensation and a year off with full pay by the EU. If she admitted that she'd enjoyed a night of extreme passion with a wandering author, half way through her period of recovery. Someone might just smell a rat.

Tiggy was just wondering whether he would have to sleep in the car when he came across a line of traffic. Outside of Auckland the only times you see a traffic jam is when there's been an accident or when there's some kind of event going on. Tiggy hoped that it wasn't the former and that he didn't have to pass through any police barriers. After a while he saw the hand painted sign stuck in the verge and realised with relief that it was an event.

The sign said 'Geraldine Trots' and Tiggy was curious enough to turn with the flow and see what was happening. He'd had a teenage girlfriend called Geraldine who'd been particularly grateful and attractive in that long auburn haired, pale skinned, willowy way that some well-bred young ladies used to have. After a few sessions at the Tiggy Foghorn training camp – she'd become a lot less restrained. So he looked back at the name with huge nostalgic pleasure.

Ten minutes later, he was still following the other cars and not found anything. The mountains ahead were dramatic as always but this immediate patch of land was flat, fertile and littered with cows, deer and the occasional river. Ahead a few miles he thought that he could see something large and white on the horizon that could be a tent and more cars.

Geraldine Trots turned out to be an impromptu horserace organised by the local farmers and it was similar to the Point to Points his parents had taken him to as a kid. There was one big difference which was this racing was not steeplechasing over fences like at home, this was trotting behind carts that looked like racing chariots. Other than that, the bookies, bars and general atmosphere of hard working country people out for a day's fun were like he remembered.

Tiggy looked like a bit of a toff compared to the rest of the people and so he wandered over to the members tent, mumbling his way in when the guy on the door was having a quick fag. He felt a little exposed without the right ID so managed to borrow a member's badge from a jacket hanging on a nearby chair back and poked it through his own buttonhole. He went over to the bar and ordered a whisky and water and picked up a sausage roll. There were about a dozen people wandering around the tent and a few thousand round the race course, so he felt quite confident that he wouldn't be questioned now he had a badge. Farmers tend to be quite solitary and visitors to this sort of event tend to come from quite a large area. So strangers are not that unusual but Tiggy had forgotten about that famous Kiwi friendly curiosity.

"Haven't seen you before – are you a new member?"

"Pretty new." Tiggy turned to his questioner and realised that this female would have looked perfect in a Jilly Cooper novel. Tall, shapely in her jodhpurs and hacking jacket with blonde hair tied back in a bun and a face that looked ... fit.

"Since you obviously know what's going on here," Tiggy looked her up and down in the same way that she probably looked at a new stallion. "What's the hot tip for the next race?"

"Well I'm in a race at 4.00 p.m. and I'm listed as number 5 – you might bet on me if you're new to the game," she said archly. "The odds will be quite good, I suspect."

"What are the odds of us meeting to discuss your performance after the race?" Tiggy asked with a smile that tried to excuse such a clichéd line.

"You're a little old for this kind of going on, are you not?" She giggled.

"There's only one way to find out ...?"

The smell of horses would be associated with intense but dangerous pleasure for years and Tiggy would be finding straw in his clothing for months. But we are getting ahead of ourselves and first must remember that Tiggy had a betting system to test.

Before the woman's race he tried out a theory that his father had told him about in those Oxfordshire races many years ago. Always put your money on the same horse that the blacksmith's lad does and you won't go far wrong son. His dad Horatio wasn't a big gambler but he always seemed to have winnings at these country races so Tiggy tried the same. There wasn't a blacksmith here but there was a farrier which he guessed was the nearest thing these days, so he waited until a young lad left the workshop and went up to the Tote tent.

"I'd like to put fifty dollars on the same horse as the lad." Tiggy had queued behind a boy who looked and smelled like a person who lived in a stable.

"I'm sorry mate...?" The woman behind the glass looked a bit concerned.

"I know it's strange but my dad came from Ireland and he always said put money on the same horse that the blacksmith's boy did – I don't bet normally but thought I'd give it a try." Tiggy tried to give her his most winning smile.

"Where in Ireland?" the teller asked with genuine interest.

"Kildare. County Kildare." Tiggy answered bluffing unmercifully and trying to add a little touch of brogue.

"Good horse country," the woman answered. "The boy put money on Pete Varney's horse ... strange system your dad had but who knows ... here's your ticket."

Tiggy looked down at the Rolex he'd so recently rescued and realised that the race was due to start in ten minutes. He couldn't quite forgive or forget Fran's betrayal but the pain was starting to fade and the reaction in his trousers when the rider had spoken to him earlier, showed that the experience hadn't quite put him off young women.

He went back and watched the next race from a seat at the front of the members stand and it was a novel experience. He'd never seen trotting before and everything seemed strange, the dirt track was an oval much smaller than most British racecourses and the jockeys sat in a streamlined two-wheeled cart. The horses looked like thoroughbreds and the riders looked like jockeys in their colourful strips. Nothing else was the same apart from the hysteria of the crowd towards the end when after a tight final circuit Number 7 came in first and Tiggy won 300 dollars.

He picked up a race card and looked up the 4.00 p.m. race. There were eight runners and the beautiful bit of female flesh he'd seen earlier had a horse called 'Mad to be here' racing in blue and white livery and carried number five. Her name according to the card was Katherine Wynne.

Whilst he waited for her race Tiggy decided to explore the course and look at the many stalls and tents that surrounded the main stand. There were plenty of bars with very happy punters outside but he was after some food that wasn't the sausage roll/sandwich selection available in the member's tent. Eventually he found a small barbecue stall that was selling bluff oysters and cones of fries and ordered a large portion. He ate these on the trot and they were glorious.

Half way round the circuit he came across a place selling organic vegetables, lovely meat and delicacies like really high quality stock and

Italian style meats. Without really thinking it through he bought a whole range of stuff that he thought he would be able to keep for a few days.

It was odd, he thought just how much he had missed cooking for himself. After weeks on the ship and in the restaurants of Dunedin, the food had been plentiful and mainly good but nothing was quite as good as a favourite meal cooked at home, hopefully with some female company to add a little spice to the event.

Tiggy wasn't a spectacular cook and the Riva galley didn't encourage complicated dishes, but what he did, he reckoned he could do well enough to impress most people. When he was in the Royal Navy, a fellow officer had been of Italian parentage and a fanatical cook. On shore leave once they had a few days free and the guy gave Tiggy a few lessons. Quality ingredients was one of his basic rules and New Zealand was now a much easier place to find them. The country used to be just 'meat and two veg' but in recent years it had got hugely better. Akaroa had a strong French influence and Tiggy had been able to get all kinds of good ingredients. The deli here proved that that attitude was spreading across the country. The stuff in his bag was excellent.

The most likely place for him to stay tonight would be a motel. Most of these – especially the remote ones – tended to have kitchen facilities. So he might just have a chance to eat some home cooked food after all.

The public address system interrupted his thoughts by announcing the runners, non-starters and owners for the next race and Tiggy wandered over to the enclosure. 'Mad to be here' was an extremely attractive black stallion carrying Number 5 as listed. Also, there was an extremely attractive Katherine Wynne who looked even better in her full kit on her racing chariot then he'd anticipated.

Whilst they were assembling the runners (or does one call them trotters?) at the start, Tiggy wandered over to the Central Otago Wine Association and asked what Pinot Noir they had on taste. Fortified by a huge glass of Dry River he went back to the stand as the competitors completed their first circuit. Number Five seemed to be last but there was plenty of time for her to make her move.

It was odd, he thought how strange it was to see these horses going round as if on tracks – no fences, no spills and not as much drunken shouting as in the point-to-points at home.

This was a big sport over here with around twenty thousand spectators attending the national events. Here this was minor league in comparison but still something the locals took seriously. He hadn't put money on his favourite this time or followed his father's advice again. He'd kept his winnings in his pocket and watched the race carefully. 'Mad to be here' was in the middle and making up ground but even Tiggy could see that unless she could get out of the crowd, she might be boxed in. On the last lap she pushed diagonally and her horse seemed to find an extra gear. The blue and white strip stood out and she pushed on and the over excited announcer seemed to be mentioning her every second. He pushed closer to the rail and she appeared to be in the leading group as it passed through the finish.

Tiggy waited for the announcer to state the places but there was a hiss of interference as the officials conferred almost off microphone. The delay was explained that there was a steward's enquiry and the final places would be confirmed in a few minutes. Groans from the spectators, some of whom were scrabbling on the floor trying to find the betting slips they'd thrown away in disgust. After what seemed to be ten minutes, it was stated that Ms Katherine Wynne had been disqualified and there was a collective cheer.

He went over to the collecting ring and found a white-faced Ms Wynne holding the reins of her horse accompanied by a little guy who might have been a trainer or stable boy or something. As he got closer, he could hear her swearing using words that most young ladies never learn. The boy looked terrified and even the horse looked abashed.

"Sorry about the result but I have an urge to make you dinner – it must be something primeval after seeing you battling in the arena or something." Tiggy whispered in her direction.

"I'm so fucking angry – I don't think I could eat for a week?" Katherine didn't seem fazed, she looked angry but just a hint of a smile was starting to show.

"I have a patented method of helping female competitors relax and I'm dying to try it on you." Tiggy tried to look like her favourite physiotherapist and failed. "Where is your horse box and is it large?"

She looked round at him with a quizzical look but Tiggy realised that that he had definitely got her attention and that sometimes fortune favours the brave.

The horse box was the size of an international truck and liveried in an elegant dark blue with 'Wynne Racing' in fine gold script. Katherine had only hesitated for a few seconds before leaving the horse with her assistant and leading him to the competitor's area at the back. She was obviously a game girl but losing did not suit her and she was still swearing as she pointed a remote control at the side door of the box. A large door slid sideways and she led the way up the chrome steps giving him a chance to see that shapely arse again.

Inside was a leather bench seat and everything the professional rider might use on a long trip to nowhere. Galley, loo and pull down, bunks were designed beautifully to stow away when not needed. The whole interior reminded him of the larger Riva boats he'd seen online where space was at a premium but luxury was still a necessity.

All Tiggy needed was the bench and using a tone of voice that he imagined might have been used by top-class trainers he instructed Katherine to remove all her clothes. She didn't hesitate.

He then gave her what his father would have called 'a good rogering'. It was lacking in his customary finesse but his instincts were right and she came good within just a few minutes and he was able to massage her shoulders and back to show how much he cared. The relaxation exercise worked and she stopped swearing and started giggling.

A few minutes later they dressed and left the horse box, both feeling as though the exercise had done them a power of good. Tiggy remembered his promise and was concerned about where he was going to spend the night and do his cooking.

"I have all the ingredients, so where can I cook this meal for you?"

"Do you live round here?"

"No, I'm travelling North."

"I thought I hadn't heard of you – after all, someone with that sort of cure for hyper tension, would be famous round here" Katherine said with a knowing smile.

"One tries ... there are so few decent bodies worth using my skills on ... but one tries." Tiggy bowed modestly.

Katherine looked him over and seemed to consider things for a few minutes, then she grabbed his arm and smiled.

"I'll tell you what, follow me home and you can use my kitchen – it doesn't get much use with me there as I'm not much of a cook."

They arranged to meet at the North exit of the course in 45 minutes and Tiggy went back to the deli tent to get some more food. He picked up some local fizz as well and wandered back to his car, thinking that anybody who could afford a truck like hers probably had a kitchen that was out of this world. His speciality was normally cooked on a bottled gas stove, so he hoped that he was up to it. But nothing ventured, nothing gained he thought to himself, practising his mental proverbs rather than listen to the local Kiwi radio which was starting to irritate a little.

He was in the Subaru and waiting as agreed when he spotted the big horse box in the queue and pushed in behind the Wynne Racing truck as it roared on to the main road. The roads here were long straight and flat with a river to the left and a mountain range to the right and Tiggy was able to dawdle behind at 60 without ever losing sight of his quarry. The only thing that passed him was a mad kid in a souped-up Subaru with big bore exhaust who overtook both of them at around 120 and nearly gave him a heart attack.

After about half an hour the horse box turned right and he was on an unsigned gravel road, so he had no idea whether he was on a private drive or a minor road. He found out a few miles later when he turned on a sharp left-hand bend coming out of wood and saw a white building perched on a hillside. It looked like something out of 'Architects Monthly' or 'Grand Designs' and turned out to be where Katherine Wynne lived in splendid isolation.

She said later that her estranged husband was away buying art in the US or in his Auckland apartment most of the time. He had designed the house and was tremendously artistic but apparently found married life a little difficult. He loved beautiful things and was kind to her whenever he was home but they lived separate lives. Katherine hadn't said much more about their relationship but Tiggy got the drift.

The kitchen still had the protective plastic covers on the hot plates and the controls looked like something out of the bridge of the starship Enterprise. But Tiggy had taken an electronics course in the Royal Navy to operate advanced weaponry and after consideration he thought he could master this device. After a few button pushes and a prayer to Escoffier the lights on the hob started to flash and Tiggy was in business.

First, they had a glass of New Zealand fizz and got to know each other. As always Tiggy had a number of surnames and ranks he could choose from but chose Eugene Fenton for old times' sake. To make it easier for himself he said that Tiggy was what his friends called him. Really, he should have been more inventive as this was the formula he'd used with the last young woman in his life – Fran. But he wasn't superstitious and using his real name of Terrence Foghorn would have felt ridiculously out of character.

Risotto was what he intended to cook and he found that many women found the idea of preparing it intimidating. Tiggy always quoted Elisabeth

David – 'Italian Risotto is of a totally different nature to other rice dishes and uniquely wonderful'. Tiggy knew that as with most dishes, the quality of the ingredients was important and he had managed to get some superfino arborio rice, some local mushrooms, Parmigiano cheese and some wonderful chicken stock from the deli at the racecourse.

First, he had to search round for a heavy sauce pan and this took some time as the kitchen was obviously not often used as a kitchen. Eventually he found a Le Creuset pan at the back of a cupboard and dragged it over to the cooker.

Risotto had originally been just a northern Italian dish because rice grew there and was a peasant dish using whatever other ingredients were available. In the south pasta was the staple ingredient.

because it could be made from the wheat that grew there. The unique thing about risotto was the combination of al dente rice with the creaminess of the other ingredients. Even Escoffier declared it to be a wonderful dish.

Tiggy took his time and was careful to stir at the right time and add the cheese and mushrooms late. Risotto is not a dish you can ignore – it demands your total attention and his navy mate said that each cooking took a little bit of your soul. Tiggy was not sure that he had any soul left but was really happy to repeat the story to Katherine who was sitting at the end of the island unit, still wearing her riding gear. She looked suitably impressed.

In the end Tiggy was moderately happy with his version of Cep Risotto which he served on big stoneware plates immediately it was ready. They ate on a large kitchen table which had been sliced from some local hardwood tree and sat on chairs that looked like vintage Conran in bent steel and basketweave. Our itinerant chef found a bottle of 2016 Barolo in the wine store and opened it with due ceremony. Unlike the kitchen this cabinet looked well used and was state-of-the art temperature controlled and huge.

Katherine was absolutely gobsmacked. The rice glistened with a sauce she couldn't quite identify but which was absolutely sumptuous and rich. She would never have thought about having red wine with the dish but the combination was stunning. Tiggy had made enough for four people but Katherine went back twice. The Italians often fry up any risotto left over the following morning as a torta. In this case Tiggy realised that wasn't going to be possible.

After all that indulgent food, bed afterwards could have been an anti-climax (in more ways than one) but she managed heroically. Tiggy was also satisfied that after his recent problems with younger women, he hadn't lost his magic touch. The lessons were still working even after all these years and Katherine was a quick learner.

He slept the sleep of the just and woke up at 6.00 a.m. There was no one to be seen anywhere so he wandered round the house whilst she was still asleep. The interior seemed stark in the morning light and Katherine had said that every surface had been made out of concrete which had been polished or moulded to give different effects.

The scenery was stunning and every glass wall showed a view like something out of a New Zealand tourist poster. There were deer on the hills, miles away and sheep in meadows closer by but no human beings visible anywhere.

The only colours in the whole place came from a huge handmade sofa in burnt orange wool that curved round the sitting room for around 15 feet. Also, from four large abstract paintings that hung on the interior walls and were rich in reds, ochres and yellows.

Tiggy eventually found a small room at the back that looked as though people lived in it, which was probably a boot room and laundry. There were a few dozen wellies and outdoor shoes on racks and a large Belfast sink and loo. Tiggy went for a wee and noticed a painting that looked like it was by an Aboriginal or Māori artist on the wall. Tiggy quite liked it.

It was an abstract or primitive painting of a figure squatting by a fire and it was in vivid reds and blue oils. Tiggy removed it quietly from the wall and took it out to the Subaru, where he hid it below the tailgate floor wrapped in a shirt.

His view that it wasn't really thieving - it was probably worth absolutely nothing otherwise it would have been in the living room with the other paintings and displayed properly. As far as Tiggy was concerned, it was a small gift to cover all his cooking and lovemaking efforts the previous night. Also, it was a keepsake to remind him of his day at the races and the young filly he'd ridden. Bloody hell Tiggy thought, 'Young Filly' was the sort of phrase his father would have used and embarrassed anybody under the age of a hundred. He must guard against inherited Terry Thomas tendencies he thought as he shut the tailgate.

Tiggy wasn't quite sure where he planned to put the painting as boats don't have much wall space. But when he sold the Riva and made a fortune, then he might just buy a house. Where it might be and what sort of house, was a question that he needed to think about. He hadn't lived anywhere onshore for years and Australia and New Zealand were attractive but might be a little dangerous whilst the authorities were interested.

To avoid thinking too deeply, Tiggy stripped off his clothes and wandered back to the bedroom where Katherine was still fast asleep, with her blonde hair spread out across the pillow and just an enticing bit of brown shoulder showing out of the duvet. This is the life he thought and drifted off himself and only woke when someone gently touched his side.

"Can you ride? "Katherine asked with that smokey early morning voice that a man could learn to love.

"I rode as a kid, but I'm no kind of professional."

"Let's ride out – the morning is absolutely lovely and there's something I've always wanted to try."

"I haven't got any gear" Tiggy added sleepily.

"For what had in mind – you really won't need any clothes at all – come down in five minutes and I'll saddle up Gregory."

Tiggy was intrigued and after attending to his morning ablutions he wandered over to the window. This place was absolutely stunning with glass walls facing in every direction. In the distance he could see a small range of hills and miles of fields covered in what he thought were deer, who had moved further up into the hills since he'd looked earlier.

He couldn't see any other houses or signs of human occupation in any direction and wondered whether Katherine really enjoyed this kind of isolation.

Walking out of the back door he felt a little self-conscious, wearing just a pair of shoes, but in the yard, he saw a totally naked Katherine holding on to the reins of a large cob which looked a much more stable platform for a naked amateur such as himself.

Tiggy remembered how to hold on to the reins and mount on the left and managed to swing his leg over the horse and get his feet into the stirrups, gripping both sides of the horse with his thighs as his riding tutor had insisted all those years ago.

"Where's your mount?" Tiggy asked looking down at the tall and wonderfully athletic figure below, naked apart from a pair of brown leather riding boots.

"You are," Katherine answered as she held the front of his saddle and swung herself on to his lap, facing him, which was a surprise.

His male member had already got the message before Tiggy's brain had and was standing proudly erect as Katherine manoeuvred herself on top of him, wriggled with a happy sigh and fastened her arms tightly around him.

"Walk on," she said and the horse obediently walked out of the yard with its mistress moving slowly on top of Tiggy and starting to gasp with pleasure. The horse seemed to know its own way down the track, which was just as well because Tiggy was starting to lose control and worry that if this beast ever broke into a canter, then his lovemaking days could be over and he would be singing castrato.

This was an erotic experience that would wake Tiggy up in the middle of the night with a tremendous stalk-on for years to come and though Tiggy prided himself on his skills, this was all down to Katherine's imagination. She eventually shuddered to another climax about half a mile later after showing signs of physical dexterity in the saddle that definitely wouldn't have been recognised by the Pony Club.

"That was absolutely wonderful," she said and slid down off the horse grabbing hold of the reins and leading the poor nag back to the yard.

Tiggy looked down at that lovely blonde head and wondered whether he was changing. Katherine was not the older, larger, model that he'd been attracted to most of his life since Maddie, but she was incredibly attractive. Part of the attraction was that she was well-bred in the same way that her horses were. Looking down at her, she was fit and had muscles in her arms and legs, not just softness. Her breasts and bum were a work of art and you knew instinctively that she would look just as good in twenty years' time as she did now.

The other difference was she knew her own mind and had led much of the lovemaking, appreciating his skills, but also demanding more than most women he'd ever met. Her husband must be gay or mad, life with her could be extraordinary – as long as you didn't weaken.

Talking about weakness, he realised that the inside of his thighs and calves were rubbed raw with the effort of trying to grip the horse. He desperately needed a bath, some breakfast and then to find out where the hell he was.

He reckoned that Akaroa was still about three hours away and he needed to remember to be careful. There had been nothing about him on TV that he'd seen recently but he hadn't really had time to check. He had to presume that the forces of evil might still be searching for him and even Katherine Wynne was a potential risk as she knew his nickname.

The beard had developed into a full set that he thought made him look a little like an old royal and Katherine quite liked. As a disguise it worked reasonably well but any decent police officer would have predicted this sort of effort and had artists mock up a bearded Count.

He almost felt guilty as he drove away after breakfast and left her looking at her laptop, pretending not to care that he was leaving. This place was one of the most spectacular houses he had ever seen but it was around twenty minutes off the nearest blacktop road and far too remote for a red-blooded woman like her. She'd said that there were a couple of farm workers helping to run the farm but they had their own cottage around half a mile away. Tiggy almost felt like taking her with him but that would have been crazy.

What he did do however was make a call to an old friend in Akaroa.

"Hello this is Pierre's fine restaurant how may I help you?"

"Bruce this is Tiggy – how's you doing?"

'Tiggy … or perhaps I should call you Count Jergov … it's been weeks and we thought you might have been kidnapped by one of those rich widow ladies you were with."

"Bruce, you have no idea but first ... the good Count may well be in a little trouble with the authorities, so can you please forget that you ever met him?"

"Err ... well I guess so, but we really liked him," Bruce answered with regret thinking about the extra turnover the good Count had generated.

"I know Bruce and I'll tell you more in a couple of days. First do you still have that apartment in town and is it empty?"

"Sure, the last of the people left on Tuesday."

"Can I rent it for a few weeks? The boat won't be usable for a while."

"Course you can Tiggy."

They discussed rates for a couple of minutes and then came to an agreement. The rent charged was extortionate really but Tiggy was in no position to bargain too much. The apartment was hidden above some shops on the very edge of town and had a great view of the bay. They agreed handover details and Tiggy swore Bruce to secrecy as he wanted to pay a surprise visit to the boatyard and see just how well that shyster Roberto had been spending his money on the Riva.

Tiggy was now a little more confident. Nothing regarding the good Count had been mentioned on this morning's TV or on the radio news in the car. He was on Highway 1 filling up with diesel and the attendant was talking to him like a local. The sun was shining, the car was going beautifully and he was planning to find a bar or pub where he could get quietly drunk and

176

fall into bed before making the final stage of his journey tomorrow.

Had Tiggy had any conception of the forces who were trying to find the Count or his alter egos then he might well have been less sanguine.

Sergeant Lawrence had been back from Auckland for a day and chased up as many enquiries as possible. The name Foghorn seemed to be genuine as not only had the Brazilian woman seen it on the evil Count's credit cards. Miriam Bender, the woman off the cruise ship had employed an investigator and he had come up the same surname after finding some other evidence recently. The nationality of the man or where he lived were still unknown.

It was possible that a bank search for such an unusual name might reveal more detail but the paperwork involved in getting financial information with data protection, human rights and every other piece of legislation getting in the way meant that it wouldn't happen quickly. This guy was not stupid and Max was convinced that by the time he had got answers from the banks then the Count or Mr Foghorn or whatever his name was, would have left the country. After all, judging by the number of people he had probably conned, he had well over a hundred grand and with that kind of money, you could be anywhere by now.

Max would have been tempted to quietly let this case drop down to the bottom of his in-box but the Australian woman, was calling everyone senior in his office every few days and had some contacts in the Wellington party office who were also giving him hell.

Max had pinned a NZ map on his wall with red pins showing possible sightings which so far including Port Chalmers where the Count had almost certainly conned the Chinese couple, Central Dunedin where he had stayed with the lovely Francesca. And recently he had an embarrassed call from some sort of Euro MP, whatever that was, complaining about a similar publishing con in Wanaka. She had been staying at the Invercastle hotel – a hotel that Max had only read about in the gossip columns. The MP was anxious to get her money back but not get any publicity.

So, the good Count had obviously moved out of Max's patch but sadly his boss had talked to his equivalent in Central Otago and they were both anxious to for Max to carry on with his enquiries. With the political complications growing rapidly alongside this investigation, Max had the gentle feeling in his guts, that he was being stitched up by the top-brass again.

The other problem was that Max was developing a sneaky admiration for Count Jergov, as his crimes were so well executed that you could tell that many of his victims really seemed to love him. Having talked to Miriam and Elmer separately they were as concerned about the Count's wellbeing as well as the amount of money he had extorted from them. Elmer quoted the passage he had written about his partner verbatim and would have been happy to drop the whole thing if the Count could have finished it.

Max had read stories about this sort of behaviour in the text books but never encountered the loyalty and affection that a good fraudster can generate as directly before. The physical descriptions were all the same and the man was obviously tall, slim, good looking with dark hair and around 40 years old. He was well - if occasionally eccentrically dressed and extremely presentable. So, he was handsome and people like good-looking people, but his personality and presentation skills must be extraordinary.

When Max first heard about the scam – paying for the chance to become a character in a romantic novel – he thought it was a great idea. But when he heard what people had paid for it, he was astonished. Given, the people targeted were rich, but still Max couldn't quite get his head round paying tens of thousands of dollars to be named, even if it was going to be the best book in the world. The other mystery was the man's nationality. According to different witnesses he could be Lithuanian, Canadian, Kiwi or English, people had different opinions.

Max tried to plan his next few days. First, he fired up his computer and reviewed every bit of information he'd got in over the last few days. Despite his admiration for this guy, he had to make some progress and maybe he'd missed something that might help.

He went through the files till it was dark outside which at this time of the year meant that it was around nine o'clock and he was late. He'd been due to go with his wife and kids to a neighbour house for a barbecue and forgot to phone. He'd already been away in Auckland for a few days and though his wife Kaylene was very understanding normally, this might be taking the Mickey.

"Where are you - as if I didn't know?" Kay answered his call sounding a lot more friendly than he deserved.

"Sorry ... really sorry. I just got hung up on this case."

"It's OK, Greg said come over, there's a steak on the barbie now and a new Pinot he wants you to try."

"OK, half an hour and I'll be there." Max really didn't want to go but didn't want to upset Kay more. Greg was a nice guy but his insurance business was going like a train and all you normally heard was what car, what holiday or what new house they were planning and it tended to cause problems when he got home. Not that Kaylene was money mad or anything but a Sergeants pay wasn't going to buy them anything like that.

He parked the squad car round the corner and took off his tie and jacket, so he looked a little bit off duty and pushed open the tall gate to the property. He could smell the food and hear the chatter from the back and walked round with his hands raised in mock surrender as an apology. Kay smiled from across the yard and Greg handed him a glass and plate.

The steak was wonderful Brazilian rib-eye and the Roaring Meg Pinot Noir was absolutely stunning. Kaylene was not annoyed despite all the delay and was enjoying a few glasses herself, so Max was relaxing for the first time in ages. Then Greg started on about the latest acquisition he was planning to make when he got his bonus.

"We've never been into boats – Nichola didn't like them. But she saw this boat featured in Auckland Life magazine and fell in love. It's 20 metres, sleeps four, has a sodding great engine and she's persuaded me to get it…"

Max had a eureka moment and pretended that his mobile was ringing. Shouting over to his wife and waving apologetically to his hosts, he ran out of the house and got in his car, putting his jacket back on and yelling into the radio.

Back in the office he was trying to get his sub-conscious to work because Greg's story had triggered something. There was something in the Count Jergov witness statements that he'd forgotten – something insignificant at the time but vital now. It took half an hour and a grovelling call to his wife but he knew what it was.

The guy who had teamed up with Miriam Bender to report the Count Jergov fraud on the cruise ship had mentioned something in one of the early reports about a boat. A quick email to Elmer Flannigan had given him more detail. Apparently, the Count had said that he was having to raise money to restore a really valuable boat and that was why he was charging people to be in his book. Elmer said that as he was a marina owner himself, he'd shown interest and Count Jergov had shown him a photograph of a boat that looked like something out of an old movie.

Elmer said that the boat was a vintage Riva speedboat and it was extremely rare. He said that these boats were much sort after now and

179

that when auctioned it might make millions. Trying to be helpful Elmer said that the Riva would probably be easier to find than the Count himself. Max hadn't really registered that fact at the time but now it might be a possible way of locating Count Jergov, Eugene Fenton, Tiggy Foghorn or whatever name he was using this week.

Max knew he was in for an all-nighter at the office and fired up his computer again.

Roberto Carlotti loved restoration jobs that were money pits. His family had been boatbuilders in New Zealand since his grandfather came over in 1970 and though Roberto had been born in NZ, he'd been getting more and more Italian every year. He looked Italian which helped and the permanent tan, stocky build and dark hair had won him plenty of admirers. He'd got into the part so much that he'd had to learn Italian which meant that now he could speak English with a perfect Italian accent and Italian with an appalling Scottish accent. He'd never realised that his tutor was one of the Italians who'd come back from Glasgow many years ago and acquired a pronounced Jock accent.

So Roberto had been a bit of a laughing stock on his first trip back to the ancestral homeland and locals kept on joking about when he was going to open the chip shop in Venice or Como. But he hadn't really understood the jokes and he'd spread the cash around liberally and money was tight, so he became quite a celebrity.

One thing they respected was craftsmanship and the emigrants to New Zealand had built up a good team of boatbuilders, who were all Italian background and in some cases second generation from those his grandfather had trained. Roberto had visited Riva at exactly the right time when they were looking to expand their market and after-sales business in Australasia. They were impressed and after a lengthy induction course a year later he was officially agent for Riva and a number of other European boats.

The company had not made much money out of the connection so far as the big sales push into Asian markets had been interrupted by Covid and other global trends but Roberto loved having the Riva name on his masthead.

Then the ex Royal Navy guy had come in with the 1920's Riva over a year ago and it had contributed greatly to the company profit margins ever since. The 1920's boat had had a wonderful Ferrari engine – at least it had until the fire had meant a complete rebuild. It had lovely lines and a unique cabin but as both client and himself knew – it wasn't quite Kosher. Somebody many years ago had done a bodge job on the hull and that could vastly reduce its value if it was ever revealed. Which is why Roberto had charged him a fortune to rectify and why the client had never really questioned it.

If the Riva ever went to auction and Roberto was pretty certain that was the plan, then the boatyards certification of work done along with all the authentic Riva stamps he could find, could well be worth an additional few thousand. And that point was coming soon, because he'd heard from the village gossip that Tiggy was planning a surprise visit soon. Roberto realised that he must put together an expensive snag list before he arrived.

He knew the guy wasn't an engineer so a little bit of crap in the fuel would make the engine sound rough. A few deliberately loosened connections would mean that some of the instruments would fail. Both of which the yard could get away with charging a couple of thousand dollars in cash to remedy.

It helped that Roberto really didn't like the guy. He was too smooth and handsome in a kind of British way and distracted the women away from himself. Until the naval guy arrived Roberto had his pick of the local and tourist girls as his Italian accent and his tan were irresistible.

What made it worse was that according to the women in Pierre's Restaurant, the guy was a lover of staggering quality and credited with lots more notches on his bedpost than Roberto could claim in his wildest dreams. Akaroa is a very small town and a reputation like that can be very valuable for a single man over the cold winter months.

He had one other concern about his customer and that was he didn't know his full name. Everyone in the town called him Tiggy and money requested came in by bank transfer from a Panamanian bank so his identity was a bit of a mystery. Roberto always hated mysteries and vowed to find out more when the man returned to Akaroa. Which would have to be soon because he had to see the work so far and sign off the last few thousand dollars of contract which was mainly upholstery and trims. Plus, of course the engine and electric faults he was going to manufacture tonight.

Roberto had looked on the internet and seen that companies like Christies and Sotheby's in London, New York and Beijing had sold vintage boats in the past. Some of the boats had gone for millions because in recent years the Russians and Chinese had got interested.

Roberto would offer to buy the boat first (at a discounted price) because he thought that he would make a fortune out of the deal. He didn't think the guy Tiggy was stupid but if he couldn't afford the highly inflated prices that the boatyard would charge in order to get its certification, there was just a chance he might weaken and accept. After all, 500K in your hand and no more boatyard bills to pay might just be attractive to a mystery man whose provenance was as doubtful as some of his boats for sale.

Roberto went to the yard where the Riva was on blocks and took some photographs. He then sent them to some family contacts in Milan and in Las Vegas, where there were a number of people with plenty of money and a good eye for Italian quality. Judging by what he'd seen on the previous sales, the market for vintage boats was good and this Riva could easily make 2.5 million dollars – US.

Tiggy was in a library in the town of Roberts Creek looking at a computer and charging his mobile. His only aim was to check the news and find out a convivial place to stay before he made his push into Akaroa tomorrow. Knowing the friendly curiosity of most small-town Kiwis would be aroused by a stranger in their library, he had to decide what name he was going to use from his repertoire of

identities. Over the last few weeks, he'd cheated by using the nickname Tiggy rather than any of his full personas. He needed to think fast because the curiosity of the volunteer on the desk was obviously driving her crazy as she kept on looking in his direction. She'd been too polite to enquire when he'd first arrived and been put off by his studious looking at the screen but he knew that in the next few minutes she'd break and have to ask who he was, where he was from and so on.

There was nothing concerning Count Jergov on the online news but using that name would be unprofitable in both senses. It was too memorable and Tiggy had vowed to kill him off.

Eugene Fenton was his favourite author and Tiggy still carried his book in his backpack. He'd done a great job in Wanaka but he too was probably on the wanted list and needed to go into hiding.

Tiggy was cursed by having a real name that was also highly suspect- Terence Foghorn was a proud English name but not right for this occasion. In the end Tiggy did what many people do when looking for a code name or security question – he thought of his Mother.

"Terry DuPont from Oxfordshire." Tiggy stood up and introduced himself to the woman who'd eventually cracked and come over in the guise of offering him a coffee.

She was called Jaylene and was a short fair-haired woman who looked as though she spent most of her life mountain biking, hiking or running marathons for fun. Her Lycra fitted her like a second skin and her bright blue eyes and taut skin made her look the picture of health. After a decent cup of Watties tea for him and some sort herbal concoction for her she had settled down to some serious interrogation.

She was not fanciable in any of the normal ways that brought a rise to Tiggy's manhood but a lovely woman. She was 28 years old and she was planning a trip abroad. Every Kiwi female he'd met seemed to talk about trips to the old country they were planning or had been on in their youth. This one's ancestors were from Scotland and England and she was planning to save up enough holiday and money to go in a year.

She asked where he lived and he said he'd moved to North Island, NZ which seemed to disappoint her. Then he realised that a friend in Akaroa had told him that Kiwi's abroad always take advantage of foreign contacts and stay when they can. They are nearly always good company and welcome in Scotland, England or anywhere in the UK and it saves them money. So remember if you say to a Kiwi – 'next time you are in MacTavish, Bog Guinness or Newton Burgoland or whatever out of the way place in the UK you are from,' don't be surprised if they turn up.

Tiggy – or Terry Dupont as he needed to remember his name was, had disappointed by being resident in NZ. But he had a good chat and he checked out a couple of the places close to Akaroa that he'd seen online and which looked like they might be entertaining. He realised after a while that she was not likely to be a good source as fitness freaks don't generally go on the piss or attend drinking sessions. The one hopeful remark she made was that she wouldn't suggest that he went to the 'Goldminers Arms' near Copper's Creek, as she'd heard that they'd had some trouble. To a parched and hungry for male company Tiggy this looked like a good place to start.

He still had a few thousand dollars in cash and so had no need to use any cards. Tiggy realised that his phone had plenty of juice and that he needed to get on the road, so he thanked Jaylene and walked out of the library and back to the car. The days were getting colder now and there was a strong wind blowing up the high street and there were dark clouds massing ahead. He thought that the Swan-Dri coat he'd bought all those weeks ago in the Dunedin charity shop was going to get some use.

He was starting to really enjoy driving the Subaru. It may be a few years old but it was well equipped and comfortable and purred along for hours. Tiggy turned on the heated seat and looked forward to the journey. The only downside was local radio in New Zealand, which meant that listening in the car could be a little boring unless you were interested in agriculture or 1950's country music. He put the radio on search and eventually found a news channel and listened to the mid-day update. A metal bridge had been stolen over the weekend which impressed everyone apart from the guy who'd plunged into the stream that morning. Vineyards were forecasting another good grape harvest and asking for volunteers to help with the picking. Internationally there were more concerns about the immediate imprisonment of rioters in Hong Kong. Nothing was mentioned about a notorious Lithuanian Count, a romantic author called Fenton or a mysterious conman called Foghorn.

Tiggy was relieved and popped in to a service station cafe for petrol and a cup of tea. Seeing them on the menu, he also couldn't resist a blueberry muffin which arrived warm and the size of a small boulder. He gave the young woman behind the counter his appreciation and she popped round the counter wiping her hands on her tea-towel.

"Will you be having a wee desert? I've got some homemade Lemon Meringue you might like."

Tiggy could tell by the white spiked hair, the tattoos and facial piercings that she was some sort of punk revival enthusiast but a genuinely beautiful woman underneath. What's more her muffins were spectacular.

He ordered the desert and asked her about places to stay, thinking that this kind of woman probably knew more about where the action was round here than the fitness freak he'd met earlier. Also that to her, he probably looked a hundred years old. She mentioned the Goldsmiths Arms outside Coopers Creek and that there was live music that night so probably worth a try. He said that he hoped it had decent beer and she confirmed that it had a range of good ales, but added that it could get a little raucous at closing time. Tiggy said that he'd been away at sea for a few months and needed some fun. She nodded understandingly and went back behind the counter.

The desert was excellent and Tiggy realised by the pressure on his waistband that he was getting back into bad Kiwi habits. He never used to eat muffins or deserts and what food he normally had was good meat or fish and vegetables. Any calories were normally used up during his extensive nocturnal liaisons.

He realised that he had a difficult decision to make. No cake or more sex.

As over the last few weeks he'd sustained himself during a ménage à trois, satisfied an Anglo-Irish sex fanatic and brought a new meaning to bareback riding, he didn't think rejecting sex was possible. So regrettably, he vowed never to touch a muffin again.

The last hour on the Canterbury Plains was fairly boring. It is one of the few extensive flat areas in the country and very fine agricultural land. The monotony was only broken up by lines of high conifers that presumably acted as windbreaks or borders. Also, he noticed that some farms had oval tracks and it took a while to work out what they were.

As he remembered from a couple of days ago, trotting racing was big in South Island and these farms were obviously big enough to have their own racing stables. After another few miles he noticed signs to the right and turned. The Goldsmiths Arms was just another few miles and it looked just the right sort of place.

Many people don't realise that New Zealand had a gold rush that was even bigger than California and that the country still produces it by the ton. The Goldsmith Arms looked pretty old by Kiwi standards and dated back to 1829 according to the date above the porch.

Tiggy pushed open the old plank front door and almost fell down the two steps into the room. His eyesight adjusted gradually and he could see a bar open to the garden at the far end with sunlight streaming through. He carefully pushed his way through the tables and chairs to where he could see an old bloke talking to someone in the outside bar.

He scanned the pumps and was gratified to see not just Speights and Lion but Black Sheep, Bass and some locally brewed stuff which might be palatable.

"My names Dupont, I've booked a room for tonight." Tiggy realised that the old guy wasn't really into customer service because he turned round with a look of annoyance that anyone would deign to interrupt the pearls of wisdom he was spouting to another local.

"You seem to have some decent beer here at least – I hope you don't serve them all at minus 20 degrees though?" Tiggy added.

"What are you some kind of fuckin Englishman?" The landlord added with a half-smile.

"I'm a bit of mongrel – a bit of everything – but I like to be able to taste a decent beer."

The guy handed over a key and a piece of card with all the normal stuff hotels are supposed to tell guests and directed him over to some rooms on the other side of the garden.

The rooms were lovely. Obviously, they had been converted from stables or outhouses and they had exposed beams, stone walls and real character. The bed was comfortable and the bathroom was almost as luxurious as the one on the cruise ship. Tiggy reckoned that he had around an hour before things started to get busy so lay back on the bed and switched the TV on.

He woke up two hours later to the urgent opening music of a documentary programme he'd not seen before. Following the formula of most programmes, it was fronted by a black female and a white male both in their middle thirties:

Discovery Tonight asks. "Are we all becoming too trusting or just Gullible?" The Māori presenter handled the question with huge gravitas, as if the world was ending.

"Recently off our shores 10 women and 1 man were conned out of nearly half a million dollars." The white guy looked almost as shocked as Tiggy was about the outrageous exaggeration.

"A man pretending to be a Count carried out this fraud in New Zealand and on the cruise ship *Amazon*. Police think he is still in this country." Original photographs of Count Jergov taken by Miriam and library shots of the ship steaming through an azure sea were flashed behind the presenters and Tiggy was grateful that they hadn't mocked up him with a beard or done any more enhancement of the images. He stayed for a few more minutes where psychologists were interviewed and historic frauds like London Bridge and the Ponse scam were analysed. Luckily, they didn't mention him again specifically and he decided it was safe to go through to the bar.

Tiggy looked at himself in the mirror and decided that Terry Dupont was going to be a Kiwi, but one who'd left for Europe as a kid because his dad was in the navy and now returned. He was wearing a check shirt and jeans he'd bought all those weeks ago in Farmers and a decent pair of English style brogues he'd picked up at the races. Despite the documentary he'd just seen, he didn't think Kiwis were gullible, but he did think that off the rugby field, they were friendly and interested in strangers. So he thought that his background story had a fair chance of being believed.

As he walked over the courtyard, he noticed that it was dark and there was a good hum of male voices from the bar. There was someone putting steaks on a huge outside barbecue but it was drink that he was after with

186

a vengeance. He pushed through the back door and stood behind three blokes who looked like farmers and waited until the same old guy noticed his presence.

"A pint of Black Sheep please and make sure it's not cold."

"It's Major Disaster, the English Master." The landlord said as he pulled the pint with due deference and Tiggy ignored the racial rhyme and drank half the glass in one gulp.

"That's still a bit cold for a proper beer but if you pull another now, then it might be warm enough for a civilised man to drink when I'm ready" Tiggy said with a smile, noticing that he was now the centre of attention and realising that that was a dangerous place to be for a fugitive.

The landlord laughed and the tension was broken. Tiggy backed off and looked round the bar, realising that this was a special place in a country that had many good things but a fine old English style pub wasn't common. This had beams, stone walls and a cast-iron fireplace with a fire that looked as though it never went out. On the walls were mining memorabilia and old posters and on the flagged floor there were hand-woven rugs. Tiggy loved the place.

It was funny, our hero joined the navy when very young and knew the Plymouth pubs but hadn't really known what a country pub was until he was in his 20's and posing around in his illicit Aston Martin. Whilst he'd dated the titled stick-insect he'd visited lots of good country inns. He remembered the Tower Inn in Slapton, the White Horse in Ilminster and the exceedingly upmarket Smoking Dog in Marlborough. Each had a style that had evolved over a long drunken history and was quite often a male bastion but quite often classless with decidedly agricultural labourers mixing with executives with no problem at all. These places never had TV, they despised fruit machines and they were unique to England. The Goldsmiths Arms was the nearest thing he'd ever found to that level of importance in NZ. He told the landlord this and received his next pint at room temperature along with a satisfied nod.

The two guys at the bar had turned round with good-natured interest and plied him with questions as Tiggy started his third pint of Black Sheep. Tiggy remembered his story and introduced himself as Terry Dupont and explained that he'd grown to love country pubs whilst he was in England.

The two large men lived in the area and one was involved in agricultural machinery and seemed quite affable whilst the other didn't seem quite as open or friendly. They looked as though they'd been there for a lot longer and were ordering yet another jug of Speights with local whisky chasers.

Tiggy moved back to a table which was made from some kind of up-turned barrel. With all that beer on-board and the pints, he intended to have over the next few hours, he certainly didn't want to sit and the barrel was a wonderful leaning post. The old man behind the bar lifted the flap and wandered round the room picking up glasses until he reached our author.

"Major Dupont, I'm afraid that you have drunk us out of Black Sheep, but I have a local ale brewed just half a mile down the road that I don't mind wasting on you."

"As long as it isn't as cold as that Speights, I'm willing to give it my expert opinion" Tiggy answered.

"By the way" the landlord whispered. "Watch out for Dylan at the bar – he's a bit anti English and I think he's a bit of a psycho."

Tiggy looked over at the large guy at the bar and wondered what the problem was but was distracted when the landlord brought a pint of the local beer. This was apparently called Gold Digger and was a dark winter ale that looked pretty respectable. He sipped the pint and got a real malty, smokey taste that was somewhere between a stout and a bitter. He downed a third of the pint and sighed with very obvious satisfaction.

"Civilisation ... I do believe that this is probably the best Kiwi beer I've ever tasted."

The landlord was happy and Tiggy ordered a burger and kumara chips from the barbecue and looked round the pub. The food was excellent when it arrived on a big wooden platter and Tiggy tucked in realising that he had consumed around six pints and was feeling a little like the barrel he was leaning on. Despite that he was feeling a lovely buzz created by good beer and good food that he hadn't felt in years.

In the corner a couple of people were tuning up their instruments and Tiggy remembered that the girl that afternoon had promised that it was live music night. Tiggy wasn't exactly a fan of folk music so when the duo started with the opening chorus of Sheep Gut Blues he shuddered with distaste.

I worked in the Berwick slaughter house
killin daggy ewes and rams by the undred
now I got the sheep gut blues, the deep shit blues ...

Tiggy was starting to consider moving to another bar, another town or another planet when a gentle hand touched his shoulder.

"Hello stranger, I told you it was good."

Tiggy turned round and saw the white-haired punk he'd met earlier was smiling down at him. He decided that after all, he could handle the music and realised what a lovely young woman this really was – despite the tattoos and piercings. She accepted a Rye & Dry and leant on the barrel next door to him and tried to explain in the din that the band opened with the song as a piss-take and would be on their real stuff soon.

By the time she was on her third drink and Tiggy was wondering whether another pint would take him past his plimsol line. He was aware that a large obstruction was blocking out the light and that it was the guy the landlord had warned him about.

"Listen, you Pommy bastard, get your hands off this woman - she's a Kiwi and far too good for a tosser like you."

"The girl in question didn't let him answer, she just picked up a wine bottle from the table next to them and smashed it over the top of his head like she'd been practising for years. Tiggy felt a compelling need to go to the loo and reversed out of the bar as the blood started to flow out of the yokel's cranium.

By the time he'd drained off the six pints and returned, the guy was slumped in a seat by the bar with a load of paper towels clamped to his head. The punk waitress had disappeared out of the door and out of trouble. Tiggy walked to the opposite end of the bar to get his room key and the landlord gave him another pint as an apology.

"Sorry about that trouble Mr Dupont but Tracey is a lovely girl but she won't take any shit from blokes like him," the Landlord pointed over to the bloody guy.

"Won't there be any trouble with the police?" Tiggy asked for obvious reasons.

"He is the fucking police."

Sergeant Max Lawrence had emailed a database of all boatyards and marinas in the country with a request for information on any Riva or other classic boat they had on their books and explained that it was part of a major fraud enquiry. He also updated all regional police offices with the new information about Mr Foghorn and all his various aliases along with the various photographic evidence he'd gathered so far which now had a photo fit of the criminal with dyed hair, a beard and/or a shaven head. **The quality** was now as good as anyone could expect and Max had sent a copy of the photo fits to the people who'd seen most of him like Miriam Bender and Elmer Flannigan in the US.

189

Coincidently those two had taken to zoom calling each other every few days and were able to compare reactions to the photo mock-ups. After all the fuss created by that gorgon Florence and her loyal band of protesters had died down, Miriam reckoned that most of the victims had decided that finding Count Jergov was impossible. Most of them were wealthy and 10 or 20 grand was not so significant that it was worth getting an ulcer over. In fact, many were probably already booking their next cruise at more than that. Miriam's sister was a prime example.

But something in Miriam's background made her different. She'd not grown one of the largest retirement businesses in the US without showing some grit. She'd not suffered one of the most boring marriages without developing some determination. Miriam had enjoyed her bed-time with Count Jergov tremendously but now she wanted his balls on her bedpost. Elmer Flannigan looked like a heavy which could be useful in the future but his determination was almost as great an advantage. Miriam didn't know whether it was his partner Bruce or himself but Elmer had been positive in every meeting and his knowledge of boats was invaluable. He'd already contacted Riva in Italy and though he'd got a fairly negative response at first, he'd not given up, he'd got some pretty high price boats in his own marina and knew how to apply leverage.

They saw the mock-ups from Sergeant Lawrence and thought they were just about OK and passed on any comments. It was funny for Miriam looking at the shots again gave her a thrill in a part of her body that she'd thought was dead until she'd kidnapped him but she still wasn't going to let him get away with it.

Looking at the various photographs gave them an appreciation of just how difficult it was to find someone who didn't want to be found. Tiggy with a beard or a blonde wig or a shaven head, would be difficult for even Miriam to recognise. The sergeant had said that credit cards and bank withdrawals were a way of tracking fugitives but the Count hadn't done anything traceable for weeks. He was an intelligent man and she was sure that he'd avoid all the normal traps. The boat, however, might be his achilles heel.

Flannigan was convinced that the Riva boat the Count had shown him was worth millions. A little research with Riva online had gleaned enough for him to believe that a boat of that size in the 1920's with a cabin was rare – maybe even unique. Just about every other example he'd seen from the early 1900's was an open speedboat of the type used by glamorous stars like Loren and Grant. The lines were absolutely beautiful, though not those of an ocean-going boat like those who moored at his marina. He could see those sleek lines suiting Lake Como or Cannes where the vessel never had to deal with real weather, but just transported its owner close to home in maximum style.

Aged cars like rare Ferrari's or Bentleys had been a popular investment for ages with some examples fetching three times the guide price. Boats had lagged behind the trend for a few years but now the market was exceedingly good as billionaires realised that a stylish boat by their huge waterside house in Geneva or the Black Sea was the ultimate status symbol.

So, if the Count wanted to sell it, it would probably be at an auction organised by one of the big houses like Christies or Sotheby's. Flannigan checked and there were no classic auctions scheduled in the next few months but ensured that he was on the mailing list with all of the big houses.

He and Miriam consulted together and decided to send everything they knew to the cop in New Zealand who seemed a really nice guy, but seemed under great pressure at the moment.

The Sergeant saw the incoming emails but parked them for the moment. He was pissed off about the TV documentary he'd seen about gullibility because they were still using the old photos of Count Jergov and not the enhanced versions he'd sent out to all the regional offices. He emailed the producer he normally dealt with but wondered whether they would ever use them.

It was weeks since the original broadcast and stories died very quickly if there are no new leads. Count Jergov was an extraordinary story but he didn't seem to have conned anyone since that woman in Wanaka. Even that terrible woman in Australia – Florence Hasty – seemed to have stopped her calls and threats to come over. That was a profound relief and meant that the pressure from his senior officers might die down. He hoped so.

Max Lawrence tried to work out what the good Count would be doing now. He walked over to the wall and looked at the map where he just had a couple of red pins indicating the sitings of Count Jergov in Port Charlotte, Dunedin and Wanaka. His deliberations were interrupted by a call on his mobile that he didn't recognise. In trepidation that the Ginger monster might have renewed her pressure he answered with trepidation giving his rank and serial number.

"Sergeant Lawrence, this is Adele Lang and I'm speaking to you from the European Parliament Building in Brussels."

"Yes Mizzz Lang." Max answered with a certain lack of respect for her political or marital status.

"In your search for the Fraudster who pretended to be an author called Eugene Fenton I did some investigation myself and think that he was staying in Queenstown and used a driver called George who had a Bentley and who was a local man."

"Thank you Ms Lang, I will check that out."

"Are you any closer to an arrest – I lost a considerable amount of money, you know."

"Our investigations are on-going Ms Lang and we now know a lot more about the man including his real name. We think he is still in New Zealand, but we haven't found him yet."

"Thank you Sergeant – I would be grateful if you would keep me apprised as to progress."

"Rest assured Ms Lang, we will be following up every lead and making an announcement in due course."

Max hung up the phone and put a red pin on the town of Queenstown, firing off an enquiry to the local police requesting that they checked out hotels and limo drivers who might have dealt with our infamous author. Personally, he thought that his quarry would be hiding in the crowds of Auckland by now or have used another identity to get out of the country.

He had loads of cash and the fact that he seemed to have entered the country without using Foghorn or Count Jergov or Eugene Fenton, probably meant that he had another passport or the means to source one. The only hope Max had was that the boat that the Count had been trying to restore was genuine and able to be located.

He read the incoming emails from the US with interest. Looking again at the map, he realised that one red pin was missing and that it might be important. Miriam Bender and her sister were the first victims of Count Tolstoy Jergov and they had been on the cruise ship *Amazon*. It was on this ship where most of his other victims were located. But it wasn't where the two sisters first met Jergov. They met him at a harbour side cafe in the town of Akaroa which had that lovely bay on the east coast that he'd always wanted to visit.

Roberto Carlotti had received an email from Riva in Italy and also from the local police requesting information about any vintage boats being restored in his boat yard. There was an opportunity to be honest about the project that had been helping his profits for the last 18 months and enhance his reputation with Riva. There was also the chance to be a good citizen and help the police with their enquiries. There was an even more attractive possibility, which was to get his own back on the annoying British bastard who'd cramped his style ever since he'd arrived. Also, to squeeze a few more thousand dollars out of him when he tried to sell the boat. Some might call this blackmail but Roberto called it being opportunistic and reacting to market conditions.

If he had a conscience Carlotti might have had it eased by the research he'd done online and with Riva head office. His boat was unique and even though he said it himself, his team had done a brilliant job with the restoration. Recently a Riva from 1926 with far less provenance had sold at auction for 3.5 million US dollars to someone in China. At a conservative estimate the Riva with the cabin could fetch 4 million – maybe 5 – the market was so good.

The other opportunity which looked golden was the Las Vegas connection. Carlotti had sent a photograph of the fully restored boat to a few rich Italians now living in the US. Some of these had family connections and weren't short of a few billion dollars. One, in particular had a vast empire in Las Vegas including an Italianate palace of a casino. He had emailed back and been very positive about the boat and offered to send someone over to look at it.

Now in the cold light of day, Roberto was a little scared. He had been trying to show off a little when he sent the photographs to the people with mob connections and now he regretted sending them. These people may have billions but they didn't operate using civilised methods. Dealing with them could be dangerous, so he sent a general email back thanking them sincerely for their interest and promising to keep them informed. After all god knows what his father had done when he had met the Don all those years ago and Roberto didn't want himself subject to 'omerta' or whatever it was.

Terry (DuPont) Foghorn had an almost superstitious regard for some of his other personas. Count Jergov and Eugene Fenton had been incredibly good to him and made him thousands of dollars. As characters they'd also put him in the beds of some of the most attractive and grateful women he'd ever hoped to meet. The nickname Tiggy had been given to him by his mentor all those years ago and was sacrosanct as well as successful.

As he woke up in the luxury of his room in the Goldsmiths Arms, he realised that the use of his mother's maiden name the previous night had not been lucky. Despite doing nothing to offend anyone or con money out of them, he'd had to leave one of the best drinking sessions in years because someone had taken against him. That person had been the local cop.

He loved the pub and would have stayed another night but for safety's sake intended to sneak out early, so he crossed the garden to the main building, hoping to get out to the car and get on his way.

"I suppose Major Disaster the English Master is trying to sneak out without paying," said a voice from the far end of the pub.

Refusing to be intimidated and with a certain amount of national pride he couldn't help responding:

"As you took payment last night, you colonial misfit, I think that was unlikely. I would have stayed for the breakfast I already paid for, but thought that it would probably be as cold and bad as your beer."

The landlord was almost forced to break into a chuckle and fifteen minutes later Tiggy found himself sitting behind one of the best breakfasts he'd ever seen including poached eggs, kidneys, bacon and black pudding. All washed down with a mug of tea the size of a bucket.

Tiggy had to admit defeat and sigh in happy satisfaction. The landlord came over and whispered that the cop who'd been on the wrong end of the bottle the previous night had gone to hospital for a checkup and no-one knew what the result was yet. The cop knew the punk waitress from old times but didn't know Tiggy, so the landlord suggested that he got out of town as quickly as possible as the guy was a vindictive sod.

He promised to help cover DuPont's tracks by saying that he paid cash and left the name Jones. The cash statement was true but Tiggy thanked him sincerely for the help with the false name. In his present circumstances and with the TV coverage, he was starting to feel like Public Enemy Number One and he'd prefer to be a little less famous.

Tiggy pushed his way out of the front door carefully and scanned the road both ways. The car park was across the street and he hoped that no-one had bothered to notice his car the previous night. His green Subaru was still there as was an old Morris Oxford and a couple of Toyota pickups he seemed to remember from when he'd arrived. It was dusty and old like most of the vehicles and certainly didn't look like a getaway car. It started reassuringly quickly and Tiggy swung on the side road, knowing that he had around ten miles of minor roads before he hit Highway 1.

Tiggy had a mobile but was loathe to use it because he knew how easily they could be tracked. He'd invested, however, in a couple of cheap ones in Queenstown and got the last of those out of its wrapper and fired it up.

"Bruce, I'm arriving at around mid-day and I'll come to the bar to get the keys to the apartment – is that OK?

"Er … yeh mate, that's fine."

"What's the problem Bruce, you haven't told anybody I'm coming have you?"

"Er ..."

"Listen Bruce, I bring a lot of business to Pierre's and I need to know you're not going to blab every time I tell you something – who've you told?"

"Just the girls here – they miss you."

"No more gossiping Bruce – please."

"Oh. Sorry Tiggy ..., sorry."

Tiggy pulled back on the road and couldn't help being angry. Pierre's was a great bar and he'd pulled in some great fish like Miriam and her sister there but it had more gossips than a ladies hairdressers. He had better presume that Roberto in the boatyard knew he was coming and that just about everyone else did too.

Another problem was himself and his weaknesses. They didn't stop the cruise ships coming for at least another month and he knew that if he saw any large ladies from Florida or Texas, he'd be tempted to put them in his book. Trying any of his Count Jergov tricks on incoming cruisers would be suicidal but the challenge of creating another lucrative scam might be too much to resist.

Tiggy brought his mind back to the present. The last bit of the route down to Akaroa was testing with a narrow road crossing the mountains and always the possibility of meeting a tour coach on one of the blind bends. The first time he'd done this route had been terrifying as it was foggy and there was a yahoo in a powerful pick-up up his arse trying to pass. In the end he'd let him go by and tried to match him on the bends. He'd no chance in keeping up but had developed a little more confidence in handling mountain roads.

The Subaru was fine and before he knew it, he was looking down at Akaroa on the final stretch and admiring the sheltered bay that had attracted all those French and English whalers so many years ago. He could see a couple of ships in the bay and suspected that they were cruise liners, closer in he could see a couple of leisure craft and the harbour where he normally moored his Riva. At the far end of the bay was the sailing club and the boatyard where that shyster Roberto Carlotti had his business.

The sun was high in the sky and there was a warmth in the air that belied the fact that it was late Autumn. Tiggy thought that it couldn't be a better day for him to return to his old stamping ground and renew a few old acquaintances.

Tiggy had enjoyed the few pints at the Goldsmiths Arms despite the violent encounter with the cop but was feeling a little recycled as he made the last decent and decided to have a refreshing glass of wine and snack at Pierre's. It was risky but as the rumour mill had betrayed him, he might as well test the water.

He parked round the back of the shops so no-one knew whose vehicle he was in. He started to pull his overnight pack out of the car, then realised he had a reputation to maintain, and opened up the bag on the passenger seat. Tiggy had the image of an elegant if somewhat eccentric gentleman all the time he'd been in Akaroa. Most of the last few weeks he'd been trying to blend in with the locals and look as different from Count Jergov as possible. Now he had to consider his image or people might think he was trying to hide something.

Luckily the car park was empty as it tended to be used by the shop owners and they were all busy earning dollars. Changing trousers in a car is difficult and likely to result in either a hernia or a charge of exposure – neither of which Tiggy needed in a business like his. So the local denims had to stay, but at least the brogues he was wearing were respectable and not the trainers or jandals half the world was wearing. He had a light blue shirt and dark blue blazer that he'd kept from the Miriam purchases on the *Amazon* and the dark blue bow-tie he'd purloined from the apartment in Dunedin. After he'd hand-tied the bow in the car mirror (a gentleman should be able to tie a bow in total darkness if necessary as he remembered from his Dartmouth, navy days) he looked respectable.

The beard was different but he needed that and as he stepped out of the car and buttoned up the blazer, he looked in the car window reflection and thought – just for a second – that Count Jergov's rich cousin might have arrived.

Tiggy gave himself a severe telling off for the thought and walked slowly but ramrod straight round the front to the outside of Pierre's. There were around ten people who didn't look like tourists enjoying the sunshine and Tiggy sat in his normal table as close to the promenade as possible.

One of the girls came over and asked whether he was eating and obviously didn't recognise him. He asked for a plate of Calamari and a bottle of New Zealand Alberone and still she didn't know who it was and wandered back to the bar looking at her order pad.

Tiggy didn't know whether to be relieved or annoyed that the waitress hadn't recognised him. She was a lovely woman and Tiggy had shared a bed with her for a few nights when he'd first arrived in town and paid for his accommodation with pleasure given. She claimed to love him shortly after that and Tiggy had a difficult few days extricating himself from that situation. Now the little madam didn't even recognise him. Sometimes women were so fickle he thought ruefully.

The food and wine arrived as did a tender from one of the ships out in the bay and Tiggy was subjected to the temptation of seeing what appeared to be a mixed herd of European and American matrons getting off the tender and on to the coaches. His prey had never been the masses, however, it had been the rebels who decided to reject the standard tours.

Looking down the harbour he couldn't help remembering the wonderful moment when he spied Miriam and her sister and had shagged his way into one of his most lucrative adventures.

At that moment the object of his fantasies was ten thousand miles away and thinking of him too. She'd sent the email with the summary of their findings to the cop in New Zealand a few hours ago and now she had very little to do other than consider the important things in life.

Miriam's first husband had been boring and dependable. He'd help her make a fortune but the retirement business suited him perfectly. Many of the 80 year olds in their homes had more entertainment value than George Bender.

She realised that she had wasted a lot of her life thinking about money and that meeting Count Jergov or Tiggy or whatever name he was called, was the most exciting thing that had happened to her since she'd lost her virginity in the back of a Cadillac. Miriam wanted some more excitement – most of all she wanted Tiggy back in her bed – but on her own terms.

Her sister Elsie wanted vengeance but wanted decent sex even more. The trip had been meant to bring the sisters closer together. It had worked perfectly when Tiggy had been between them and they had something interesting in common. Now he'd gone, they realised just how little they really liked being together.

She walked around the house trying to distract herself by planning the new sitting room and looking at swatches and colour charts. But it was boring and too early for a drive to the country club or a drink. She sat down again and tried to concentrate on emails but found herself opening up the iPad to look at some photos from the trip. Apple were brilliant and had labelled the shots with locations that were incredibly accurate. It was just as well because some of the many places they had visited looked so similar and when you saw a beautiful harbour with mountains behind it was difficult to tell whether it was Italy or Australia. Sadly, it didn't do the same with people and the number of friends they had made on the trip was extraordinary and apart from a couple of the crew it was very difficult to remember who anybody was.

Inevitably she found the one shot they had of the Count pretty quickly and was sad that it did him so little justice. How he'd managed to avoid being photographed all those days despite being the centre of attention was absolutely extraordinary. Looking at him pissed and slumped in the corner of the saloon after they'd kidnapped him was hysterical and Miriam couldn't help but giggle.

Scrolling back a few frames was fascinating and the more she looked, the more Miriam felt the excitement rising. There was another shot a beautiful bay and harbour but this one was very, very special because it was where they had first met Count Tolstoy Jergov. Looking at the caption it said Akaroa, New Zealand. Miriam made a call to her travel agent and emailed Elmer.

Tiggy was wondering whether to make himself known at Pierre's or just have another glass in wonderful anonymity. He wouldn't have admitted it, even to himself, but his pride had been hurt by the fact that no-one recognised him. Given that his mate Bruce aka Pierre, the patron, hadn't been over but both girls had served his table had been close and not a flicker.

"Pierre, where are you – you snail eating excuse for a restauranteur?" Tiggy couldn't help shouting in his best aristocratic drawl after trying to draw attention for another few minutes.

The owner looked over in annoyance from the bar and did a double take. Still unsure, he took off his apron and wiped his hands to come across and see who was being so familiar and yet so rude.

"Tiggy, you lovely man what's with the Captain Birdseye look?"

"I'm afraid I'm on the run from my fans Bruce – some of them are getting a little too close for comfort- so the beard is essential."

"I think it makes you like one of those old kings like George 1st or maybe it's Rasputin I'm thinking off – not sure."

"As long as it's not an old queen?" Tiggy added quietly. "That would definitely be bad for business."

Tiggy asked the patron to sit down and share a glass whilst he brought them up to date with what was happening locally. He trusted the guy generally and knew that he had a few secrets of his own he wouldn't want shared so told him that it was just possible the cops might be after him. He may be a gossip but now he knew the seriousness of the situation Tiggy reckoned he could be trusted.

The manager had seen one of the TV programmes about Count Jergov and loved the fact that he had started everything here at Pierre's. It was sad that his place hadn't been mentioned by name and that all the coverage had been about the ship *Amazon*.

"Did you tell Roberto Carlotti that I was coming?"

"No, what kind of friend do you think I am – I wouldn't tell that pseudo-Italian gigolo anything. Did you realise that he's been trying to chat up Francine over there?"

"No" Tiggy looked over at the leggy blonde and didn't blame him. "No, she bats for the other side so he had no chance."

Tiggy thought that on balance he trusted that the manager hadn't told Roberto directly but better assume that the girls or one of their friends had told him to be safe. What his father had called the Jungle Telegraph was as strong in Akaroa as it had been in his home village. Tiggy reckoned that if he started a juicy rumour at the coffee shop at the Southern end and walked slowly to the other end of the bay, then his story would be told back to him with interest in Pierre's at the other end.

He needed to presume the boatyard knew and that a surprise inspection would be pointless. In any case Tiggy realised that he hadn't really decided what he really wanted to do with the Riva yet. He'd been putting the decision off for weeks and though he had more dollars in his Panama account than he'd ever had, the only way he was ever going to get enough to retire early was to sell the boat.

The manager made his excuses and went back to the bar and Tiggy ordered another large glass of wine and a plate of cheese and tried to concentrate.

He normally thought that he did better thinking with a pen in his hand so pulled out the old pen from his blazer pocket. This was probably the most serious thinking he'd done for years, so he listed the options for the Riva and their relative merit on his notepad:

1. He could get the boat back on the water and motor somewhere quiet and live onboard for a few months.
2. He could get the boat transported to somewhere they had classic boat auctions – probably Italy, USA or UK.
3. He could sell the boat immediately in NZ where they had a large boating tradition and good flights – probably only Auckland would meet that brief.
4. He could get an agent to sell it anonymously on his behalf.

Each option had disadvantages though the thought of motoring off to some Kiwi backwater had to be dismissed - tempting as it was – because the Riva was built for lakes and sunny bays and not the deep water of New Zealand. Tiggy may have spent years in the Royal Navy but he knew that life on board a frigate did not qualify him to attempt the Pacific in a 50ft gin palace.

To assess the second or third option he needed to get a copy of 'Classic Boats' or one of the other specialist magazines to find when auctions were scheduled. Transport would be a consideration as the Riva would have to be taken across the mountains by specialist truck or put in a container and taken by sea to wherever was needed. This wasn't going to be cheap, even if it was just to Auckland.

The fourth alternative was a possibility if he could find an agent he trusted. For a man on the run from the police and whose exploits had been seen on TV, this had an obvious attraction. Though there had been nothing in today's papers, it was only a couple of days since the work of the nefarious Count had brought the gullibility of the whole nation into question.

He had to presume that the police or the victims were still after him and that he stupidly had mentioned the Riva on a number of occasions and so it was a weak spot. It was reassuring that the locals hadn't recognised him with his beard but he needed to keep a low profile whilst he was in Akaroa.

Before he made any final decisions Tiggy decided to walk round the bay and stow his bags in the apartment. On the way he changed his mind and decided pop in the boat builders and see the restored Riva. Carlotti had apparently taken to having a siesta in the afternoon because he thought it made him seem more Italian so it was quite possible that it would be shut but Tiggy decided to chance it. He was dying to see the boat and felt a tight knot of excitement as he got closer.

The boathouse was next to the sailing club and Tiggy could see the double doors were shut but he scrambled up the slipway to have a look. The surface was slick with weed and his smart brogues didn't help him make progress. Neither did the bottle and a half of good Kiwi wine that he'd consumed over the last hour. Eventually, however, he crawled up the ramp, feeling a little like a guilty sailor returning late from leave.

There were two vertical perspex windows in the concertina doors and Tiggy peered through. What he saw gave him a greater thrill than any mere woman. The Riva was up on blocks and it looked absolutely magnificent but he could only see a section of the bows. He had to see more.

There was a narrow walkway down the side and Tiggy crept down, knowing that there was a second door into the boathouse which led via Roberto's office. Eventually he found it and turned the handle, going in quickly so no-one on the quay could see him. Inside was a cluttered desk and a wall covered with drawings, post-its and old sailing calendars. In one corner there was an inner door which led to the rest of the workshop and so Tiggy pulled it open with a mounting sense of anticipation. This had been what everything had been all about – all the cons – all the sex – all that money. Everything had been for that 1920's classic the Riva Weekender and restoring it's etherial beauty.

"Whata da fuck are you doin ere?" A coarse male shouted.

"Aaaaaaaaargh" the female voice got higher and higher until it was a scream.

Tiggy nearly bolted but then he had the chance to look at the apparitions that were screaming at him from the semi-darkness. Firstly, there was someone who appeared to be a Roman Centurion but who actually was Roberto, the boathouse owner.

Secondly there was someone dressed as some kind of slave dominatrix in leather complete with whips and flails. She appeared to be Lucinda the mayor's wife.

Seeing a unique opportunity to capture a classic farce for posterity, Tiggy pulled out his mobile and flashed off a couple of shots before carefully putting the phone back in a zipped pocket. He then pushed past the twosome and into the main workshop, thinking that the phrase 'having a Roman holiday' now had a rather different meaning.

Tiggy was in no position to judge Roberto morally for his sexual infidelities but as a man with a strong sense of survival he knew his choice of woman was definitely unwise. He didn't know Lucinda biblically thank goodness, though she was attractive in a blonde Valkyrie sort of way. The mayor was the big man whose money had already got him out of a couple of serious GBH and assault charges and who's reputation for casual violence on the rugby field had been legendary.

Tiggy pushed through, turned the lights on in the workshop and looked at his real love. The long-raked hull stretched as far as he could see and he carefully walked round checking the workmanship. The bodged repair that had been done before he had bought the boat was gone and everything looked wonderful. He wouldn't be able to see the deck and cabin properly until later but he climbed up a workman's ladder and touched the deck. The mahogany decking looked magnificent and the woodwork of the cabin looked to be showroom quality.

"Giva me da phone." He heard Roberto whispering below him.

"Roberto – stop using that ridiculous accent, I know you were born in Greymouth – not Napoli."

Tiggy reversed down the steps until he was level with Roberto. It's sometimes helpful being 6ft 2inches and used to bluffing your way through officer training when you are facing someone considerably shorter and someone who is still wearing his Roman outfit.

Roberto backed off and sat down heavily on the sail locker opposite with a sigh. Tiggy averted his eyes as he had no wish to learn whether Centurions wore anything under their skirts or not.

"You obviously like living dangerously – the mayor is not someone I'd want to get on the wrong side of." Tiggy needed Roberto to realise that he recognised the woman with the whip. He was not disappointed and the pseudo-Italian collapsed with his head in his hands and started to sob in a manner that was decidedly non-Kiwi.

"It's all her fault ... she forced me ... she's a demon."

Tiggy ignored the sobs and ordered him to have the Riva in the water by 8.00 a.m. in the morning and be ready to take the boat on the water for a full equipment test. He then pushed his way back out through the office and on to the quay. He moved back to the car to pick up some stuff and then took a circuitous route to the apartment so that as few people knew where he was as possible.

The view was as good as he remembered. The apartment was on the third floor on a corner above the shops and had a small balcony looking over the harbour. He couldn't quite see the boathouse but just about everything else was in view and there were still a couple of cruise ships waiting at the entrance to the bay but apart from that there was little to see. Whilst he had a few minutes he decided to see what one of the auction houses had to say about the boat and emailed a photograph of the Riva with a brief outline of its provenance to Chris Arnold of Chartwells. Arnold had been a fellow officer on a frigate Tiggy had served on and had shared many drunken escapes on leave and Tiggy remembered that he had family connections with the auction house. It was a bit of a punt but our heroic seafarer realised that the more advice he had about the sale, the better and Chris had been a good mate. Tiggy leaned back in the easy chair and decided to rest. When he awoke it was dark and the stars and planets shone as brightly here in New Zealand as they did anywhere. Only at sea did Tiggy remember night skies that were as beautiful. He just missed someone to share all this glory with and worried that a few days without sexual gratification was turning him soft in the head and hard in the groin.

He pulled his shoulder bag over and took out the leather folder, notepad and fountain pen that he'd used so successfully last time he'd been in Akaroa. His handwritten notes were still there and on the top was a note of "George Bender – loyal, boring and rich but with bad teeth." This was the note on Miriam's late husband he'd written so that he could be included in the book and had been his first ten thousand dollar fee and the beginning of a very profitable voyage.

He realised that he missed Miriam almost as much as he had missed Maddie Quimby his original love guru. This was astonishing and the first time that anyone had replaced his teenage teacher in his fantasies since the age of 12 years old. Even his recent exploits in the saddle paled into insignificance compared to the few days with the Bender sisters. Of the two, Miriam was by far the most lovely, and the ache for her was a little embarrassing.

Tiggy looked at the notes again and decided to add a few more sentences on George in the style of Eugene Fenton, thinking that if he ever met Miriam again, then she might find it amusing. An hour later he told himself to stop and go to bed before he started believing in himself too much and went loopy.

Riva loss Vegas?

Akaroa was about to get a few more visitors. Not tourists in the normal sense and less interested in the beauty of the bay or unusual quality of the French inspired food. Sergeant Lawrence was one of them and he knew some of the rest but the visitor normally resident in the Coliseum Hotel in Las Vegas was not really known well by anyone in New Zealand. Roberto Carlotti however, knew him by reputation.

Through an odd series of coincidences that sometimes happen in policing Max Lawrence had a call from Elmer Flannigan to say that he and Miriam were coming over immediately and that he'd heard that a notorious gangster was also coming over. Max vaguely remembered that his brother was a US cop dealing with organised crime and presumed that this was the source of his information. What had alerted Elmer was the fact that the gang boss was coming over to buy some kind of Italian classic boat that was worth millions. The boat was apparently in Akaroa in South Island, New Zealand.

Max didn't normally believe in good fortune but the fact that this was where Count Jergov aka Tiggy Foghorn had first enticed Miriam and her sister was a coincidence too good to ignore.

Miriam and Elmer had drawn the same conclusion and were already on the long flight from the US. Max had advised them on transport from Auckland and made a tentative arrangement to meet them in about three days.

The police computer gave Max access to the gangland boss's background. Al Romano had been born in New York fifty years ago in a family that had strong Mafia connections. By 20 he was apparently a trusted lieutenant for one of the most successful crime syndicate bosses and credited with three kills. Over the next ten years he forced his way to the top of the organisation and was suspected of being involved personally in the deaths of ten competitors. The gruesome method of his attacks gave him the nickname of 'Al Machete' and a fearsome reputation amongst criminals in the US. Despite all the suspicions the police had been unable to make any charge stick and Al still had a clean record. For reasons unknown to the authorities Romano had retired in his 40's and bought the failing casino and hotel in Las Vegas called the Coliseum. Since then, the man had spent billions of dollars turning the complex into the most luxurious hotel on the strip and trying to bring Vegas back to its

20th Century high. The hotel had a huge lake at the front with a half size replica of the Hotel Splendido and marina on Lake Como and apparently Romano was obsessed by acquiring a boat to go with it.

Sergeant Lawrence knew that if he mentioned a visiting gangland boss to his superiors, then all hell would break loose and his chance to capture Count Jergov himself would be made impossible. The top brass had been delighted to pass the enquiry to him when things were looking political and the Euro MP and terrifying woman from Australia had been making a fuss. Now he reckoned that he deserved to get the credit himself and just said that he was continuing the investigation in Akaroa and would be back in a couple of days. They were delighted to leave him to it and blame him if he failed but step in with alacrity if things had glory.

Max couldn't quite rationalise why he was so keen on catching up with Jergov. He didn't seem to be an evil man and the police legal officer had reminded him a couple of days ago that the case against him was not easy as there were contracts that victims had signed and real issues of jurisdiction with many of the crimes having been offshore. At least three of the crimes had taken place in New Zealand and there was something fascinating about someone personable enough to dupe intelligent, worldly people like Miriam or the Euro MP and so he had to be found.

Our upholder of the law decided to drive from Dunedin which would take a few hours but he knew a good place to stay en route and planned a few pints tonight then an early start tomorrow. The Goldsmiths Arms was one of the few original pubs in the South Island that hadn't been turned into a hobbit themed rest house or a high-price restaurant. He had a liking for good ale too which is how he'd found the place many years ago. The only downside was the local copper who unlike almost everyone else he'd ever met in the force was a bigot and against anyone who wasn't himself. Max hoped that he wouldn't be around.

Miriam Bender had sensibly booked first class aircraft seats for her and Elmer Flannigan but could see that he was struggling. British Airways seats were like pods and large enough to carry most human beings in luxury but Elmer was huge. When you are six and a half feet tall and built like an all-in wrestler you try to avoid air travel, which is why Elmer and his partner normally travelled by sea. The flight in total was around 15 hours and Elmer was having to get up every hour to stretch and walk round. The flight attendants did their best and fed him champagne, food and anything else he might want in order to give him rest but it was impossible.

About half way over Elmer leaned over and asked her a really difficult question, which was why she really was coming over all this way and what result she was hoping for. Miriam suspected that now they were on the way, he was starting to wonder that about himself and really gave it thought. She had grown to like Elmer – he had a gay guy's sensitivity and was a genuine sort – he deserved an honest answer.

"Thinking it through I want my money back but as we kinda kidnapped the Count I wouldn't want him harmed or in jail."

"You kidnapped him?" Elmer asked with astonishment.

"Yes I guess so. Elsie and I were both captivated with his story and I guess we just took him with us ... it all seemed so easy at the time to get him on the tender ... we were all drunk at the time."

"What did the Count say?" Elmer was still reeling a little by this revelation.

"He was even worse on Miami slammers than we were and barely conscious."

Miriam realised that she'd told no one about the incident and that only her sister was aware of the part they'd played in the deception. She could see that Elmer was shocked and re-calibrating as she spoke and realised that she needed to add something important.

"Listen, it's important you know that we believed the Count Jergov story totally and both paid lots of money to get characters in the book."

"But you still smuggled him on board?" Elmer questioned.

"Yes, we did and he shared our bed – it was wonderful," Miriam added with a sigh. "All I really want is to have him back - if I'm honest, that's why I'm here."

Elmer seemed stunned and heaved his body back to his seat and tried to sleep.

Miriam realised that anyone hearing the same story would consider her and her sister to be complicit in the crimes of Count Jergov and that she really better try not to be so honest with the cops as she had been with Elmer. He looked pale and withdrawn in his seat and could easily be a problem when they got to New Zealand. She hoped not.

Al Romano hadn't flown long-haul for years. In fact, the last time had been ten years ago when he 'retired' from organised crime and decided to visit his ancestral homeland in Sicily. That had been a disaster and if anything had been less like the scene in Godfather 2, then he's yet to see it. The old village was a shit heap, the family members were incomprehensible and he'd returned to the US with such a bad case of food poisoning that he'd been hospitalised.

He'd only ceased to be a full time leader of one of the major families when a number of his supposed colleagues objected to him chopping a new recruit in half for showing a lack of respect. His machete had been his companion during his early years and though some traditionalists said it was more suited to a rasta than a don, he loved it. He thought that it allowed self expression, sadly the rest of the syndicate thought that it didn't help their ambition to turn the syndicate into a respectable business. Thinking back on his apprenticeship when he'd done everything from running drugs in souped up boats from Columbia through to assassinating non compliant policemen, the thought of his business seeking respectability was laughable. But times change and the money was still obscenely good.

Romano had been retired with a huge golden handshake and realised that he needed somewhere to invest it and hide it. The casino and hotel in Vegas had been perfect and he had lavished millions on it over the last few years. In the golden years the Coliseum had had stars like Sinatra, Dean Martin and the rest of the rat pack appearing on stage and millions had been gambled nightly. Things had declined in the late 20th Century but in recent years dirty money from people like Romano had flooded in and big boxing matches had returned. There were even top class European bands considering appearing because the money was so good. The fees meant that bands like U2 or Motorhead could make more money out of a couple of nights at the Coliseum than they could during a complete US tour. The audiences were small but the rates of pay offered by Romano was so generous that it didn't matter.

Romano's favourite film stars when he was a kid were Sophia Loren, Gregory Peck and those glamorous actors who appeared in the great Italian movies of the 1950's. The epitome of sophistication was a movie he saw with the two of them speeding across Lake Como in a stylish speedboat and mooring at the hotel Splendido. Since then, he'd seen the movie dozens of times and built a replica of the hotel frontage outside his casino. The other thing he'd tried to find for years is a replica of that beautiful boat, which he knew was a Riva.

The email from that peasant Roberto Carlotti in New Zealand had been passed to him a couple of days ago and he'd nearly ignored it. When he saw that sleek shape, he nearly creamed himself and told his associate to tell Carlotti that he was on his way and he wanted the boat.

207

It had taken a few hours to get things arranged but now he and one of his few staff who didn't have a criminal record were on a private jet which after a couple of stops would take him to New Zealand and then to Crakatoa or Flackatao or Akaroa. Where ever the fuck that was ....

Al Romano was rich and prepared to spend almost anything to get the boat but normally his reputation and look helped him get good value. But he felt vulnerable this trip because he didn't have Luigi and Frank his two enormous minders because their records meant that they would have been detained at almost any airport in the world. He just had Nico his financial director who was about as intimidating as a pastrami on rye. The other problem was that his team had insisted that his machete had to stay at home so he felt powerless – except for the Glock made out of some kind of resin he'd managed to hide in his luggage. He was told that it had a magazine of fifty bullets but to him it looked like a toy and didn't have the tactile charm of the blade.

Chris Arnold was another man with a mission on his way to Akaroa. Chartwells Sydney office had started to question his expenses again on a regular basis and despite the family connections with the founder, he knew he was in danger of being gently fired. They might call it 'garden leave' or 'taking a sabbatical' but it would end up the same way. His debts were too great to have an involuntary pause in his income.

When Chris Arnold had left the Royal Navy, he walked straight into his Uncle's business but at the bottom. Unlike his fellow officer Tiggy Foghorn, Arnold had been expensively educated and spoke like a member of the Royal family, so a career in Chartwells was a natural. The fact that he knew little about antiques, other than the Aunt he hoped to inherit a fortune from sometime, didn't seem to matter. This was an auction house that had a history going back to the 16th Century and it may not have grown to the size of a Sotheby's or a Christies but it wasn't far off. It had grown so far with a mixture of privilege and nepotism driving it and it wasn't going to change any time soon.

Chris had challenged those principles sorely. He'd started well in London and was a regular for lunch at the Ritz grill room or Quaglinos with well-connected people. Then a few bad deals and a slightly unusual attitude to what was legal or principled had put him in the Managing Partners bad books. Knowing the family connection, the partners hadn't fired him – they'd sent him to Australia – in their minds that was a far worse punishment.

After a few months Chris Arnold had proved them wrong by finding a new market in classic cars and boats that they really hadn't known existed over there. One Ferrari he'd found in a sheep farmer's garage had made 3.5 million dollars and with the Chartwell fee of 10% to his credit, the bosses had started to say that they'd always known he'd come good in the end. But that was a year or so back and Arnolds' expense account was again amounting to a small fortune and Chartwell was not seeing anything worthwhile in return.

The Royal Navy background hadn't helped Arnold judge the shot of the Riva boat, but the the long days in the Hamble, Poole Harbour and Nice as a youth had helped considerably. Many rich men enjoyed their Sunseekers or exotic sloops but the uber-rich liked to find something even more rare. These days that was a classic with a great provenance and the best of them never seemed to go down in price. With sail, a classic J2 racing yacht in great condition could fetch ten million, with motor, the market was less developed but experts had predicted its growth for months.

Tiggy Foghorn's description and shot of the Riva Weekender looked wonderful and if it had the right background then it could break new ground at auction. There was a huge affection for things Italian and rare Ferrari's, Alfa Romeos and Lancia's all had that classic design style that had sold well for years. He was pretty confident that Italian boats were going to be even more successful and his route to continued employment.

He'd enjoyed serving with Terrance Foghorn though his background couldn't have been more different. Foghorns success with the fairer sex had been legendary but Chris had been no slouch either and they got on. On shore leave abroad, they reckoned that if they worked as a team then no attractive pair of females was safe, anywhere.

The two both had a healthy disrespect for the rules and shared a couple of schemes that weren't quite legal but which had made excellent money. Despite his expensive education Arnold wasn't rich and his navy pay seemed to be spent on the finer things of life well before the end of the month, so extra money from one of Tiggy's schemes had been extremely welcome.

They were both tall and good-looking and popular amongst the females at the endless parties. Tiggy nicknamed him Lord Collywobble after his uneasy first trip on the frigate and constant trips to the heads during bad weather. The name seemed to stick and there were still dozens of good-looking women round the world who thought that it was his genuine title and his aristocratic looks and Eton drawl made it believable. When you have a real name like Foghorn, he supposed that it helped to have a partner in crime with a name just as silly.

The thing was Tiggy wasn't a bad man – he was just a bit of a rascal and a very stylish one at that, so Chris was sure that if he'd acquired a boat like the Riva, then something would be a little risky about it.

Chris Arnold had sent a text to Tiggy a little late and was already on the three hour flight from Sydney to Christchurch by the time he'd thought to confirm their meeting. He hadn't seen his shipmate for years but knew that they'd enjoy his company and his nefarious schemes just as much as he used to. In the meantime, he realised that he'd better call too just to make sure, as communications from aircraft weren't always that reliable.

"Tiggy is that you?" There was a hesitation at the other end as the recipient muffled his voice, then eventually an answer.

"Lord Collywobble – can that be you after all this time?" said a breathless Tiggy, who still sounded a little uncertain.

"Yes, you uncouth peasant, I'm here about that worm-riddled boat you're trying to sell."

"Ahh ... well Collywobble – where are you now?"

"Looking out of the window of this bi-plane that Air New Zealand are using – it looks like we're just approaching Christchurch."

"Goodness – you do move quickly when you think there might be some money in it," Tiggy said with a smile in his voice.

"Somebody has to get you out of trouble Tiggy – is this Riva actually yours or did you steal it from Sophia Loren's granny or one of your other girls?"

"All mine Collywobble, but there are some forces of darkness around as usual ... we might need to be a little careful."

"There always were with your deals Foghorn – where shall we meet? I can be in Akaroa or anywhere local in about three hours."

"I'm not quite ready yet Collywobble, so don't bust a gut."

They arranged to meet at Pierre's for lunch the following day and Chris settled down for the landing. He sent a confirmation of his meeting to his boss at Chartwells and said that he might need to set up an auction over the next few days. He appreciated that this was short notice but since Covid most auction houses had become expert at sales where bidders could bid online or attend the sale personally. The Riva looked incredibly photogenic and once they got it on the water and got it filmed Chris reckoned that a number of the rich on the Chartwell lists would be captivated.

Sergeant Lawrence stopped at the Goldsmiths Arms and checked that they had a room. It was the only decent pub with accommodation for miles so he was relieved that they had some space. If he'd known that his quarry had stayed in the same place a couple of days previously, he might have been tempted to swab for DNA or something. In blissful ignorance he dumped his bag and wandered back to the bar for a pint. So far that ape of a local cop hadn't turned up which was a huge benefit as he didn't want to have to explain why Max was on his patch unannounced.

It was difficult to work out the International time differences but after wandering around the pub for a few minutes he got enough signal to check emails from Miriam Bender. It seemed that they were still in the air but anticipated that they could be in Christchurch in 24 hours and Akaroa as soon as they could hire a car. Max reckoned that they hadn't really allowed for jet lag and that any human being would need to get their head down for a few hours first. He just asked them to email him when they'd arrived in Christchurch and confirm things.

He'd only done long haul once himself when he'd taken the wife on a special trip but it had taken him a week to get his head back together. The US was even further and they would need some rest if they were going to function properly and be with him when he apprehended Foghorn or Count Jergov or whatever ID he was using now.

"What's the boy from the big city doin on my patch," Max sighed inwardly at the gruff voice behind him and wondered whether he could get out quickly before he had an argument. He turned and looked at the cop who'd always given Neanderthal Man a bad name and noted the bandage strapped round his cranium.

"What happened to you?" Max asked hoping that it would distract from his question.

"A fuckin pom loving bitch hit me with a bottle a couple of nights ago," the ape answered.

"A girl injured you?" Max asked knowing that he might draw maximum discomfort from the constable, who was undoubtedly misogynist as well as bigoted.

"You can't hit women any more, can you? And she was with this huge bearded pom and by the time I'd turned round they'd legged it – 10 stitches this is!"

Max tried to look sympathetic but failed, though his interest was slightly piqued by any mention of a pom, though to this cop anyone not born in South Island or with 6 toes like his family, was probably what he called a pom.

It was funny how New Zealand varied with Kiwis whose parents or grandparents came from Scotland, Ireland or Wales often becoming more enthusiastically Scots, Irish or Welsh than those in the home countries. Others like this ape just became anti English.

Despite all that Max realised that he really couldn't avoid asking everyone at the bar about his target and pulled out a the wanted poster.

"Have you seen this bloke?" Max showed the Constable and the Landlord the photo fit images of the Count. The landlord looked studiously blank but the Cop immediately pointed to the bearded version of the image mocked up by the computer guys.

"That's the bastard ... that's the bastard who was with the bitch who bottled me ... are you after him for murder or something?" The cop drew himself up to his full height and looked maniacal.

Max looked at him and the pale white gut bursting through his uniform shirt and thought that some people give policing a bad name. He had to think quickly as the last thing he needed was Constable Bigot on the case in Akaroa with him, so he had to be devious.

"No, he's a star witness for the prosecution on the run from some gangsters in Auckland...When did you seen him?" Our Sergeant asked with commendable restraint.

"Yesterday, he was in here – wasn't he Jack?"

Another barfly called Jack picked up the photo fits and nodded enthusiastically. The ape grabbed the sheet and studied it with enthusiasm.

"Wow he's important then – and I saw him first. This is the break I've been looking for. Do you realise that I've been in this shit heap for ten years? This could be my ticket out of here."

By the look on the landlord's face and one or two regulars, Max could see that the locals would be delighted if anything from a hole in the ground to a hole in the head would rid them of this horrible man but he had to end their hopes.

"Constable Dylan it is incredibly important that you stay here. You are the only man to have seen him in the flesh and he could be staying in the area or on his way back. It's vital that you stay here and keep watch – I'll tell the Chief, believe me you'll get the credit you deserve." Max could see the information being processed slowly by the brain of the beast and decided to leave the bar and go to his room before it had time to compute.

Max couldn't remember whether he'd said that he was on the way to Akaroa or not but hoped not. The thought of him turning up and ruining everything sent Max into a cold sweat and so he drained his pint and made his excuses to the constable. His plan was to stay in the bedroom for a couple of hours and hope that the cop left, so he could have some food and a pint.

Tiggy had a very basic problem to resolve and after a few hours sleep in the emperor size bed and another glorious dawn through the windows of the apartment in Akaroa, he felt strong enough to start thinking. That problem was how much was the Riva worth.

There was a reasonable signal but his phone was so basic that it was difficult to get real information but he'd done some research over the last few weeks and knew that new Rivas can be much larger but cost between ten and thirty million dollars. Judging by the waiting lists, they were in great demand.

Looking at used or classic Rivas was quite easy at first. He found a 1966 Riva Super Aquamarina that was selling at nearly a million US dollars, a 26ft Riva Tritone which was quite rare and was around 700K and a few 1970's boats that were a couple of hundred thousand. The rarest boats were fetching lots of money and there was nothing like his boat going back to the 1920's or 30's and nothing with a cabin like his. In his book when it came to rare things of beauty it always made sense to aim high.

He was going down to the boat yard in a couple of hours to see the boat on the water and have a full test. The thought of Roberto being beaten by the mayor's wife whilst wearing a Roman soldier's outfit still made him laugh and the shots he'd taken had come out surprisingly well, considering the bad light. He'd been expecting all kinds of problems and demands for money from the shyster, so it was helpful to have that leverage.

It was going to be useful to have Chris Arnold over from Sydney. He'd always got on with Lord Collywobble and Chartwells was a respectable auction house. Provenance might be a difficulty with the boat however, as the contract he'd signed in ignorance from De Glanville in that bar in Palma all those years ago, appeared to give him ownership but who really knew. He'd certainly paid a fortune for its mooring fees then and an even greater fortune for its repairs since and had boxes full of receipts to prove it, but would that be enough?

Just to stir things up a little Tiggy emailed a wonderful shot of a Centurion being whipped by a slave to Roberto's address and reminded him to have the boat in the water first thing for a proper sea trial. He was tempted to copy it to the mayor's official email but restrained himself with difficulty. The Mayor was a thug and quite likely to eliminate the boatbuilder in a particularly nasty way and Tiggy needed him at the helm putting the Riva through its paces in a couple of hours and needed the official Riva stamp on all the work he'd done.

Tiggy had a shower and walked back to the balcony with a cup of Costa Rican coffee and looked out at the view. The sun was shining on the bay and there was one cruise ship on the horizon already and there were a few leisure boats out on the bay. This was a beautiful place and the air smelt clean and the sky looked that bright light blue that New Zealand seemed to specialise in. Tiggy breathed deeply and wondered whether he would ever be safe or rich enough to live here. The next few days could be the culmination of all his plans. As a 40 something Englishman of dubious parentage and with few skills except for love-making, this was a major turning point.

In his dreams all his efforts were rewarded and the Riva sold for millions of dollars and the police never found him. Much to his surprise Tiggy realised that his dreams had developed a new ryder and that was he was sharing that perfect existence with someone else. That was a large shapely woman from Miami who had the most cheerful disposition of anybody he'd shared a bed with – Miriam Bender.

Tiggy realised that he couldn't afford dreams. Count Jergov was a calculating bastard who had used his skills in bed and ability to con good women in order to make hundreds of thousands of dollars to feed his real mistress - a Riva Weekender. Over the next few days Tiggy needed all that selfish determination and not get distracted by any piece of skirt. If he succeeded then he might be able to indulge in such romantic crap.

Looking over to the boatyard, Tiggy could see that Roberto and his team were already winching the boat down the slipway to the water. Looking at the Rolex, Tiggy realised that he was due to meet them down at the harbour and that he'd better get dressed. The watch was a bit of a totem and it seemed like years since the hard-hearted woman from Brazil had stolen his heart and then his watch. He'd used his wits to get the collectors piece at cut price from its original owner and had to use equal cunning to get back from the pawn shop in Dunedin. Apart from the Riva it was the most valuable thing he owned and one had sold for a fortune at Sotheby's recently.

Looking down on his wrist he needed to remember that he was not impervious to charm and that sometimes he was his own worst enemy. He put on his Swanndri and put wallet and mobile in the zipped pocket and went downstairs, soon he would get the chance to see what that pseudo-Italian bastardo had done to the Riva and listen to his demands for more money.

Al Romano, recently resident in Las Vegas, had landed in what he was told was Christchurch Airport and had given his assistant his bags to carry through. It was always easier at the private jet terminal in most countries and this appeared to be no different. As long as you had your passports and other paperwork in order there wasn't normally much formality. In this case that was important as the bag carried by his finance guy contained around three million dollars which had come out of a couple of arcade machines in his Coliseum Hotel that the IRS didn't know existed.

The guy was also carrying a personalised golf bag by Fletcher and Steel that had a Glock 19 lookalike hidden that was made from some material that according to the armourer didn't show up on most x-ray machines. Romano knew fuck all about golf but knew that he needed some kind of weapon to help him through negotiations.

Romano felt naked without his normal two minders and Nico hadn't exactly been his normal companion on the trip over, spending hours worrying about money laundering rules in New Zealand and tax laws. But he was a useful organiser and bag-carrier especially when the contents of the bags might be a little risky.

The flight had been long and so he got Nico to book a suite at the best hotel at the airport and check out limos for the trip over to Akaroa. There was no hurry as he had told that idiot Roberto that he wanted the boat and no one was going to deny him especially some third generation peasant who thought that his grandfather was part of his family.

He'd watched his favourite film again on the flight and seen the lovely Sophia Loren and the handsome Cary Grant (who was so cool that he must have Italian blood) go across Lake Como in the Riva. He knew the story by heart and the two had been married for only a year before war broke out and had been staying on the boat for weeks and speeding from cove to cove ahead of the Nazi's in the Riva Weekender. At the end of conflict, there was a lovely scene where the boat – battered but still lovely moors outside a lovely hotel and they go in for a romantic dinner.

That hotel frontage was the one Romano had re-created on the water outside his hotel in Los Vegas and contained the VIP suites that were so popular with visiting stars and gangland bosses. The boat was the last piece in his plan to bring back the great days of his hotel and the city.

The suite in New Zealand was crap and the food in the hotel would have had any Italian chef tearing his hair out with embarrassment but Romano had around seven hours sleep before Nico was hammering at his door asking stupid questions.

He'd thought that jet-lag was an invention of the first class wankers who'd blighted his early life by playing stressed executives on some of the worse American movies ever made. If they wanted stress Al had thought to himself, these suited warriors should try pushing their way to the top in a group of psychopathically ambitious teenagers, like he had and not get tired on an international trip by drinking too many Martinis.

Now he knew better, he felt feverish, tired and like he was coming down from some bad trip – drug induced, not travel. He told his assistant to leave him in peace for another few hours and go out and find him some decent Italian food and not come back empty handed. Nico scuttled away looking pale and knackered but knowing that a mistake when the boss was in this kind of mood, could be fatal. He went down to the reception and slipped the guy a hundred dollars to find him some genuine Italian pasta or something and have it fresh in the hotel reception in four hours and he would get another hundred US dollars.

The receptionist was called Francanelli and obviously had some kind of Italian in his ancestry along with Polish on his mother's side and had seen the two guests arrive earlier. The Nico guy handing out the dollar bills looked fairly normal but his boss looked scary in a way you don't normally see in downtown Christchurch. About 5ft 9inches tall but built like a rugby prop forward in a black handmade suit that couldn't disguise the muscle in the arms and the black hair that crept over his silk shirt wherever it could. But it was the face that was really frightening – swarthy, unshaven and dark with eyes that looked at him like a reptile. Really scary and not a man he wanted to deliver a Pizza Hut meal to.

Luckily, he had an answer and called his Papa and explained the situation, saying that there was fifty NZ dollars in it plus whatever the meal costs if he could deliver something authentic to the hotel in three hours. Luigi Franconeli said to his wife that there was 20 dollars in it for her if she could rustle up some decent pasta for an Italian staying at the airport hotel. She was delighted to do anything for anyone from the old country as she knew that the food there was an insult.

Before her husband had finished the call, she was hand making fusilli and making her famous Carbonara sauce. She knew that spaghetti would have been more traditional but fusilli had more class in her opinion and no-one had ever complained about her pasta. Three hours later the sauce was bubbling on the stove and it was rich, creamy and with some of her best pancetta for bite. For fun she also included a fresh green salad and some of her home baked bread. Her husband hadn't mentioned quantity but she'd done enough for two people.

When Luigi delivered the pasta in a basket covered in a tea-towel the smell was enough to make the receptionist salivate copiously and he had to stop himself from dipping in. He called the suite and waited as a drowsy voice with a strong American accent answered and said to the man that his home made genuine Italian meal was ready and that it needed to be collected without delay. The assistant Nico came down immediately and was given the full provenance – aged female cook from Puglia who'd been on the staff of the Bertone family in Florence whose pasta had been legendary etc etc. Nico could smell something good, handed over the money and rushed up in the lift to the suite whilst the food was fresh and repeated to provenance to his boss with the embellishment that the cook had been on the staff of a major Italian hotel in Lake Como.

Al Romano tucked his napkin into his shirt collar as he had seen in the movies and knew that there was a god. The pasta may have been basic food but it was wonderful and only bettered when he'd been in Chicago as a kid. The sauce was sumptuous and if that cretin Nico thought that he was getting any – he had better get real. The only regret was the lack of a bottle of Amarone to go with it but as his body didn't quite know whether it was breakfast, lunch or dinner, he was prepared to live with it for once.

The desert was also wonderful and as he was feeling generous, he offered Nico a couple of scoops to try. In truth the meal had been fantastico and his assistant had done well – but now was not the time to show it anyone. He growled like a wounded bear and Nico exited like a scalded rat. Now he was feeling more human Romano pulled over his bags and started to assemble the Glock 19 from the parts in the golf bag and check the rolls of US dollars in the other case. It was extremely relaxing and after a couple of hours Romano was ready to plan his trip to Akaroa.

The Riva Weekender was 50ft long and powered by a V8 Ferrari engine that the Chief Designer at Riva had negotiated with Enzo Ferrari to have specially designed for the boat. This had been estimated to be 410 HP and supposedly capable of propelling the boat at speeds of up to 60 mph which was considered insane by many engineers at the time. Sea trials had shown that they had been right and that the hull was in danger of self destruction at that speed. The engine was de-tuned so that it could propel the boat at a more manageable speed which was still record-breaking for its time.

The boat had obviously rammed something solid in its early days that had seriously damaged the hull and been kept out of sight during the second world war, though no-one had real knowledge of who had hidden it. The first time it had appeared back on the scene seemed to be the late 20th Century when a mysterious owner called De Glanville tried to sell it – first in Positano then in Palma when a certain amount of work had been done to make the craft sea worthy.

Riva itself seemed uninterested in the boat during this period as new boats were all that the market wanted with their new designs getting larger and more sophisticated as bankers, hedge fund cowboys, web kings and oligarchs wanted a vessel that looked good anywhere from Dubai to Beijing and kept a crew of twenty on permanent standby. Then as Super-Yachts became commonplace in the rich harbours of the world then the people who guide taste amongst those who have serious money started to look for something that was rarer – something that was not made anymore. That was when someone in a drawing office in Italy came upon the plans of a boat that was a dream of a wonderful designer and engineer many years ago.

It started when a Riva agent in New Zealand sent an email of a damaged boat that was supposedly a Riva to their head office but no one recognised it. The boat had obviously been restored there and looked every inch a Riva. But as it had no provenance and was larger than most boats of that era, the bosses first thought it must be a fake – a very lovely fake- but a fake worth suing someone for. Then someone had dug down in the oldest plans chests, which hadn't yet been digitised or dumped and found that this was possibly the most significant find in the last fifty years. One unique boat created by one of the most influential people in the family with one of the most ionic names in motor racing. The plans were there but no-one had thought that the boat had been produced.

The next thing seen at HQ was a notification from the auction house Chartwells that a boat thought to be a Riva from around 1920/30 was being sold by public auction in 48 hours. It was evident from the email that this was the same boat and a call was made immediately to the Riva agent and to Chartwells to say that they wanted the boat as it was of huge significance but were concerned about its lack of documented history.

The call was received by Carlos on his mobile as he was with Mr Foghorn and just about to take the boat out on the water

"Meester Foghorn as you cana see, the boat looks wunnerful."

"Yeh, Carlos, but if you are about to stitch me up with another load of surprise bills then I promise you the photo I sent on your email will be copied to the mayor's office before you finish the sentence."

"Noa ... pleasa dona do dat – no more bills ina fact Ia want to buy de boat ofa you."

Tiggy ignored the statement and fired up the engine which burbled like a caged lion behind him. The wheel was old-fashioned wood and aluminium and felt better that any mere steering device. Even better than the Aston Martin he'd owned in his mis-spent youth.

Trying not to show the love he was feeling he handed it over to Carlos and ordered him to take over and give it some stick. Over the next twenty minutes the boatman quartered the bay at great speed in sweeping curves and tight turns that showed the Riva's amazing performance. The decking sparkled and the engine noise was divine bringing people out of the boat club and shops to wonder at that Ferrari roar.

Tiggy pushed down through the saloon doors and pulled up a few hatch covers to see whether the manoeuvres had created any leaks. There was a tiny bit of water under the forepeak but really nothing to worry about. Whilst he was wedged in the cabin, he remembered the Carlos offer to buy the boat and sensed that the phone call he'd taken just before they'd boarded had been something to do with it. In some ways it might be an attractive option as anonymity was safer and Carlos was a plausible seller but he was a total shyster and unlikely to offer anything like the value or have the money anyway. If he'd done some research and had a buyer already, then what he offered would be interesting

"Carlos, there is a leak under the forepeak hatch and the engine was starting to run a little rough, but you've not done a bad job of the interiors. I was relieved to see that you hadn't decorated the saloon in the style of a Roman Generals tent or with manacles after what I saw yesterday."

"Err... upph," Carlos gurgled nervously, for once speechless.

"What would you offer for the boat ... should I be insane enough to sell it?" Tiggy asked as he sat down on the seat and Carlos slowed to a halt close to the harbour and drifted.

As Carlos furrowed his brow and tried to work out just how much a fool Tiggy was and what might be a plausible offer, Tiggy noticed a tall fair haired figure stood on the quay who looked very much like Lord Collywobble and he had a camera in his hand.

"Listen Carlos, you better tell me soon – that's my agent from Chartwells, the world famous auctioneers, so your price better not take the piss."

"Three undred thousand dollars and I'll forget all the resta my bills," said Carlos more in hope than expectation.

"You haven't got that kind of money anyway you charlatan," Tiggy exploded. "And unless you want to see the wrath of the mayor, don't mention extra bills again."

"I'da find it quick."

The Riva slid into the mooring and Carlos leapt off to tie the bow lines whilst a familiar figure handled the stern line. Privately Tiggy was astonished by the size of his offer because it was far higher than he was expecting from a guy who was notoriously tight-fisted. All Tiggy managed to do as he got off was to shout, "millions you shit – it's worth millions – now fix that leak."

Tiggy congratulated himself that he'd held his composure and walked over to his ex shipmate and shook him warmly by the hand. He'd still got the long fair hair and high tanned forehead with cool Ray-Bans pushed back from the blue laconic eyes. There were more wrinkles, maybe the suspicion of a belly but he still stood tall and slim in his rumpled linen jacket, blue trousers and battered suede shoes.

Chris and he were ship mates in many ways but it was good that they had separated after the navy. Despite the good times they had shared, there was still an edge of blokey competition and Tiggy could see him sizing him up too. If they'd stayed together, they would have competed so much for women, money or status and they would have ended up shooting each other, being shot by a jealous partner or sharing a jail cell. But it was great to see him.

Chris Arnold spent a couple of minutes looking round the boat whilst Carlos glowered at them from the stern seat. Arnold didn't really know anything worthwhile about boats of this type any more than he'd known much about classic cars. But he could look like an expert in anything and after he'd taken a few shots and opened a few hatches with a look of intense concentration on his face, the boatbuilder was convinced at least and shouted that he might be able to get a better offer for the Riva if he had chance to call someone.

The two ex officers ignored him and walked round the harbour and back to Pierre's place. Arnold said he'd taken some footage of the boat when it had been speeding around the bay and it looked fantastic. He asked permission to send it out to all their database of buyers and Tiggy agreed but said that they needed to have a detailed planning meeting over a bottle of Kiwi sparkling now and that Chartwells was paying. Also, that he needed a large plate of Eggs and Bacon after his sea trip. Chris always knew when an expense account meal was worth having and ordered two bottles immediately.

If the two men had known just how much interest the boat was creating, they might have targeted even higher when it came to the reserve. Al Romano had three million US dollars in his Gladstone bag and would use it to buy the boat if the usual amount of intimidation and violence didn't get it for nothing. That approach was purely just a matter of principle – the fact is Romano had an embarrassment of dollars hidden in the vault of his hotel that he would never be able to explain if the IRS came to call. So being seen to spend a few mill on a real legal transaction might help.

Another very interested party was Carlo Fontaine who had realised that he was a direct descendent of the iconic designer who'd been behind the collaboration with Ferrari in the 1920's. He'd made billions by selling out his social media empire in 2020 to one of the major platforms, who then made such a bad job developing it, that he bought it back for a pittance. Since then, he had revolutionised that side of the market and was in danger of making billions all over again. Carlo Fontaine was obsessed with Italian and Scandinavian designers of the early 20th Century and already had some lovely Ferraris and extraordinary bits of Swedish furniture. When the mailing came in about the Riva auction and he realised its significance, he told his agent that he would buy it at any cost.

Chartwells had another dozen expressions of solid interest within five hours of sending out their email. Head Office had seen the film that Chris had sent and seen just how lovely the boat looked. The Riva was unique and boats were new territory for the auction house but some experts were already predicting that this boat could outperform his last auction in Australasia which had been the Ferrari. Arnold was astonished that his boss was trying to reach him despite the fact that it was 3.00 a.m. in London but decided to have lunch with his old mate first.

The other people on their way to Akaroa were mainly interested in the boat because it was the only way they might find Count Jergov aka Tiggy Foghorn.
Miriam Bender and Elmer Flannigan were the first of the searchers and they had been in New Zealand for a couple of minutes. The journey had nearly crippled Elmer and he had demanded a spa and hotel room for himself or he would be unable to continue. Miriam was fitter and anxious to get on but could see the pain he was in and called the police sergeant to tell him they would be delayed. He made some suggestions and within a few minutes they were on the way to an expensive but excellent health resort.
Sergeant Lawrence realised that he wouldn't be able to meet them for another couple of days and booked into the Goldsmiths for another night. He decided to mitigate the risk of meeting the ape of a cop again by instructing the idiot to check all the empty holiday homes and Baches in the area and keep one or two of the nearest under undercover surveillance. There were dozens of such properties in the beach area and up in the hills so Max was convinced that he would be occupied for at least 48 hours.
Back on his computer Max had informed headquarters about the extension to his trip and gone back to the pub for a lunchtime pint of Speights and a Venison Pie. As he sat in the garden feeling the late Autumn sun on his back, he didn't feel a trace of guilt. He spent twelve hours a day keeping the evil powers at bay round Dunedin. So a little me time was called for and there was no point in arriving before the two people who could ID the fugitive anyway. The pie arrived and it was rich and full of gravy but sadly the pint had disappeared and Max had to order another. He sighed deeply and wondered whether the Spanish trick of

siesta was worth trying. The room was really comfortable and Max thought it would be worth experimenting.

"If Chartwells want to handle this, they will need to do the auction in the next 48 hours." Tiggy looked through the empty bottles on the table at Pierre's and tried to focus on Chris Arnold's face.
"Jeez, why?"
"Because the powers of darkness are getting close and I need to get this whole thing over with ... listen Chris, you're going to have to do it or I'll sell the boat direct," Tiggy whispered intently.
"But that might mean you get a lower price – you haven't told me what you want for the boat yet!" the auctioneer said, seeing the chance of his commission disappearing. It was funny he thought, Tiggy had been an impulsive, instinctive man all the time they had served together but when he made his mind up, that was it. "OK, let me make a call."
Chris Arnold pulled out his mobile and left the hubbub of the restaurant so he could call London. It was still an anti-social hour there but his boss had tried to get him in the middle of the night, so he decided to return the favour.
Tiggy still hadn't decided what he wanted for the Riva. The 300K offered by Carlos had been a huge surprise as he had no idea where the man could find that kind of money and so it was likely that there was someone financing him. Also, that it was a fraction of its true worth.
Whilst Chris was phoning the office Tiggy decided to come at the problem from a different direction. He was in his 40's, he had a miserable Navy pension and few skills other than plausibility and lovemaking that might earn him a living in the future. So the Riva needed to finance his next 40 years. So the big question was – how much cash does a gentleman and a scholar need to finance a future of travel, good clothes, debauchery?
"Three million dollars – US dollars that is," said Chris Arnold, as he sat down after his call.
"Whaa..." was all Tiggy could manage in shock that his friend could read his mind from that distance.
"That is what head office think should be your reserve after the amount of interest they've already had online to the email we sent out to clients," he said smoothly.
"Four million is what I was thinking." Tiggy realised that he needed to think big and hide his surprise – after all he'd been sacrificing his body for years so that the Riva could float.

"OK, but remember that we need to pitch the reserve just right – it's not what we expect to get."

Tiggy nodded sagely as if he knew everything about auctions. In fact, he'd only seen them on TV and that was when the odd Renoir hit the market or at the other end of the market on the Aussie programme, "Cash in your Granny."

Feeling as though he was entering some kind of drug induced fantasy, Tiggy played mental games with the figures and liked the result. When he was a kid there was a programme about a family of Hillbillies who discovered oil on their land and had every luxury money could buy thrust upon them - huge cars, ranch style mansions and lovely women. He was starting to feel the same.

He forced himself to concentrate and Chris confirmed that they could set up the auction in 24 hours. Some people might come directly but Chartwells expected most of the action to be online. Chris would act as auctioneer and the fee would be 10%. Tiggy was tempted to complain but decided that the figures were so outrageous he just shut up.

There was discussion as to where to hold the auction and Tiggy favoured Pierre's Restaurant but space was an issue and regrettably the Sailing Club had more space and was even closer to the boat. So Arnold said that he'd sort it out whilst he paid the bill and they retired to the apartment.

Tiggy said that Arnold could stay at the apartment and gave him directions. Yet another day had nearly passed in Pinot Noir fuelled glory and Akaroa was looking wonderful. As he wandered down the front of the shops he looked out to sea and this time there was a cruise ship coming in that looked a little like the *Amazon*.

He sat drunkenly down on a bench that had a brass plaque commemorating some Kiwi couple who been here looked at the view and obviously died. In a moment of absolute genius Tiggy vowed to himself that when he made a few millions, the first thing he would do was buy a bench for himself whilst he was still alive. Then he could enjoy the wonderful scenery without being dead.

The cruise ships were almost over for the year and Tiggy imagined that he would miss them. As a matter of pride, he went through a memory check of those onboard *Amazon* who had contributed to the Riva fund by buying a little bit of the Eugene Fenton book. He pulled his leather folder out of his case as a double check.

Firstly, there was Miriam and sister Elsie. Secondly Elmer Flannigan and partner Neil. These originals had a special place in his heart. The horrible red headed gorgon Florence Hasty deserved to be boiled in one of her cut-price crematoria. Ms Anders and her cadet son had been important targets as anyone who thought that John Lennon had been supporting the National Rifle Association with his record "Happiness is a warm Gun," **needed to be shot**. Tiggy was trying to remember any of the others and mentally shuffled through each lounge or bar on the ship until another contributor reared their head. The last and most beautiful of his donors came to mind - De Candole Von something, the lovely blonde haired Aryan woman from Panama who'd decided that a place in Eugene Fenton's book might explain how her Nazi grandfather had a collection of fine art acquired during the war.

Tiggy was proud of himself and glad that all the sex and alcohol hadn't totally pickled his faculties. He opened his notebook and cursed – he'd forgotten the Chinese couple who he'd taken on dry land at Port Chalmers. Unlike some of his victims they didn't seem people who deserved it – then he remembered that they were buying property in New Zealand on the cheap for the Chinese government. That made him feel much better – New Zealand should be owned by the locals.

And how could he forget Adele? Beautiful Eurocrats of conveniently mixed parentage who knew how to use Woke to rip off the system, deserve all they got too.

With a clear conscience Tiggy had a triple slug of Lagavulin he'd kept from Dunedin and staggered to bed thinking of tomorrow. The bed was huge and he realised that it felt a little empty without someone large, round and warm to share it with. There had been a time only a couple of weeks ago when he thought a well-rounded, young woman with an all over tan and a Brazilian accent might have been his answer. Now he knew that he needed to think bigger.

Miriam Bender had not slept well. The jet lag had meant that she'd lain for hours on the hotel room in New Zealand with a body that was convinced that it needed to get up for breakfast. She'd tried everything – counting all the golf clubs in her late husband's bag, listening to George's golf jokes in her imagination and nothing worked. Then, just as she drifted off, her phone rang and that nice local cop was trying to tell her to wake up and get to Akaroa in a hurry. It took a cup of strong coffee and a return call to Sergeant Lawrence for her to concentrate enough to really get the message.

Apparently, there was to be an auction of a Riva boat that was worth millions and it was suspected that it was the one owned by Mr Foghorn. Miriam didn't get the drift for a while but when Max said that this was the real name of the felon called Count Jergov, known to many as Tiggy, she got a real jolt in a part of her body that hadn't really had any action since she'd last met the aforesaid Tiggy.

The cop tried to emphasise that the auction was in less than 24 hours and that after that, he was sure that he would be on the move.

Miriam called Elmer Flannigan and passed on the message. He had been in the Spa and had a massage that had helped his body unkink after the flight. He had also hired some sort of vehicle so they could make the last part of the journey from Christchurch airport to Akaroa, which was about a three hour drive across the mountains. At around 6ft 6inches and 20 stone and with the build of an all-in wrestler, Miriam was astonished that he'd found a vehicle big enough, but said nothing and arranged to meet in the hotel cafe in 30 minutes, packed and ready to leave.

The vehicle turned out to be a Range Rover which was large enough for Elmer and had every conceivable luxury from leather seats and real wood facia through to clever all-wheel drive systems and satnav that knew where you were before you knew it yourself. By late morning they were on the road and Elmer was an excellent driver remembering to be on the left hand side almost all of the journey.

As a precaution they had tried to get hotel rooms in Akaroa and found none available as some visiting American had block booked a floor in the main hotel and there were other visitors arriving for some kind of sale. In the end they had rented a place through Air B&B overlooking the town en route as a precaution. Neither of them knew exactly when the sale was and the thought of travelling on too far was beyond anybody.

The only car that passed them on the first part of the journey was an extremely garish white Volvo stretch limo which looked as though it spent most of its life carrying hen-parties or prom guests. The girlie look carried on onside which mock fur seating and a drinks cabinet that seemed to contain lots of small bottles of cheap Prosecco and play a tune when you opened the door. Inside was a very unhappy Al Romano and a very scared Nico who was driving the limo and slunked down in front of the sliding screen which separated the driver normally from the party goers.

In the US Romano had two limos – a large black Cadillac and a dark grey Mercedes. He also had a number of Range Rovers in black with smoked windows so he could look like the motorcade of a visiting monarch.

Finally, a couple of Ferraris and Alfas that kept his Italian image cool but he was unable to get in or out of.

The driver had been asked to get a limo and the only one available was this. The driver hadn't helped his survival chances by driving it round a roundabout the wrong way and forgetting what side of the road they drove on in New Zealand. This is created a fish tale skid on the main road out of Christchurch and curses from the back as Romano was thrown round the mock fur interior and ended up on the floor where all he could see with his head wedged under the seat was what appeared to be a used prophylactic. This did not help his temper and had he been able to assemble the Glock, then the driver would have died on New Zealand soil. Eventually, however, the car pulled into a cutting and they both got their breath back.

"Yer mudderfucker, yer mudderfucker, yer a dead man." Al Romano repeated until he managed to drag himself off the floor and would have smashed his fist through the glass partition and grabbed the driver by the throat until he realised that for the moment, he needed him. He was in a strange country where the cops weren't on his payroll and he had no idea where Akaroa was. A dead driver would not be productive at the moment so he pulled himself back on the seat and waved him on reminding him forcibly that these limeys drove on the left and had these strange things called traffic islands.

After they had got out of town the driver started to gain confidence as it was relatively flat and there was little traffic. He'd never seen roads so empty and shouted through to Romano that he'd booked an entire floor at the best hotel in Akaroa and said that they'd be paying cash which had meant that he'd succeeded in getting a discount. This meant a lot to the driver whose normal job for the mob was finance but just got curses from Romano. Thinking it through later he realised that with over three million in illicit cash in his bag, the boss was probably more interested in other things like the boat he was after.

The boss had played the Sophia Loren/ Cary Grant movie on the plane video system and tried to explain why he loved the Riva but the accountant had to pretend that he understood. To him the boat looked old -fashioned and the film ridiculous. But he knew better than argue as Romano's life would not be complete until he had the Riva moored on the lake on the front of his hotel.

After about an hour the car started to flash that fuel was low and they had a panic trying to find a filling station in such a remote area. Thank goodness a small country store came on the horizon with a few pumps outside. Much to his surprise a guy came out and they realised that it wasn't self-service. After a few minutes pumping, the guy said it was a hundred dollars and Romano buzzed down the rear window and handed a wad of dollars through. The attendant nearly complained that the currency was US not NZ, but decided against when he saw the look of the guy. Also realising that he was quietly making about an extra 15% on the deal if he kept his mouth shut. He shut the filler cap and wished them both an ironic 'have a nice day' and walked slowly back to the workshop counting the notes again.

The journey got considerably worse after that as the plains east of Christchurch started to end and they started to hit the mountain ranges. The stretch limo was not designed for hairpin bends and neither was the driver who'd only got experience in Las Vegas and Nevada which were either crazy busy or empty but always wide and straight. What made it worse were the lumber trucks which were few in number but huge in size and who seemed to take an instant dislike to the limo. One such behemoth overtook them on the first of the bends and he panicked and pulled on to a secondary route which seemed fine until it got steeper, narrower and they were faced with a line of chequered tape across the edge of a drop.

Despite his fear of the boss, Nico had to stop and get out. He could hear the door opening and knew it was the boss because of the expletives and what made it worse he could hear an engine labouring up the hill behind and it sounded like the sort of truck he'd being trying to avoid.

"G'day mate, who's drivin the tartmobile?" The guy in the big tartan jacket was hairy, tall and wearing what appeared to be a hat made from some kind of dead animal. He repeated the question but louder and the driver knew the boss wasn't going to answer without a gun in his hand so admitted the fact in his best US accent.

"You from Melbourne are you?" The guy asked with not a little amount of piss-take.

"No, we're from Las Vegas" the limo driver answered.

"Well Mr Las Vegas, would you mind moving this …. this shit heap out of the way so I can get through?"

"I'm real sorry ... I don't think I can," said Nico looking over the brink at a drop that seemed to go on forever.

"For fucks sake give me the keys – I'll turn it round – go back to the main road. If you carry on this way, you'll reach the quarry and if the guys see this car, they might think it's party time."

The truck driver went to the limo and put in reverse so fast that it banged into the cliff face, then slammed it into first and accelerated on full lock to the edge. There he reversed again and skidded the Volvo round on its axis so it was facing the other way. He then got out and climbed up into the truck and carried on his journey with a blast of air horns that nearly killed the two Americans.

It was a quiet journey after that and not much was said, even when the limo was having to negotiate hair bin bends on the last bit if the journey. After the mountain track everything was easy and the fact that a big farmers truck had passed them half a mile previously with bald tyres and sheep in the back, meant that Nico could just follow their line with more confidence. Eventually they saw the bay of their destination below them and realised why everybody came here. Even Al Romano, whose idea of a nice view was the butt of big woman playing one of his machines in Vegas, was looking out at the bay and the mountains and smiling to himself.

The car swept round the last few bands and narrowly missed an oncoming coach but it didn't matter, the driver had survived the precipice of a mountain pass, the attack of killer lumber trucks and he was still alive. The last bend into town was wonderful and the big white Volvo entered the beach road in confident style, much to the amusement of locals sitting outside the cafes and shops, who thought they'd been invaded by the most riotous hen party ever seen. Every panel seemed to have a dent and the rear end looked as though it had collided with a mountain.

The hotel that Romano had booked looked more like a guest house. Mr and Mrs McDonald who ran it were respectable second generation Scots from Stirling and they kept a clean and orderly house. The sight of the hen party limo sliding into their car park horrified them so much that they were going to refuse entry, The sight of a thin white face man opening the door for a man who looked like he might have been in the Sopranos, did not help. In the end it was only the weedy man pushing hundreds of US dollars through the front door that got their interest.

Eventually Nico explained through the letter box that they were a film crew from America and so they'd booked the first floor of the hotel. Mrs McDonald had actually liked the Gangster series on TV and so relented.

She rationalised the fact that they weren't really gangsters, they were actors playing gangsters, which made the thing OK. The fact that they were paying in cash also made them extremely excusable too.

The descendant of the original designer of the Riva was in a quandary. When he was a kid his father's favourite record was The In Crowd by Brian Ferry and even then he'd understood the elite style being a rich Italian could give him. Carlo Fontaine looked on every day as an episode in his own personal soap opera. From his hand tailored suits from Marchetti of Rome and his hand made shoes by John Lobb of London, he looked the part. Even before he'd sold out his media empire, he was worth millions, now he was worth billions.

Fontaine was a perfect example of his heritage with a medium build, dark haired, brown eyed look that women found irresistible. Cars had been his first love and he was often seen in the VIP suites or pits of Ferrari race team at the F1 or Le Mans. His second love had been tall Scandinavian women and Inga had become his wife two years ago. The marriage had not been a great success because she was a woman who radiated loveliness and in the end, he didn't like the fact that she got more attention than himself. Also, she wanted kids and he didn't, which was a constant cause of arguments and he was paranoid that she'd trick him into parenthood.

His latest love was boats and he'd spent time in Nice and the West Indies learning how to sail the big yachts. Here again Inga disappointed him by being a natural sailor and winning races, also by distracting everyone's attention by having such a beautiful tanned body, which always looked at its best stretched out on a boom or winding the sheets.

He decided to move to power and here he felt that he'd found his true vocation. Inga didn't have a natural advantage and showed a reassuring amount of fear as he took the power boats up to their maximum speed. He was about to buy a Sunseeker Predator from the UK when he saw the email about the Riva and realised that fate was knocking on his door. His quandary was whether to buy just the Sunseeker or acquire both.

Carlo was a great believer in fate and was convinced that the spirit of his father had guided him when he was choosing who to sell his company to. His father was a great business man who'd grown his traditional media empire and pushed him into social media years before anyone else. Sadly, his judgement didn't extend to women and he'd been shot by a Russian hooker who'd decided his money was more attractive than his lovemaking.

His grandfather was a superb designer back in the 1920's but virtually unknown at the time. His fame had come later and the Riva Weekender had been the pinnacle of his achievements, recognised only briefly after his death. Carlo had never met him or seen much of his work but was convinced that his spirit was calling him from that great marina in the sky. Having seen the film of the boat now Carlo understood which is why he was hiring the only Ferrari available in Christchurch and about to cross the country to Akaroa.

Twenty hours later, Tiggy was in disguise and sitting at the back of the sailing club waiting for the auction to be set up. His disguise was a Riva boiler suit in blue which the mechanics wore when important customers were coming in. It looked a little like a Formula 1 or Les Mans pit crew outfit, was an all padded material which was incredibly high tech and zipped up the front. It had electric blue piping down the sleeves and trousers and a large Riva embroidered logo on the chest. Tiggy felt that it made him look rather racy.

The addition of a baseball hat pulled down on his head and his luxuriant beard made Tiggy reasonably confident that many of his old friends would not recognise him. From where he was sitting, he could see the seats that had been laid out leading down to the auction desk with the screen behind it in one corner. Through the large open doors at the end Tiggy could see the harbour and the road leading down to it.

The Akaroa Sailing Club eventually had agreed to be the venue, though a number of the crustaceans on the committee had objected for a while. Only Chris Arnold in full Royal Navy mode had got them to agree by mentioning in the second world war the close links between the NZ Navy and the Royal Navy and just about everything else. The fact that the auction was being televised and Chartwells agreed to sponsor an off-shore sailing competition also probably helped.

Tiggy and Chris had talked for hours about how to handle the sale. Chartwells had updated the figures and at least three bidders were coming personally from different parts of the globe and all had satisfied the auction houses criteria that they had enough wealth to deal with any likely bid.

In addition, there had been numerous expressions of interest from people on the database who might be bidding online for themselves or clients. The minimum qualification for these was the ability to handle bids of up to five million US dollars.

Chartwells had tried to send the boss from Sydney to handle the sale but Tiggy had insisted on Chris Arnold but allowed one assistant to be sent to handle some of technology. As part of the sale Tiggy had insisted that the seller remained anonymous and that provenance for the boat be 'taken as seen'. He had emailed the original contract of sale between De Glanville and himself and added all the work invoices from Palma and here to show that the boat had been restored professionally.

Tiggy had been worried about this aspect and made acceptance of the provenance a condition of Chartwells acceptance of the sale. So far, they had said that they were happy and that the sale would go ahead in precisely four hours' time, which was the most civilised time for bidders in both hemispheres and most likely markets.

Three million dollars was still the reserve that had been agreed for the boat. Tiggy had started to get concerned that it was too much but our auctioneer told him to hold his courage and remember just how much a gentleman of means would need to survive another 40 years in the manner to which he wanted to become accustomed.

Tiggy relented and started to imagine just how much fun he might have with someone like Miriam Bender with that kind of money. Always presuming that she wanted to share some fun with him and that the police didn't throw him in jail first.

"Howamucha money are you goin to give me to keep quiet?" The boat builders false Kiwi/Italian accent had returned as the little shit slid into the seat next to him. That was bad news because he didn't need anyone causing problems at this late time."

"Let's wait until the sale is over Roberto – but I will be generous – believe me I'll be generous." Tiggy whispered out of the corner of his mouth.

With a final muttered threat, the boat man left the hall and Tiggy knew what he had to do. It was cruel, it might even be fatal but he had to do it.

The photograph of Roberto in centurion gear being whipped by a large female slave was sent immediately to the mayor's personal email and his office. The mayor's wife was a fearsome creature so it was obvious who the mayor would want to punish.

In fact, it was 30 minutes before the large Mercedes owned by the mayor pulled up along the way. His honour looked extremely red and he had a large assistant with him. Tiggy moved across to the window where he could see more clearly and after a few seconds Roberto Carlotti was dragged bodily out of his workshop and thrown into the boot of the car. Tiggy suspected that Roberto would not be demanding money from him for some time.

The remaining hours went quickly and technicians installed a large screen linked to the online bidding system and TV cameras delivering a live streaming of the process to key media agencies. Tiggy was shocked by just how big a deal it was and from an anonymity point of view the whole thing was becoming a little threatening. Despite that, he couldn't resist a last look at the boat that had been such a big part of his life for the last few years since he'd been conned into buying it by De Glanville.
He had to admit that the Riva looked superb with the decks shining with teak oil or something similar and the bright work gleaming with hard polishing. The lines were so graceful and the long-raked prows seemed to make the boat look fast even when it was moored. Very few shapes have that quality – the early E-Type Jaguar or the MTB being notable exceptions - of being as truly iconic as this Riva. The other stunning feature was the Ferrari engine. The cover had been left off and the sheer brilliance of the engineering was obvious to anyone with a bit of Soul. Tiggy thought that the team had done well and wandered back to the quiet seats at the back where he could observe the arrivals.
The odd thing sitting down was that he realised that he had a hard-on and he had no idea why. He reckoned it was an hour before the bidding started and some primeval part of brain was telling him he needed sex. He didn't know whether it was the thought of making millions or the thought that he might be locked away for life, but his prick, his old man, his penis needed action.
The waitress from Pierre's was a good sport despite the fact that she'd not recognised him earlier and Tiggy had enjoyed her company when he'd first arrived in the town. She had enjoyed his masters level lovemaking and Tiggy had her number on fast dial, which was an advantage in urgent situations like this.
"Sadie, are you available this very minute?"
"Errr ... yeh if that's the super stud cowboy I used to ride with?"
Tiggy didn't quite get the symbolism but after seeing two other locals dressed as Roman soldiers and sadistic slaves, he wondered whether the whole town had turned into a sensory theme park like Westworld.
He mumbled an affirmative and told her to come to the Sailing Club now and sneak into the secretary's office on the first floor without being seen.

He remembered the body which was younger, slimmer and less voluptuous than his normal taste. But she was appreciative and adventurous and when she arrived, she was wearing a long mac that Tiggy vaguely recognised as a Driza Bone and as the weather was warm, he couldn't quite see why. Then she opened the front and he understood.

"You think your God's gift, don't you old man? Let's see whether you've still got it."

"We seemed to enjoy ourselves when I first came to town...and less of the old man."

Tiggy had Sadie across the old Victorian desk which was just tall enough for standing entry. It was wonderful for the posture and Sadie gradually pulled him onto her and wrapped her legs round his waist. The fact that she found the position exciting was obvious by her mounting cries and Tiggy became concerned that they might be heard by those setting up the show downstairs. Actually, that was the least of their worries because Sadie was leaning with her shapely bum on the switch that operated the PA system. This was used to call boats from the bay or announce winners and was sufficiently powerful to be heard in most parts of Akaroa.

Miriam Bender and Elmer Flannigan met Sergeant Lawrence at the library in Akaroa. There wasn't a police station anywhere near the town as with a 0.005% crime rate it really didn't justify one. Miriam thought he was an instantly likeable man about 6ft tall with a build that his wife would call comfortable and a ready smile underneath his rather unfashionable moustache. They had talked many times on the phone and tried a FaceTime once but nothing beats a face to face.

Max was obviously a little intimidated by Elmer but gradually relaxed as the guy talked about his brother the US Cop and that the fact that he was even larger. It only took a couple of minutes for Elmer to convince most people that despite his appearance, he was actually a sweetie.

Everyone in the library had been talking about the auction and how it was the biggest thing to hit town since some of the America Cup winners had sailed into the bay in 2021. The street was obviously busy and looking out of the front windows Max saw media trucks and one of the worst limo wrecks he'd seen still moving in years. If he'd been on traffic duty, he'd have pulled the thing over in minutes.

Akaroa was an upmarket area and it had its share of nice vehicles but the Porsches and what appeared to be a million dollars' worth of Ferrari 420, that passed over the next half hour, showed that big money had come to town for the sale.

Max's conversation with Miriam stopped abruptly when a middle-aged lady violently pushed into the front doors of the library obviously desperate to find someone. She was red-faced, giggly and started whispering to the woman on the front desk. The two women then pushed out of the doors in a big hurry and the cop didn't have to be a genius to realise that something gossip-worthy was kicking off outside.

Excusing himself he rapidly pushed past the racks of books and out of the door. Miriam was not averse to a bit of excitement herself and found herself outside on the pavement with the Sergeant. She looked up and down the main street and couldn't see anything worth all the fuss. She then realised that Max was listening and that there was some kind of low moaning sound coming from the other end of the bay.

"Ooooah … Ooooah … Oooahhh … Tiggy you clever bastard … don't stop."

Miriam recognised the ecstasy and the name of the bounder who'd created it. Sadly, for the other person involved there was a hammering clearly audible through the speakers and the pleasure was suddenly interrupted.

"Well Sergeant, we certainly know now, where Mr Foghorn aka Count Jergov is," Miriam whispered to the cop.

"Sorry Ms Bender what do you mean?"

"That groaning noise - and I hope genuinely that you recognise such noises – if you don't then you need counselling – that noise was a female orgasm and the Count produced more for me in a week than I'd had in the previous ten years of marriage."

The cop didn't quite know what to say and grinned embarrassedly at the longing look on the female Miriam Bender. Luckily before he needed to come up with a sort of answer that could be used against him, Miriam started again.

"And if you listened the lucky girl mentioned Tiggy … and we all know who that is don't we?"

By this time, they were back in the library, sitting on little seats normally used by the school kids and Miriam was trying to explain what the noise was to Elmer who'd stayed inside. The frank description caused most of the other people in the library to go silent and make Elmer wonder whether heterosexuals had all the fun anyway.

Tiggy was suffering what he believed was called Coitus Interruptus as Chris Arnold had burst in just before he was about to deliver what they used to call below decks, his Vinegar Stroke. He was happy that his legendary powers had not diminished even with the younger members of the opposite sex, but a little unfinished. The fact that her orgasm had been amplified across the whole bay might have been a little embarrassing for her had she not jumped out of the office window and hidden under the sailing club until the fuss died down. It was an interesting philosophical point Tiggy thought to himself as to how many people might recognise the sound of anyone – especially a well-bred young lady – by the sound of their orgasm.

Anyway, his deliberations were interrupted by the sound of people starting to arrive at the auction. Tiggy was back fully zipped up in the crew overalls and with the baseball cap pulled down over his ears. He was starting to feel slightly unreal and not too much unlike when as a little boy he used to hide under the big oak dining table with its huge overlapping cloth and listen to his parents talk to their friends. He felt invisible, he felt safe and dangerous at the same time, he really wasn't there. Yet this was the most important event in his life since he'd joined the Navy.

"I'ma goin to have that boat whadever ita takes." An accent straight out of the gangster movies woke up Tiggy from a few rows down.

"Boss da tree million may nodda be anuff – dis is goin for big bucks," said a secondary voice with a similar provenance.

Looking from his corner down at the two people who were sitting diagonally three rows down, he wouldn't have wanted to meet them on a dark night. But presumably they had qualified financially or Chartwells would not have allowed them in. According to the latest information there were going to be around twelve people allowed to bid about ten of which might be attending in person. From his viewpoint Tiggy could see the desk and screen at the end of the room and through the open doors in the far corner he could see out to the harbour and the approach to the sailing club.

Only a few bidders had requested a run in the Riva and Arnold had been at the helm on each occasion. That engine noise was unmistakable and the boat looked magnificent as it wove around the bay during the test runs. The fact that repairs had been carried out by an authorized Riva specialist in Akaroa was important to some but strangely Roberto Carlotti, the man involved, was not available, having been unavoidably detained in the Mayor's Mercedes. One of his assistants had to field any technical questions and was doing a good job.

There were now a dozen people sitting in the audience and spread out in groups of two. Everyone as they arrived peered around and tried to make out who the competition was. Chartwells said that this was an unusual sale and that unlike selling a Picasso, where the bidders might be limited to a few people who probably knew each other by reputation. The bidders in this sale could be anybody from any number of spheres and could be classic car dealer, a successful businessman or a movie star. All they needed to prove was that they could bid up to twenty million dollars. As a recent Picasso had sold for one hundred and thirty million dollars this was chicken feed but Chartwells was convinced that it was an area with huge future potential.

Tiggy looked down at the Rolex that was his secret reserve if all else failed and realised that it was exactly ten minutes before proceedings started. It was late evening and he decided to stand up and go for a final pee before the show. He looked out through the open doors down the harbour road and nearly wet himself.

Just a few yards down the quayside there were three people picked out by the early evening sun. One was a stranger, a stocky middle-aged man with a bushy moustache that was visible even from this distance and the flat-footed walk of a policeman. He looked like a Kiwi.

The second man was twice the size of the first and was looking down at the other man waving his hands expressively. Even from this distance he looked intimidatingly muscular and most people would have thought that he was a wrestler, weight-lifter or minder. Tiggy wasn't sure yet but he looked like someone he knew quite well.

The third figure was female and she was wearing a bright orange dress that enhanced the tan which he knew to be nearly all over. She had blonde hair pulled back from her forehead and a pair of sun-glasses perched on top. As she got closer, he could see that voluptuous figure almost bursting out of the dress top and realised that some women like his original mentor Maddie Quimby were always meant to be large and welcoming. This woman could diet for years, go vegan, become a marathon runner and she would still be larger than life. Tiggy knew exactly who she was and he really didn't know whether to run to her or hide in shame.

For the moment he decided to sink down further in his seat and watch. He could hear a certain amount of fuss as the three tried to enter the hall but they obviously managed it because a few minutes later he could see them sitting on the front row talking to Chris Arnold.

Over the next few minutes, a number of strangers came in and there was the roar of an expensive engine as someone ignored the no entry signs on the final stretch and drove in. From what he could see it was a Ferrari 422, an absolutely beautiful classic, worth conservatively around four million dollars. Out of it stepped a man who was nearly as beautiful and who threw the keys at a tall blonde headed woman who got out the other side. The man put a silk jacket over his shoulders and waited until the woman had presented his invitations to the desk. He then processed regally through the room and sat three rows back – ignoring everyone except the supermodel at his side. Having looked down the list of invitees, Tiggy would put money on the chance that this was Fontaine, the Italian guy whose ancestor designed the Riva and who had sold out his social media empire for billions the previous year.

A TV film crew turned up late as usual and fussed around trying to get lighting and sound checks done. He could hear Chris Arnold shouting in his best Royal Navy voice that the auction would start on time as everyone worldwide was geared to the same timetable.

"Good evening Ladies and Gentleman, can I first say that Chartwells are delighted to be handling the sale of this magnificent boat - the property of a Gentleman."

As the screen showed original footage from Riva in the 1920's intercut with glamorous black and white images of stars of the era Arnold gave an excellent description of the boat and its uniqueness plus the fact that it had been found almost beyond repair fifteen years ago by a gentleman who recognised its importance and nearly went bankrupt trying to restore it. He added a considerable amount of other detail – most of which was total fabrication – but even Tiggy was impressed. He also reminded bidders of the conditions of sale (basically that Chartwells took responsibility for nothing other than charging commission to both buyer and seller). He then confirmed that bidding would commence in precisely three minutes.

"Tree million dollars – US!" The rather swarthy guy a few rows down obviously lost patience a shouted his bid very loudly whilst his sidekick tried to stop him. This was rather a painful for him and the boss gave him a rather enthusiastic sideswipe which threw him onto the floor.

"Thank you, Mr Romano, – your bid is noted but please just raise your hand next time and we'll come to you."

Nobody else in the room seemed interested for a while but the online bidding was just getting warmed up. "I have a bid of four million dollars online." Chris was able to see that this was a bid from a Chinese buyer but had the feeling that there was a lot of interest on the internet and that this could be a big day.

"Tree fuckin million US dollars – cash you motherfuckers," Romano shouted so loudly that the cameras turned on him. Tiggy could see him holding up a large leather bag and continuing to swear whilst Arnold tried to explain that the current bid was four million and would sir like to increase his own bid. Romano slumped down in his seat and appeared to be fumbling in his case.

"Five Million dollars." The elegant Italian stood and raised a languid arm whilst the red head alongside looked up adoringly.

"Mr Fontaine, thank you for your bid and thank you for being patient." Arnold said pointedly whilst looking back at his screen. "The bid stands at five million in the room so if there are any other bids..?" Arnold had just thought that the sale price had reached its natural level when a flurry of online action silenced him." Just a moment, we have two more bids." The team were looking to the middle of the room and a girl was starting to scream.

The stocky guy Romano had stood up and he appeared to be carrying a big black weapon that looked as though it had come out of a Rambo movie. "Tree million is wot I bid and dats all yur gonna get." Some people threw themselves on the floor and Arnold stood transfixed as the gangster moved to the front and demanded the keys.

Uttering a stream of obscenities Romano burst through the doors and ran to the Riva. A few seconds later there was the characteristic roar of the engine as Romano untied fore and aft with practised ease and pulled at considerable speed away from the harbour and out to sea.

Everyone except Tiggy froze with shock for a few seconds and then ran forward and out of the room to see where the boat had gone. Tiggy went a few rows down to where Romano had been sitting and checked out a few things. The assistant looked as though he was just coming too so he went back to his dark corner and pulled his hat down to hide his face, his emotions in turmoil.

Chartwells were trying to restart the auction despite the fact that its attraction had just sped off at 50 mph.

"For those still with us, I should say that the last bid was from an anonymous bidder and it was for ten million dollars," Arnold paused. "But as the Riva may have been stolen, I should say that my assistant will note all the bids and that we will postpone for now and hopefully reconvene when the boat has been recovered."

There was excited chatter from the TV crew and the bidders in the room who were now standing and comparing notes. Auctions can be highly competitive affairs but having a bidder pulling out a Glock 19 during the process was unique.

Tiggy didn't know quite how he felt. The whole day had felt unreal and the figures being quoted in the auction had been unbelievable. When he'd been a kid in Portsmouth being a millionaire had been the pinnacle of being rich and though billionaire replaced it as the ultimate description in recent years the fact that he might have been worth ten million dollars a few minutes ago was just crazy. Then just before he was going to strike it rich, some crazy gangster pulled out a gun and had stolen his pot of gold. He realised that everything he'd planned, everything he'd dreamed, had all probably gone to shit.

"Hello darlin ...." Tiggy felt a lovely warm hand on his right thigh and realised that another part of his dream or nightmare was about to come true. "I don't think that you've met Sergeant Lawrence?"

The Sergeant thought that you don't get times like this in a normal job. A couple of days away from the drudgery of the office in Dunedin in the beautiful surroundings of Akaroa and what do you get? Something that sounded like the audio track of one of the most extreme pornographic films ever made, broadcast to the entire town. Then the company of a delightfully attractive Miami woman and giant of a Florida bloke listening to his every word with rapt attention. Finally, the chance to look efficient and handsome in front of an international TV crew whilst he organised the capture of a notorious gangster and recover stolen property.

Max had a few minutes looking like someone out of Police Squad phoning Auckland HQ and loudly ordering a helicopter search for an armed man, thinking that this would do wonders for his reputation. He made sure that he turned his right side to the cameras as he was convinced that his moustache - considered rather old-fashioned by younger members of the team - was more luxuriant that side. All this excitement was happening and he hadn't even found the quarry that had started all this - Terence Foghorn. He was looking forward to it.

The boat that had been stolen was apparently worth ten million dollars, so the recovery of that would also be another feather in his cap. According to auctioneer that shouldn't be too difficult because after the test runs earlier there was little fuel left in the tank and the big Ferrari engine used it like an oil sheik.

The fact that all this drama had happened today helped his case immeasurably, because his bosses had started to lose interest in Count Jergov. He could only presume that the political pressure from that Eurocrat politician and the terrifying Aussie Florence Hasty had diminished. Because he'd had a couple of emails complaining about his expenses and demanding that he returned to clear his case load of local offences. He suspected also that the strength of the legal case against Jergov was worrying them because all the victims had signed a contract that the experts thought might just be bulletproof...

Max was a persistent bugger however and had resisted all pressure to give up. Now he had an armed robbery on international TV to solve and it would be at least an hour before any senior officer could get here to claim the credit. That was just enough time.

Miriam Bender interrupted his thinking with an urgent tug on the sleeve of his fleece and pointed to the back of the room where he could see a figure slumped in the semi-darkness with a hat pulled down over his eyes. Miriam whispered to Elmer, pointed and asked him to use his considerable bulk to block the exit. He nodded and took up station in the one gangway that led to the exit, looking like not even Jonah Lomu was going to get past him.

Lawrence had a call on his official mobile to confirm that the helicopter and armed response squad were just leaving with an ETA of 30 minutes and by the time he had hung up, Miriam was already sitting next to the figure at the back of the room. Max had to establish his authority quickly before anything else happened to disrupt his plans so he joined the two of them, taking a pair of handcuffs out of his pocket.

"You are Terence Foghorn also known as Count Jergov or Eugene Fenton and I arrest you for grand ...."

"No!" said Miriam Bender much to everyone's surprise.

"Whaa..." was all the good Sergeant managed before Miriam called Elmer over and they had a whispered conversation in the corridor.

"Listen, Mr Foghorn is willing to pay back any literary fees paid by people on the ship Amazon with interest, the minute the boat is sold – Isn't that right Tiggy?" Miriam turned to Tiggy.

"Aarghh…" was all our favourite author had to say. He tried to rise in his seat but was discouraged from further movement by a large hand pushing him down from Elmer.

"So" Miriam drew herself up. "As Mr Flannigan and myself are not pressing charges, don't you think you better go and find that rather valuable boat Sergeant?"

"Arrm … yeh …." Lawrence decided that he needed some fresh air and that, as the cameras were still facing up to him, he better look as though he knew what he was doing. He pulled out his mobile and chattered urgently in to it pushing past the crew and out to the harbour. His phone rang then which nearly spoiled the charade but he just got away with it.

The helicopter had spotted the Riva beached on the next cove where it had presumably run out of fuel. He ordered the chopper to pick him up immediately so that he could help in the search for Romano. The pilot hesitated for a few seconds thinking about police fuel budgets but Max shouted that he was the only person of authority who might recognise the gangster.

Two minutes later the chopper was in Akaroa and Max had to work out how to climb aboard a chopper full of armed men in full body armour. The only training he had was looking at old programmes like MASH or Apocalypse Now so he kept his head down and ran for it.

Somebody strapped him in and they ascended almost as fast as his breakfast, but luckily, he was able to swallow that a second time and not decorate anyone's Kevlar. The boat was clearly visible after a few seconds in the clear New Zealand air and the shingle cove was deserted.

En route Max was able to brief the team that they were looking for a roughly 50 year old man in a black silk suit who looked like an Italian gangster. With all the Woke silliness that had infected everywhere in past years, Max wondered whether he was infringing the gay gangster liberation front or something, but everyone knew what he meant. He added that he was armed with a weapon that looked similar to a Glock or similar automatic weapon and seemed to know how to use it.

The helicopter did a swift pass over the stretch of land behind the beach but couldn't see anything. This was not surprising because it was marsh covered by thick undergrowth growing to around 10 feet tall where you could have hidden a regiment. Sadly, they were not carrying thermal imaging stuff so the search would have to be the old-fashioned way. Two men were dropped at the far end of the marsh and two would act as beaters from the beach end. The Sergeant didn't envy them as Kiwi Sand Flies are vicious and would find Kevlar no deterrent at all. Max asked to be dropped back at the harbour and gratefully left the specialists to their tasks.

Tiggy and Miriam were chatting like old lovers and Elmer felt so jealous that he phoned his partner, forgetting that it was a rather uncivilised time on the West Coast. As always Neil, his partner, was a bit more hard-nosed about the Count Jergov situation than Elmer was but eventually warmed to the idea of a full repayment of the literary fee with 20 % added interest. Whilst Miriam was contacting some of the other *Amazon* people she knew with the same offer, Tiggy called Chris Arnold over and asked him to quietly talk to the Italian on the other side of the room who was descended from the designer and ask him whether he was willing to get closer to the ten million dollar bid that had come in online. If so, Tiggy indicated that he'd be willing to agree to the sale now.

He wandered off with a thoughtful expression on his face and Tiggy could see that the idea appealed to him. The auction had gone pear-shaped in a big way and even though the Riva would probably be recovered in the next few hours, the chance of getting the auction running again with all bidders was much reduced. A bid in the hand was worth two in the bush etc etc etc.

Whilst everyone was distracted Tiggy picked up a bag left by the seats and took Miriam by the arm and walked out of the sailing club. He called to Chris that he'd be back soon and to tell Sergeant Lawrence when he returned that he'd only be up the road and not to call the dogs out. The sun was virtually down as the two walked down the harbour and along the road where his apartment was. He opened the door and they climbed the stairs to the top where Tiggy pointed to the seats on the balcony and offered her a drink.

By the time Tiggy had found a decent bottle of wine and opened it, Miriam was sat on one of the easy chairs looking at the view.

"I can see why you love this place Tiggy."

"Yes, it's lovely but I'm not sure the authorities would let me stay – I came into New Zealand rather unofficially and half the world seems after me, so I'm probably going to have to leave in a hurry. But I need the money first."

It was wonderful Tiggy thought how understanding, how simpatico,

Miriam Bender was and our lothario was convinced that he'd found his soul mate. Unless he had lost all his instincts for women, which was unlikely, he was pretty sure that she felt the same. With a moment of sheer madness, he got down on one knee in front of her.

"Will you be my partner, my soulmate, my cohabitee, forsaking all others for life?"

"You're not offering marriage then?" Miriam asked with a laugh.

"I thought we were both too grown up for that - but I am offering you fidelity, which is more than I've ever offered anyone." Tiggy answered sincerely but worrying that his knees were starting to creak in the kneeling position, he stood up and kissed her hand whilst she considered the matter.

"Actually, I do really appreciate the offer but I have another form of partnership in mind. It's important, however, that we keep you out of jail." Miriam touched his face tenderly.

Over the next few minutes Miriam and Tiggy discussed the future and then they went back to the sailing club. Everyone there had dispersed apart from the auctioneer and Fontaine who were talking animatedly by the desk and Tiggy realised that he had to step out of the shadows if he was to get the Riva sold. He tapped Arnold on the back and asked what offers had been made on the boat.

"Mr Fontaine went up to eight million, but I was trying to tell him that it wasn't good enough to match the Chinese bid."

"Do you have the money immediately available?" Tiggy asked the Italian.

"Si"

"What will you do with the boat?"

"My Grandfather said that it was meant to be used, not put in a museum – so I would use it." The Italian said with tears of pride in his voice.

"In that case Mr Arnold, please arrange the sale to Mr Fontaine at eight million. I loved the boat and though it nearly broke me, I think it needs to go to an Italian, not an investment company."

Tiggy shook hands with them both and returned to his seat with a feeling that he'd done the right thing.

Two minutes later Sergeant Lawrence returned by helicopter and pushed his way back into the sailing club. He had the feeling that whilst he'd been away, he'd lost control of the situation. Ms Bender and the big guy were sitting with Tiggy Foghorn looking like long lost friends and not exactly like criminal and victims.

The tall auctioneer interrupted the cops progress, demanding to know when the boat was being returned because it had been sold. The cop was able to confirm that one of the police had put fuel in and was on his way back to Akaroa with it now. He'd had news whilst he'd been travelling that the gangster called Romano had tried to shoot his way out of the marsh and had been killed by police marksman.

Max looked round for the thin pale guy from Las Vegas and he had disappeared. He put out an alert for him on his radio and then wandered over to the group including Foghorn.

Ms Bender saw Sergeant Lawrence coming and intercepted him

"Mr Foghorn has made an extremely generous offer which I am authorised to accept on behalf of the passengers of *Amazon*."

"I'm not sure that ...." the good Sergeant started to say when he was interrupted by an effusive Miriam Bender.

"Because identifying recipients may take some time, Mr Foghorn has agreed that three million dollars of the eight million raised by the sale, will go into trust with the Auckland State Bank. That is hugely in excess of the amount raised by Mr Foghorn as literary fees and a reputable lawyer will be employed to administer the fund." Miriam gathered her breath again. "Furthermore, Mr Foghorn has agreed that one million each goes to three charities, Cancer Research, Oxfam and Red Cross."

Sergeant Lawrence felt as though he'd entered some outrageous reality show where criminals gave their ill-gotten gains away on TV. He almost applauded when Miriam mentioned the charity donations – three million dollars could do some good in the world.

Then the sergeant put his thoughts in order. Mr Foghorn was about to leave and surely he was a shyster, a conman or a fraud? Or why the hell was Max here and why had he chased him half way across the country? He stopped the group at the door.

"Not so fast Mr Foghorn, apart from the cruise liner passengers there are still accusations from people in China and Europe who claim that you contracted with them to write a book."

"That is certainly correct," Tiggy answered with as much levity as he could manage.

"In which case you are guilty of fraud and though passengers on the ship *Amazon* might be willing to accept compensation, the New Zealand police will still press charges."

"Why?" Tiggy asked with an anticipatory gleam in his eye.

"Because you are not an author, you have never written a book and that in my book is fraud." The good sergeant stated with as much authority as he could muster.

"I *have* written a book, so I'm afraid your case fails," Tiggy said with a new confidence.
"What's more," he added." You, yourself have read it!"
"Don't be ridiculous," the cop added, feeling his grasp on reality starting to fade.
"The book is called **The trials and tribulations of Tiggy Foghorn.**"
"Whaa ..."

"I hope that you enjoyed reading 'Trials and Tribulations' so far Sergeant ... and that you enjoy the final few chapters as much as I intend to," said Tiggy, taking Miriam by the arm and leaving the scene.

Going on a final Bender

It took three months for the authorities in New Zealand to release Terence 'Tiggy' Foghorn but as he was held in a comfortable private house and allowed complete freedom to wander round the restaurants and bars of Auckland, it was no great hardship. Funnily enough one lunchtime he went for a pint in the very Irish pub that his near nemesis, Fran Capelle had worked in and never knew its significance.

Every time he looked down at his Rolex, he remembered the dalliance with her but he had no regrets. The days spent with Miriam Bender had made him complete, though she had been back to the states once with Elmer to sort the compensation deal out with her fellow passengers.

Tiggy's book was nearly genuinely finished and he already had given Elmer Flannigan two or three pages of script where he had reimagined his partner Neil as a ship's officer in Nelson's time. Elmer choked up when he read it and was incredibly grateful. A few days later he even had an email from 'Captain Neil Davies' in the US thanking him too.

Remembering his first commission, he also drafted ten pages about a boring man with bad teeth and little ambition who had been lucky enough to be married to a vital, beautiful woman who made his life a success. That man was the late George Bender and his ex-wife almost imploded with laughter when he gave it to her to read on the last trip...

Tiggy had his passport back and a clean record. Now he could go anywhere but Miriam still hadn't accepted his proposal of fidelity and though they'd shared some wonderful nights in bed when she'd been in NZ, Tiggy wanted more.

Sergeant Lawrence had been given a bravery award for his part in apprehending the notorious gangster Al Romano and was back in his office in Dunedin. He still wasn't sure whether he should have detained Tiggy Foghorn too, but had been warned by the legal eagles that the case wouldn't have stuck and by the press department that imprisoning someone who was about to give three million dollars to charity, wasn't good press.

In truth Lawrence rather liked Foghorn – you don't see many likeable rascals these days. So Max was happy, though Nico the gangsters apprentice had disappeared and the private plane they came in had also gone. Everyone involved had agreed that there was no place for gangsters in South Island and that it was good riddance.

Miriam had emailed Tiggy to say that she would be back in the next few hours and that they needed to have a planning meeting. She'd arranged for a jug of Miami Slammers and a seafood platter to be ordered for 6.00 p.m. at The Captain's Table, which was one of the best restaurants overlooking the Americas Cup harbour.

A few hours later he was thinking how radiant Miriam looked and how strong those blue drinks called Miami Slammers were. It was after a lot of those that Miriam and her sister had abducted him and he wanted his head clear for when she answered his proposal.

"According to my reckoning, after the money you've put in trust and the three million you have donated to charity, you only have two million dollars for immediate use," Miriam looked questioningly across the table."

"That's not quite true ..." Tiggy responded quietly.

"Ah ... yes I forgot, there is the Chartwell commission on the sale of the Riva ... which I thought was outrageous, by the way."

"Ah well, it did seem the right idea at the time..." Tiggy added defensively.

"And the other thing was the donations to charity ... I'm a charitable person too but paying that upfront seemed a bit too much if you ask me."

"Well, that three million went down well with the Kiwi authorities and it didn't cost quite as much as it might have seemed at the time." Tiggy whispered across the table.

"Tiggy Foghorn, stop being so mysterious, what are you talking about?"

"There was some money that no one here knew about – it really didn't exist in any sense that the police knew about and I thought that it could be used to do some good."

"What are you talking about?"

"When the gangster Al Romano pinched my boat, I went down to his seat and pinched his bag."

"OK ... why did that help? Was there something valuable in there?" Miriam asked, half-knowing the answer.

"You could say that ... strangely enough, there was just under three million US dollars in used notes there," Tiggy said with a satisfied smirk.

"You are an incorrigible rascal Tiggy Foghorn – a real hard case as they say round here."

The Miami slammers and the extra three million dollars had made Miriam incredibly randy and it was the next morning before Tiggy finally got an answer to his proposal. By then Tiggy had almost been ready to offer marriage rather than just fidelity, but Miriam had her own ideas.

"The thing is Tiggy, I want to go on a cruise – call it our honeymoon or a test of our fidelity vows if you like."

"OK but why – I thought you might have had enough cruising for one lifetime?"

"In some ways I have, there are more over privileged, pretentious people on some of these cruises than you find anywhere else – I made my own money, I didn't get it on a silver spoon," Miriam said.

Tiggy couldn't quite get her drift but agreed. Looking back at his experience on the *Amazon* there were people there he had been glad to take money from. People like Florence Hasty the cheapskate funeral director, Ms Anders the gun loving tobacco soldier, Alexandria Wolfberg the second generation Nazi art collector. Even on shore Adele Lang may have been very bedworthy but she had been happy to exploit her sexuality to gain political power and compensation.

Miriam and her sister and Elmer Flannigan were the only people looking back, that he had felt guilty about.

"So what is your plan, Miriam?"

"I want to bring back Count Jergov or maybe his cousin Count Vangov or something plausible. We made a great team on the *Amazon* and I had more fun than I'd ever had before. Let's bring back Eugene Fenton or his uncle and do the book character scam again." Miriam looked across at him and the sparkle in her eyes said it all.

"I love it Miriam, we're rich but life is about adventure. Let's go to Bermuda, Jamaica or somewhere warm where the cruise ships call ... but I have one condition."

"What is that?"

"I don't want to be talking in a Lithuanian accent all the time and I would prefer not to sleep with the clients .... is that OK?

"I think that might be arranged," Miriam said with a smile.

....

249